FireDrakes

Chronicles Of The Daemon Knights

David Korinetz

David Korinetz
Unit #6, 477 Martin Street
Penticton, BC
V2A 5L2

www.davidkorinetz.com

Cover design by Sharron Middler, www.artistoutofcanada.com

Library and Archives Canada Cataloguing in Publication

Korinetz, David 1954 -
        FireDrakes : Chronicles Of The Daemon Knights
        David Korinetz

        ISBN : 978-0-9783824-0-7

        I. Title.

        PS8621.075F47 2007
        C2007-904053-5

Printed in Canada

FireDrakes

Chronicles Of The Daemon Knights

David Korinetz

Books By David Korinetz

Chronicles of the Daemon Knights
FireDrakes
Sorceress
Halfling (forthcoming)

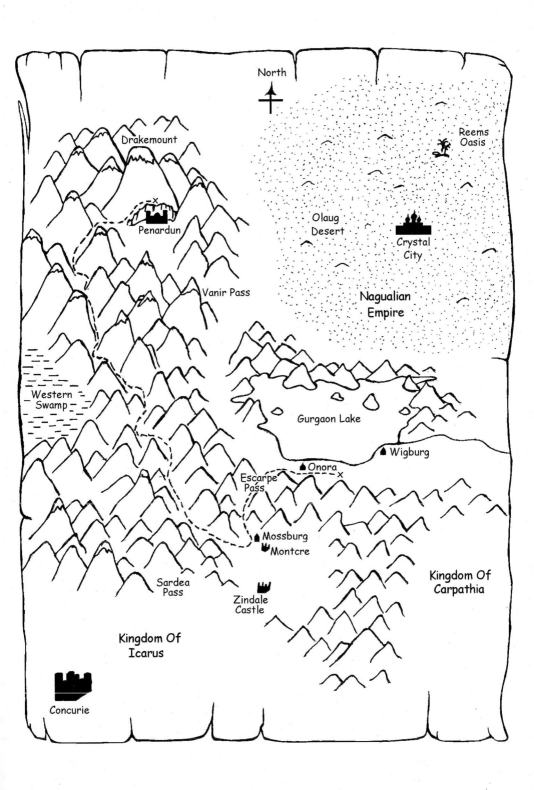

Chapter 1

MAGDALEN

Deep inside the ancient elfin keep of Penardun at the base of Drakenmount, Magdalen leaned over her scrying pool. What she saw reflected back was not her own youthful face, framed in flowing flame-red hair, but that of a wrinkled old man with long wispy hair the colour of freshly fallen snow.

"A score of FireDrakes have secured the northern passes," Magdalen said to the image in the inky black water. "Any army foolish enough to try marching through there will be turned to ash. I have kept my part of our bargain, Gamel. Now it is time for you to keep yours."

"You are hardly in a position to carp about not keeping bargains, my dear," the old man replied. "If anyone has a right to complain, it is I."

In spite of herself, Magdalen experienced a twinge of guilt. "I took all the risks. You would have done the same in my place." She was being defensive, and with Gamel that was a mistake. The slippery old weasel would goad her into doing something stupid if she wasn't careful.

Calming herself, Magdalen walled away her emotions. "What is done is done. We have a new arrangement now, and I expect you to abide by it."

"We are both reasonable people," Gamel replied soothingly. "I am only asking for one FireDrake, and for but a short time. Surely you can spare the one."

His slippery words had a seductive timbre that Magdalen found irritating. It served to remind her of just how much she despised the old man. "It was not part of our arrangement. The answer is no," she growled.

"Such hostility is really unbecoming, my dear. I require the beast for a little reconnoitring, nothing more. What harm could that possibly do?"

The old man held out his hands palm up. To anyone else his demeanour was that of a benign and even sympathetic grandfather, but Magdalen knew better. She had been taken in by this pretense of benevolence before and not all that long ago.

"I do not like it. Not one bit," she said, losing some of the edge to her anger despite her resolve. His request was minor, and his reasoning sound, but she couldn't be seen to cave in to his demands. Give Gamel a slice and he would take the whole pie.

"My men will take very good care of your pet, I can promise you that."

"One fortnight," Magdalen said, not quite sure why she was agreeing. Perhaps it was some misguided lingering gratitude, or just a way to end the conversation and forgo having to look at the old man's face a moment longer than necessary.

"That will suffice. Tell it to look for a legion camped near Onora one moon from today. I will inform the Captain to expect a FireDrake. Once it arrives I will personally instruct the beast in its duties. Since that concludes our business, I bid you farewell, my dear."

Even after the old man's smiling image had faded away, Magdalen continued to gaze upon her own reflection. She knew it was petty, but it still pleased her in some strange way to defy the vile old man. She would put an end to their alliance when it suited her purposes, once she no longer needed his legions, but for now she found solace in exploring new ways to irritate him.

Gamel hid it well, but Magdalen had been close to him long enough to know how deeply disturbing it was when a woman refused to grovel at his feet. Right now he needed her, or at least her control over the FireDrakes, so he would bear it behind a greasy smile until he found a way to wrest Aedon away from her. Magdalen clutched the amulet that hung from her neck by a glowing red chain and smiled. That was never going to happen.

Using Aedon to amplify her thoughts, Magdalen summoned Gytha. She immediately felt the link through the amulet's magic, heard the beating of the FireDrake's great heart and drew warmth from the fire in its blood. Leagues away, Gytha would feel the irresistible pull of Aedon. Every fibre of the FireDrake's being would force her to respond. In the case of Gytha, it was not necessary, but the magic of the amulet was indiscriminate in such matters. Magdalen let Aedon fall back to its resting place. She felt its lingering warmth even through the thick material of her dress.

It had taken Magdalen two full seasons to gain the trust of just a handful of female FireDrakes. Gytha, the dominant female, was the first to befriend her. Sympathetic to her cause, Gytha shared similar views about their male counterparts among other things. It was likely this common ground that had prompted the FireDrake to aid in the theft of the amulet. Gytha had been her closest friend and ally ever since. If only the other races followed the example of the elves. Male, female, it made no difference to them. Power and responsibility was shared equally. It was a refreshing change from the rest of the world.

Magdalen grabbed her cloak and headed for the tower stairs. As she trudged up the steps, she mulled over what to say to Gytha. She would ask her to obey the Emperor, within limits of course, but only to act as his eyes and ears, and not to get involved in any fighting. By the time Magdalen reached her destination, Gytha was perched on the edge of the rooftop courtyard.

Magdalen formed the words in her mind. *Gytha my friend, I have a task for you.*

The FireDrake's reply was pleasant. As always, the words seemed to originate in the centre of her forehead. *What do you wish, Magdalen?*

The big Female was scratching at her belly. A flash of pink told Magdalen that Gytha had lost a scale. That could be a problem. *Is your molting time near?* she asked.

Not for another two moons, Gytha replied. *Just lost a scale to the antlers of the buck I had for dinner two days ago. I must admit, for such a small thing it is most irritating.*

Magdalen touched the amulet and focussed on the area of concern. The scale had not come out cleanly and a jagged piece of the root was lodged just under the skin. Magdalen sent a thin tendril of Aedon's magic, in the form of fire, to incinerate the offending piece of scale. The tiniest plume of pink smoke drifted up from the spot.

Ahhh, my thanks, Gytha purred.

Hold still and I shall grow a new one for you, Gytha.

No need to bother yourself with that. It feels much better now.

Well then, Magdalen said, *a favour for a favour. It would please me for you to serve with one of the Emperor's legions for a time. Just a fortnight. They will await you near a place called Onora, exactly one moon from tonight.*

Humans! Forgive me Magdalen, but if it were not for humans elfin kind would still flourish. Instead we are confined to Drakenmount and the northern forests.

You forget I am human too.

Only part of you, my dear halfling, Gytha said sweetly. *If you had no elfin blood, Aedon would be nothing but a shiny bauble in your hands.*

You have a point, Magdalen conceded, *but will you do as I ask?*

You could always compel me. You possess Aedon, after all.

Magdalen felt a little insulted. *We are friends. If you don't want to do this thing for me of your own free will, then I will ask one of your sisters.*

Magdalen stared into the FireDrake's large unblinking green eyes and sighed. The anger quickly drained away. *It is just that I trust your judgement, Gytha. I am fearful of sending one of the others. Gamel is a slimy toad and cannot be trusted.*

Do not fret, Magdalen my dear, the FireDrake cooed. *I will do as you wish.* With that, the big FireDrake spread her wings and leapt off the roof. Magdalen's hair blew back in a gust of wind when Gytha flapped her wings.

Thank you my friend, Magdalen said, pulling her cloak tighter around her shoulders. *Stay safe, and under no circumstances are you to involve yourself in any fighting*, she added as the shape of the FireDrake shrank into the distance.

Gytha's soft voice was as clear as if she were still perched on the roof. *Rest easy, Magdalen. I will return by the coming of the second full moon.*

All seemed well, but as she made her way back to her scrying pool Magdalen could not shake the feeling of foreboding.

Chapter 2

ALDUS

West of Balor, high above the mainland coast, a long sleek FireDrake soared across an icy predawn sky. Leagues sped by as he floated skilfully from one updraft to the next. Though the wind was raw and wintry, it was of little consequence to a being like Grigor who called the frozen peak of Drakenmount home. The same could not be said for his passenger. Bitter wind whipped Aldus Lasairian's long hair and beard back and forth, stinging his face and neck. It was most annoying, but at least it kept him alert. On each of the past two nights he had fallen asleep only to awaken with aching leg cramps and nearly frozen to the bone.

In an effort to stimulate his circulation, the hoary old wizard shifted back and forth in the makeshift saddle strapped to the base of Grigor's long neck. To avoid unfriendly eyes they had limited travelling to between sunset and dawn. On this particular night, the stars were obscured by dark clouds and the moon was new. Even with eyes superior to most humans, Aldus could barely see past the back of Grigor's head.

As if freezing cold wind wasn't hardship enough, in the darkness time seemed to drag on forever. Occasional conversation with Grigor was the only relief. Unfortunately, though an amiable companion, a FireDrake is physically incapable of speech. The only way Grigor could communicate was by telepathy. Though a common trait among FireDrakes, elves and halflings, for Aldus telepathy was a newly discovered ability, and one he was finding difficult to master. At times it was easy, but when his mind was preoccupied it was a struggle to reform his raw thoughts into coherent patterns that Grigor could understand. *Do you think we will reach Balor before first light?*

Grigor's reply came swift and clear. *The ocean lies below but I cannot yet see the island. With dawn less than a sun-mark away I suspect we will not reach our goal before sunrise. Should I turn back? We still have plenty of time to find a suitable resting place on the mainland.*

It was still too dark to see, but the smell of the ocean was indeed heavy on the wind. Aldus contemplated turning back, but the thought of being delayed another day, when they were so close, was most unwelcome. *No, I think we will press on. As I recall, it is but a day and one half journey by ship so it cannot be much further..*

As you wish, Grigor replied.

Having another's thoughts bouncing around inside his head was a sensation Aldus still found discomforting. At times it took great effort just to separate Grigor's ruminations from his own. In the process of accomplishing the task, it occurred to him that Grigor had been flying all night without a moment's respite. Engrossed in his own discomfort, Aldus had neglected to consider Grigor's needs. *You've been aloft a long time, my friend, and with my added weight. Are you sure you have the strength to continue on?*

Fear not, Grigor replied. *A scrawny halfling like you is a nothing to me, however it has been a while since I have eaten. Is this island of yours good auroch country? An elk would suffice, but I really do fancy some roast ox.*

Balor is a large island with much of its interior still wild and unsettled. I am quite confident you will find excellent hunting there.

That is good news, Grigor said. *I will try to go a little faster then.*

In the silence that followed, Aldus found himself absently caressing one of Grigor's scales. They fascinated him. Tough as steel, yet smooth as silk and light as a feather. Formed from thin layers of a diamond-hard carbon material, as were his hollow yet nearly unbreakable bones, the scales made Grigor effectively fireproof. A fortunate thing, considering a FireDrake could exhale a stream of fire hotter than any blacksmith's forge. Spontaneously combustible stomach fluids, mixed with a little magic, were all part of a FireDrake's unique body chemistry.

Prior to meeting Grigor, the sum of Aldus's knowledge regarding dragons had been gained through an apprenticeship with his aging halfling uncle, Pewlin Lasairian. When departing the world of the living, after almost four centuries, Pewlin had bequeathed many wondrous things to his nephew. Gweneal, the talisman Aldus wore around his neck, was his greatest legacy. Fashioned long ago by elves, it was one of four very special bloodstone amulets.

Grasping Gweneal through his heavy wool cloak, Aldus could sense the power lying dormant within. The warmth in his palm was a subtle reminder of the constant draw on the amulet's magic to support two wards he had constructed. The first surrounded Grigor, to shield his whereabouts from the

Nagualian Emperor's former apprentice. It was barely a year since Magdalen had brazenly stolen the most powerful of the elfin talismans from under the very snouts of its keepers. With Aedon the FireDrakes had been created, and with it they could be controlled. Grigor was too far away to be compelled, but Aldus wasn't willing to risk being thwarted when they were so close to their goal. The ward around Grigor was tenuous at best, however, and if Magdalen even suspected what they were up to, all would be lost.

The second ward was a clever spell of his late uncle's design. Under normal circumstances, Gweneal's internal protective spells blocked unwanted magical probes by projecting a magical barrier many leagues wide. Unfortunately, that also meant it left a hole in a scrying pool that more or less pinpointed its position in the world, if someone knew what they were looking for. The ward Aldus maintained simply modified Gweneal's own to render both the amulet and its wearer invisible to all forms of a scrying without creating a telltale hole. *You will not be spying on me, Magdalen.*

You think very loudly, Grigor said, interrupting Aldus's line of thought.

Sorry my friend, Aldus replied. *I have not yet mastered this elfin mind speech. To my knowledge, Pewlin never used it, and until your coming, neither had I.* Aldus would have to be careful. Grigor was trustworthy, but he would need to guard his thoughts around others. The gifted could be anywhere.

As Grigor had predicted, they reached Balor just after sunrise. They emerged from a patch of low cloud to see rippling deep blue water a thousand feet below and catch a fleeting glimpse of the island through a convenient hole in an early morning mist that drifted off its shore. The breeze was fresh, heavy with salt and the smell of the sea. Soon, green and yellow patches within the mist below told Aldus they were once again over land. The mist grew thinner as they progressed inland, but still obscured everything below the tree tops.

Once again, words manifested inside Aldus's head. *I do not understand how a handful of mundane humans will be able to rescue Aedon. The sorceress has her own halfling magic, augmented by all the power of Aedon, the support of many female FireDrakes and the might of the Nagualian legions. Has one of these champions of yours some secret weapon? A magical sword perhaps?*

It took Aldus a moment to organize his thoughts. One of his gifts was prophetic visions, and it was just such a vision that had drawn them to the island. *I do not know how they will accomplish the task, but I have seen it. My visions have not failed me in over two hundred years. You must trust me in this my friend.*

Oh, I trust you well enough. You are a Lasairian after all. It is the only reason I am here, so far from home. I was but curious.

It was easy to forget this fearsome creature was really a gentle being of great intellect, mostly because he was so big which in turn was also misleading. At forty feet from crown to tail, Grigor was larger than average for a male FireDrake, but like all flying dragons he was relatively light despite his bulk. Riderless, he would weigh little more than two large Carpathian war horses.

As their journey neared its end Aldus reviewed individual images from his vision, trying to capture some identifying facial feature, but it was of no use. Each face was shrouded in a haze of uncertainty, as if not yet fully formed in reality. Just as with every other attempt, the only thing clear was the red dragon on their belt buckles. The fact that the Daemon family of old Sidon had been the only noble house to ever adopt that symbol was precisely what had drawn Aldus and Grigor to the island. The men they sought would be found in Balor.

The faceless images were erased by Grigor's voice. *You realize, of course, we can be seen now that the sun has risen.*

Yes, yes, I know, but it cannot be helped, Aldus replied more sharply than he intended. His irritation stemmed from a lack of control over his thoughts and had nothing to do with Grigor. *I beg your pardon Grigor. We are very high up and it is unlikely that anyone here has ever seen a FireDrake, so perhaps in ignorance they will mistake you for a bird. On the other hand, we will need to convince these men to aid us and seeing you can only help in that regard.*

Instead of a reply, Grigor abruptly changed course and dove toward the ground with alarming speed. "What are you doing?" Aldus screamed as he hung on for dear life.

Breakfast, the dragon replied with a booming laugh that echoed in Aldus's head.

As they continued their dizzying descent, words from one of Pewlin's books of magic came to mind. *The FireDrake is highly intelligent and normally gentle. This is the passive elf half of the creature. However, when it comes to hunting, or battle, the aggressive instincts of the common dragon have sway. In this state, the FireDrake is an unfeeling and dedicated predator.*

Chapter 3

RODNEY

The peal of steel against steel broke the spell of an otherwise peaceful spring morning on the grounds of Vincent Castle. The young lord of the estate had been coerced into a sparring match with his brother-in-law, Sir Jason. Shamelessly, Sir Rodney had positioned himself with the rising sun at his back. Without complaint, Jason held his shield close and his eyes narrowed to slits below a polished conical helm.

Clad in full field armour, both men stood three fingers over six feet. Both men were also clean shaven with short cropped hair, as was the custom for knights of their order, but any similarity ended there. While Rodney's face was plain and scarred, Jason's was unmarred and exceedingly handsome. Rodney was the more heavily muscled and, though admitting to a lack of finesse, could deal blows of greater force. Jason, on the other hand, had the grace of a cat paired with the speed of a striking snake.

Enthralled and wide-eyed, despite the early hour, their teenaged squires stood out of harm's way, wrapped in long wool cloaks to ward off the morning chill. For a fleeting moment, Rodney's eyes wandered to his squire, Morton, who shivered despite the heavy cloak. It was hard to believe he was Jason's nephew. Already eighteen and still far too frail for knighthood.

A short cough drew Rodney's attention back to the business at hand. Jason had obviously noticed his distraction, and the cough was his way of letting Rodney know without bringing undue attention to it. Most men would have taken advantage, but not Jason; he was above using such conveniences. Rodney gave his opponent a slight nod, lowered the tip of his weapon, and then stepped

15

to the side. At least he could give up the advantage of the sun to even the score.

The two men began to circle, each waiting for the other to make his move. Despite a well-earned reputation for rashness, Jason had so far been content to plod on with his shield close and sword steady. Rodney had a little surprise in mind, but he needed the right opening. He flicked his sword to the left, but then quickly rotated his wrist to swing the heavy weapon in from the right. With Jason's shield positioned a fraction too low, the tip of Rodney's sword struck a glancing blow against the front of his helm. Jason raised both shield and sword as he stepped back. It was just the opening Rodney had been waiting for.

Without further delay, Rodney lifted his shield and rammed it hard into Jason's, forcing him aside even as Rodney pivoted to the left. At the same time, Rodney swung his sword backhanded in a downward arc. The back edge of the blade struck the unprotected rear of Jason's left knee. He crumpled. If the blow had been delivered with a sharp edge, instead of a blunted practice sword, Jason could have been badly injured or even maimed. Satisfied, Rodney stepped back without pressing the advantage. It was a rare occasion when he could put the Order's best swordsman on his knees. No doubt he would pay for it, but it was worth it.

Though favouring his left leg, Jason was up quickly. "When did you learn that move?" he asked through clenched teeth as they resumed the circling.

"Lionel demonstrated it to me just yesterday," Rodney replied, "and in the very same manner I have just shown you."

Even though he smiled and offered a friendly nod, Jason's face had taken on that dangerous look Rodney remembered so well from their squire days. Rodney was definitely in some serious trouble, but he still couldn't suppress a satisfied smirk.

"Well, since I am in your debt, I shall endeavour to repay your kind deed." Jason's sword was moving downward even as the words slid off his tongue. Rodney tilted his shield to block, but somehow in mid-swing, Jason spun around to Rodney's left side and delivered a hard chop to his shield arm.

"Shit," Rodney swore as he backed away. His gauntlet was twisted and he was having difficulty righting his shield. Jason stood back graciously foregoing any advantage to even the score.

Once sufficient feeling had returned to his arm to enable a solid grip on his shield, Rodney charged. Jason met him head-on and they went at it toe-to-toe exchanging blows until their tin-covered wooden shields were both splintered and cracked.

Breathing heavily, their faces wet with sweat, both men finally backed away. If it came down to stamina, there was no question as to who would outlast the other. While Jason's breathing was rapidly returning to normal, Rodney's chest still heaved like a blacksmith's bellows. In desperation, since waiting would only work against him, Rodney threw all his superior weight into ramming Jason's shield with his own. At the moment of contact however, Jason deftly sidestepped and Rodney stumbled. Jason stood back, patiently waiting.

"Blast it," Rodney roared. Jason was granting him too much grace. It was unseemly. Rodney was a belted Daemon Knight, not some half-trained squire. He'd worn the Order's red dragon for six years. He could not be that hapless a swordsman. His anger grew hotter with each silent self-inflicted insult, then, just when it reached a fevered pitch, his training resurfaced. Instead of making a fool of himself, he let all emotion flow away until his thoughts were as cold and hard as the sword in his hand; then he launched himself at Jason with a vicious downward slash.

The blow slid off Jason's shield as he nimbly danced to the side. Rodney's momentum carried him past his opponent. In passing he felt the thrust of Jason's blade as it stabbed him in the ribs. The jab was painful even through mail and padding. Rodney exhaled sharply. His breath mixed with the steam rising from his overheated body. It formed a swirling cloud of mist before his eyes, bringing on a sudden dizziness.

Rodney shook his head in an attempt to clear his muddled thoughts. Expecting Jason to stand back and allow him to recover, he failed to raise his shield. All Rodney heard was a short whistle as Jason's sword cut through the air. There was an explosion of pain as it struck his left ear guard and cheek. His head twisted with the force of the blow, followed by a ringing in his ears. *Gods, is he trying to kill me?*

"Ha, what sport!" Jason bellowed. Then his broadsword hammered into Rodney's battered shield. A wood fragment, or piece of tin, must have hit Rodney's sweat-covered face, because it burned like a demon. When he licked his lips he could taste blood.

Swaying with the force of the attack, Rodney backed away. His left arm ached terribly. The upper regions had swollen enough that he could feel the pressure against the unforgiving links of his mail. His sword felt like it was made of lead and his face was on fire, but the worst of it all lay in the knowledge that Jason was just toying with him.

Almost too late, Rodney raised his shield just in time to block another blow. The force proved too much for his injured arm, however, and he toppled backwards. The fall knocked the wind out of him and by the time he regained his wits, Jason's blunted sword point was levelled at his throat. His own weapon was pinned beneath Jason's left boot, and his battered shield lay in the dirt six feet away.

"I yield, Jason," Rodney croaked, "but you must joust with me this afternoon so I can at least attempt to reclaim some of my injured pride." He wasn't serious, of course. Losing to Jason did Rodney's pride little harm. He had done it too many times to be of any consequence.

After handing his sword and shield to his squire, Lewis, Jason extended his hand to Rodney. "So be it. You have my promise, even though we both know how it will end. You are unbeatable with a lance."

Grasping Jason's hand, Rodney groaned as he pulled himself up. When Rodney lifted his helm, he winced in pain as the ear guard rubbed against his injured face. After plucking a thin sliver of wood from his cheek he stared in wonder. It was awfully small to have caused so much pain. He flicked it away in disgust. Now, he would have to find some excuse to avoid the joust he had just foolishly arranged.

"Some cold water will bring that swelling down," Jason said.

Glancing up, Rodney grunted a reply. When Jason removed his own helm, a look of dismay crossed his face at the sight of a scratch that marred the black crossed swords painted above the nose guard. He rubbed at the offending blemish as the four of them set off across the courtyard toward the stables.

As they walked, Rodney's thoughts drifted. Vincent Castle had been passed down from father to son in an unbroken chain for two hundred years. Rodney was the last living male Vincent and a bachelor. Would the next Lord of Vincent Castle be a Lambert, or a Tait? In truth, he had felt deserted ever since Sylvia had left the castle the year before as Jason's bride. With both Jason and Lionel lodging at the castle, and his sisters sleeping in their old rooms, it was reminiscent of when his father was alive. Their company did wonders to dispel the oppressive loneliness that had crept into his life as of late.

Sparring with Jason stirred up memories of his father because, like Jason, Sir Frederic had been a master swordsman. Even though his father was twenty-five years older, and past his prime, Rodney was never able to best him in a contest of blades. The ache in his arm served to remind him of his lessons. Pain was a necessary thing for a knight. What didn't kill him, only made him stronger. "The trick," as his father used to say, "is in knowing how to tell when a thing will kill you."

Normally, at the age of seven, a Knight's son would be sent off to page within another's household. For undisclosed reasons of his own, Sir Frederic had elected to go against custom and had trained Rodney himself. Rodney suspected it had much to do with his mother's untimely passing. The Lady Beatrice died giving birth to his second sister, Sylvia, shortly after Rodney's fifth birthday. Heartbroken, his father mourned her loss for the rest of his life. Frederic courted many fair ladies afterward, but none could hold a candle to the flame Beatrice had ignited in his heart. His father's anecdotes of their six short years together, retold time and time again, were etched into Rodney's mind. He could remember little of her himself save a warm smile and infectious laugh.

Upon reaching the water trough, just outside the stables, Rodney gripped the sides and plunged his head in, breaking the thin layer of ice that had formed overnight. The chill numbed the pain in his face. He shook off the water like a wet dog, and took a deep breath. When his eyes opened, he could see the tops of apple trees sticking up above the wall behind the stables. Though still bare, soon the air would be filled with the sweet perfume of apple blossoms. In the heart of the orchard lay the flower garden, preserved exactly as it was these past twenty-two years in memory of Lady Beatrice. When Rodney strolled along its stone paths, he felt her presence. For the last five years, ever since his father had gone to join her in the otherworld, Rodney could sense Sir Frederic's presence as well. It pleased him to think their souls were together again, in the place they had both loved so much.

"Your mail will rust."

"What?" Rodney asked, his reverie broken.

"Your mail," Jason said, "it will rust to uselessness if you leave it wet." Jason knitted his brows as he peered deeply into Rodney's eyes. "Perhaps I hit you a little too hard on the head. Shall I send Lewis for a physician?"

Rodney finally noticed concern in evidence on Jason's face. "What, oh, no need for that. Right as rain. Just thinking."

"Ha, too much of that will addle your brains."

"I was thinking of Sir Frederic."

"Ah, those were the days," Jason replied softly. "The years spent within these walls I remember with great fondness. Your father made good knights of all three of us. Did he not?"

"Yes, he truly did, in spite of how vexatious we must have been," Rodney replied with a childlike grin, and then winced at the pain it caused his swollen cheek.

"I have no doubt we were that."

"Do you remember the time I dared you to jump from the mill? You know, I never believed you would actually do it."

Jason frowned and shook his head. "The river was not as deep as I had believed. As I recall, Sir Frederic took considerable pleasure in stitching me up afterwards."

"It shames me to admit it now," Rodney said, "but I have been remiss in our friendship by keeping something from you all these years. In my defence, I can only say I was young, foolish, and more than a little resentful. I hope you can forgive me."

Jason opened his mouth to speak, but Rodney raised his hand to signal that he was not finished. "Later that day, my father confided in me that he was much impressed with your courage, if not your stupidity. He said he gave you ten stitches, rather unkindly, and yet you never flinched or complained. He said you were fearless, and the toughest little beggar he had seen in a long time."

"He said that?"

"Yes he did. I was envious, so kept it to myself. Do not let it swell your head though, for in the next breath he swore no one could train such an undisciplined and headstrong boy."

"I did not care much for Lionel back then," Jason said obviously trying to change the subject.

His friend's inept attempt at subtlety brought a smile to Rodney's lips. "He was a bit of hard cheese back then, I will say that."

"Just two years older and ordering us about as if we were his squires. All fast comrades in arms now though," Jason said slapping Rodney on the back. Rodney flinched at the renewed pain in his arm, but Jason seemed oblivious.

After pulling off his gauntlets and coif, Rodney handed them to Morton who was still holding his practice sword, shield and helm in outstretched arms. Unlike Jason, who wore a short mail shirt, Rodney preferred his knee-length. Lewis stepped forward to help peel off the heavy mail, and then draped it over Morton's already sizable burden. The backside of his mail was covered in dirt turned to mud by the water from the trough. Rodney pulled off an equally soiled padded vest, and tossed it on top of the mail. Morton's burden appeared to be taxing the limits of his strength. What was Rodney going to do with him?

"Return the equipment to Master Gilbert if you please," Rodney said. "Then clean the mud from my mail and dry it by the forge."

Weighted down with a mountain of harness and steel, Morton looked toward the smithy. It was a large squat stone building attached to the stables. A curl of black smoke drifted up from the chimney. A smile appeared on Morton's blue tinged lips. The forge was never allowed to go out. He was no doubt thinking the smithy would be warm and comfortable.

"Lewis, would you be so kind as to clean and dry my mail as well," Jason said, handing Lewis his own equipment, all of which he had removed himself.

As the two young men trotted off to the warmth of the smithy, Rodney could not help but notice that Jason had barely worked up a sweat. There were but two small stains below the arm holes of his tunic. As for his mail, aside from a small patch of dirt on the back, it was as spotless and shiny as ever. His equipment needed neither cleaning nor drying so Jason must have wanted to give the young squires more time to gossip. Most knights took on just one, with perhaps another once their current squire neared knighthood. That left squires with little opportunity to spend time with someone of their own age and station, except at tourneys or visits. Rodney and Jason's experience had been the exception, not the rule.

"Ah, here comes Lionel," Rodney said upon catching sight of the tall lanky knight crossing the courtyard with his easy stride. He was as dashing as ever with his blond curly hair and winning smile. "You seem well-rested Jason. Perhaps Lionel would like to spar with you for a bit."

Jason's eyes lit up. "Oh, I needs call Lewis back." Rodney laughed and Jason smiled meekly once realizing it was a jest.

"A good morning to you, sword brothers," Lionel said in his rich baritone. He glanced at Rodney's face and frowned. "You've been in a major battle I see.

I thought the tourney was not until the day after next."

"Just a lucky blow," Jason said.

"I doubt that," Lionel replied with a knowing smile. "A sound drubbing I would wager."

"A wager you would win," Rodney said before Jason could reply.

"Your modesty is misplaced Jason," Lionel said shaking his head. "You bested me even after I was knighted, and you with nearly two years left to squire. I take great solace in the fact you also bested Sir Frederic himself the following year. I had not thought it possible, and would not still if I had not seen it with my own eyes."

"Nor I," added Rodney. Never seeming comfortable with praise, Jason blushed.

Lionel winked at Rodney. "Ah, now for the reason that I am here, instead of relaxing by a warm fire. Lady Sylvia requests the company of both her wayward husband and dear brother for an early breakfast. My own sweet wife is famished and wishes you to know that she will be most angry if you do not make haste."

"As impatient and demanding as ever I see," Rodney said before he could stop himself. "No offence, Lionel" he quickly added.

"None taken, Rodney. I have known Elinor since I was seven and she but a babe. Your observation is most accurate. She ordered me about when I was a page and teased me relentlessly as her father's squire."

"Then wed and bed you the moment she came of age," Jason quipped and the three of them laughed together.

"I am glad for your company," Rodney said when their laughter had subsided. "The castle becomes a lonely place over a long winter, however, since I have no desire for another drubbing, especially of the verbal sort, we had best not keep my sisters waiting any longer."

Chapter 4

JOHN

In a lush open meadow two leagues south of Vincent Castle, John Coch watched his flock graze lazily on dandelion tops and the first new grass shoots of spring. He was perched comfortably on a small rock at the edge of the meadow with his back resting against a large gnarled oak. The sun had risen, but a thick cloud of morning mist clung tenaciously to the tree tops and the air remained brisk.

Like most mornings, John was saddled with the responsibility of safeguarding the family's livestock. The Coch family had been shepherds and vassals to the Vincent family for as long as anyone could remember. When the first Lord Vincent had set sail for Balor with Baron Carl Daemon, there had probably been a Coch in his retinue. In spite of much grander dreams, John was following in the footsteps of his father and every other Coch before him. It had been more than twenty years since anyone had even seen a wolf in this part of Balor, however, so in reality his job was simply to ensure the sheep didn't wander off and get lost.

The boy's attention this particular morning was not on the flock, however, but on the nearly finished longbow resting in his lap. Four and a half years had passed since he chanced upon the bowyer's yew tree just south of his cottage. He remembered the day well, it being his eleventh birthday. When he triumphantly displayed the find to his father, he was rewarded with a smile accompanied by a fatherly slap on the back. High praise from Peter Coch. John and his father spent the rest of that afternoon rough-cutting staves.

The yew had yielded four perfect six-foot lengths. The grain was straight, with no knots or rot in the heart wood. The elder Coch had told his son that in all his days he had never seen better, but then came the bad news. John would have to wait four years for the wood to age properly. It seemed like a lifetime, but as the previous summer's end drew near, his father finally declared them ready to work. Keeping the best quarter for himself, John had made a gift of the second best to his father. The other two he sold at the Riverside fall market. The sale had earned him a tidy sum, amounting to what was a small fortune for a fifteen-year old sheepherder.

John was keenly focussed on the final sanding with a patience only a shepherd could possess. He had worked at the stave in stages over the winter. To achieve a fine smooth finish he was using a piece of dried shark skin. The skin he had purchased for the exorbitant price of three pennies and a reed flute. Knute, the fisherman's son, had driven a hard bargain, but John was pleased with the finish and well satisfied with the transaction.

A gust of wind gave John cause to look up just in time to see a large dark shape break through the mist and descend on the flock. He stared in wide-eyed horror as the thing passed directly overhead with a bleating ewe in each of its wickedly hooked rear talons. Frozen with fear, he watched it soar back up and disappear in the swirling mist. A moment later, first one ewe, then the other, punched through the mist and slammed into the ground with sickening thuds.

By this time, the rest of the flock had fled in the general direction of home and their pens. John, however, was still unable to move when the creature returned and landed, surprisingly lightly for its incredible bulk, next to the bodies of the ewes. It stood so tall that everything above the base of its neck was hidden by the mist. John had barely recovered his wits when the monster lowered a long neck, which ended in a large and hideous head. A stream of fire flowed from its open maw, engulfing the dead ewes along with the patch of grass around them. When the thing finally closed its mouth, black greasy smoke and the stink of burnt wool filled the air. Lowering its head once more, it released yet another blast of red-hot fire.

Once the flames had died away, the creature reached out with its two short front legs. They could have been arms, except they ended in smaller versions of the same claws on its hind legs. Despite their clumsy appearance, those claws deftly grasped a blackened leg on the nearest charred ewe and bent it back until the bone snapped. Then it tore the leg off and flipped it up. The serpentine head darted down and snatched it from the air, its sizable jaws snapping shut with a crunch.

The creature's mouth moved rhythmically as it chewed the mutton leg. That's when John noticed a smaller head at the base of the monster's neck. A knot of fear and revulsion formed in the pit of his stomach. The second head looked human. Somehow that made it all the more terrifying. Self-preservation finally overcame fear and John crawled silently back into the trees. Once in the relative safety of the woods, he leapt to his feet and ran for his life.

It was a full quarter league between the meadow and his cottage. John was determined to cover the distance as quickly as his long gangly legs could manage. On the way he caught up with the sheep. Using his bow as a shepherd's staff, he hurried the last one along with a slap on the rump. Somewhere along the way he dropped the shark skin. "Pathos's bad luck," he cursed, realizing it was no longer in his hand, but he wasn't about to go back and search for it.

Upon his arrival, John herded the sheep into an empty pen as quickly as he could. Without even counting them, he latched the gate closed and darted for the cottage. Gasping for air, he yanked on the door and stumbled inside.

When John burst through the door, his parents were sitting at the table sipping tea from clay cups. They looked up in unison as their son leaned against the table trying to catch his breath. His father put down his cup. looking very annoyed. "What the blazes are you doing home at this time of day?"

His mother Annabelle set down her cup. "Are you well son? You look as white as a ghost."

"A monster... A monster is eating the sheep," John managed between gasps.

"What nonsense are you on about now, boy?" his father said sharply, the frown on his face a perfect match for the irritation in his voice.

"Father, I swear, it's bigger than this cottage and flew through the air. A dragon, that's what it is. A two-headed dragon and it's eating the livestock."

"Flew you say boy. Pair of eagles by the sound of it. I have heard tell a big one will sometimes take a lamb."

John looked at his father dumbfounded. He couldn't believe his ears. Somehow he had to make his father understand. "It picked up two ewes, one in each claw. It has two heads and spits fire. Do eagles spit fire!"

"Calm down boy. Calm down. I'll get my bow and we'll deal with this eagle or whatever it is." His father put on his cloak and grabbed his longbow from the corner. He bent it around his knee, stringing it in one quick practised motion before grabbing a quiver from the wooden peg by the door on his way out. John stared at his father's back through the open doorway. Recalling the gigantic proportions of the beast, he just shook his head and followed.

It took considerably longer for Peter Coch to retrace his son's steps, John following impatiently on his heels. At the edge of the meadow John's father turned to face him. "Do you want to admit now that you were just trying to pull the wool over your old father's eyes?"

When John made no reply his father just shrugged. It was one of those disappointed long-suffering shrugs that only a father could give to his son. Then he stepped out from the protection of the woods and strode boldly into the meadow.

With some small satisfaction, John observed his father's demeanour wilt at the sight of the beast swallowing down the last of a charred hind leg. When it belched, the quiver slipped from his father's fingers spilling its shafts onto the grass. His father backed away woodenly. Once in the trees, he just stood and stared with a vacant look in his eyes.

John finally broke the silence. "Is that a dragon?"

The elder Coch nodded his head in silence until another loud belch from the meadow sent them both running. By the time they arrived home, his father was too winded to speak. "Go John," he gasped. "Go to the castle. Warn Lord Vincent... a dragon... has invaded... his estate."

John nodded once before turning down the trail leading to the main road. Pacing himself, he settled into a steady gait that allowed him to cover the two leagues to Vincent Castle without stopping for rest. Upon reaching the gates he paused at the portcullis to catch his breath and figure out what to do next. Though he had been to the castle countless times, John normally went straight down to the docks to visit with his friend Knute. While leaning against the stone wall, panting, he spotted two guardsmen crossing the court yard. They were an odd pair; one was tall and thin while the other short and fat. After gulping down one last quick breath he sprinted toward them.

"Dragon," John blurted out as soon as he was close enough to be heard.

"What?" said the taller of the two guards.

"A fire breathing two-headed dragon is eating our sheep," John managed between deep breaths.

After a moment of dead silence both men guffawed. "You hear that Garrick," the short, fat one said, slapping his thigh with the flat of his hand. "A dragon he says. With two heads, no less."

"We had better warn the Master-at-arms before it burns the castle down, Shem," Garrick replied in mock seriousness. Both men roared with laugher at the jape.

"It's true, I swear it's true by all the Gods," John wailed. "The dragon was as big as a mountain and spit fire. Turlough strike me dead with a lightning bolt if I tell a lie."

The smiles disappeared. Shem crossed his chest with the sign of Ulrich and Garrick glanced up to the sky. "Careful what you say to the Gods, lad," Garrick said softly. "You never know when they are listening."

John stood defiantly in silence. Why were adults so mutton headed? The dragon will have eaten all the sheep, both his parents and burned the cottage to the ground before he got them to listen.

Garrick placed a strong callused hand on John's shoulder. "All right lad, we'll take you to the bailiff, he'll know what to do with you, but mark my words, if you are up to mischief you'll be switched for sure." John blanched but stood his ground. Garrick spun John roughly around and then pushed him in the direction of the inner keep.

At the main door he was turned over to Albert Beane, Lord Vincent's bailiff. Albert was very old and wore heavy wool robes that only partially concealed a hunched back. John tried not to stare as they walked down a long hallway. It was his first time inside the keep and he was awestruck by its grandeur. It was even bigger than the Riverside Inn, where he and his father stayed on their yearly trip to sell wool at the fall market.

The bailiff took John through a series of hallways until they stopped abruptly in front an open doorway. When the aroma of fresh baked bread drifted by his nose, a rumbling in his stomach reminded him that he had missed breakfast. "Are you ready Fabian," Albert barked through the doorway.

Curiosity got the better of him and John peeked around the bailiff's robe to see two men standing by a huge rack of steaming bread. His stomach growled again. Luckily, no one seemed to notice.

The man whom John assumed was the baker, because of his long white apron, tapped his index finger on a few loaves. "They have cooled enough to be removed from the rack," he said in a shrill voice. "Mouse, give Pantler Fabian three loaves."

A young boy, the baker's apprentice judging by all the flour on his face, plucked three loaves from the rack and deposited them on the pantler's platter next to three little dishes of melted fat. "It's about time," Fabian snapped. "Eunice, Gretal, to the hall."

As Fabian marched out of the kitchen, a pretty young girl followed with a platter of cold sliced venison. Behind her came an even prettier girl carrying a platter of cheeses. The second girl turned her head and smiled at John as she passed. The ends of her long light brown hair brushed his face briefly. Grand castles and two-headed dragons were quickly forgotten. Her smile seemed to be all that mattered. John felt his face redden as he sheepishly smiled back.

The baker's shrill voice snapped John out of his pubescent fog. "Get back to work, Mouse. There are still plenty of loaves to rack before we can start on the tart shells."

The bailiff placed a thin gnarled hand on John's shoulder and gave him a little shove in the direction of the departing bread and cheese. John gladly followed on the heels of the beautiful brown haired serving girl.

Chapter 5

RODNEY

A cosy fire blazed happily in the great hall's hearth. Its warmth extended all the way to the raised main table where Rodney sat slumped in the Lord's high backed padded chair. Elinor, by virtue of being the eldest sister, sat on his right next to Lionel. Sylvia and Jason were seated to his left. Two pages, the young grandsons of Lionel's uncle Philip, stood on each side of the Lord's chair waiting to serve. Kyle, the younger boy, held a jug of chicory root tea while the older Walter held one of mulled cider.

It had been a while since Rodney was last granted an opportunity to entertain guests. As luck would have it, he was too distracted with his own discomforts to play the good host. It had been pure folly to cross swords with Jason, especially just two days before the annual tourney, but after a long winter with only Morton and the guards to spar with, the temptation had been irresistible. The match had left him with a throbbing headache which so far showed no signs of abating.

The son of a physician, his man Garrick was skilled in dressing battlefield wounds. He had seen to Rodney's face at the bequest of Sylvia, who steadfastly refused to start breakfast until her brother's injuries had been seen to. At least it no longer felt like his face was being prodded with a hot poker. One of Garrick's unpleasant smelling salves had dulled the pain. Unfortunately, the only cure Garrick knew for a headache was willow bark tea. It was a vile brew Rodney couldn't stomach at the best of times.

When reaching for his cup, Rodney was rewarded with a sharp pain in his ribs. He had failed to mention his injured side to Garrick, an oversight he was beginning to regret. Switching hands, he snatched up the cup and drained it in one gulp. Young Kyle quickly stepped forward to refill it with more chicory tea.

Raising the warm cup to his lips, Rodney closed his eyes and paused to savour the aroma. The castle well produced plenty of sweet water, but it ran dry every summer forcing them to use the river until after the fall rains. The estate's proximity to the sea meant the river was slightly brackish and its bitter taste tended to spoil the flavour of his tea. Most everyone drank chilled cider in the summer's heat but Rodney had never developed a fondness for cider warm or cold. At this time of year, however, he could enjoy chicory tea to his heart's content.

"Have you found a suitable young maiden to take to wife?" Elinor asked in a tone that was as sweet as honey, yet cut like a knife.

Rolling his eyes, Rodney remained silent in the hope that ignoring her question would end the matter, but no such luck. A satisfied smile formed on Elinor's full lips. "I thought not," she said rather smugly. "Lionel's sister is comely enough, and I think quite taken with you. You might find her willing if you were to but court her. She is without question the perfect match for you." Elinor leaned forward and glanced down the table. "Would you not agree, Sylvia?"

From the corner of his eye Rodney caught Sylvia wince. Setting her cup down, she gave Rodney a long-suffering look. "It is true that Colette would make a wonderful bride for Rodney," she said politely before her voice turned sour, "were he interested in finding one."

Once his sisters got started there would be no stopping them, so Rodney thought it best to nip the conversion in the bud before things got out of hand. "Colette is a beauty, there is no doubt, and as fine a bride as any man could hope for, but alas, I have no desire for a wife. This castle and my knightly duties consume me." At that moment, Fabian and his retinue entered the far end of the hall. Rodney seized upon the opportunity to extricate himself from an uncomfortable conversation. "Ah, here comes our breakfast."

The pantler led the rest of the servitors up to the table. With a flourish he placed a loaf of bread and a dish of congealing fat on each of the three platters. The serving girls transferred generous portions of meat and cheese onto three smaller platters resting on the table before taking their places off to the side next to the pantler.

Jason sliced off a small piece of meat and offered it to Sylvia skewered on the end of his belt knife. She made a face and shook her head. Jason shrugged and tore off a chunk of bread and dipped it in the fat. Folding the meat into the bread he stuffed it all at once into his mouth. Sylvia reached over and wiped the grease tenderly from the corners of his lips with her forefinger.

Their actions forced the corners of Rodney's lips to rise despite his pounding head. Jason and Sylvia were like happy children at play. Glancing back to his right, Rodney's eyes locked onto Elinor's. For a moment he was worried she would broach the subject of marriage again, but then Lionel came to his rescue. "Jason, what contests strike your fancy in the tourney?"

After kissing his wife's finger, Jason responded without taking his eyes from her face. "Master-of-the-sword of course, and then perhaps the melee."

"I understand Sir Martin intends to ride for the red in the melee," Lionel said flatly.

At the mention of the name Jason's face clouded over. "Then I shall ride for the yellow," he snapped back.

Rodney rubbed his temples. It was fortunate Jason had friends. Left to his own devices, he would have been killed thrice over no matter how expert a swordsman he was. Rodney cleared his throat. "You know the rules, Jason. You cannot ride in the melee against a knight with whom you have a quarrel. If your cousin rides for the red then so must you, or not at all."

"I'll not ride with Martin Neville, rules or no!"

"Then stay out of the melee," Rodney said softly. "Be content to defend your title as Master-of-the-sword."

Lionel leaned forward to look Jason in the eye. "Rodney is right, Jason. Besides, Sir Talbot and Sir Joel will undoubtedly be at his side. I doubt Martin can take a piss without Talbot getting his boots wet."

Jason's anger immediately turned to laughter. Rodney nearly choked on a mouthful of tea while his sisters covered their mouths, attempting to hide their amusement at such a rude remark. It would seem no one cared much for ferret-faced Sir Talbot.

The only one at the table maintaining any kind of serious expression was Lionel. "You may all laugh, but Sir Talbot can put a dagger in a man's eye at twenty paces nine times out of ten. It would be extremely foolish to be caught among those three, Jason, and you know it. I would wager your cousin is most eager to avenge that nasty scar you gave him last year. You had best watch your back, that is all I have to say."

"I do not understand why you and your cousin maintain this animosity between you," Rodney said. "You and Sylvia have been wed now for over a year. Martin has taken Bella Malet as his bride, and I understand she is now with child. It is just plain foolishness. The matter must be settled. The only honourable thing now is to let bygones be bygones and offer him your hand in friendship."

Jason's face went as white as new snow. You would think Rodney had asked him to kiss a viper.

31

"After all Jason," Lionel said, wearing an innocent looking smile, "you cannot fault the man for desiring Sylvia as his bride. She would be a prize for any knight."

The remark drew an icy glare from Sylvia. "I am not some prize war horse to be won in a bicker," she said raising voice. "Knights! You all act more like spoiled children!"

Rodney groaned. Lionel had an uncanny knack for saying just the right thing to annoy Sylvia to distraction. It had been so ever since she was five years old.

"Master-of-the-sword it is," Jason said, once again smiling. Elinor wore a smile as well, but hers seemed insincere and did not touch her eyes.

A series of coughs, coming from the end of the hall, finally caught Rodney's attention. Albert Beane and a rather nervous looking young lad were waiting at the entrance to the hall. Once noticed, Albert led the lad in. They stopped an arms length from the table and the Bailiff bowed. His charge made an awkward imitation of Albert's long practised performance.

"What is your name boy?" Rodney heard Albert whisper from the side of his mouth.

"John... John Coch, sir," the lad whispered back.

"John Coch," Albert said indicating the young lad with an open palm, "one of your vassals, a sheepherder I believe, requests an audience, Sir Rodney."

Rodney looked John over. As tall as a man, but no more than fourteen or fifteen years old, he reminded Rodney of himself when he was about that age. Even his straight cropped light brown hair was much like his own. The sight dredged up bitter memories from his fifteenth year. It was his first, and last, experience with love. A new governess had taken up residence at Vincent Castle that summer. Her name was Selina, the daughter of Sir Desmond Bailey. Even though she was five years older, Rodney was smitten the moment he laid eyes upon her. He professed his love in the garden. She laughed, called him a silly boy, and then tussled his hair as if he were a child. Rodney's young ego was crushed, but he kept it to himself and they spoke no more of it.

For days Rodney moped aimlessly about until one evening he chanced upon his father and Selina walking hand in hand through the garden. Rodney stalked them, staying hidden in the shadows. When they parted, Selina reached up and kissed Sir Frederic on the cheek. They may as well have plunged a knife into his heart. On that day Rodney made a solemn vow to never love. Physical wounds were painful, but love was a cut that never healed. Six months later Selina left Vincent Castle to wed Sir Duncan Breen.

The bailiff clearing his throat pulled Rodney back to the present. Rodney nodded his permission and Albert nudged the boy with his elbow. "Speak up boy," he growled.

The sheepherder gave an outlandish account of a winged two-headed dragon that swooped down and devoured two of his flock. The hall was cloaked in silence by the time he had finished. Rodney had to give the lad credit; he was a convincing liar and had all the makings of a fine bard. Obviously the lad lost two of his sheep and had concocted a wild story to cover up his negligence, but it did give Rodney a good reason to excuse himself from both an unwanted discussion on marriage and the joust with Jason.

"Sir Lionel, Sir Jason," Rodney said as a broad smile spread across his face. "Would you be so kind as to accompany me? It appears we have a dragon to dispatch."

"Ha, what sport," Jason cried, slamming his fist on the table.

"You can't be serious, Rodney," Lionel said aghast. "At the very least the lad is suffering from delusions."

Lionel was right, it was ludicrous, but Rodney was determined. "Nevertheless," he said boldly, "it is a short ride and might prove an entertaining distraction, besides, what knight worth his salt would pass up an opportunity to slay a dragon."

"Right, wouldn't miss it for the world," Lionel replied shaking his head.

"Come lad," Rodney said. "You shall ride with me."

Even though midday was fast approaching the air remained cool and fresh. It made for an invigorating ride. If not for a persistent headache, Rodney would have called it perfect. Spring was his favourite time of the year, warm enough for comfort but without the annoyance of the summer season's buzzing and biting insects. He was in such good humour, despite his head, that the reason for being out in the countryside was all but forgotten until he heard the young sheepherder's voice. "The clearing is just up ahead."

The lad slid down from behind his saddle the moment Rodney reined in. For a long heartbeat, Rodney feared Thunder would kick. It wasn't normal for the big black destrier to tolerate anyone near his backside, not even Rodney, and Thunder had more than enough power in those hind legs to crush a man's skull. Luckily, the horse stayed calm and the lad had enough sense to not linger, but then Thunder's behaviour had been unusual all morning. He made no fuss when

Rodney hauled the lanky sheepherder up behind the saddle. Such was never the case with Morton. Perhaps John, by profession, simply lacked fear of animals. Rodney's father had once mentioned that horses could sense such things and would respond in kind.

The young sheepherder was quick to disappear down the narrow trail. Rodney touched heels to Thunder's flanks and followed at a trot until the trail disappeared in a tangle of crisscrossed overhanging branches. He was just about to stop when he spotted the sheepherder pressed tight against a small twisted oak. The lad was peering into an open meadow. Ducking his head, Rodney coaxed Thunder to push through.

The moment they cleared the branches, Thunder stopped short as Rodney's jaw dropped in amazement. The dragon, for it could be nothing else, was just as John described. The giant rust-red creature sat balanced between two thick hind legs and a long coiled snakelike tail. Great folded wings protruded from the shoulders and extended down the sides of the body to end just above the hind legs. Holding an unrecognizable piece of bone to its mouth, it appeared to be sucking out the marrow like some giant dog. Intent on its meal, the dragon didn't seem to notice Rodney, or Jason and Lionel when they reined in on either side. Rodney glanced quickly at his companions. Lionel looked startled but Jason seemed pleased. Controlling Thunder was taking more and more effort with each passing moment. When the dragon stretched its wings, Lionel's horse snorted and tried to back away.

With its wings extended the dragon seemed even larger. Its quick jerky motions were bird-like and somewhat awkward, as if not accustomed to being on the ground. Perhaps it was preparing to take flight. If they were going to act it would have to be soon. Rodney drew his sword, but the blade seemed most inadequate for the job at hand. In hindsight he wished he had brought a steel tipped war lance. Calming himself, he tried to think the situation through logically. What would his father have done? He would formulate a plan of attack. Since the dragon appeared ill suited for moving about on the ground, they should slice its wings to render it incapable of flight. Then, the three of them working together could dispatch it at their leisure. The beast seemed incapable of moving with any great speed, so it would be just a matter of time before they wore it down.

The plan was simple enough. Rodney just needed to inform his companions; unfortunately, he never got the chance. Before Rodney could say a word Jason charged on ahead waving his sword in the air and screaming like a madman. Dumbstruck, Rodney let him get thirty feet away before he thought to put heels to Thunder.

The moment Jason neared the dragon, its head spun toward him with surprising speed for a creature of such bulk. Accompanied by a thunderous roar, one of its broad wings swung out to knock both Jason and his mount to the ground. The horse struggled to regain its feet with Jason's left leg pinned beneath it. By the time Rodney rode past, the terrified horse had finally rolled upright and was galloping away in the opposite direction leaving his injured rider laying in the grass.

While Lionel approached their quarry from the right, Rodney veered in from the left. This time the beast reared up and pumped both of its massive wings. The wind from those powerful strokes literally blew Lionel from his saddle. White-eyed with panic, the riderless horse followed Jason's mount off into the forest. By some miracle Rodney managed to stay in the saddle, but Thunder was of a mind to join the other horses. By the time Rodney had reasserted his will the dragon was sniffing at Lionel's unmoving body.

With no desire to see his brother-in-law eaten, Rodney dug his spurs frantically into Thunder's sides. Long hours of training overcame fear and the big war horse lurched forward. Ducking under the right wing, Rodney hacked away at the dragon's hind leg in a desperate attempt to hamstring it. To his shock, sparks flew from his blade as it glanced off with little or no effect. The beast's scales were as hard as flint. Finally, after much persistence, the tip of his blade found its way beneath one of the scales. That produced another great roar as the creature swept him from his saddle with a jerk of its injured leg. Rodney was hurled to the ground. He heard something snap. It felt like a hot knife being driven into his side and he barely managed to hold on to consciousness.

Thunder had also gone down, but he rolled back up bucking and kicking until the spirited destrier finally delivered a good solid blow to the Dragon's belly with both hind legs. The dragon howled and staggered back. When it extended its long neck, a stream of fire erupted from its maw. The flames missed Thunder by less than a single arm's length, close enough to singe his mane and send him bolting for the trees.

While the dragon had been preoccupied with Thunder, Jason had somehow managed to get back on his feet and limp to within striking distance unnoticed. The dragon's large green eyes were still fixated on the retreating horse, leaving its rounded belly exposed. Holding his sword levelled at his waist, with his right arm drawing back and his left gripping the blade near the hilt, Jason appeared intent on driving the blade straight into the creature's belly. Rodney watched as Jason tensed his shoulder for the thrust, but at that angle he was never going to penetrate the beast's armoured hide.

"Up under the scales," Rodney screamed. The effort brought on an explosion of pain in his side just as a loud and unnatural voice boomed across the meadow like a crack of thunder.

"Enough!"

His ears ringing, Rodney finally noticed a white-haired man astride the dragon's shoulders. The dragon-rider clutched at his chest with his left hand while thrusting out his right. Jason's sword flew from his grip with enough force to land twenty feet away. Oddly enough, Jason just stood there motionless without trying to retrieve it. Despite the excruciating pain in his side, Rodney forced himself to stand. Dizzy and nauseated, he picked up his own sword from where it lay in the grass. Painfully he raised the blade above his head only to have it torn away by some unseen hand.

Without pause Rodney pulled the dagger from the scabbard at his belt. He managed one agonizing step forward before finding his feet would no longer obey him. With unseen bonds holding him fast, the dragon now turned its attention to him. Rodney stood helpless as the dagger slid from the numb fingers of his outstretched hand. All he could do was swallow down the lump that had formed in his throat, and wait for the end. He hoped it would at least be quick.

The dragon lowered his ugly horned head until his lower jaw lay flat on the ground near Rodney's feet. Although unable to move, Rodney could still observe. He noticed the beast had two small horns near where he imagined ears should be. He would have laughed, if he could. His last worldly thought was going to be about where a dragon's ears might be. With the beast's head out of the way, Rodney could clearly see the dragon-rider seated in a saddle of sorts at the base of its long neck. The man slid down the beast's neck and dropped to the ground. He was unsteady and stiff, like someone too long in the saddle.

Ignoring Rodney, the dragon-rider set about inspecting a small wound on his mount's leg where Rodney had struck it. There was a trickle of copper coloured liquid that must have been the dragon's blood flowing from between the scales. After fumbling around in a leather pouch at his side, the old man withdrew a small vial and poured the contents into his hand. Reaching up under the scales, he applied it to the wound. The dragon closed its large green eyes and made purring noises like a cat. The corners of its great mouth seemed to curve up into a smile. The procedure was repeated at the location on the creature's belly where Thunder had kicked it.

When he was done, the dragon-rider placed the vial back in his pouch, which then seemed to disappear somewhere within his long robe. He approached Jason and stared at his face briefly before reaching out to touch his helm. The dragon-rider's face registered a reaction to the crossed swords he found painted there. Rodney tried to speak, but he had no more control of his tongue than his feet. All he could do was watch and wait. The dragon-rider knelt down and placed his hand firmly on Jason's thigh. Rodney swallowed another lump in his throat as a ghostly glow formed around the old man's hand.

When the glow faded away the dragon-rider stood and walked over to Rodney. He smiled as he reached out and touched Rodney's hand. A pleasant warmth flowed into Rodney's left arm and ribs almost immediately. When the strange old man removed his hand, there was a pins-and-needles sensation as if Rodney's arm had been asleep. Amazingly, when the sensation faded, the pain was completely gone. Unfortunately, Rodney still couldn't move.

As if possessing all the time in the world, the old man casually reached down and touched Rodney's belt buckle. He stood back with his head cocked to one side and, resting a forefinger under his lip, obviously considering something, then waved his hand across Rodney's face. Rodney staggered as the rigidness drained from his body. He felt as weak as a new born lamb, but at least he could move again.

"You had a badly broken rib so I took the liberty of mending it," the old man said still smiling. "The method of healing I employed is fast but taxes your reserves of strength. Broken bones require a lot so you can expect to feel weak for the rest of the day. By morning you will be fit as ever."

"My thanks," Rodney said, not quite sure he understood what was happening.

"Ah, but where are my manners? Let me introduce myself. I am Wizard Aldus Lasairian." He waved his hand toward Jason as he spoke. When Rodney saw Jason sag, he knew his friend had been released from the same invisible bonds that had moments before held Rodney prisoner.

"And this," Aldus said indicating the Dragon, "is my good friend Grigor." The dragon gave a snort at the mention of his name. "Now, if you will excuse me, I must see to your unconscious friend over there."

The wizard walked over to where Lionel lay in a heap. Kneeling by the fallen knight, he placed a thin white hand on Lionel's forehead where a long and ugly purple welt had risen. Lionel wasn't going to be happy about that. He was rather vain about his appearance. A few moments passed and then Lionel moaned. When Aldus removed his hand, the welt was gone.

"This one had a minor head injury," Aldus said. "He will still have quite a headache when he comes around, but it will pass in time."

With genuine sympathy, Rodney nodded silently in response. The old wizard looked tired as he walked back to take his place beside the Dragon, which now lay on its belly with its head flat on the ground and its eyes level with the wizard's waist.

As Rodney and Jason helped their disoriented friend back on his feet, they tried to explain everything that had happened since he was thrown from his mount. By the time they finished, the sheepherder had found enough courage to venture out from the safety of the trees. He seemed nervous, but once Rodney introduced everyone the lad visibly relaxed. His eyes, however, remained fixed on the dragon.

"I am sure you all have many questions," Aldus said as he scratched at his chin through his long beard. His eyes roamed back and forth as if considering each one of them before he finally settled on addressing Rodney. "I came seeking the descendants of Carl Daemon's followers; the Daemon Knights. I assume by your belt buckles that I have found them."

"We are of the order," Rodney replied cautiously.

"Good, because the people of Coronis are in desperate need of your help. The continent is on the verge of war. One that will arrive on your shores all too soon, perhaps even next spring."

The wizard paused and looked at each of them in turn as if to gauge the effect of his words before continuing. "Legions of Imperial Dog Soldiers are even now on the march. The Emperor's interests lay far to the east for the moment, but that will change once he has defeated King Solon and has a firm grip on Icarus."

"You wish for Balor to go to war?" Rodney asked.

"No, no, not at all. I have a mission much more important in mind. One that is vital to stopping Gamel and saving us all."

"Who is this Gamel?" Jason asked.

"I forget how isolated you are here," Aldus replied. "Gamel Cola is the Emperor of Nagual. A very ambitious man, and a powerful wizard in his own right. What brought me here, however, was not the Imperial threat. The Emperor's one-time apprentice, a young sorceress by the name of Magdalen, poses the greatest threat to Coronis now."

"No offence to you, Wizard," Lionel said, "but magic aside, how can one woman possibly threaten an entire continent?"

"You have demonstrated your power, wizard," Rodney said. "Why not just dispatch this sorceress yourself."

"If only it were that simple," Aldus replied, shaking his head. "If you will bear with me for but a moment, I will attempt to answer both of your questions. Now, beside the fact that where magic is concerned sex has no bearing at all, Magdalen possesses Aedon, an ancient and powerful talisman. It was with Aedon the first FireDrakes were formed, and from them that all others like Grigor have sprung. Before the wizard who made them died, he gave Aedon to the FireDrakes for safe keeping. He feared it would one day be used against them, and with good reason, for they are immune to all magic save Aedon's. It was kept hidden well enough for many centuries, but this Magdalen was somehow able to worm her way into their confidence and snatch it out from under them. Now they are completely in thrall to her."

"Is that why you used an ointment on Grigor instead of your magic," the sheepherder said. "He is... immune."

"Ah, bright lad," the wizard replied, smiling at John. "You are correct in your assumption. Only Aedon has power over our friend Grigor here. For good or ill."

Aldus's smile faded as he turned back to Rodney. "Now you understand. Magic alone is no defence against a FireDrake. On a whim, Magdalen can command hundreds like Grigor to lay waste to Solon's kingdom, or to Toth, Carpathia, perhaps your own little island. They will have no choice but to obey. Even now, by her command, a score of FireDrakes blockade the northwest passes to Icarus, cutting them off from their only seaport. Only the eastern pass to Nagual remains open, and soon Gamel will invade. Once Icarus falls, it is only a matter of time before Toth and Carpathia capitulate. Their long standing hatred of each other will prevent them from ever forming an alliance to defend their borders. The north is already effectively under Gamel's control. That would leave Balor, and the Daemon Knights, as the only opposition to the Nagual Empire."

"The Order can muster two thousand knights and perhaps four times that number in foot soldiers," Rodney said.

"Such a large force would never get close to Penardun without drawing the attention of the Empire," Aldus replied. "In a direct assault you would drown in a sea of Imperials. Gamel has twenty legions at his disposal. That is one hundred thousand hardened desert warriors. No, the force that undertakes this mission must be small enough to travel unnoticed. No more than two score of your knights."

"Numbers matter not," Jason said. "Can we get to the meat of the matter?"

"In a nutshell then, my impatient friend" Aldus replied. "A small band of brave men must travel five hundred leagues west, into the heart of the Hagstrom mountains to Drakenmount. There, at the ancient elfin fortress of Penardun, they must confront Magdalen and recover the amulet. Aedon will then be returned to Grigor and the other FireDrakes for safe keeping. Without her support, the balance of power would be restored and Gamel would have to think twice before starting a war with the south."

"Why don't you just sneak in and take it back while she sleeps?" John asked. The lad tensed when every eye turned toward him.

Rodney ignored John's presumptuousness. "The lad has put forth another good question, Wizard Aldus. What say you to that."

Aldus smiled at John. "Magdalen will not risk Aedon being beyond her grasp for an instant. She will also use it to set powerful wards preventing anyone from coming near her while she slumbers. No, the only way is face to face while she has full use of its power."

"Sounds impossible to me," Jason said. "When do we leave?"

"Tomorrow we travel to Daemon Castle," Rodney said, ignoring Jason's remark. "You may accompany us and plead your case before Baron Basil and the Knight's council."

"My thanks, good Sir," Aldus replied. "I accept your kind and generous offer with all due respect."

Rodney looked at the old wizard. "Can you ride?" He glanced up at the FireDrake and quickly added, "A horse."

The wizard laughed. "I was riding horses long before you were born, Sir Knight."

"Very well. Once we get to Vincent Castle you may choose one to your liking from my stable, but for now you will need to ride with one of us. I would not recommend riding him to Daemon Castle," Rodney said pointing a thumb toward the dragon.

"Never fear," Aldus replied. "Grigor cannot remain here in any event. He will be missed, and we cannot afford that." With a look from the wizard, Grigor stood up, stretched his wings, and then lifted off in a cloud of grass and dust. Within moments he was but a red speck in the sky.

"Well, now that your beast has gone perhaps we can retrieve our mounts," Lionel said.

Rodney put two fingers in his mouth and whistled. After a moment he whistled again. Thunder emerged from a stand of oaks at the far end of the meadow. Stepping cautiously at first, he soon broke into a quick trot. Coming to a stop next to Rodney, the horse butted him playfully in the chest. Rodney reached up and patted his neck. Thunder extended his nose and whinnied in delight. Rodney took the time to check his horse's legs. Only when satisfied he was sound did Rodney climb into the saddle. The effort took nearly all his strength.

"I will find the others and return shortly," Rodney yelled back as they trotted off toward the trees. He felt weak, but his ribs no longer pained him and his headache was gone. As they entered the trees, he heard the sheepherder's voice far behind him. The lad must have been addressing the wizard. "Sir, my father will want to know who is going to pay for the sheep Grigor ate?"

Chapter 6

RODNEY

Fortunately, the wizard's prediction of a quick recovery proved true. Rodney awoke the next day feeling as fit and robust as ever he was. As promised, he offered Aldus the pick of his stables, excluding Thunder, of course. To his amazement the wizard selected Frederic's old war horse. Beside the fact that no one but Rodney's father could ever ride the ill-tempered beast, Demon was near twenty years old and tended to bite. Rodney tactfully suggested a ten year old grey mare named Daisy, which Ferdy Riggs, the stable man, had vouched would not be in season for at least another ten days. Though a little skittish, she was as gentle as a lamb. Even Morton had no trouble with Daisy.

They set out for Daemon Castle at first light. With Aldus as his shadow, Rodney led the way south along the winding road to Daemon Castle. Elinor and Lionel rode abreast behind them. Rodney's elder sister had chosen a ruffled green dress for the journey which necessitated riding side saddle. It was a rig Rodney had always thought to be utterly ridiculous. Sylvia and Jason rode behind them. Unlike her sister, Sylvia had chosen a more suitable tunic and loose-fitting britches. She had always been the more practical of the two, and also controlled her spirited six year old gelding as well as any man. Sir Frederic had not been remiss in ensuring that all his children were well acquainted with good horsemanship.

The squires rode in the three wagons that followed. Morton and Lewis sat atop Jason's wagon with his driver, while Lionel's squires, Julian Gail and Lewis's younger brother James, rode in the back of Lionel's. Rodney's woodsmen, Tyko and Yvon Kreel, brought up the rear with Rodney's wagon. The woodsmen were twins, and most anyone would be hard pressed to tell them apart. Though they were three summers older, Rodney and his woodsmen had more or less grown up together. To Rodney the differences between the two were plain for all to see. Tyko was a finger taller, Yvon's nose was turned a

42

notch to one side, the result of being broken when he was seven, and his hair was a slightly darker shade of yellow.

The twins were along to compete in the archery contest. It was one of the three contests open to commoners, the other two being pole-arms and bare knuckle fighting. Since both bow and crossbow were considered un-knightly weapons, archery had the distinction of being the only contest in which no self-respecting knight or squire would compete. Unlike his brethren, Rodney didn't hold the bow in such contempt. He did, however, keep his opinions on their value in warfare to himself.

As the good host, Rodney had introduced Aldus to his sisters at supper the evening before. During the meal the wizard had entertained them with tales of elves, FireDrakes and magic. The high point was Aldus's account of meeting a young Carl Daemon while he was still the King's champion and known as the Red Dragon of Sidon. The wizard was a likable sort, and Rodney enjoyed his stories, but by the next day his enthusiasm had begun to wane and he found himself longing for the bliss of silence.

After a sharp turn in the trail, the trees gave way to open grassland. Rodney hooded his eyes with his free hand to gauge the sun's position. It was two sun-marks past midday by his reckoning. At their present pace they would reach Daemon Castle by three. "What in the seven Gods is that," Aldus said, cutting short his dissertation on the dire state of affairs in Coronis.

When Rodney looked in the direction of the wizard's outstretched arm he saw only a faint thin line. If he hadn't known what it was he would have been unable to distinguish it from the horizon. "You have incredibly good eyes. That is the South Curtain Wall. It is almost two leagues from here. Though I believe it has now fallen in some disrepair from years of neglect, it runs from east to west extending into the sea at either end. It was built long ago to keep out the Kelatch."

The wizard raised his bushy eyebrows, "The Kelatch?"

"We were not the first to lay claim to Balor. When Carl Daemon and his followers arrived, they found the island inhabited by wild half-naked savages. They named them Kelatch. It is an old Sidonese word that means a disembodied spirit. I've never seen one myself, mind you, so I can only tell you what my grandsire told my father. They are a race of little people who cover themselves head to toe in white chalk and go about nearly naked. Their victims, when they left a body behind, were said to bear no marks or wounds. Black magic most say. Until I met you I did not believe in magic, but now..."

"Wouldn't it have been much simpler to just bargain with them?"

43

"To treat with them proved impossible. They spoke in clicks and grunts that no civilized man could ever hope to understand. According to my grandsire, they shrink the heads of their enemies down to the size of a man's fist and hang them around the entrances to their homes as trophies. Before the wall, they would attack common folk and knights alike. Each time a force was sent to give chase, the Kelatch would just fade back into the forests and disappear like smoke on the wind. Most foolish enough to follow them into the forest never returned."

"Such an undertaking is quite remarkable for so small a nation," Aldus replied thoughtfully. "You Balorians must be a determined and strong-willed people."

"I suppose," Rodney replied. "It took two score years to complete. A watch was kept for five generations, but by my grandsire's day it had been abandoned. One of the last to venture over the wall, he and five brave companions, all belted knights, went in to explore. Only my grandsire returned. The Kelatch may have died out by now, who can say, but no one goes over the wall just the same."

"Interesting," Aldus said, absently scratching the side of his face through his beard, "but walls are no defence against FireDrakes. We will need to make that very clear to your brethren. I cannot stress strongly enough how..."

Rodney interrupted by raising his hand. "You have already convinced me, my friend. I have seen first hand what a FireDrake is capable of. You had best save your arguments for the Baron. It is he you must convince now. Those of the order will follow his wishes without question." Aldus opened his mouth, as if to reply, but then obviously thought better of it.

"Rest easy," Rodney said in a conciliatory tone. "I will speak in favour of your request, as no doubt will Jason and Lionel." Aldus nodded once and to Rodney's great relief they rode on in blessed silence.

Even from a league away Rodney could see the castle. Small blotches of colour hinted at the silk and canvas village being constructed just outside its tall walls. When they reached the first outlying tent, Rodney called a halt. They were still too far from the castle gates for his liking. He rode back to his wagon and grabbed a red griffin pennant affixed to a long pole. "Wait here," he shouted as he rode on between the tents.

Worming his way back and forth through a jungle of cloth and equipment, Rodney searched for a suitable site to pitch their tents. He passed by many banners in the process. The single red wolf of house Vennell, the red cross and lion of Lionel's house and the black crossed swords of house Lambert to name but a few. Finally he chanced upon a large unclaimed area adjacent to two yellow tents bearing red lions. It was the Darnell coat of arms, Rodney's cousins on his mother's side. It was as close as he could hope to get, so he stuck his banner in the soft churned earth and trotted back to his companions. Navigating the wagons through the maze of tents to where Rodney had placed his pennant proved no easy task. It was four sun-marks past midday by the time they arrived.

Leaving Sylvia and Elinor to supervise raising the tents, Rodney, Jason, Lionel and Aldus set off on foot for the castle. As they crossed the drawbridge that spanned the narrow moat surrounding Daemon castle, Rodney noticed Aldus staring at the pennant flying atop the outer wall. It bore the same red dragon on a white field that adorned Rodney's oval belt buckle. He recalled the wizard's interest in it the day before.

"Carl Daemon's arms," Rodney said. "We wear the dragon to honour Him."

Aldus nodded. "Yes, I remember it well," he said. "I was a young apprentice, still green behind the ears, when first I saw one. Carl was a most impressive man. Did I tell you he had hair very much like your own. He wore it long and tied back like a horse's tail."

"I am familiar with the style," Rodney replied. "The horse tail was a long standing tradition among Sidon's fighting men. Carl Daemon and his men cut off their tails to leave behind in Sidon along with their shame. We keep our hair cropped short, lest we forget."

"I see," Aldus said softly. "Daemon Castle is most impressive," he added as they passed through the gate.

Rodney had never considered it before. It certainly was much grander than Vincent castle. The high wall of Daemon Castle proper was five hundred feet back from the eastern outer wall. At each corner rose a round tower with battlements fifty feet above the ground. The tops of the crenels were nearer to sixty. The inner keep had been built to house the original knights, as well as their families and retainers. It was a true fortress, designed to withstand a prolonged siege, even though its walls were never tested.

With a warm late afternoon sun in a clear blue sky, the large courtyard was a beehive of excitement. Scores of knights, squires, and ladies milled about in its centre. The sound of hammering rang out from where wooden stands were being erected on either side of the jousting curtain. A long table had been placed at the far end under a canopy of dark blue cloth. A handful of scribes and tournament officials were seated in the shade of the canopy. In a high-backed chair at the centre of the table sat a red faced portly man in blue robes. Rodney recognized him as the Baron's bailiff, Manfred.

"Ah, Sir Rodney. Come to defend your title I see," the bailiff said as Rodney approached the table. Manfred had spoken with such enthusiasm that it set his jowls to jiggling. When Rodney nodded, the Bailiff turned to his scribe. "Sir Rodney Vincent, Lord of Vincent Castle and Master-of-the-lance."

The scribe's quill bobbed back and forth as he wrote. Rodney moved aside as Lionel stepped forward. Manfred looked up and smiled. "Sir Lionel Tait, Lord of Quimbly Manor. What event this year, my good Sir?"

"I will compete for Master-of-the-sword and ride for the yellow in the melee," Lionel replied.

Jason stepped up to the table next. "Ah, our renowned Master-of-the-sword," the bailiff said. "Here to defend your title, Sir Jason?"

"Of course," Jason replied.

"Anything else?" Manfred asked with one brow lifted expectantly.

Jason glanced at the sour look on Lionel's face, and then at Rodney before replying, "Not this year."

Just when Rodney thought all was going smoothly, a familiar voice spoke up from off to the side, "No stomach for the melee, Jason?"

Rodney, Jason and Lionel turned as one to face the speaker. Arms folded across his chest, a dark-haired knight stood six feet away. His broad smile only further exposed a long white scar that started in his left eyebrow, touched the bridge of his nose, and then ran down his cheek where it carved a line through his short and immaculately trimmed beard. From the corner of his eye, Rodney saw Jason tense and tighten the grip on his sword hilt.

"Sir Martin," Jason said in a tone as tense as folded steel.

Ferret-faced Sir Talbot stood next to Martin. His right hand crept slyly toward the brace of throwing knives attached to his boiled leather breastplate. Rodney leaned closer to Jason and covered his friend's sword hand with his own.

Without even a sideways glance, Martin placed his own hand on Talbot's as he nodded to Rodney. "And how is your sweet sister Sylvia, Sir Rodney?" Martin asked.

"Well and happy I am glad to say," Rodney replied coolly.

"Pleased I am to hear it," Martin said in return.

Jason hawked and spat, just missing Martin's shiny black boots. In the silence that followed the smile slowly faded from Martin's face. "Good day to you, sirs," he finally said before he abruptly turned and walked away. Talbot followed like a well-trained dog, all the while casting back narrow-eyed sneers until they were lost in the crowd.

"I really must speak with your leader," Aldus said, breaking the silence. "Would it be possible to see him now?"

"Yes of course," Rodney replied. He looked to Lionel and nodded toward Jason. Lionel's eyes flicked once toward Jason before he smiled knowingly and nodded back.

"This way," Rodney said as he started off toward the inner keep.

When they approached the archway that led inside, two burly guards stepped out from dark recesses in the wall. "Sir Rodney and Wizard Aldus to see the Baron," Rodney said. The guard on the right eyed them both suspiciously before he signalled to the other and they both melted back into their dark alcoves.

"So Baron Basil, is Carl Daemon's descendant," Aldus said.

Rodney laughed. "Half the knights on this island, and I would wager as many commoners, all claim they can trace their lineage back to Carl Daemon, but the truth is he had but one child, a daughter, and there is no record of her begetting an heir."

"What happened to her?" Aldus asked.

"Eloped with her father's squire. They were last seen heading south. Those were dangerous times to stray too far from the castle. Kelatch got them both, most likely."

"So then the title is not his by blood."

"Some say the brotherhood of Daemon Knights was born from the ashes of Carl Daemon's funeral pyre because before they were cold his knights had chosen one from among them to take his place. That tradition continues to this day. Basil Vennell was elected Baron shortly after Elinor was born. His nephew, Silas, is the favourite to replace him, but the knights will make their choice when the time comes."

"I must say, you have a unique system in Balor," the wizard said. "In all my travels, I have never seen the like."

"I never really gave it much thought," Rodney said absently as he waved to the Baron's chamberlain standing in the doorway.

They were escorted to just outside the door to the Baron's study where the chamberlain knocked once and then left them to wait. A considerable amount of time passed before the door was opened by a hard-faced knight in his mid forties. Aldus came instantly to life. "Baron Basil?" he asked with a wide smile.

The knight raised an eyebrow and looked to Rodney. "This is First Knight, Sir Silas Vennell," Rodney said. "Sir Silas, may I present Wizard Aldus Lasairian."

Silas replied with a short grunt. "The Baron will see you now," he added, stepping back inside.

It had been years since Rodney had ventured into the Baron's study. The last occasion was when his father died. It smelled musty despite the small but robust fire burning brightly in the hearth. The centre of the room was dominated by a great oak desk. Though somewhat frail, in the twilight of his years, the baron still cut a regal figure sitting behind its polished surface.

"Sir Rodney and Wizard Aldus, my lord," Silas said after closing the door.

When he saw Rodney the Baron smiled. "It is good to see you again, Rodney. Will these old eyes have the pleasure of watching you joust tomorrow?"

"They will, my lord," Rodney replied.

"Ah, I look forward to seeing it. I must say, with each passing year you remind me more and more of your father. I miss him sorely, you know. Frederic was a brave knight and a true friend."

When Basil turned his head to face Aldus his smile melted. "So, wizard, you would have us go to war. You would have the blood of our young knights spilt on foreign soil."

The Baron's harsh tone took Rodney somewhat by surprise but Aldus appeared unruffled by it. "On the contrary, my lord," he said. "I desperately seek your aid in preventing such a war, though I was unaware you had been briefed."

Aldus cast a sideways glance at Rodney. He said nothing, but his narrowed eyes conveyed a clear message. Not privy to Basil's sources of information, Rodney felt the need to convey his innocence in view of the wizard's implication. Unsure of what to say, he just opened his hands and shrugged.

The wizard must have understood because his eyes relaxed before switching back to the Baron. "As I have already explained to Sir Rodney, you can expect Imperial Dog Soldiers to invade Balor within the year, with FireDrakes in the van, unless something is done before Icarus falls."

The Baron raised a shaky skeletal finger. "If you think I have no eyes or ears outside these walls you are mistaken. I am well aware of the trouble brewing on the continent. Your request will go before the council after the tournament. You may attend and address the assembly at that time."

"I understand your word carries much weight," Aldus replied. "Will you endorse my request?"

"I have not yet made up my mind," Basil replied evenly. "Now, whatever else needs be said can wait until the council convenes," he added with a wave of his hand.

"Rodney, Wizard Aldus," Silas said as he motioned them to the door. They had been dismissed.

Rodney appreciated the silence as he and Aldus made their way back to the tents. It was dusk by the time they arrived and Rodney retired to his tent. Morton appeared in very short order with a platter of bread and cheese. It was accompanied by a most welcome pot of chicory tea. Rodney thanked his squire and released him to his own devices until the morning. He ate little of the food but finished off the pot of tea before laying down on his pallet. Thankfully, he was rewarded with sleep the moment his head touched the pillow.

Chapter 7

SYLVIA

Her husband may have slept soundly, but for Sylvia the night had been long and restless. Their energetic lovemaking had left her content and she should have slept soundly even on the less than comfortable bed, but her lack of sleep was due to more than just a lumpy sleeping pallet. It was her deep and growing concern for Jason's safety that had kept peaceful slumber at bay. She loved her husband dearly. The thought of him travelling so far away, only to face unknown dangers, filled her with such dread that she found it difficult to think of anything else.

With great effort, Sylvia shoved fears of the future aside for later consideration. The imminent threat to her husband was the tourney at hand, and Sir Martin. As one of her former suitors, she knew Martin well enough. It was before that ridiculous duel of course. In his own way, Martin was just as honourable a man as Jason, but he also possessed a single mindedness that made him an extremely dangerous enemy, and Jason had done his very best to make him one. *Men can be so stupid.* Even though her husband was the finest swordsman in the land, Sylvia could not shake the fear that his rashness would be his undoing. She knew from experience that his reputation as a hothead was well earned. If not for her calming influence, this feud between her husband and his cousin would have already ended in more bloodshed.

With all the worrisome thoughts swirling around in her head as she dressed, Sylvia nearly forgot to stop and inspect her appearance in the small mirror resting on her night table. One glance was enough to tell her Elinor wouldn't approve. Aside from the state of her hair, the simple pale blue dress she had selected for the tourney had long ago fallen out of style, but it was comfortable, practical, and about as far as she was willing to go to dress up like a lady. Elinor would never allow herself to be seen in anything but the latest fashions. If not for the embarrassment it would cause her husband, Sylvia would

50

wear nothing but tunic and britches. The thought that Jason seemed to prefer her wearing nothing at all made her grin. On a whim, she wrapped a white silk scarf around her neck to hide the old-fashioned collar.

Jason awoke while Sylvia was brushing her hair. Like a true warrior he made the transition from a sound slumber to total alertness in a blink of an eye. His first action was to give her a smile before walking naked across the tent to gather his clothing from the hanging rack. Sylvia watched her cheeks redden in the mirror as her thoughts wandered to lust. Such a beautiful man, and every bit as wonderful on the inside where it truly mattered.

Jason had barely pulled his trousers up when Lewis arrived to assist him in preparation for the tourney. Sylvia left the tent with the excuse of needing to wash her face, but instead of visiting the nearby stream, she soon found herself standing before the entrance to her brother's tent. There she waited in silence, nervously twisting the ends of her long brown hair between her fingers, until she finally she found the resolve to speak. "Rodney, it is Sylvia. May I enter?"

"Come," was the terse reply.

The tent was sparsely furnished. Besides a sleeping pallet, there was a night stand on which rested a teapot, a single cup and a pair of gauntlets. The pungent aroma of metal polish and oiled leather hung heavy in the air. Morton was tightening the straps of her brother's jousting breastplate. It was the one he wore only for tourney jousts. It appeared a little snug at the waist. As Sylvia stepped into the tent, Rodney glanced up with a look of annoyance. "I seem to have added a finger or two around my middle since last year," he said.

"Do you want me to find an armourer, Sir Rodney?" Morton asked.

"There is no time Mort," Rodney replied. "I will make do," he added with a sigh.

Her brother tended to be overly dramatic. He reminded her of an adolescent boy at times. The notion caused Sylvia to release a sigh of her own. More than a year had passed since her wedding and she was still without child. The fault was certainly not for lack of trying. Elinor's son, Philip, was born within the first year of hers. Surely something could be done. Perhaps Sylvia should speak to the wizard; he might be able to suggest a potion.

A sudden muted clash of wood and steel, accented by a distant cheer, reminded Sylvia of why she had come. "I wish to speak with you before you leave," she said. Her eyes darted to Morton and then back to Rodney. "Alone," she added softly.

A look of surprise crossed Rodney's face, but he smiled and turned to his squire. "We'd best hurry, Mort. It would be most unseemly to be late. Strap up my greaves and then see to Thunder."

The squire turned green around the collar at the mention of the horse's name. *A squire who is afraid of horses. Whatever is Rodney going to do with him?* She had warned her brother after Morton's first year that he seemed ill suited to knighthood, but Rodney would hear nothing of it. He was convinced the lad would come around.

Nodding a silent response, Morton went back to work on the greaves. He left immediately after the last strap was pulled tight over her brother's calf. Sylvia waited another few moments before she spoke. "I am worried about Jason. I fear Sir Martin, or one of his lackeys, will find some way to do Jason grievous harm this day."

"Jason can take care of himself," Rodney said as he picked up his gauntlets from the night table. "He is the finest swordsman in the order after all."

It took Sylvia a moment to collect her thoughts. She had to make her brother understand, and without slighting her husband in any way. "I know that," she said finally. "My faith in his ability is unwavering." Moving forward, she touched Rodney's arm to ensure she had his undivided attention. "It's trickery I fear. Promise me you will look out for him. Watch his back for me this day, and should he accompany you on this fool's quest, which he undoubtably will, please bring him back safe."

When she had finished, Sylvia gazed into Rodney's eyes searching for some sign of understanding. Rodney cupped her hand in his and smiled. It was her father's smile and it warmed her heart. "Fear not for your husband," he said. "I will watch over him, and so too will Lionel."

Hearing Lionel's name soured the moment. Sylvia could never put faith in Lionel's protection. They exchanged one last look before Rodney broke eye contact to hang his gauntlets on a small hook attached to the side of his breastplate. Sylvia relaxed. Her brother meant well, he just didn't see the truth about Lionel the way she did. She smiled and kissed him on the cheek. The short bristles on his face stabbed her lower lip. She wrinkled her nose. "Brother dear, you need to shave." Altering her voice, to what she thought was a fair imitation of her elder sister, she added, "We simply must find a wife to look after you."

They both laughed as Rodney reached over to hold the tent flap open for her. When they emerged, Morton was waiting at a discreet distance with Thunder. The big war horse looked splendid in his jousting armour and appeared just as restless for the lists as her brother. He shifted his weight back and forth from one foreleg to the other in anxious anticipation. Morton was having no end of trouble keeping him in place. Lewis and James stood back out of harm's way.

Morton's left arm was wrapped tightly around Rodney's war lance which wobbled dangerously back and forth threatening to strike anyone who came near. Thunder chose that moment to sidestep, pulling the squire along with him. Sylvia marvelled at the lad's determination. He hung on to both reins and lance even though it must have taxed his abilities to their very limits. Rodney rushed over to take the reins, allowing Morton a chance to steady the lance. Once Rodney was in the saddle, he relieved Morton of his burden and locked the back end into the lance grip. It was only for show. When he reached the lists he would exchange the war lance for an array of the hollow tourney lances provided by the Baron's officials.

"Remember your promise," Sylvia said as she waved to her brother. Rodney waved back and then set out at a trot with Morton following a good ten paces behind.

When Jason emerged from their tent, Sylvia turned to greet him. A broad smile spread across his handsome face when their eyes met. "Rodney is on his way to the lists," she said, returning the smile. "He did not wish to be late."

"Ha, they would have to wait my love," Jason replied. "He is last year's champion after all."

Sylvia pulled the white scarf from around her neck as she drew close to her husband. "For luck," she said, tying it loosely around his neck.

Enveloping her hands in his, Jason kissed her tenderly on the forehead. "Just knowing you are there is all I need to make me invincible," he whispered softly in her ear.

Just be careful, Sylvia thought as Lionel and Elinor emerged abruptly from their tent. Elinor was speaking in low harsh tones. They were still too far away for Sylvia to make out her words, but whatever she was saying did not appear to sit well with Lionel. He was wearing an uncharacteristic scowl that on him looked positively dreadful. *They deserve each other,* Sylvia thought and then quickly admonished herself for thinking such a thing. By the time Elinor and Lionel had drawn near they were both smiling pleasantly, as if nothing was amiss. *How can they do that?*

"Good morning Elinor, Lionel," Jason said with a slight nod of his head.

"Lady Sylvia," Lionel said bowing more than was necessary. "Good morning Jason," he added nodding to Jason. Lionel looked to the castle and held a hand above his eyes. "I see Rodney is even now at the gates. We best escort the ladies to the viewing stands before we miss his first run."

Sylvia took Jason's outstretched arm and the four of them started out for the castle with the squires following in their wake. Sylvia was only vaguely aware of the conversation as they walked. Her mind was much too busy to pay proper attention. Tourneys tended to dredge up memories of her father. She could still recall, all too vividly, the way her world had come crashing down when he died. She had been only seventeen, so her distress was understandable. Just the same, her feelings for Jason were so much stronger, she did not want to contemplate how it might feel to lose him. She would have tried to talk him out of it, if she thought it would have done any good, but he was a Daemon Knight, and his honour was everything to him, just as it had been with her father. No, she had done what she could to protect him. It was now up to Jason's skill with a blade, her brother's vigilance and the will of the Gods. There was also Lionel of course, but she put no faith in that. No matter how hard she tried, she just could not bring herself to trust that man.

Before Sylvia knew it, they were across the courtyard and seated in the viewing stands next to Wizard Aldus, who had apparently been there all morning. Shortly after they had taken their seats, the castle pages sounded their trumpets and the crier announced the end of the trials. Even though the air would likely remain cool all day, the jousting would be finished before breakfast. It was a custom carried over from the days when their ancestors had lived in a much warmer climate. On the mainland, jousts had always been conducted before the heat of the day made wearing the heavy armour and padding unbearable.

"We are just in time for the finals," Lionel remarked cheerfully.

"Look, the first match has Rodney up against my brother Ernest," Jason replied.

"No offence Jason. But your brother has no chance against Rodney. He has done well to make it this far."

Sylvia felt her cheeks flush with anger. *Lionel is such a boor*, she thought, but said nothing. If Jason was insulted, he didn't show it.

"It is as you say, Lionel," Jason replied. "Ernest has done well to make it to the finals and I am proud of his accomplishment."

Well, if it didn't bother her husband, then Sylvia wasn't going to let it bother her either. Her attention was drawn back to the field as the knights began their course. Rodney looked magnificent charging down the field in his gleaming tourney armour. The red griffin of house Vincent almost seemed alive against the fresh snow white paint on his shield. A long red streamer fluttered from his helm like a trail of flame.

There was a loud crack of breaking wood when the knights met. Ernest's lance glanced off the side of Rodney's shield while Rodney's struck her brother-in-law square in the chest. Her brother's lance shattered, but not before Ernest was raised from his saddle to tumble over the rear of his mount. Ernest hit the ground hard but was back on his feet before Rodney had turned around. The defeated knight saluted Rodney as the crier called out his win. Sylvia smiled as her brother returned in triumph to the end of the list.

"I see cousin Maynard has made the finals again this year," Lionel said as the next jousters took their positions.

"He rides against Sir Lewis," Jason replied. "I fear his chances are no better than my brother's were against Rodney." Lionel's eyebrows went up in surprise.

"No offence Lionel," Jason said with an innocent smile only Jason could pull off with any credibility. Sylvia put her hand to her mouth to hide her grin and then watched Jason's prediction prove true when Maynard was unhorsed on the second course.

The next knight to enter the list was Joel Neville, her husband's second cousin. His opponent was Edgar Hale. It was an exciting match. Both men were excellent jousters, but Edgar's superior size tipped the scales and he unseated Joel on the third course.

The following match was over quickly. Daniel Buxton rode against Claude Dunn, and either Daniel was nervous, or his horse made a misstep, because the knight's lance missed his opponent completely. Sir Claude's, however, stayed true. It struck Daniel in the right shoulder knocking him sideways from his saddle. The unlucky knight's right foot caught in his stirrup and he was dragged for the balance of the list. The spectators fell quiet until he was rescued from his entanglement and carried from the field. The trumpets sounded the ending of the first round.

The first match of the second round pitted Edgar Hale against Claude Dunn. Like Edgar's previous match, it proved to be another exciting one. Both jousters made a good show of themselves on the first three courses. Claude appeared to have been injured on the third however, because on the fourth he was unable to keep his lance steady. Edgar unseated him easily with a hit to the head. Claude got up of his own accord, but seemed disoriented and needed his squire's guidance off the field.

The crier called the names of Rodney Vincent and Lewis Buxton. Sylvia felt butterflies in her stomach as they mounted their horses. Lewis was the very knight Rodney had faced in the final joust of the last tourney. This would be a spectacular match and everyone knew it, as evidenced by the loud cheer that erupted when they levelled their lances to signal their readiness.

"Buxton, Buxton," someone behind Sylvia bellowed. Sylvia turned her head and recognized Lewis's brother Gavin. The knight was on his feet waving. Gavin looked down to Sylvia. "Your pardon, Lady Sylvia," he said with a bow of his head.

Sylvia laughed. "No need for pardons, Sir Gavin. Please do not let my presence spoil your merriment." Gavin bowed once more, and Sylvia returned to watching the joust.

The two knights charged. Both lances struck shields on the first course, and again on the second. Rodney had knocked Lewis from the saddle on the third course the previous year. He repeated the feat by unhorsing Lewis cleanly with a high chest hit. Rodney rode back to his end of list amid cheers. The trumpet sounded again, signifying the final round.

It was now down to Rodney and Sir Edgar Hale. Rodney was a big man but Edgar was a full hand taller and considerably heavier. They met in the centre of the field, and for the first time Sylvia could remember, Rodney was struck a blow that truly seemed to rock him. When his own lance struck Edgar it shattered, but the big man seemed unaffected and the response from the spectators was deafening. Sylvia's right hand went to her mouth. Jason took her left in his, no doubt sensing her worry. The strain evident in his grip told her he was concerned. It wouldn't be the first time a knight was maimed or even killed in a tourney joust. Her brother was in for a real challenge. It would be his skill and stamina against Sir Edgar's size and strength.

After four more courses, both knights were bloodied. It was more likely from wood splinters that anything else, but Rodney was also showing signs of weakening. He was leaning to the left and favouring his ribs. Sylvia feared that he had not yet fully recovered from his battle with the FireDrake two days before. Perhaps his injuries were not truly healed, in spite of the wizard's claims. She mouthed a silent prayer to the Gods as she squeezed Jason's hand.

When the two knights began the fifth course, Sylvia could no longer recognize the Griffin on her brother's shield because of the damage to the paint. The shield was also buckled somewhat above and below the centre. It was a testament to the force behind Edgar's strikes.

As the charging knights closed in on each other, Rodney appeared to be having difficulty keeping his lance steady. Suddenly, less than a second before impact, Edgar's horse stumbled and the big knight was pitched from his saddle. He hit the ground head first. Edgar valiantly tried to rise but fell once again. It wasn't until his squires arrived to assist him that he finally managed to stand.

Sylvia couldn't believe it. Perhaps the Gods had actually answered her prayers. She glanced at Jason. Her own relief was mirrored on his face. Then from the corner of her eye she noticed the wizard smiling. It was an odd sort of satisfied smile. His hand was resting on his chest. Recalling what she had been told, a possibility suddenly occurred to her. She decided to say nothing of her suspicions to anyone, especially Rodney.

Amid all the cheers and excitement, Sylvia stood up and half-heartedly joined in as Rodney rode the length of the list with his pennant dangling from the tip of his war lance. He dismounted in front of the Baron to be presented with the Master-of-the-lance medallion. Sylvia clapped her hands and cheered once more with everyone else. This made his third year as champion. Father would have been so proud. If only the wizard's smile didn't mean what she feared it did.

"Ah," Lionel said. "Time for breakfast."

Chapter 8

MAGDALEN

Penardun's library was a magical place, existing outside of normal time and space. Even after an extensive search through numerous books, Magdalen still hadn't unravelled the secret of how it worked. From without, nothing more than a thick windowless stone wall, but from within, a cavernous expanse of row upon row of book shelves, flanked by clusters of polished tables and high-backed chairs, all set against a long wall of impossibly tall windows. Completely invisible from the outside, the windows offered a panoramic view of the entire valley.

While the rest of the keep turned dark and lifeless after sunset, the library remained warm and bright. Aside from the comfort Aedon could provide, it was the only respite from a long bleak night. The ceiling was clad in lumin, a stone-like material that radiated both heat and light. The builders had quarried the lumin from Drakenmount's interior to render the library void of darkness even in the remotest corner.

The light was pleasant and easy on the eyes. Magdalen could read all night without adverse affects, which suited her just fine. Even as a child she could not abide sleeping more than three or four sun-marks at a time. The confines of Penardun's cold grey walls had exasperated her restlessness to a level where she rarely slept at all. Once her business with Gamel was over she would be free to leave, but until then the only joy available within the old keep lay in its vast store of books. Without the library, where she spent the better part of every night, she would surely have fled long ago.

For the third straight night Magdalen had slept not a wink. Engrossed in her latest find, she had spent the entire night reading. The journal in her hands was written seven centuries earlier by a halfling who had not only created the first two FireDrakes, but was also the last to possess Aedon. The text not only reaffirmed what she already knew about the four bloodstone amulets, it also

58

contained an ominous warning. Aedon came with a price. Prolonged exposure to the magic imprisoned within would eventually drive the owner insane. Unfortunately, his last entry ended in mid sentence leaving her to wonder what else he had discovered.

A barely perceptible movement in her peripheral vision alerted Magdalen to a presence. There was no need to wonder who it was. In all of Penardun there was only herself and the librarian. The same elf who served double duty as her self-appointed keeper, or guide as he called it. A nuisance she called it; but he did no harm and had even proved useful on occasion so she tolerated his presence with cool indifference. "Greetings, Merflyn," she said without looking up.

"It's so good to see someone finally making use of the library after all these years, mistress," the librarian said. "I trust you have found something of interest."

"I have indeed," Magdalen replied as she flipped the cover closed to display the title, *The Life And Times Of Rendalt Lasairian.*

"Ah, Rendalt's journal," Merflyn said thoughtfully, in a rare display of emotion.

"Quite a remarkable book. Did you know him?" Magdalen asked. It was entirely possible after all, given the aging process and long life span of an elf. The librarian could be anywhere from twenty to a thousand years old.

"I did have the pleasure," Merflyn replied. "Both I and my grandsire's grandsire considered him a friend. Like you, he made good use of the library in his day."

"What was he like? Was he as noble as he sounds?"

"As for noble I cannot say, but in disposition he was more elf than human. He had lived a long life, even for a halfling, and in the end wanted only release from an aged and failing body."

"The halfling's curse," Magdalen said. "I too am doomed to spend most of my life being old and feeble, if that excuse for rodent droppings, Gamel, is any example. Considering that age tends to be kinder to men than women, I am not looking forward to the prospect."

"Rendalt was old but I do not believe anyone would have called him feeble," Merflyn said. "His passing was a great loss."

The indignant edge to the librarian's voice caught Magdalen unaware. "You admired him," she said in surprise. "A halfling held in high regard by an elf. Imagine that. Tell me, Merflyn. Are all his words true? He successfully melded elves with dragons; FireDrakes are proof of that, but according to his journal he accomplished the deed by just reading the spell from a book. Was he really so skilled and powerful?"

"Power, skill, greatness, they can all be measured in innumerable ways, mistress. You will have to be more specific with your question."

Talking with elf-kind was always an exercise in self control, but Magdalen found the librarian more trying than most. He tended to respond to her as if admonishing a juvenile and Magdalen was not in a mood for it. Her temper flared. She quickly changed the subject to give her ire a chance to cool. "Tell me. How is it you can come and go from the library without the aid of magic. I could not even find the door without Aedon."

"Penardun is older than you might think, mistress," the elf replied, once again as if addressing a wayward child. "Built long before the first human set foot on Coronis, it recognizes its own."

"So none but an elf or the holder of Aedon may enter," Magdalen replied, keeping her rising ire in check. "That is good to know."

"I did not say none may enter, mistress," the elf said in reproach. "The library is not infallible."

Magdalen drummed her fingers on the table in frustration as she formulated her next question. "Alright then, please tell me how a human might gain entrance."

"A human could never enter without the aid of magic, mistress," the librarian replied.

Magdalen slammed her hand down on the table. "Enough games, Merflyn. Just tell me how someone could get in! Someone like Gamel for instance."

Merflyn seemed unaffected by her display of temper. "It would take a very powerful glamour to fool the library into mistaking a full-blooded human for an elf, but any halfling with enough skill, like your Emperor of Nagual for instance, could mask his human side and pass through as an elf. That is assuming he could first locate the door."

"So, the library can be fooled," Magdalen said. "My thanks for the information, Merflyn. Our conversation has been most illuminating."

"Glad to be of service, mistress. Now if you have no further need of me, I shall see to the books."

"Of course," Magdalen replied with a wave of her hand. "I have no wish to keep you from your duties."

Once the librarian had disappeared among the maze of bookshelves, Magdalen turned her gaze to the window. She had chosen a table with a view of Drakenmount in order to catch the transformation brought on by the rising sun, which was well underway, but she found the spectacle difficult to enjoy. It was hard to put her finger on it, but something was amiss among the FireDrakes. Through the bloodstone, she could sense a hint of foreign magic. It was evasive and difficult to identify. She had ruled out Gamel, being familiar with the slimy taint of his power. This was something different, something new.

She could, of course, be mistaken. It might not be magic at all. It could be that a FireDrake was ill. If she could just pinpoint which one then she could help. Perhaps there was more knowledge to be gained from Rendalt's journal. She flipped the book open and began again with the first page, but the nagging sense of brewing trouble had settled in her craw and refused to go away.

Chapter 9

RODNEY

Considering the battering his body had taken, Rodney felt better than he had a right to expect. Immediately after accepting his medallion, the wizard had pulled him aside to heal his various cuts, bruises and abrasions. Along with the healing he also did something to reduce the pain jousting had caused to his newly mended rib. Aldus's constant talking might be trying, but it would appear having a wizard around was a useful thing and any annoyance could be overlooked.

It reminded Rodney of the time he brought a complaint before his father, incensed over some trivial infraction by one of the servants. "No one is perfect," his father had said. "You are young, Rodney, and I realize it may be hard for you to understand right now, but along life's twisted path a man eventually discovers that the hardest things to endure are his own shortcomings. You must learn to be tolerant of others and accept a little bad with the good, otherwise you run the risk of becoming your own worst enemy."

The wizard did not linger long once he completed his task. Rodney barely had time to thank him before he was off to administer his gift of healing to all the other injured jousters. Rodney knew Aldus wasn't doing it strictly out of the kindness in his heart. The wizard was simply attempting to win over as many knights as possible to his cause. Rodney found no fault with that; it was a sensible thing to do.

With Morton's assistance, Rodney shed the remainder of his armour and sweat soaked padding. Once the equipment was removed and draped over Thunder's back, Rodney turned the reins over to his squire. "Store my gear in the wagon. Then see to it that Thunder is well watered, brushed and given a double portion of oats. He has earned it."

"Yes Sir," Morton replied with little enthusiasm.

"After that, you are free for the rest of the day to do as you wish."

Morton's face brightened considerably. "Yes Sir. Thank you Sir." Rodney watched his squire's determined struggle with the big destrier as he led him away. Hopefully, Thunder would not give the lad too much trouble.

As with every spring tourney, thousands of knights and ladies were in attendance. To avoid offending anyone's honour, since only five hundred could be seated in the castle's great hall, both breakfast and dinner were served out of doors. Long rows of tables and benches had been constructed behind the viewing stands. Once the jousting was over, the tables were expeditiously arrayed with a plentiful supply of cheeses, bread, fat, smoked fish and cold mutton.

The savoury odour of roast mutton and freshly baked bread, mixed with the faint scent of fresh-cut pine, was pleasant enough to elicit an eager growl from Rodney's stomach. There would be no shortage of servants to keep the platters full either. Over the past few days, commoners from leagues around would have flocked to Daemon Castle. It was an opportunity for the common folk to earn extra coin at a time when their resources were worn thin after the long winter. The Baron's hirelings rushed about filling cups with mulled cider, which would have come from the Baron's finest stock and been warmed to just the right temperature.

Rodney walked between the rows until he found his sisters and their husbands. When he sat down to breakfast with them, Jason, Lionel and other nearby knights congratulated him once again on his win. The table was noisy, with everyone talking at once. On top of the sounds of the festivities it was almost too much for Rodney's sensitive ears. A young boy reached down to fill his cup with cider. Rodney sniffed at it and then wrinkled his nose at the unpleasant odour.

"Compliments of the Baron," a soft female voice said to his right. Rodney turned to see a young common woman push the lad aside with her hip. She was very pretty, with a round freckled face and voluminous curly straw-coloured hair that tumbled down her back. The woman held out a silver tray. On the tray rested a glazed kiln-fired pitcher along with a matching cup. The set was well crafted and most likely imported from Toth, where the finest dishes were made.

"Fresh chicory tea my lord, compliments of the Baron," the serving woman said with a pleasant smile. As she lifted the cup from her tray Rodney noticed the Toth potter's guild stamp on the bottom. It was no doubt a piece from the Baron's own table. The wonderful aroma of chicory drifted up as she filled the cup before placing the pitcher close to hand on the table.

"Please give the Baron my deepest thanks," Rodney said offering the woman a warm smile. She curtsied and turned to leave, but Rodney grabbed her wrist. "Just a moment," he said as he reached into his tunic for his purse, "I have something for you." The woman responded like a frightened rabbit and tried to pull away. He could understand her trepidation. It could be a dangerous thing when a noble took too much interest in a commoner, one whom he would never marry, and she was certainly pleasing enough to interest many.

"Rest easy," Rodney said softly. "All is well," he added placing a silver coin in her palm.

The woman remained tense and hesitant until Rodney released her. Only then did her smile return. "My thanks, Sir," she said as she curtsied once more before rushing away.

Raising the cup to his lips, Rodney sniffed the rising steam before taking a sip of the hot fluid. It was like ambrosia, momentarily relieving the discomfort of all the noise. Falling into a familiar state of melancholy, he paid little attention to the multitude of conversations until Aldus flopped down beside him. "You look worn to the bone, my friend," Rodney said, after seeing the wizard's haggard face. "You must have healed a score of jousting injuries by now."

"I do what I must," Aldus replied as he attacked a large slice of mutton like a hungry hound.

While he nibbled on a piece of cheese and sipped his tea, Rodney watched in utter amazement as the old man dispatched a whole platter of mutton along with half a loaf of bread between gulps of cider. Aldus caught him staring and smiled. "You Balorians play rough games," he said between bites. "By the sound of it I will need all the strength I can muster for the melee."

Watching the wizard eat was fascinating. Rodney refilled his cup and took a long swallow before speaking. "By the look of you, I would conclude that magical healing must be difficult work."

"It is a drain on my resources, to be sure," Aldus replied as he chewed. He paused only long enough to empty his cup and wipe the spillage from his long beard on the back of his hand. "But healing one person uses very little magic. It is mostly a matter of using my mind, you see, with a small thread of magic of course, to coax the body into doing with more speed what it would normally do on its own, given time. Even so, after so many, I must eat to restore my vigour."

Rodney nodded as the wizard plucked a thick slice of cheese from a nearby platter. Mouth crammed with food, he held out his cup to a passing servitor, while grabbing still more cheese with the other hand. Across the table, Elinor eyed the wizard with a look of distaste while Jason and Lionel remained embroiled in a private disagreement over the finer points of sword play. Sylvia stared vacantly, as if her mind was leagues away.

With breakfast over, Sylvia and Elinor excused themselves to search for a place in the stands that offered a good view of the upcoming matches. Aldus hastily filled the pockets of his robe with fistfuls of cheese and bread before following after them.

While knights and ladies had leisurely breakfasted, six walled rings had been constructed in the former jousting field. On the south side of the list there were three rings for pole-arms and the bare-knuckle fighting contests. To the north were three more for blades. The south rings were open to anyone, while the north were restricted to knights and their squires. Rodney followed Jason and Lionel to the north side. When they arrived, Lionel and Jason's squires were waiting with their equipment. By the way sunlight sparkled on helms and breastplates, the squires must have stayed up half the night polishing them.

The fighting rings were thirty feet across with four foot high walls made of rough pine poles lashed together. Most of the spectators viewed the matches from the stands, but the participants and their seconds surrounded the rings leaning on the pole ends. Of the three rings for blades, the first was for the Bohort. It provided the older squires an opportunity to test themselves against each other with blunted training weapons. The squires fought until one was knocked to the ground or lost his sword.

The second was the elimination ring, where most of the contests would take place. In the second ring the combat was until first blood was drawn, or a knight yielded. The third was the Master-of-the-sword ring itself. The best eight swordsmen would compete there for the title. In the third ring, the fighting continued until one of the knights yielded or was rendered unable to continue.

The first match was underway in the second ring and two squires were pummelling one another in the first. As defending champion, Jason would not compete in the second ring. He was one of the eight by virtue of being the current Master-of-the-sword. Jason and Rodney leaned on the poles to watch, while Lionel was being strapped into his armour.

It was the fourth match when Lionel first entered the ring. He faced Sir Joel Florentine, eight years his junior and a Daemon Knight only since the last tourney. The young knight was a fine swordsman but eventually Lionel's greater reach and experience won out. "First blood!", the judge called out. Sir Joel bowed to Lionel before he limped out of the ring holding the wound in his thigh. Lionel entered the ring four more times over the next two sun marks winning all four matches and securing a position as one of the eight.

The sun had moved well past its zenith before the final elimination match was underway. Rodney could see Jason tense as Martin entered the middle ring. "I best go put on my armour," Jason growled. Martin turned his head in time for them to exchange a sour glare before Jason walked away.

Leaning forward, Rodney rested his forearms against the side of the ring to watch the match in comfort. He was pleased to see Eugene Florentine enter the ring. Eugene was a superb swordsman, one of the eight from the last tourney. Martin was good, grudgingly better than Rodney, but certainly not as good as Eugene. Rodney gave a sigh of relief. With Eugene drawing first blood there would be no possibility of Martin meeting Jason in the third ring.

Most of the match went as Rodney suspected it would. Martin was hard pressed to defend himself from his opponent's constant attacks, but he managed to prevent Eugene's blade from drawing blood far longer than Rodney would have thought. Then, when both men had begun to show signs of tiring, it was Eugene who made a mistake. He pressed too hard and Martin sidestepped with speed completely unexpected from a tired man. *The crafty devil. He was faking.* The moment Eugene's sword arm passed by Martin he was exposed, and Martin took full advantage by neatly slashing the back of Eugene's arm with the edge of his blade.

With first blood the match was over. Rodney was stunned. Martin had become far more cunning and dangerous since his duel with Jason. The melee rules, unfortunately, did not apply to Master-of-the-sword. How could Rodney possibly keep his promise to Sylvia now? He looked up to search the stands until he found Sylvia, but she was too far away for him to read her expression.

Jason had returned just in time to witness Martin's victory. Rodney tried to read his face, but whatever Jason was feeling was well hidden behind a mask of seeming indifference. Rodney felt uneasy. It was very uncharacteristic of his friend. Jason slid his sword from its scabbard and checked the keenness of its edge. Picking up his spiked shield, he stepped into the third ring. In the centre of the thirty-foot circle he waited calmly until Edward Austin entered. With his left hand, Edward drew a wicked looking bastard sword from the scabbard strapped to his back. "There will be a new Master-of-the-sword this day," he bellowed.

Since all squires were trained to fight with their right, left-handed swordsmen were extremely rare. Rodney could vividly remember the tourney match four years back. Edward had lost the first two fingers of his right hand, when his opponent, Sir Charles Dunn, had chopped through Edward's gauntlet with one swipe of a two-handed broad sword. Rodney noted that though Edward wore no breastplate, he did have a heavily armoured gauntlet on his left hand.

As the two knights touched blades, Rodney tried to imagine how he would deal with a left-handed opponent.

The spectators took an audible breath when Jason discarded his shield and faced the challenger with just a naked sword. Edward, moving with a speed that belied his bulk, swung his hand-and-half in a deadly arc toward Jason's head. Rodney held his breath as Jason ducked under the blade at the last possible moment, and then with his left hand gripping the upper part of his sword, he rammed the point under his opponent's shield, stabbing him in the solar plexus. Rodney winced remembering the sharp pain he had felt two days ago when Jason had done the same to him, and that had been only one-handed with a blunted sword.

All of Jason's pent up animosity toward his cousin Martin must have been behind that blow. Edward staggered back coughing. He spat and then wiped his mouth with his right hand. Edward looked at the blood smeared on his glove and swore. He raised his sword but began to cough again and lowered it. "I yield," he gasped and left the ring still coughing and holding his chest. Jason picked up his shield and followed him out of the ring with concern etched on his face.

"Shall I find a physician?" someone asked.

"The wizard," Edward gasped. "Bring me the wizard," he repeated before another fit of coughing prevented any further speech.

Lewis stepped up to take Jason's sword and shield, but Jason refused to give them up. "Lewis, go find Wizard Aldus," he said softly. Lewis nodded and trotted off in the direction of the stands.

Rodney's attention was drawn back to the ring when Lionel stepped into the circle closely followed by Gunther Darnell. Rodney exchanged a smile with Lionel, genuinely pleased for his friend. This would be his first time in the third ring. Rodney had never been able to get this far and had finally given up trying. Lionel and Gunther wasted no time with preambles and went instantly at each other toe to toe. Unfortunately, just when Lionel seemed to be gaining the upper hand, he slipped. As quick as that he found himself on his back with Gunther's sword levelled at his throat.

As he left the ring, Lionel gave Rodney a wry grin. Sir Daniel Buxton passed him on his way in. Rodney watched with interest as Sir Charles entered the ring next. The man was large enough to handle his four and a half foot long two-handed blade with more ease than Rodney did his own three and a half. Daniel landed but one blow before Charles dispatched him with a crushing blow to the head. The big knight used his weapon more like a club than a sword. Daniel was carried from the ring unconscious.

The next two contests were over quickly. Maynard Emson yielded to Martin and Gunther to Jason. Then Martin stepped into the ring with Charles. Like Edward, Charles wore no breastplate, only heavy mail and a broad grin. "Why not yield now and spare yourself a lot of pain, little man," Charles said in his deep gravelly voice.

Martin's reply was a lightning fast stab to the big man's ribs. The knights lining the ring cheered and banged their shields and armour. If not for his thick mail the blow could have been fatal. Charles grunted in pain and stepped back, keeping Martin at bay with the point of his longer sword. Rodney was impressed with Martin's speed, even Jason could move no faster. The smug look that had been on the big man's face was gone. In its place was one of stone-cold determination.

Charles moved in like a charging bull, wind-milling his sword at Martin's head. The swing was backed with enough power to split his opponent's head in two, if Martin had been foolish enough to still be there. Twice more Charles swung his sword and missed as Martin danced aside. Then Martin made his mistake. He tried the same quick stab to the big man's ribs for a second time. As he moved in, Charles twisted sideways and slammed the iron edge of his heavy shield into the side of Martin's head. Martin was thrown back against the poles of the ring where he collapsed in a heap.

The men standing around the ring fell silent. When it became apparent that he was not going to rise, Charles raised his sword and shield in triumph. A few cheered for him, but not many, and not whole heartedly. Martin appeared to be held in higher regard by his brethren than Rodney had thought. On the one hand, Rodney was relieved it would not be Martin that Jason would face next, but on the other, Charles might be far more dangerous.

Talbot and Joel carried their dazed companion from the ring. As they passed Jason, who was waiting his turn by the entrance, Talbot's face was a contorted mask of pure hatred. To Rodney's surprise, Jason watched them remove the limp form of his sworn enemy with a frown. Rodney would have expected a look of anger or possibly satisfaction. What the frown meant was a bit of a mystery.

As Jason walked into the ring, Rodney could not help but think how he resembled a child holding a long dagger, compared to the mountain that was Sir Charles and his massive two-handed sword. Jason's blade was a foot and a half shorter. He would be at a disadvantage in reach as well as power.

Without any warning, Charles swung at Jason's head. Jason ducked, and to Rodney's surprise, tried to stab the other knight much like Sir Martin had done in the last match. In a similar response, Charles swung his shield and knocked Jason to the ground. A loud cheer erupted as the champion hit the ground. The big man quickly placed his left foot on Jason's sword and levelled his own at Jason's chest. Rodney was stunned.

"You disappoint me," Charles said. "My squire could have given a better account of himself. I was expecting more of you. Do you yield?"

"Nay," Jason said, as he delivered a swift kick with his armoured right boot straight into Charles' groin. At the same time, Jason released his sword and rolled to the left, just in time to avoid the big two handed sword as it bit three fingers deep into the dirt. With only his shield, Jason stood to the side waiting. After a few moments, Charles dropped his sword and toppled like an old oak to lay on the ground clutching himself and moaning.

Jason walked over and picked up his sword. He touched the tip on Charles' shoulder. "You really should wear a cod piece," he said softly. "Do you yield?"

"Yes, you son-of-a-bitch," the big man croaked.

It took two men to help the stricken knight from the ring. After that, Rodney and Lionel fell in to either side of Jason and escorted him before the Baron, who personally placed the Master-of-the-sword medallion around his neck. This was Jason's third consecutive win.

As First Knight, Silas presented the lesser medallions to the bare-knuckle, pole-arm and archery champions. The only other champion Rodney recognized was Sir Duncan Breen, Selina's husband. As Duncan accepted the bare-knuckle medallion, she stood off to the side with their two young sons. Time had not been kind to Selina. She looked pale, thin and sickly. Her once bright reddish blond hair was dull and streaked with grey. She looked many summers older than just thirty-two. It reaffirmed something that Rodney already knew; love was a cruel and merciless curse.

After the medallions had been bestowed, the nobles returned to the long tables for dinner. While they supped, the rings and jousting curtain were cleared from the field to make room for the melee. Some eighty knights in total took part in the event and nearly a quarter of those sustained injuries serious enough to require immediate attention. Largely due to the presence of Wizard Aldus, who was on hand to deal with the more gravely injured, there were no fatalities this year. Lionel managed to stay on his horse and received only minor bruising. Notably, Martin was absent, as were Talbot and Joel. All in all, for a melee, it was a relatively benign affair.

By dusk, nearly two thousand men had crowded into the inner courtyard of Daemon castle proper. The air was thick and surprisingly warm for early spring. Four large braziers had been filled and set ablaze. Their light had begun to dance along the walls with the darkening sky. It had been a long day. The wizard's healing, along with the heat, had left Rodney weak-kneed and drowsy. He yawned as he wiped the sweat from his brow.

Many of the men gathered in the courtyard were dressed in leather, with some even wearing chain mail. Rodney was thankful he had removed his own leathers and wore only a tunic and britches. He was standing just outside the entrance to the great hall along with the small group of men who faced the gathering. Aldus stood to his right, still in the same thick woolen robe he'd been wearing when they met. Even so, the wizard's brow was dry and he seemed comfortable despite the closeness and his heavy garment.

Both still in their fighting leathers, Jason and Lionel were to Rodney's left. An ugly purple bruise was spreading down Jason's left arm from his shoulder. He had declined the wizard's offer of healing, with the excuse that he would rather suffer a little pain than be left as weak as a newborn lamb. Considering how he presently felt, Rodney was forced to concede that he had a valid point. Perhaps he had been too swift to accept the wizard's gifts. As his father used to say, "Everything in life has a price. First be sure that you are willing to pay it."

A few paces away, Baron Basil was resting on one of two chairs placed by the archway leading to the grand hall. The way Basil's eyes sagged, Rodney couldn't help but think of how taxing the festivities must have been for a man of his years. Silas stood to the Baron's right, stone-faced, with his arms crossed. Leaning over a small wooden table, Basil's scribe sat with quill poised above a thick open book. It was the latest in a series of journals that had been used to record events in Balor since the founding of the order. Preserved with care for future generations, they were referred to collectively as the Daemon Knight Chronicles.

"If I was smarter, I would be sharing a warm cup of cider with Elinor right now, not trapped in these close quarters with you two," Lionel said just loud enough for Jason and Rodney to hear.

"Council meetings grow more crowded every year," Jason said in reply.

Rodney felt the beginnings of a headache and growled under his breath. The noise and close proximity of so many bodies was annoying to the point of being unbearable. A movement to Rodney's right caught his eye. Silas was bent over whispering something in the Baron's ear. It was too muffled for Rodney to make out, but the thin smile that cracked the old man's face seemed to chase some of his weariness away.

"Thank you for reminding me," Rodney heard Basil whisper back. The Baron stood, with the aid of Silas's arm, and raised his hand. The courtyard fell silent.

"Before we begin," the Baron said in a strong loud voice which was at odds with his frail appearance, "it will be my privilege to conduct a knighting." Rodney winced at the deafening uproar that followed.

The Baron smiled, waiting until he could be heard once more before he spoke. "Sir Herman Austin, step forward if you please."

Herman's hulking form made ripples through the sea of bodies as he made his way toward the Baron. Save for one or two others, Herman was the tallest man in the order. His balding pate could be seen bobbing just above the rows of heads. Finally the crowd parted, and Herman stepped out. Though close to fifty, he was still a powerful and dangerous man. Both his face and head bore countless battle scars accumulated over many years. What little hair he had left was snow white and confined to a narrow horseshoe-shaped ring just above his ears.

"I am told that you have a squire to be submitted for knighthood," Basil said.

"I do my lord," Herman replied as he turned to face his peers. "I, Herman Austin, knight in good standing, do submit Squire Gregory Vennell to my brethren for acceptance into the order of Daemon Knights. Gregory is just today of age and I vouch for both his skill and his courage."

A clamour of hoots and clanking metal followed the squire as he stepped forward. The young man glanced briefly at Silas before his eyes returned to the Baron. The resemblance between young Gregory and Silas was striking. Rodney had never before seen the First Knight smile, but any attempt Silas was making to suppress the overwhelming joy at his only son's impending knighthood was in vain. An ever widening grin was threatening to split his chiselled face in two.

Basil raised his hand again until the courtyard was relatively silent. "What say you my fellow knights," the Baron shouted. "Do you accept this young man as your new sword brother?"

"Aye," roared the crowd.

"Any nay-sayers?" he asked. There was only silence. Basil smiled at Gregory. "Kneel before me squire," he said. Gregory knelt with his head bowed low.

Basil drew a thin ceremonial sword from the ornate silver scabbard at his side. "Gregory Vennell, son of Sir Silas Vennell, heir to the Vennell family estates, will you swear the oath of the order for all to witness?"

Gregory's head came up and he met the Baron's gaze. "I forsake all kings, queens and potentates. I pledge my life to the preservation of Balor, its people, and the Daemon Order. This oath I do swear to uphold until my last breath, before all men and Gods."

Basil tapped him lightly on the head with the flat of his sword. "Then arise Sir Gregory, Daemon Knight."

A servant appeared at the Baron's side with a black leather belt draped over his arm. The Baron took the belt and fastened it around Gregory's waist. When he stepped back, the torchlight glinted off the highly polished edge of a silver buckle. The face was round and painted snow white. In its centre glowed a bright red dragon. Cheers bounced off the tall stone walls as Silas rushed forward to hug the Order's newest knight. By the time the clamour had faded to a low murmur, Rodney's ears were ringing.

Basil allowed them a few more moments before he once again raised his hand. "We must set aside normal business today in order to respond to a threat to our homeland." The gathering fell completely silent. "First you will hear from three fellow knights and then from a visitor to our island. All I ask is that you hold your tongues until you have heard what they have to say."

The Baron turned his head to Rodney and lowered his voice. "Rodney, you may begin," he said before he sat back down.

Rodney stepped forward. Feeling a slight tickle, he nervously wiped away a bead of sweat that was threatening to fall from the tip of his nose. His chest constricted as the smell of stale sweat and heat of the crowd pressed in on him. Feeling both warm and cold at the same time, he rubbed his face and tried to calm his nerves. When jousting, he always focussed on winning the match and was never really aware of the eyes of spectators upon him. It was another thing entirely to stand and address such a large body of men. His throat went first dry and then numb as he worked desperately to remember what he had planned to say.

When Silas made a loud coughing noise, Rodney finally found his voice. "I trust many of you have had the opportunity to meet Wizard Aldus." Rodney's voice was hoarse and sounded strange to his ears. "I know most of you have witnessed him applying his craft this day and I suspect he has shared his views with at least some of you. I for one have no reason to doubt his claims."

A ripple of nodding heads was followed by murmurs of agreement. Rodney waited until he had regained their full attention before continuing. "Now, I will tell you of our encounter with the FireDrake Grigor two days ago. You may know this creature better by the name Dragon."

Half the gathering burst into laughter while the other half began asking questions in spite of the Baron's instructions to the contrary. The ruckus was deafening. Basil raised his hand until the noise died down, then he smiled and nodded for Rodney to continue.

The Baron's smile put Rodney at ease. "As I was saying, two days ago we attempted to slay a FireDrake and would now be dead if not for the intervention of Wizard Aldus. This FireDrake stood two thirds as tall as these walls." Almost to a man, heads turned to look at the castle walls. Rodney didn't need sensitive hearing to note the sound of two thousand men pausing to take a breath.

"Its hide is armoured with scales harder than good steel. I did strike it several times with my blade, but to the FireDrake I was no more than a troublesome gnat. After much consideration, there is only one course of action I can conceive. To defeat a FireDrake on the ground would require experienced jousters and hard fine-tipped lances. Should one attack from the air..."

Rodney paused knowing his fellow knights wouldn't appreciate what he would say next. "We could try bolts and quarrels, though I doubt such would pierce its armoured hide at any distance if at all." Rodney stepped back. There was a low mumbling. Whether it demonstrated their distaste for using a commoner's weapon, or disagreement with Rodney's conclusions, he didn't know.

Jason and Lionel each came forward in turn to tell their own versions of the encounter with Grigor. Though their stories varied, and there was no further mention of un-knightly weapons, they confirmed all Rodney had said. After that, Aldus moved to stand closer to the Baron before turning to face the gathering. He addressed them with arms folded across his chest and hands tucked into the sleeves of his thick robe. The heat from the nearby brazier seemed to have no effect on him whatsoever.

"Three of your fellow knights have just testified as to their experiences," the wizard said in an unnaturally loud voice that Rodney recognized from the encounter with Grigor. "Taking up arms against FireDrakes is pure folly. Salvation lies in defeating the sorceress who controls them, but to this end FireDrakes are but one of the dangers. It is true that the sorceress must be stopped by force of arms, but an army would never be able to cross Nagual unnoticed. The Emperor's Dog Soldiers number one hundred thousand strong. A large force would be doomed to failure, but a small group, say forty knights, could pass through without drawing undue attention. These brave men must travel through Carpathia, Nagual, Icarus and then on through the mountains to

Drakenmount. Time is critical. Since it will take more than a full cycle of the moon to get there, it is imperative to leave at once."

The wizard paused to look upon the faces of the men before him. "I must warn you," he said. "The journey will be hard and perilous. A safe return is doubtful, but those who go will be saving the lives of their friends and loved ones." With that, he returned to his place next to Rodney.

The courtyard remained silent until Sir Duncan spoke up. "What say you, Baron," he yelled.

"Aye, what say you, Baron," echoed another voice.

Using Silas's arm for support, Basil got up slowly. "I know that for many of you this is hard to swallow all at once, but for the last two seasons I have received reports confirming much of what you have just heard."

The Baron paused and gazed out at the faces of the men before he continued. "There have been strange happenings on the mainland involving dragons. In Nagual, Imperial legions have indeed been moving south. I believe we must take this request to heart and act accordingly."

Basil held out his hand toward Rodney and his friends. "Our own sword brothers have stated how dangerous these FireDrakes are. Wizard Aldus tells us this sorceress has hundreds of them at her disposal. As I understand it, without her, they are no longer a threat. Distasteful as it seems to take up arms against a woman, for the good of Balor I can see no other recourse. She must be stopped. Killed if necessary."

"I will go," Sir Gavin shouted. Shouts of approval, and many more volunteers, drowned out anything else for a time.

"I anticipated that too many would offer their services," Basil said, "so I took the liberty of preparing a list of those I consider best suited to undertake this quest. Our First Knight will lead the company." There was more shouting and murmurs of approval until the Baron raised his hand for silence. "Since Rodney has first hand knowledge of what you may face, he will act as Second."

Rodney was shocked. He looked at Basil and then at Silas. The Baron's face was unreadable, but Silas wore an undisguised scowl of disapproval. With a nod from the Baron, his scribe stood and read out the remaining thirty-eight names. Jason and Lionel were the first two called while the newly knighted Sir Gregory was the last.

When the scribe was done, Silas stepped forward to address the assembly. "Each of you will be allowed four retainers, and that includes your squires. Bring who you will, but bring no less than two seasoned arms-men. Arrangements are underway to secure passage by ship to the mainland. Wagons and provisions will be provided. All of those named must be at the Riverside docks no later than sunset the day after next. Now, with this business done, I suggest we join our families for the evening meal."

"Wait," Aldus yelled as he stepped out from beside Rodney and raised his hand. "I meant forty men in total, sir. You are suggesting two hundred. That will never do. It is far too many."

Silas turned to the wizard. "You asked for two score knights. You have been given two score knights. We will need squires, camp guards, scouts and wagon drivers." Silas glanced at Rodney. "Perhaps we may even need a few skilled archers."

The wizard's face turned stony as he and Silas stood eye to eye. Then Aldus bowed politely, turned, and walked away without another word.

The assembly broke up into noisy groups, each discussing what had transpired as they drifted out of the courtyard. As Rodney turned to leave he felt a hand on his shoulder. It was Silas. "In addition to whatever you require," he said, "I expect you to supply a large freight wagon, driver and enough supplies to sustain the company for six days."

Since the First Knight's request didn't appear to be open for discussion, Rodney just nodded in agreement before accompanying his friends back to the tables for supper. He walked in silence hoping there would be another pot of chicory tea and vowing to reward the server with a gold piece if by some miracle there was.

Chapter 10

RODNEY

It was the morning of the second day after the tourney. Rodney was wide awake long before first light, but he was not well rested. His mind had been far too preoccupied with recent events to allow him any kind of a peaceful sleep. After buckling up his leathers, he made his way by the light of a single candle down into the kitchens where he brewed himself a fresh pot of chicory tea. He had little trouble finding the ground chicory root, as he knew very well where things were kept. Years serving as page in Vincent Castle had its rewards.

After filling his cup for the second time, he returned to his bed chamber. Impatient, he had not allowed the water to come to a full boil before the brewing, so the tea was weak, but he felt much refreshed just the same. By the time he reached his bedchamber, the first light of dawn was filtering through the thin window coverings. Picking up his travel pack, he dropped in a small flax sack of chicory root that he had pilfered from the larder. Next he stuffed in some clean small cloths, an extra tunic and a pair of britches. He tied the pack shut before slinging it over his shoulder and taking one last look around the room. How long would it be before he could enjoy sleeping in his own bed again?

When Rodney stepped outside, Aldus was there waiting for him. As he walked across the courtyard, the wizard fell into step at his side and renewed his protests regarding the number of men the Baron had seen fit to send. Aldus waved his hands about in the air while he spoke, as if swatting unseen insects. Rodney finally stopped abruptly and turned to face him.

"It is pointless for you to continue arguing the matter," Rodney said softly, but with an edge to his voice that he hoped would convey his desire to end the discussion. "All has been decided. We travel to Drakenmount. You may accompany us or not. That, is of course up to you."

Mostly it had all been a bluff on Rodney's part. He didn't have a clue how to get to Drakenmount, but the wizard's hands dropped to his sides in apparent defeat. "Very well," he said, "I shall speak no more of it, but mark my words, you will all regret ignoring my counsel in this matter."

Rodney doubted he had truly heard the last word on it, but he let it go with a silent prayer it would be so. The men he had picked to accompany him were ready and waiting at the gate when he and the wizard arrived. The castle staff were lined up near the gate as well, to pay proper respect to their Lord. They bowed as he passed them by. He could sense the apprehension hiding behind their smiles. It was the first time their Lord was to be away from the castle for an extended period of time, not to mention leaving Balor altogether.

Two big draft horses were hitched up to the long freight wagon. The expedition would need to carry enough supplies to last at least a moon. To supply over two hundred men and fifty horses required five large wagons. Since the wealthiest landholders could best afford the cost, Rodney was to supply a wagon, driver and one fifth of the supplies. Silas, Martin, Gavin and Herman would supply the rest.

After securing the pack to his saddle, Rodney walked over to inspect the wagon. It looked sound enough. The axles had been recently greased. A water barrel and three steel tipped war lances were strapped to each side. He tested the lashings by giving them a hard tug. It was not that he mistrusted the reliability of his people, but rather a simple precaution he had learned from his father. "Scrutinizing his own gear will keep a man alive in both peace and war. Always take the time to look things over for yourself, Rodney."

A smile spread across Rodney's face as he remembered the countless times his father had left a strap undone, a tie loose or a sheath empty. Frederic acted as if it had been an oversight, but Rodney caught on right away that they were really tests of his diligence. Nevertheless, it did impress the lesson on him. Mindful of that, Rodney untied and lifted the oiled tarpon to inspect the contents and mentally checked off the items against a list in his head.

A tent large enough for eight men. Four bundles of travel bread wrapped in cloth and sealed with beeswax. Two small barrels of dried apples, six small barrels of cider, two large barrels of salted fish, six sacks of flour and six, no, seven large sacks of oats for the horses. The stable master must have thrown in an extra sack. Well, no matter, there was still enough room at the back of the wagon for extra arms to be stored. Silas had restricted everyone to leathers and mail as it would be too long and difficult a journey to transport heavy armour. His coif and mail lay in the corner next to his shield. Rodney pulled the tarpon tightly back in place and retied it.

Satisfied with his inspection, Rodney walked silently back to Thunder and climbed into the saddle. Morton was perched on the wagon seat. His eyes followed Thunder warily as Rodney passed by. Could Thunder smell the squire's fear? Was that why Morton had such difficulty in handling him? A mysterious thing, that. Morton was a Lambert after all, and had spent the first seven years of his life at Lambert Castle where the finest destriers in all of Balor were bred. The Lamberts were renowned breeders and horsemen. Thunder was of Lambert stock, purchased by his father back when Rodney was still a squire. Frederic had presented the three year old destrier to Rodney on the day he was knighted.

Clicking his heels to Thunder's side, Rodney rode toward the gate. Aldus followed alongside on the mare like a grey shadow. As an afterthought, Rodney looked back and waved to the castle staff as he passed through the gateway. Coll Dunn, his Master-at-arms, flicked the reins of his team and followed with the wagon. At fifty, Coll was too old to be going on such a long and perilous journey, and Rodney had not hesitated to tell him so, but Coll had been Frederic's man since before Rodney was born and maintained it was his sworn duty to the father to look out for the son. When he pointed out that Sir Herman was of the same age, Rodney finally relented. Besides, as well as being an experienced soldier, Coll was an excellent cook.

Corporal Jasper would fill in as Vincent Castle's temporary Master-at-arms. Though the corporal was not the most reliable of men, old Albert Beane practically ran the castle on his own, so Jasper could do little harm. Rodney could rest easy that he was leaving his holdings in good hands.

Morton looked tired, but otherwise seemed happy enough riding along in the seat next to Coll. Truth be told, Rodney had strong reservations about bringing his squire. Leaving him behind, however, would have been a grave insult to the Lamberts. Even though this would be his eighteenth summer, Morton had not yet come into his growth. Rodney was beginning to suspect he never would. After more than three years of training, Morton had developed only minimal skill with a sword. His training with the lance had not even begun, since he had not yet mastered riding and never would unless he overcame his fear of horses. If Rodney could not cure him of that then nothing else would matter. In hindsight, he should have listened to his sister and turned him out at the first sign of trouble, but he just didn't have the heart to do it.

The twins, Tyko and Yvon, followed behind the wagon on foot along with Garrick. For venturing into unknown lands, Rodney wanted an experienced woodsman and tracker. His woodward Garth Foster was one of the best, but he was even older than Coll, so Rodney had elected to bring both Tyko and Yvon instead. They were both experienced hunters as well as two of Balor's finest archers. Taking both men left the castle without a warden, but the larder was full and it couldn't be helped as the twins were inseparable. Garrick had been an easy choice. The tall arms-man was deadly with a pike, and like Yvon and Tyko he had no wife or children to leave behind.

The air was warming quickly, even though Rodney could hear the occasional crunch of thin ice under Thunder's hooves as they passed between the garden wall and mill. The mill was a solid three story whitewashed structure with a ten-foot water wheel. Farmers from Rodney's fief, as well as others, brought their grain to this mill to be ground. A tenth of the grain was kept by the miller for Rodney's granaries as payment for use of the mill, and another fifth from Rodney's vassals for the use of his land. Profits from trading in excess grain, wool and cider had made the Vincent family rich. With no heir, should Rodney fail to return, the estate would go to the next in line, Elinor.

Wearing a broad smile and covered in flour dust, the miller stood in the entrance to the mill waving a farewell. Rodney could hear the squeaking of the wheel and the crunching of last season's grain between the stones. He doubted anyone else in his party would notice. At an early age Rodney discovered he had an unusual talent for hearing things others seemed to miss. He had been quick to speak of this ability, but soon found he was rarely believed and often ridiculed. After being severely punished by Albert for making up slanderous stories, he decided to keep what he heard to himself. As Rodney grew older, he found it proved quite useful to know what people said when they thought he couldn't hear.

After the mill came the dock. Two vessels were moored there, a small fishing boat and a large square barge. The barge was too small for the wagon and horses, so they would ride the ten leagues to Riverside. There was no hurry. They would arrive in plenty of time to board ship before the evening tide. Silas had sent word that Rodney was assigned to the Swift. Well, the name was certainly promising anyway.

The Fisk family stood by the dock and waved an enthusiastic farewell to Rodney's party as it passed by. Jakob Fisk was the fisherman. He lived next to the dock with his wife Viola and their son Knute. The Fisks kept the castle supplied with both fresh and salt fish. Besides helping Jakob clean and salt the fish he caught, Viola worked in the castle laundry.

Knute appeared nervous. When Rodney waved back, he noticed that the boy was staring at the wagon like he'd never seen one before. As Rodney entered the trees he glanced back. Jacob and his wife had gone about their business, but Knute stood as if rooted to the spot still wearing that same blank look on his face. *Well, maybe the lad is weak minded,* Rodney thought before he put it out of his mind.

As the morning wore on, Rodney passed the time by listening in as Coll told Morton stories of Balorian history. In spite of the distance between them, the noise of horse's hooves and the creaking of the wagon, Rodney heard almost every word.

"Two hundred years ago, before he came to this island, Carl Daemon held a large Barony in old Sidon," Coll said. "He was sworn to King Brian."

"Brian the Betrayer," Morton said enthusiastically.

"The very same," Coll replied. "Now Galen, the King of Carpathia, threatened to invade Sidon and remove King Brian's head if he didn't bend his knee to Carpathia. His subjects would have fought to the last for King and country, but Brian was weak. To save his own cowardly head he swore fealty to Galen and betrayed the good people of Sidon. Well, the Baron was enraged when he learned of what his King had done. Like everyone else, Carl Daemon was prepared for a fight to the death. In a fit of anger he disbanded his levies and abandoned his barony. Rather than live under foreign rule, he set out with his wife and daughter for the wilds of Balor Island. Four score and ten of his loyal knights followed him, with their families and retainers in tow."

"I have never understood why King Galen did not send his army after them," Morton said.

"Ah, well now, it's a good thing we're talking then. The Baron was a very wealthy man, you see. He had more than enough gold to purchase every last ship at the port of Celia. All those ships sailed to Balor, but only one sailed back. The Baron had the rest of the ships burned to the waterline and sunk in the bay. He allowed only one to depart loaded with all the sailors who wished to return, in exchange for their word to scuttle the ship or never return to Celia. It was a long time before enough ships could be found to mount an attack and by then Castle Daemon had been built."

Rodney smiled. He was sure that he had heard every story Coll knew, thrice over, but was just as sure he would never tire of hearing them.

"What happened after that?" Morton asked.

"Well now," Coll replied, "after the baron died, the knights agreed to form the Daemon order in his honour." Coll chuckled. "And I dare say for their own mutual protection. Carpathia was just across the sea after all. The first elected Baron was Hugh Vincent, Sir Rodney's ancestor. He had been Carl Daemon's First Knight, and most trusted friend."

Coll lowered his voice and took on a conspiratorial tone. Rodney had to strain to hear his words. "Murdered in his sleep within a year of being named Baron. Stabbed once through the heart he was. Real professional like. The hand of Galen was suspected of course, but nothing was ever proven one way or another. He was succeeded by Amos Vennell. In two hundred years, no other Vincent has ever offered to stand as Baron."

"Is this Riverside?" Aldus asked, breaking Rodney's concentration.

"What?" Rodney replied, "Oh yes it is." He had been so intent on listening to Coll that he had failed to notice they had entered the outskirts of the city. It was two sun-marks past midday, the busiest time of day. People went about their business and paid little or no attention to their passing even though they rode down the centre of main street. Riverside was Balor's only port and the hub of trade on the island. Wagons moving back and forth were a daily occurrence. They had passed two, very similar to their own, going in the opposite direction by the time they neared the docks.

A score of Knights and their retainers were waiting in small groups along the docks. Four large ships were moored in berths, with another anchored out in the bay. Horses and wagons were being lifted by slings into three of the larger ships. They located the Swift in the last berth. Jason, his brother Garrett and cousin Ernest were waiting on the dock next to it. Eight knights had been assigned to the Swift. Lionel, his brother William and their cousins Herbolt and Maynard Emson had not yet arrived. They would be the last to reach the city, as their estates lay many leagues farther from Riverside than Vincent Castle.

"You be the leader of this here party then," a big, black, bearded man yelled down from the deck of the Swift.

"I am Rodney Vincent, and yes, I will be in charge of the this ship."

"Ah, well, I be Captain Micah Moises," the black man said, stabbing his hairy chest with his thumb, "but before we start loading, there is something you and I must be clear about. Just so's there's no trouble, you understand."

There was a long moment of silence before the Captain finally continued. "I'm the Captain of this here ship, and I'll be giving the orders. If that be not acceptable to you, Sir Knight, well, then you'd best find another ship, as you'll not be coming aboard mine."

Rodney forced down his anger over the Captain's lack of respect. "I understand," he said. "Please forgive my assumption of command."

The Captain laughed. "I can see we'll get along famously you and I, Sir Knight. This here be the Swift's first mate, Ira Duffy," he added, pointing his thumb to a bull of man standing cross-armed beside him. The first mate had a large scar that ran up the side of his face and disappeared beneath a black eye patch over his left eye. "Aboard ship we just call him Patch."

"Patch it is then," Rodney replied nodding to the first mate.

"Is this the lot of you then?" the Captain asked.

"Only half," Rodney replied. "The rest will arrive within a few sun-marks." Rodney introduced the other knights and then Aldus. Micah's eyebrows lifted in alarm at the mention of the word wizard.

"No one said anything to me about wizards, and such," the captain said. "I'll not have any spell casting on my ship."

"I can assure you Captain," Aldus said. "I will perform no magic of any kind while I am aboard your vessel. I seek only uneventful passage to the mainland."

"Well, it best be as you say. The first hint of a curse, and it'll be over the side with you." Aldus gave a slight bow and the Captain's smile returned. "Now I must see to the loading." With that, Micah and Patch disappeared from the rail.

Rodney left the task of unsaddling Thunder to Morton while Coll and Garrick unhitched the horses from the wagon. A seaman came down to lead them to their cabin. As Rodney walked up the gangplank he noticed a short brown-skinned sailor eyeing him. He was slight of build and a full head shorter than the other seamen. The little man smiled, showing a uniform row of pointed teeth, and then he was gone, disappearing among the rest of the crew. It happened so fast that Rodney had to question whether he had actually seen him or not. He shrugged and followed his guide to the cabin.

Chapter 11

JOHN

John Coch was disoriented and slippery with sweat. The air was so hot and thick he could hardly breathe. Eventually, after remembering where he was, he pulled the sack down from around his head and took a deep breath. The fog in his brain cleared a little more with each breath, until it all came back to him.

The hardest part had been convincing Knute to steal an empty sack from the mill and then show him where the wagon was kept. Sneaking into the wagon under the cover of darkness had been easy enough. Though terrified of being caught, he hadn't felt such excitement since finding the bowyer's yew. It made him feel so alive. Staying curled up in the sack all day had been another matter. The experience had been truly awful and not one he wanted to repeat anytime soon.

Unaware the wagon had stopped, until it suddenly rolled forward, John was startled by a gruff voice very close by. "Haul away," it barked. The wagon jerked forward, and then rocked slowly from side to side. A hot lump formed in the pit of his stomach as the swaying motion made him feel sick. When the rocking finally stopped, the smell of rotten fish assailed his nostrils. It made him gag and brought on an overwhelming urge to throw up. Fear, at the sudden arrival of voices, took his mind off his discomforts. He frantically pulled the sack back over his head and lay very still.

Once the voices drifted away, John relaxed, but then the nausea returned. When he could stand it no longer, he pulled down the sack to take a gulp of fresh air. The smell didn't seem so bad this time. He listened until he was sure there was no one near the wagon. The voices were still there, but they were muffled and distant.

When John tried to stretch his legs, they were so numb from lack of circulation that he had to unfold them by hand. He was surprised with the weight of his own legs and the effort it took to move them. Once his legs were straight, he rubbed them until they had regained some feeling and the ability to move on their own. Kicking off the sack, he crawled to the end of the wagon and lifted the corner of the tarpon just enough to peek out.

After the near total darkness under the thick oiled canvas, the small amount of sunlight that filtered though a grate above was almost blinding. He had to blink several times before his eyes adjusted enough to see that the wagon had been secured to a post near the end of a row of livestock stalls. His first conclusion was that he was in a stable near the docks, but when the wagon tilted he realized he must be in the belly of a ship. Leaving the corner flap raised enough to see by, he pulled some badly squished bread from a pouch tucked inside his tunic. He alternated between chewing and gulping water from the small sheepskin bag at his side.

As John drained the last drop of water, a horse neighed. There was a loud thud that he felt as much as heard. He peeked out from under the tarpon just in time to see the legs of a horse dangling from the open hatch above. When he heard voices, he quickly tugged the flap closed and scrambled to get back into his sack. He pulled the ends over his head and listened to the sounds of men leading the horse into a stall.

"What's in the wagon," one of the men said.

"Don't rightly know," another replied. "Why don't you take a look. Our passengers be rich I think, could be full of gold."

The wagon shook. John's heart was pounding so loud he feared that one of the men would surely hear it. If they found him now, all his suffering would have been for nothing.

"Get the lead out down there," someone yelled from above. The wagon shook once more and then went still. John listened as more horses were brought down and placed in the stalls, which gave him a chance to calm down. It grew very warm in the sack and at some point he drifted off to sleep.

John awoke with an uneasy stomach. This time was even worse than the last. The bread he had eaten earlier now felt like a dead weight in his gut. After freeing himself from the sack, he crawled on hands and knees to the end of the wagon. As a precaution, he squinted to protect his eyes from the light before lifting the corner of the tarpon. It proved unnecessary as very little light filtered down from the grate. John squeezed his arm between the wagon and the tarpon and felt around for the end of the lashing. After fumbling with the rope for a while, he finally managed to untie it and slip out.

After a whole day cramped inside the wagon, it was wonderful just to be able to stand upright again. John took the opportunity to walk around and explore the hold until the stiffness was gone from his legs. Now if he could just do something to relieve his queasy stomach. He counted eleven horses in the stalls. Lord Vincent's big black stuck his nose out and snorted as he walked by. John gave the animal a quick rub on the cheek before heading back toward the wagon.

Once beneath the grate, John paused to look up. The source of light shining down was a large oil lantern hanging outside. He reached up, but was a foot short of touching the well worn wooden slats. The ship swayed and then lurched. The smell of rotten fish was still strong and a wave of nausea hit him once again. He leapt up and grabbed the grate, pulling himself up for some fresh air. The ship lurched and he lost his grip on the slippery slats, falling to the planking below. He landed badly and cursed as a sharp pain shot up from his ankle. The hold seemed to spin. When the ship lurched again he could no longer hold it back and vomited.

In his misery John vaguely heard a dull thud behind him, but ignored it. Just as he was thinking things could not get much worse, a pair of strong rough hands locked onto his shoulders. He looked up into the dirt smeared weather beaten face of an old sailor.

"What have we here," the old man said. "A stowaway is it?" The man's breath was foul, smelling of fish and rotten teeth. John felt the bile rise again in his throat.

"Haul him up where we can get a good look at him," said another voice from above.

Something wrapped around John's waist and he was lifted up into the cool night air. The next thing he knew he was sprawled out on the deck surrounded by many pairs of bare feet. He vomited again indiscriminately onto the deck and one or two of those feet. The man with the fish breath cursed and John felt a kick in his ribs. The blow made him want to vomit even more, but there was nothing left and he just coughed.

"I'm not cleaning this mess up, Patch," fish-breath said.

"You will bloody well do whatever I tell you," came the reply.

"Throw the filthy wretch over board, I say," someone else shouted.

A dirty bare foot, as rough as shark skin, rubbed unkindly against his cheek forcing his head to tilt back. The foot was in front of his face, but the toe next to the big one was missing and through the gap he caught sight of its owner. His face was a ruin with many scars and a black eyepatch.

"Looks fit enough," the one-eyed man said. "Maybe we can get enough work out of him to pay for his passage."

"Looks a bit too soft to me, Patch," fish-breath said.

"Maybe he has some coin, eh," a squeaky voice said. "Check his pockets and I'll go back down to look for his purse."

A new voice boomed in John's ears. "There'll be no thieving aboard this ship, Digger." The voice had the unmistakable ring of authority and the feet all backed away.

"Ah, Captain, I was just teasing is all," Digger said. "Just having a little fun."

"He's tall enough, but just a lad by the look of him," the captain said. "He might belong to one of our passengers. Patch, bring him aft and we'll see what's what." John was half carried and half dragged along the deck by Patch and fish-breath. They stopped at a low door near the rear of the ship.

"My lords," the captain bellowed through the door. "This be Captain Micah. I've something here what might belong to you."

The door opened and a man dressed in forest green stepped out. He looked around, nodded, and then stepped back inside. John was roughly pushed through the door. He tripped over something and landed painfully on his knees. When he raised his head, he was looking directly into the eyes of Lord Vincent. John's first thought was that the knight was actually not so imposing sitting there in his tunic and leggings. The ship rocked and his stomach began to rebel, but he managed to hold it down. It certainly wouldn't do to throw up on his Liege Lord's boots.

"You're the sheepherder from the other day," Lord Vincent said. "What in Turlough's name are you doing here!"

"I want to fight for Balor," John said. He had tried to lower the tone of his voice in an attempt to sound older. Unfortunately, his voice cracked halfway through and he ended up sounding like a child.

"This is no game, boy! I will have to send you back when we reach the mainland."

"No, please Sir," John said. "I am a good archer. I can hit a knot in a tree at sixty paces."

The man who had opened the door was standing next to Lord Vincent. John saw his eyebrows raise. Then he rubbed his chin with a forefinger for a moment before bending down to whisper something in the knight's ear.

Lord Vincent looked John straight in the eye. "Very well lad, Tyko here will take you up on deck and we will see if you have any skill. I make no promises, but we have too few archers for my liking. If you are as good as you say, then perhaps we can use you after all. Do you have a bow?"

John couldn't believe his luck. "Yes Sir, down in the wagon."

Long fingers wrapped around his right arm and hauled him to his feet. Tyko then gripped the sleeve of his tunic and marched him back out the door.

What little moon there was had disappeared behind some cloud, casting the deck of the ship into inky darkness. Tyko took a lantern from a hook by the cabin door and led John back down to the hold, where he retrieved his bow and quiver from the wagon. They had been well hidden beneath the tent poles. Once on deck, they walked back to stand in front of the cabin once more. John strung his bow and waited nervously while some of the sailors went about searching for a target.

A plank, on which three concentric circles had been hastily painted with pitch, was tied between ropes at the prow. It had been tied in such a fashion that any shaft that missed would end up in the sea. Two men couched behind barrels on either side, holding lanterns which provided barely enough light for John to see the target. Many of the ship's men had gathered on deck to watch the sport. They stood well off to the side laughing and talking amongst themselves.

John had not lied about his ability but never before had he tried a shot aboard a moving ship, nor one in the dark for that matter. The target was closer than the sixty paces John had boasted, but it was hard to judge the exact distance with any accuracy under the current conditions. To make matters worse, his eyes were distracted by the main mast, which was just to the right, halfway between him and the target. He nocked an arrow, raised the bow, drew back, and then released it in one fluid motion just as his father had taught him. All he saw was the flash of goose feathers in the yellow lantern light as the shaft sailed past the plank and off into the night.

The sailors roared with laughter. John looked at Tyko, who nodded toward the target. His meaning was clear. John would be allowed another shot. Somehow, he knew if he missed the target again, it would be his last. He nocked another arrow and raised his bow, but did not let loose. As he focussed on the target, he could feel the ship rise and fall in a constant rhythm. He suddenly realized that there was a moment, just before the prow began to rise, where it was motionless. He waited until the ship stopped falling and then let fly. The shaft thudded in the lower corner of the target, outside the last circle but stuck firmly in the plank.

The silence that came over the group of sailors seemed even louder than the laughing. John glanced at Tyko once more, but his expression was blank and he gave no response. John nocked another arrow and this time put it in the centre circle.

"Good shot laddie," the big sailor called Patch yelled out. John put four more shafts all within the inner circle and by then the sailors were cheering with each strike.

"That will be enough, boy," Tyko said, putting a hand on John's shoulder. "Go get your arrows."

Lord Vincent was on deck standing next to Tyko by the time John had retrieved the shafts. Tyko said something to him that John could not hear. Lord Vincent smiled. "Well lad," he said, "it appears you will not be going back after all."

"Thank you, Sir," John said, much relieved. "You will not regret it, Sir."

"That remains to be seen," he replied.

Chapter 12

RODNEY

Contrary to Captain Micah's approbations, the Swift did not live up to her name. Even though she was the second ship to sail from Balor, she was the last of the five to arrive at the mainland port city of Celia two days later. It was near three sun-marks past midday by the time the Swift's crew had her tied off and ready to unload. Once the gang plank had been run out, Captain Micah's booming voice announced that the passengers could disembark.

Rodney was standing near the gang plank, about to leave, when he caught a brief glimpse of the same dark-skinned man he had seen two days before. The strange little fellow was there one moment, smiling with those pointed teeth, and then gone the next when another crewman passed between them. Rodney had spent many sun-marks on deck, but had not noticed him again throughout the voyage. He was beginning to wonder if the man was only a figment of his imagination, or perhaps Aldus was using his magic to play some sort of game with him in spite of the captain's warnings. In the end, curiosity got the better of him and he decided to ask the captain about the elusive little man.

Captain Micah was standing by the hatch with his burly first mate at his side. They were looking down into the hold. Rodney walked over and tapped him on the shoulder. "Captain, that little fellow, the dark one, what country is he from?"

The captain knit his eyebrows for a moment and then let out a belly laugh. "You be talking about Shark-tooth," he said. He was joined by Patch in another fit of laughter.

Rodney was beginning to get annoyed, but before he could say so the captain raised his hand. "Please excuse us, Sir Knight. We meant no disrespect, but Shark-tooth be from your country. He be a Kelatch from Balor."

"Ah," Rodney said, surprised and a little excited. "I have heard many stories about them, but I never thought to see one."

"Few men have and lived to tell of it I'd wager," the captain replied. "Cannibals they be, or so I'm told."

"How did he come to be aboard your ship."

"We found him adrift in a small dugout canoe fifty leagues south of Balor. He'd lost his paddle and been adrift for days without water. Didn't have the heart to throw him back. Been one of the crew ever since. That be four, maybe five winters back."

The captain's eyes narrowed as he looked at Rodney. "Has he been up to some mischief I should know about? You're not saying he has stolen something now, are you? I allow no thieving aboard my ship."

"No, no, nothing like that," Rodney replied. "I have just never seen anyone like him before."

"Ah, well I've seen plenty. There are more dark skinned island men south of the continent than a man could count. It be a bigger world than most landers know about. The southerners are not so short mind you, nor do they chip their teeth like that. That's how come I know he be Kelatch, and why the men took to calling him Shark-tooth. His real name be nothing a civilized man could say. No one but another Kelatch could understand that gibberish."

"Well, my thanks for the information, and your hospitality, Captain Micah," Rodney said with a respectful nod.

"Good luck to you, Sir Knight. It was a great pleasure doing business with you. Remember us when you need passage back to Balor. We ply these waters until a moon, or thereabouts, past summer's end. Then we head south to warmer seas till spring."

Just as Rodney turned away, Aldus appeared at the door to the aft cabin where the knights had spent the last two days. He waved to Rodney, who waited for him, and then together they walked down the plank. Rodney was surprised how unsteady he felt standing on the dock. It was strange to stand on a surface which did not move up and down after only two days at sea. He wondered how it must be for the men who spent most of their lives on a ship.

Cupping a hand over his eyes, Rodney gazed down along the dock. Three of the ships appeared to have been unloaded and the fourth had begun to unload horses. The ship farthest from the Swift was loading cargo. The full length of the docks, as well as many of the nearby narrow streets, were crammed full of horses, wagons and men. Like Rodney, most of the Balorians had never set foot off the island, and a good number of them now wandered aimlessly about, no doubt feeling out of place. Rodney tried to locate Silas among the crowd, but couldn't pick him out amidst all the confusion. "What a blasted mess," he said to no one in particular.

"All will be well my friend," Aldus said, "look there." He was pointing a long thin forefinger toward a contingent of knights who had gathered in one of the larger streets. "Perhaps Sir Silas is amongst those men."

With the wizard close behind him, Rodney squeezed by men and equipment in an effort to make his way along the dock toward the shore. A young squire, too quick in his attempt to get out of the way, slipped on the wet planking and fell into the foamy water. The squire didn't appear to be able to swim, so Rodney had to take the time to fish him out with a borrowed pike.

When they finally managed to reach the cobbles of the street, Rodney caught sight of the red wolf of Silas's house. It was emblazoned on the tunic of a burly arms-man. The man wearing the Vennell coat of arms stood beside one of the wagons halfway between them and the gathering of knights down the street. The arms-man was in conversation with another man who wore the white dove and black boar of house Jenour. Rodney waded through the press of bodies until he reached the wagon. Somehow the wizard managed to stay by his side.

"You there," Rodney said. "Are you Silas's man?"

"I am," the man replied with obvious pride in his voice.

"I wish to speak with your Lord. Would you be so kind as to lead me to him."

"I'm afraid Sir Silas has gone into the city with Sir Herman in search of stables and lodgings," the arms-man replied. "He left orders for everyone to remain here until his return."

"I suppose we will have to just bloody well wait then," Rodney replied in a much harsher tone than he had intended. The arms-man pursed his lips and took a half step back.

It is not his fault, Rodney said to himself. *No sense in making things worse with a bad temper.* Rodney took a deep breath, forced his irritation down, and then smiled as pleasantly as he could. "My thanks," he said.

"We might as well see to our horses," Rodney said to the wizard as they turned back toward the docks.

"It is truly a wise man who controls his emotions," the wizard said as they waded back through the press of men and horses. Rodney snorted. His emotions were hardly under control. The press of people and so much noise was making him extremely irritable.

Halfway back to the dock Rodney heard a high-pitched squeal. The crowd was too thick to draw his sword so he drew his dagger as he turned. To his surprise, Aldus was holding a small boy dressed in rags dangling two feet off the ground by his scrawny arm. The boy could not have been more than eight summers old, but the profanity that flowed from his lips would have made a seasoned sailor blanch. Rodney relaxed and sheathed his dagger.

"A cutpurse should be more careful where he puts his hands, if he wishes to keep them," the wizard said. His smile was at odds with the hardness in his voice. "You never know what you might find in a wizard's pocket."

A single tear ran down the young cutpurse's dirt smeared face. When Aldus released the young lad's arm, the boy landed hard on his backside. The smile on the wizard's face disappeared as his eyes narrowed. "Now begone, before I turn you into a toad!" he barked.

The boy's eyes went wide. Like a frightened deer, he leapt up and bounded through the crowd. As an afterthought Rodney reached for his own purse. With relief, he felt the weight of the pouch but kept his hand on it as they continued on toward the dock.

The wagon had been unloaded. They passed by Coll as he supervised the moving of it from the dock into the street. When they reached the Swift, some of her crew were just hoisting Thunder up from the hold. The big destrier was not happy about hanging from a sling, or being lowered onto a crowded dock. When Thunder caught sight of Rodney he neighed and snorted his displeasure. His ears were pinned back, the whites of his eyes were showing, and he looked ready to bite any hand that came near.

Rodney surmised the horse was having much the same reaction to steady ground as he himself had experienced. He finally managed to calm Thunder down by gently stroking his forehead and speaking softly in his ear. Only after the horse was calm did Rodney allow the men to remove the sling. It was much easier getting off the dock leading Thunder. Other men were most eager to get out of Thunder's way.

Another sun-mark had passed by the time all the horses had been unloaded from the Swift, moved on shore, and saddled. With Morton and the sheepherder's help, Coll soon had the draft horses hitched to the wagon. As they worked, Rodney noted how the sheepherder tended to the draft horses. The lad knew what he was about. If Morton was half as much at ease around them, Rodney could rest more easily.

It was yet another half sun-mark before Silas returned. "Ah, Rodney, I trust you had a pleasant voyage," Silas said as he dismounted.

"All went well enough," Rodney replied, "but I cannot say I am sorry to be on solid ground. Was your crossing smooth?"

"Yes, it went as I expected. Not my first sea voyage you know. Sailed to

Celia twice before, once with your father, but that was over twenty years ago. I have secured lodging at two separate inns. I would have preferred we all stay together, but it could not be helped. The largest has but eighteen rooms and we will have to double up somewhat as it is. You take the men from the last two ships to the Green Door. It's up the last street there. I shall take the rest to the Hammer And Spike. It's up the main street near the edge of town."

"There is a suitable stable next to the Green Door. You can stable the horses there, but billet the squires in the stable's hayloft and tell them to keep a close watch on the horses. Carpathia. Of all the people I've met here today, I trust not a one. I would suggest that every man sleep with both his purse and a dagger under his pillow."

"What of the common men?" Rodney asked.

"There is a large dry field adjacent to the road near the end of town. We have been given permission to make use of it as a camp site for our men. I have arranged for food and drink to be sent from the Hammer and Spike, but we'll need to select someone we can leave in charge."

"I've just the man," Rodney said. "Coll Dunn, my own master-at-arms. He is a veteran and most dependable."

"I believe I know the man. If I am not mistaken, he was Frederic's sergeant during the war."

"Yes, he was my father's most trusted man."

"Very good. He will do nicely. Maybe we should make it a more permanent position. Sergeant, no, Company Master-at-arms I should think. Oh, and ask him to place an armed guard on the wagons."

"I shall tell him."

"Very good. I will inform the others of the arrangement. We meet in the same field at first light tomorrow morning. Sleep well, Rodney."

"Sleep well," Rodney said. Silas grunted a reply as he slipped a foot into the stirrup. Rodney winced at the popping sound the First Knight's knee made when he climbed into the saddle.

After Silas left, Rodney informed Coll of his new rank and responsibilities before instructing him to lead all the commoners to the campsite Silas had arranged. Tyko and Yvon would remain behind to watch over the horses until the squires returned from their supper. By the time Rodney found the Green Door Inn's stable, it was getting close to sunset. He passed the word along for everyone to gather at the inn once they had seen to their mounts. After Thunder had been watered and properly secured in a stall, Rodney took out a brush to groom him. It had been a while since he had done the chore himself, but

Thunder was far too restless for Morton to handle.

The Inn was a solid two-story wooden structure completely bare of paint, except for the big double doors which at some time in the distant past were painted green. Once all his countrymen had arrived, Rodney stepped up to the doors and turned to face them. "I expect it will be a long while before any of us are given the opportunity to eat and sleep under a roof again, so I suggest you enjoy it."

"Do not worry on my account," Lionel said. "After two days of throwing up every scrap I ate, along with half my guts, I could eat my horse, saddle and all." Jason grinned and gave Lionel a friendly nudge.

"There is no need for anyone to concern themselves with the cost," Rodney said. "I will supply the coin for the expense of the inn's hospitality." That put a smile on everyone's face, just as Rodney knew it would. "Squires, after supper you can make good use of the hayloft in the stable and keep a watch on the horses." With that said, he opened the door and entered the inn.

The innkeeper seemed overly eager and greeted Rodney at the door like a long lost brother. He was a big man, but appeared to be more fat than muscle. "Good day, my Lord," he said. "You are very fortunate to have come today. Our rooms are usually in high demand at this time of year and it is only by chance there are so many available." He wiped his hands on his stained apron. "Yes, very fortunate indeed."

From what Rodney had seen so far, the inn's clientele were a rough lot. No more than one or two looked likely to have enough coin for a room, but he wasn't in a mind to quibble. "How much?" he asked.

"For food and lodging, ten golds," the innkeeper said. Rodney reached for his purse. "And, for the use of the stables, another two," the innkeeper added with a greasy grin.

While Rodney was counting out the twelve coins, the innkeeper's eyes never left Rodney's purse. The moment the last coin fell into his hand, the innkeeper excused himself and disappeared through a small door under the stairway. Its hinge creaked as the door closed. After he retied the pouch, Rodney slid it back so it rested under his dagger.

The common room was large, but many of the tables were already occupied by locals and sailors. In order to accommodate the knights and their squires, extra benches were brought in and long boards placed between the tables to extend them. Rodney sat on a bench next to Morton, Jason and Lionel. Aldus was seated across the makeshift table between Sir Maynard and the other three squires. Food and drink had to be passed along the tables from hand to hand since it was too crowded for the serving women to reach everyone. It made for a close but friendly meal.

They were served stewed lamb, at least that was what the innkeeper called it, with plates of bread and cheese. The stew was heavily spiced and salted, but hot and otherwise very good. Everyone ate heartily and sampled more than one mug of the local ale. Rodney would have preferred chicory tea, but there was none to be had and the ale was at least an improvement over cider.

During the meal, except for an occasional nervous glance at Aldus, Morton had kept to himself. There was obviously something on his mind, but Rodney waited for the lad to summon the courage to speak up on his own. "Wizard Aldus, could you please show us some magic?" Morton finally asked.

Aldus looked up from his third plate of stew and smiled. He then reached across the table and plucked a silver coin from the squire's ear. Morton clutched the side of his head in shock while everyone else laughed.

Rodney administered a good-natured slap on his back as Morton's face turned red with embarrassment. Lionel leaned forward smiling. "Learn that trick and you will never go hungry, Mort."

"Sir Lionel has the right of it, young man," Aldus said. "That was just a little chicanery. Sleight of hand, as it were. Real magic requires a spell."

"So, it is just words then," Morton said, looking disappointed.

"A spell can be spoken, yes," Aldus replied, "but it can also be eaten, drank, smelled or just created from the air by a thought and cast like a stone. It would not be wise in such a crowded room. I think another time would be more appropriate for such a demonstration."

"I heartily agree," Jason said. "It seems to me this magic is more trouble than it is worth."

"I beg to differ," Maynard said. "Seems quite useful and wondrous to me, but pray tell us more about these FireDrakes, good Wizard."

"Yes," Rodney said. "I am curious as well. Is Grigor common for his breed?"

The wizard pushed his empty plate aside and took a gulp of his ale. "It can be difficult to tell them apart, for they are all a similar shade of red, but Grigor is quite large even for a male. The females tend to be smaller and more brightly coloured."

"Can they talk?" Morton asked.

The wizard laughed. "Only with their minds," he said, tapping his forefinger to the side of his head. "Just like the elves."

"Elves!" Morton said, wide-eyed.

The wizard smiled. "Ah, yes the elves," he said. "They are kin to the FireDrakes and live with them at Drakenmount."

"What do they look like?" Morton asked. "The elves, I mean."

Aldus put his hand to his chin and rubbed his beard. "They are a fair people. Slender, graceful, not overly tall, with fine features most would call handsome. Of the four races, I have knowledge of but two. Though I have never met one, I have read that the Forest Elves have jet black hair with skin as white as snow. They are reclusive and, if they still exist, live in the far north. The Red Elves I know best of all. They look much like you or I, save for their pointed ears and hair the colour of fire."

"You said they are kin to FireDrakes," Morton said. "How can they be kin to something as large as a FireDrake?"

"FireDrakes are magical," Aldus replied. "They were created a long time ago by melding an elf with a common northern dragon."

"Melding," Morton said, looking confused. "What is that?"

Rodney was nonplussed at the wizard's remark himself, and glad his squire had asked the question. The wizard scratched his beard and then folded his hands before him on the table.

"Well now," Aldus said. "I can see I will have to tell you the whole story or there will be no end to your questions." He paused for another gulp of ale. "The bite of a dragon is poisonous, you see. If the unfortunate victim of such a bite should survive the wound, which is most doubtful given the size of dragon teeth, they would soon die from the deadly venom. A long time ago, the King of the Red Elves was dying from just such a poisoning. The wound was just a scratch, mind you, but he was near death just the same. Rendalt Lasairian, a great Wizard of the day..."

"Like you," Morton said.

Aldus chuckled. "Yes, I suppose like me," he said. "Ah, but where was I? Oh yes, Rendalt was summoned by the Elf Queen, but he could do nothing to save the stricken elf. That was when the Elf Queen presented Rendalt with an amulet of great power. He used the talisman to join the dying elf and the dragon into a single being. The dragon was immune to its own poison, you see. But that was not the end of it. The queen wanted to share her husband's fate, so she persuaded Rendalt to meld her with a female dragon. The FireDrakes of Drakenmount are their descendants, and that is how they are kin to the elves."

"Ah," Rodney said, "the talisman of which you speak is the very same we now seek."

"It is," the wizard replied. "The amulet used to create the FireDrakes is from a time when the world was full of magic. Make no mistake about it. It is very powerful, far more than you could ever imagine. Too powerful to ever be destroyed, and the FireDrakes are irrevocably tied to it by unbreakable bonds. The link is so strong, it is said the amulet grows warm whenever a FireDrake breathes fire. I have developed my own theory that the source of their fire is actually the amulet itself, but that is another matter."

Aldus picked up his ale and absently took a sip. "Now, when Rendalt was near the end of his life he turned Aedon over to the FireDrakes so they could hide it. More than one attempt was made to steal Aedon away from him and he feared that one day it would fall into the wrong hands. He warned the elves that a human with elfin blood would one day come to seek it out, and the FireDrakes would only be safe as long as they kept Aedon hidden."

"Why did the blasted elves not use the amulet themselves?" Maynard asked. "Is it not their bloody problem?"

"No elf can touch Aedon," Aldus said shaking his head. "Its touch would be deadly to them."

"Why?" Morton asked. "What happened?"

"Ah, the story of how the elves gave up their birthright is far older than the FireDrakes. It goes back thousands of years. You see, before they learned the secret of steel, and became enamored with war, humans were much closer in spirit to the elves. Subsequently they commingled. Most encounters were just fleeting exotic experiences, with little substance, but on occasion the seeds of more dangerous feelings took root. For some, even with the vast difference in life expectancy, the potency of their ardor solidified into selfless love. With this love grew the desire for family, and that desire overcame better judgement."

"In the normal course of events such couplings could not produce progeny, but, when one half of the partnership possesses magic, anything is possible. It was inevitable the elf half of such a union would succumb and use their gift to conceive a child. The offspring of such unions became known as halflings."

The wizard picked up his ale, drained it, and then wiped his beard with his sleeve before he continued. "As was their way, the elves accepted these young halflings with open arms. That acceptance was short lived, however. Very soon after the first halflings matured, their actions threatened elfin existence. The violent nature and lust for power of their human side proved to be too strong. All of these halflings possessed magical abilities to some degree, though very few had the wisdom to use their gift wisely. They began to wage terrible wars against one another, and war was something no elf could truly understand."

"Elves are very long lived and would have been satisfied to wait out the crisis, that is, if halflings had been condemned to live a relatively short human lifetime. Unfortunately, halflings also inherited an increased life span in proportion to their elfin blood. Looking forward to four or five hundred years of bloodshed was intolerable, so the greatest elfin magi came together at Penardun in a desperate attempt to stop the carnage."

"Hidden from the halflings, deep in the bowels of Penardun, the magi devised a plan to strip away the halfling's magic. This would remove the immediate threat, but many of the magi pushed for a more permanent solution. The physical differences between human and elf were such that these first born halflings were sterile. Without their magic to aid them they could not sire children, but elves could still create more. The Magi wished to put a stop, once and for all, to the proliferation of halflings. To that end, and after great debate, it was agreed that the only infallible way was to strip the magic from every elf as well."

"The final spell cast by the last elfin Magi was one of disenchantment, to eradicate the ability to use magic from all with elfin blood. Yet, the magic could not just be destroyed, or cast aside, it needed to be placed somewhere. Indestructible amulets were fashioned, one for each of the four elfin races, by their own most renowned craftsmen. The amulets were exquisitely crafted in fine spun copper, silver, gold, and ivory. Each was fitted with a large polished bloodstone in the centre. As a failsafe, the spell would also prevent any halfling from ever touching one."

"The magi worked day and night to cast the spell, but it ended in disaster just the same. Through some grievous miscalculation, the halflings had partially escaped the disenchantment and still retained some of their magic ability while the elves had not. The magi, now bereft of their power, could do nothing about it. Then came the final blow. To their utter horror the elves soon discovered that even though a full-blooded elf could not touch an amulet, a halfling could. This final revelation had been too much. The amulets were quickly spirited away so no halfling could ever possess one. Three of the elfin races severed all contact with those outside their own race and went into permanent hiding. Only the Red Elves of Penardun remain."

"You tell a most entertaining story," Lionel said. "Should you ever tire of wizardry, I dare say you could become a bard."

Aldus laughed along with the others. "My thanks, Sir Knight," he replied graciously.

Rodney looked around the table. The squires were wide eyed and obviously enthralled with the wizard's tales. Aldus seemed to be enjoying the telling just as much, if not more. Rodney could see they would easily be up half the night and it would be a tired lot he would have to deal with in the morning.

"We had best retire to our beds and get some sleep," Rodney said. "We leave at first light. Mort, gather the other squires and return to the stables. Tyko and Yvon still need their own supper." Morton seemed more than a little disappointed, but appeared to take it in good humour.

"Sleep well, my friends," Rodney said as he stood up. After navigating through the crowded room, he made his way up the narrow steps to search out a room.

So he would not have to share with anyone, Rodney had selected a small room at the end of the hall. It was all of eight by eight feet, with a sleeping pallet, a small night table on which rested a short candle, and a heavily stained wooden bucket in the corner in which to relieve himself. There was little else.

Enough light found its way through a small window that he had no need for the candle. Remembering the look on the innkeeper's face, he placed both his purse and dagger under the pillow. The thin bar on the door would not keep out a determined thief, so he removed his sword belt and leaned the scabbard against the door before stretching out on the pallet.

The straw filled pallet wasn't much softer than the floor, and he lay there for a time listening to the muffled noises drifting up from the common room below. Hopefully, most of the men would follow his example. He didn't relish the idea of having to drag tired men from their beds in the morning. The sounds soon faded as he fell asleep.

At the sound of a loud crash, Rodney leapt up with his dagger in hand. The door was ajar and his scabbard lay on the floor. He stepped out into the hall just in time to catch the flicker of a shadow down at the end. He listened to padded feet descend the stairs and then the creak of a hinge as the small door closed. He stepped back into his room and quietly closed his own door.

Before laying back down, Rodney felt under his pillow. He smiled when his fingers found the heavy pouch. He had been expecting something. Perhaps now he could sleep more soundly. After replacing the scabbard against the door, he lay down and went back to sleep. The next thing he knew, Jason was pounding on all the doors to wake everyone up.

Chapter 13

JOHN

A faint light to the east signalled the approach of dawn. It was none too soon for John, after a long miserable night huddled under the wagon for relief from the wind and rain. The other Vincent men had each taken a turn at standing guard. He offered to stand a watch too, but Tyko told him to just get some rest. John needn't have bothered, considering he hardly slept a wink on the cold hard ground. He was thankful to have his heavy woolen vest though, which he had only because it had been cold the night he snuck into the wagon. The vest had been his only source of warmth through the long night.

Coll was up and about with the first hint of morning. John helped him to hitch up the horses, which aided in loosening his stiff muscles. The knights began to arrive with the sunrise but there was hardly a smiling face among them. A few rode hunched over in the saddle as if they were ill. Coll shook his head as they rode by. "Fools," he said. "Being noble never made a man any smarter. You had best remember that, lad."

"Yes, Sir," John replied.

John was given a place on the wagon seat alongside Lord Vincent's squire. Shivering despite his long thick cloak, the squire looked as though he felt even more wretched than John did. He supposed the young noble was unaccustomed to such hardship; then again the squire didn't appear to be in the best physical condition. John couldn't help but feel pity for him. Noble he might be, but hardly what John would have expected for a future Daemon Knight. He was far too thin, with unnaturally pale skin, and stood near a hand shorter than John, even though the squire was two years older.

They departed Celia amidst a light drizzle that eventually turned into a downpour before the day was out. Tyko had found John a spare cloak. It had a few holes, but was very warm, and John spent most of his time riding in the wagon with the cloak pulled up over his head. He was wet, cold and miserable, but at least he didn't have to trudge through the mud like most of the other commoners.

They made camp at dusk. Tents were erected for the lords, but the commoners had to make do as best they could. There was very little shelter, and no dry wood for a fire, so Coll untied the sides of the water proof wagon cover and staked out the ends to provide some cover from the rain. After a cold meal of soggy bread and cheese, John lay under the back end of the wagon near Lord Vincent's tent. He watched the light from candle lanterns inside draw flickering images on the side of the tent.

Being so close, John could easily overhear the conversation inside. For the most part it was uninteresting and he paid little attention, but when he heard Grigor's name, he moved closer, right to the edge of the overhanging tarpon. Though he didn't recognize most of the voices, he had no trouble picking out those of Lord Vincent and Wizard Aldus. The knight had asked the wizard to tell them of how he and Grigor had met.

"It was last spring," the wizard replied. "I was wintering in my old master's cabin in Toth. It was a cold and blustery night for southern Toth. I was sitting before a cozy hearth sipping my tea, when a great gust of wind blew the cabin door wide open. You can imagine my fright when Grigor's great snout slid in through the doorway. As I fell from my chair, I instinctively cast a defensive spell, but it fizzled without even touching him. That was when I knew I was dealing with a FireDrake, even before I heard his words ringing in my head."

"Pewlin, my old master in magic, had never introduced me to telepathy, and I must confess, I am still somewhat of a novice at it. When I was finally able to communicate with Grigor, he told me of Magdalen and what she had done. We met three more times over the past year, to share intelligence and plan, but always in a different place to keep one step ahead of the sorceress. Finally we came to Balor."

"Where is this Grigor now?" someone asked.

"He has returned to Drakenmount to molt," the wizard replied.

"To what?" the other voice said.

"To molt," the wizard repeated. "Twice a year, FireDrakes must shed their old scales for new. The process takes from ten to twenty days and during that time they are vulnerable. Their scales are like a bird's feathers, you see. Without them they are flightless."

"Truly amazing creatures," Lord Vincent said.

"That they are," the wizard replied.

"But what of this Magdalen?" the other voice asked. "What can you tell us of her?"

"Unfortunately, not much at all," the wizard replied. "Just that she was the Emperor's former apprentice, and therefore to be considered both in league with him, and very dangerous."

"How many days travel to Drakenmount?" yet another voice asked. At that moment the edge of the tarpon dropped and a gush of cold water fell on John's head.

Quickly pulling his head back under the wagon, John shook the water from his hair. He was tired and had heard enough anyway. Beginning to regret ever having left the comfort of his parent's warm cottage back in Balor, he curled up into a damp ball and wrapped his cloak tightly over his head. The sound of the rain soon lulled him to sleep. He dreamed of his soft warm bed.

Over the next four days the sky remained overcast. It rained off and on, never stopping long enough for John's clothing to completely dry. By the sixth day, tall coastal fir, hemlock and cottonwoods had given way to birch, shrubs and grassy meadows. The rain had finally stopped and the sky was beginning to clear with the aid of a much welcomed warm breeze blowing in from the west. By midday it was warm enough for John to remove his wool vest. Later that evening, dry for the first time in days, he leaned back against a wagon wheel in comfort and sipped mulled cider. He had just tipped the cup back to drain the last drop when he heard shouts coming from where the knights had built their fire. John got up and went to see what was happening.

The big bald headed knight stood by the fire with a firm grip on the shoulder of a dark-skinned boy. At least that was what John thought until he noticed the wrinkles around the stranger's eyes. They were the kind his father had, so this had to be a man of nearly forty years. At that moment the little man smiled, showing two fine rows of white pointed teeth. John stepped back instinctively.

When Sir Silas, who John had learned was the leader, stood up, his knees made popping sounds plainly audible from ten feet away. John wondered if it was painful. *It must be horrible growing old.* "How did he get past our guards?" Sir Silas asked the other knight.

"He just walked into camp bold as you please, my lord," someone said from off to the side. "Perhaps he is a demon conjured up by the wizard. I mean look at his skin, and those teeth."

"None of my doing, I can assure you" John heard the wizard say from the other side of the fire.

"He is a Kelatch," Lord Vincent said, stepping forward from out of the surrounding darkness.

The name echoed in low whispers among the other men. With seemingly little effort, the dark-skinned man slipped out of the big knight's grasp only to throw himself prostrate before Lord Vincent. The knight who had been holding the man took a step forward. There was a scrape of metal as his sword left its scabbard.

Sir Silas stepped between them and raised his hand. "Hold, Sir Herman," he said.

"He is a crewman from the Swift," Lord Vincent said. "The captain told me his name was Shark-tooth, a Kelatch they rescued from the sea." Lord Vincent looked down and knitted his brows. "Get up man!"

Staying on his knees, the Kelatch leaned back on his heels. "Shark-tooth be your man, yes," he said.

"Well that's clear enough," Sir Silas said. "You seem to have a knack for collecting followers, Rodney. I will leave the matter in your hands."

Lord Vincent and the two knights who had battled the FireDrake took the newcomer around to the other side of the fire. Once the flames were between them, John could no longer see what they were doing. With the excitement over, he returned to his place at the wagon.

The next day Wizard Aldus announced they had entered Imperial territory. For another thirteen days they travelled east, following a wide river that shadowed the main road. Both river and road cut through the Olaug plains making easy walking for the men, plenty of grass for the horses and fresh water for both. Spring weather in the plains was as hot as Balorian summer.

To amuse himself during the endless hours of travel, John listened to Coll. The grizzled old man was a veteran of the Carpathian war and possessed a seemingly endless supply of war stories. His tales were mostly about himself, Lord Vincent's father Sir Frederic, Sir Silas and Sir Herman. They had all fought together in the war. In between war stories he gave Morton and John lessons in Balor's rich two hundred year history. Coll was a storehouse of information, and it helped to pass the time as they travelled.

The Kelatch had now become a regular sight around the camp each evening, though he left with Yvon and Tyko every morning before sunrise. Along with four other woodsmen, they formed the scouting party. John wasn't sure if Shark-tooth went along to help, or if it was just so Tyko could keep an eye on him. They returned a sun-mark before sunset every evening when the company stopped to cook supper and make camp. Though he was pretty much left alone, most of the men kept a close watch on the Kelatch whenever he was near.

It was mid afternoon on the nineteenth day out of Celia, during one of Coll's history lessons, the third time for that particular one, when the line of mounted knights up ahead came to an abrupt halt. John stood up in the wagon and hooded his eyes against the sun to see what had caused the company to stop. Coll and Morton did the same. He could see Tyko talking to the knights at the head of the column. Something important had happened, John could feel it.

Word was passed down the line that they were near the town of Wigburg. Even more exciting was the news that an Imperial legion had marched through the town just two days before. The people of Wigburg had been fearful and tight lipped, so the information gathered by the scouts was sparse. One thing was for certain; there would be no provisions available, as the Emperor's men had taken everything of value. This last bit of news was disappointing to John, who by now had eaten enough boiled fish and hard mutton jerky to last him a lifetime. Coll was a wonder with spices and such, but salt fish was still salt fish. The flour had turned to mush in all the rain, so there had been no bread or biscuits, and the dried apples had gone mouldy. The only comfort at dinner came from the dwindling supply of cider, and Coll had said it would soon run out.

Even though there was still a good four hours of daylight, Sir Silas had decided that they would make camp early. After helping Coll with the horses, John went off with Yvon to the camp perimeter for some archery practice. Yvon had taken it upon himself to teach John the finer points of the long bow. John was always eager, but he had never dreamed there was so much to learn.

"The Dog Soldiers, what are they like?" John asked as he handed his unstrung bow to Yvon.

Yvon pulled a bowstring from the inside of his tunic and strung the bow before answering. "All I can give you is the description the townspeople gave to us," Yvon replied, as he drew back on the bow to test the string. "They are short and stocky with hooked noses and copper coloured skin. From both nose and ears hang rings of copper and silver."

"You mean like women?" John asked.

Yvon's face broke momentarily into a rare smile that quickly vanished. He actually looked friendly for a moment. "They have hairless faces and long black hair braided so thick that it protects their necks like armour."

"Do they wear armour like a Daemon Knight?"

"According to the townspeople, these Dog Soldiers were dressed in woven knee length cloaks with metal rings sewn in much like mail. On their hands they wore fingerless leather gloves with the same metal rings sewn on the back sides. One old man said they have so many rings that they jingle when the walk. They had no swords as such, but each man carried a long one sided knife or hatchet and either short throwing spears or composite bows constructed of wood and bone."

John realized his mouth was hanging open and shut it. "How close are they now?" he asked.

"No more than one or two days to the west of us I should think," Yvon replied as he handed back John's bow. "Now show me what you have learned."

John notched an arrow and let fly. It struck the target three hundred feet away. John turned to Yvon and smiled., his face unreadable, Yvon held out his hand.

"Did I do something wrong?" John asked, handing back the bow.

Yvon notched an arrow and drew the shaft back until the arrow head was almost touching the bow. "Draw to the eye and you are accurate but lack power and distance," Yvon said. "Draw to the ear and a thousand feet can be made with enough striking power to kill." Yvon let the shaft fly. It thudded into the target and by the sound of it, John knew that he would have to dig it out with his knife.

"Your arm has gained strength over the past fortnight," Yvon said, handing the bow back. "I have shortened the string but it is still slack enough for you to draw the notch back to your ear. I will shorten the string again when your arm improves."

John pulled an arrow from his quiver and drew it back. "Do not try to look down the shaft," Yvon said. "Now, look at your target. Judge the angle and let fly when it feels right."

John drew the notch back to his ear. His left arm was shaking with the effort. When his arm had steadied, he released the arrow. It flew well over the target into the trees. John sighed. It was going to be a long afternoon.

Chapter 14

KASPAR

Kaspar Brun gazed at row upon row of light grey tents. They were large enough for a man to sleep in, yet small enough to be carried with a bedroll on his back. The Imperial army was the epitome of modern military efficiency. Each member of the legion carried everything he could possibly need. Food, water, weapons, clothing, everything. Only the captain was exempt in this. Six men were assigned to transport the command tent, its furnishings and supplies. The same six also served as his personal guard, mostly to watch over him while he slept. Assassination had always been a productive method for speeding up promotions in the Imperial army, providing the assassin wasn't duly executed for the unforgivable crime of being caught.

Kaspar was the Ninth Imperial Legion's senior lieutenant. Ever since the day he had twisted the red silk of his rank into his thick black hair, he had kept a watchful eye on the one thousand Dog Soldiers under his direct command. Nearing the commanding officer's tent, he noticed the Ninth's newest officer, Ramell Chatal, standing next to the other three lieutenants, Faolan, Bercan and Cathal. Kaspar and Ramell had never been friends, even though Ramell had served as one of his sergeants until recently. In fact, ever since Ramell Chatal's elevation to the status of officer, Kaspar had nurtured a general distaste for the young man into outright hatred.

The Ninth had been camped near Onora for the past two days awaiting the arrival of a FireDrake. The creature had been sent by the Red Witch; at least that was the name she was known by among the common soldiers. Kaspar had seen her but once, many years past while he was still a young corporal. He was leading a guard detail, just outside the Emperor's palace in Crystal City. She was barely more than a child at the time, and in the company of none less than the Emperor himself. Kaspar remembered her as a striking beauty, with smooth alabaster skin and hair the colour of fire. Kaspar found himself aroused by the memory, but the pleasant feeling didn't last long as his mind soon returned to darker thoughts. Kaspar was a restless man and the inaction was irritating him.

The officers were meeting with their captain, Raoul Beck, to submit their evening reports. Raoul had been in command of the Ninth Legion since Kaspar was just a black braided soldier. If not the oldest captain in the Imperial army, he was very near to it. Though his hair was more grey than black, he was still fit enough for the daily marches. As long as that remained true, he would remain Captain of the Ninth Legion.

Ramell Chatal pulled back the tent flap and extended his hand graciously. If it were not for the new bright red band braided in the man's hair, Kaspar would have ignored him completely. Looking at Ramell filled him with a loathing and disgust that twisted his stomach into knots. In spite of his feelings, Kaspar forced himself to reflect back the false smile pasted on Ramell's face as he entered the tent closely followed by the other three experienced lieutenants. Ramell entered last as befitted his lowly status.

Captain Beck sat hunched over his folding desk. The scowl on his face bespoke of a foul humour. Recognizing this was not a good time to be the first to speak, Kaspar remained quiet. While he waited, his eyes strayed to the new lieutenant. A sudden urge to rip the red band from Ramell's hair while proclaiming him unfit as an officer took hold. Kaspar felt his lips curl slightly with the pleasant thought.

"I am glad to see you in such fine spirits, lieutenant Brun," Raoul said.

Kaspar went rigid as he let his smile fade. From the corner of his eye he caught the edge of Ramell's mouth turn up. It was almost imperceptible, but Kaspar didn't fail to notice it.

"My concern is supplies," Raoul said. "By now the citizens of Onora are obviously aware of our presence. With three days to prepare, I expect there to be little in the way of supplies available for requisition." Raoul looked up and glared at his lieutenants like a hungry vole. Kaspar waited patiently, as did the other three experienced officers, while Ramell fidgeted.

"What is on your mind Ramell?" the Captain asked.

"It's all this, Captain," Ramell said, waving his hand in the air. "Witches, abominations and now a dragon. I would rather face a thousand naked blades. Those I understand."

"I can appreciate your frustration, Lieutenant," the captain replied in a fatherly voice. "But we must accept whoever, or whatever, the Emperor decrees. Besides, I would much rather deal with one FireDrake than a horde of the Swamp Witch's creatures. Those monsters prefer human flesh. FireDrakes, I understand, do not. Try to see it as the lesser of two evils, Ramell."

"As you say, Captain."

Kaspar was disturbed by all the effort Raoul was wasting on Ramell. Was there something going on he was not privy to? From now on he would keep a close eye on both Ramell and Captain Beck.

"What about you, Kaspar?" the captain asked. "What are your thoughts on this matter?"

"What, oh, it's all the same to me," Kaspar replied. "I care not what weapons we use, only that we destroy the enemies of the Empire."

"I am sure the Emperor would appreciate such enthusiasm and loyalty, Kaspar."

Kaspar smiled at the compliment. When Raoul asked each of the other officers, they were quick to copy Kaspar's sentiments. This pleased him even more.

"I will leave it up to you then, Kaspar. Make the necessary preparations to receive our FireDrake. We stay put until it arrives. Now, unless one of you has something of interest to report, you are all dismissed."

The officers saluted and turned to leave. Hanging back, Kaspar paused in the entrance to watch Raoul. The captain's attention had returned to the dispatches on his desk. Oblivious to Kaspar's stare, he closed his eyes and rubbed his temples. "Fire breathing dragons, witches and zealots," Raoul muttered. "What a blasted curse. They will be the death of me yet."

Kaspar smiled as he stepped past the tent flap. *Maybe sooner than you think*, he said to himself. *Captain Kaspar Brun*. He liked the sound of that.

Chapter 15

RODNEY

R odney wiped the sweat from his brow with the back of his hand. Right after leaving Wigburg, the road had turned to the southwest. It followed the sandy shore of Gurgaon Lake. Aldus had told him the lake was many times larger than the whole of Balor, and that trading ships much like the Swift sailed it. As cool and inviting as it was, the close proximity of the lake only added to the humidity and increased the discomfort of travelling during the day. In compensation, it offered an opportunity to water the horses as well as providing a cool and inviting bath at the end of the day.

Surprisingly, they had found supplies aplenty in Wigburg despite the discouraging initial reports. That was, of course, once the townspeople had seen the colour of Balorian gold. It helped too that the Imperials preferred to travel light. They had taken only what foodstuffs a man could easily carry or livestock that could keep up the pace of a forced march. Though there was no dried meat, fruits, or cheese to be had, there was an abundance of oats, flour, salted butter and four kegs of strong ale. One villager even produced a well fed long-horned auroch. As to how the man had kept a full grown wild ox hidden from the Imperials, well, he wasn't giving away his secrets.

The bounty of food and drink was made available once the people of Wigburg realized they would be paid in gold. The Imperials had paid for what they took with bits of parchment bearing the Emperor's seal. They called them promissary notes. These notes could be exchanged for gold at Legion headquarters in Crystal City, which lay over two hundred leagues north. The best the people of Wigburg could hope for was to receive a small fraction of their value from the occasional desert trader who might travel through their town. The Nagualian capital rested in the heart of the immense Olaug desert. When Rodney asked about it, Aldus remarked that Crystal City was a gilded cesspool of human suffering and best avoided at all costs.

Well pleased with his purchase of a fresh supply of dried chicory root, Rodney patted the pack tied to his saddle. The sack he had brought from Vincent Castle had turned to muck due to the incessant rain after leaving Celia. On the previous evening they had camped by the lake just outside of the town. Supper was as fine a feast as he could remember. It had been many days since he had tasted Col's dumplings, and the auroch stew had been most welcome. Everyone had washed down their repast with ale cooled in the lake and were all in good cheer. Rodney passed on the ale in favour of four mugs of steaming chicory tea.

A small puff of dust up the road caught Rodney's eye. Soon, the familiar shapes of Tyko and Shark-tooth came into focus. It was only four sun-marks past midday. They should not have returned for yet another two. Something was wrong. The quickness of their gait, combined with the serious look on Tyko's normally calm face, spoke of trouble ahead. It was confirmed when Tyko reported a large encampment of Imperial Dog Soldiers was waiting two sun-marks up the road.

"Herman," Silas said, turning to face the knight. "Rodney and I will need to see this for ourselves. Take charge of the company and lead them back to that clearing we passed a short while ago." Herman nodded. "Double the perimeter guard. Make sure everyone knows not to wander away from camp and strike no fires."

"It means a cold supper for the men then," Herman replied with a smile that showed a yellowed but otherwise near-perfect set of teeth amidst a growth of white stubble.

"It will," Silas replied. "Also leave the horses saddled and harnessed until I return. We may need to move quickly."

Herman nodded once more before turning his mount. The other knights fell in behind, all except for Gregory. He eased his horse forward. "I wish to accompany you, father."

Silas looked hard at his son. Rodney thought he was about to refuse but the hardness in his face melted like grease in the sun. "Very well, Gregory," Silas said as he turned to Aldus. "Wizard. You will come too, of course."

"Of course," Aldus replied.

As tired as they must have been, Tyko and Shark-tooth still managed to set a swift and steady pace that required Rodney and the others to follow at a fast trot. Surprisingly, Shark-tooth had no trouble keeping up to the tall archer, even though his stride was at least a foot shorter.

After covering about a league and a half, Tyko signalled a halt. "You will need to go on foot from here," he said. "We are close enough now that their perimeter sentries may hear the horses."

Rodney found a secluded spot near the water's edge with an abundance of green grass for the horses as well as strong willows to tether them to. With their mounts secured, they set out on foot. The sun was touching the distant mountains by the time they reached the small rise where Yvon and two other scouts were waiting. On hands and knees they crept to the edge of the rise so they could watch without being seen. Rodney was taken aback by the sheer size of the camp.

"It is a full Imperial legion," Aldus said softly. "Five thousand men." Rodney nodded and looked to Silas who just pursed his lips without responding.

They lay on their bellies in silence for a time watching the camp. Silas had just motioned for them to leave when a shadow moved across the crimson clouds, backlit by the setting sun. Muffled shouts could be heard from the camp. The fires grew brighter as more fuel was added. Rodney could barely make out the shapes of men as they ran back and forth in what he judged to be a general panic. He watched with fascination as the shadow grew larger and larger until a familiar shape dropped into the middle of the Imperial camp. The wind of its arrival fanned the flames, raising clouds of smoke and burning embers.

Illuminated by the growing firelight was a massive FireDrake. Rodney sucked in a breath. Now that it stood near men, he could better judge its size. If it was any smaller than Grigor, it wasn't by much. For all Rodney knew it could very well be Grigor. He looked to the wizard and heard the old man mutter an oath before he began to slowly back down from the rise. Rodney looked at Silas, who shrugged his shoulders and followed the wizard's example.

A score of questions came to mind, but Rodney thought it best to wait until they were safely away. Seemingly content to wait, Silas too remained quiet. Except for an occasional low mutter coming from the wizard, they walked back in silence.

It was dark by the time they reached the horses. After rummaging through his pack, Rodney withdrew his candle lantern, flint and a small pouch of sulphur. He pushed a few dried leaves together and sprinkled a pinch of the powder on top. Turning his face away, he struck the flint with his dagger twice. The leaves ignited in a puff of yellow smoke. Once he and Silas had lit their lanterns, Rodney kicked the smoldering leaves into the water. The lanterns would provide enough light to see the road but not so much as to be seen from a distance.

About half way back to camp Aldus suddenly broke the silence. "I will have to leave before morning."

"What!" Silas said.

"This changes everything," Aldus said. "My being here is a great risk. Magdalen might send her fetch to communicate with this FireDrake at any moment."

"What in blazes is a fetch?" Silas asked. "Another beast of magic like that FireDrake?"

"No, no, nothing like that," the wizard replied. "Any halfling with sufficient skill can project that part of themself you would call their spirit. All Magdalen requires is a place or person, in this case the FireDrake, to focus on and she can travel there in an instant. Though not physically present, she could see and hear everything, but more importantly, she could sense the presence of magic nearby, especially magic being used to ward one of the FireDrakes. It will only endanger our cause for me to stay with you now. If Magdalen suspects what we are about, you will never reach Drakenmount."

"Can we not go around them?" Silas asked.

Aldus snorted. "They have the services of a FireDrake. A very large female by the look of her, and possibly loyal to the sorceress. If we are exposed when she takes flight, she will see us. In fact, there is a very good possibility she already has. A FireDrake's vision is far superior to an eagle by day, and even better at night."

"But you are our guide," Rodney blurted out. "We would be lost without you. How will we find our way?"

"I am sorry, but it cannot be helped," Aldus replied. Rodney stared at him in disbelief until finally the wizard placed a reassuring hand on his shoulder and grinned. "Do not worry, my friend. Before I leave I will render a map. We will meet again, never fear, for I have seen it in a vision, and they never lie."

Upon their return, Silas ordered the horses unsaddled and the tents pitched. Since they were not allowed a fire, the men relied on hooded candle lanterns with which to see. After a cold meal of leftover stew and dumplings from the day before, Silas called the knights together to discuss this new turn of events. The men formed a ragged circle in the dull light of their small lanterns. Many suggestions were offered and argued upon, but in the end they could not agree on a course of action. The discussion finally splintered into smaller groups, each arguing the merits of this plan or that.

Rodney was beginning to believe that no answer would be found, until Gregory, who had remained silent throughout, spoke in a soft but clear voice. "I have a suggestion." The speakers among the other knights paused for a brief moment before returning to their own private discussions.

"I have a suggestion," Gregory repeated louder. This time the talking subsided.

"Well then, spit it out lad," Herman barked. "What in blazes is it."

"We look like Carpathians, do we not?" Gregory replied.

A few of the knights murmured a half-hearted response. "What of it?" Lionel finally asked.

As more of the knights turned their candle lanterns in Gregory's direction Rodney could make out a grin on his young face. "Who is to say we are not from Carpathia?" he asked and then waited, but there was only silence.

"Get on with it," Herman finally said with an edge of irritation in his voice.

The young knight turned to Silas. "Father, you once told me that many Carpathian knights travel about the countryside selling their services for coin."

"Yes," Silas replied. "Freelances. Men without honour. It is deplorable, but true."

"Well, why not the pretense of being a company of Carpathian freelances? I say we ride up to this legion, bold as you please, and offer our swords for coin."

"What if they say no?" Lionel asked.

Gregory smiled. "Then we leave. Nagual is not at war with Carpathia, at least not yet." The few knights Rodney could see shook their heads in doubt.

Rodney considered the idea for a moment. It was the first suggestion that made even the slightest bit of sense. "The plan has merit," he finally said. "It just might work."

"I agree," Silas added. "We could hide under their very noses."

Herman laughed and slapped Gregory on the back, nearly knocking him over. "I like it too, lad, I mean, Sir Knight."

"What say the rest of you?" Silas asked. There was much agreement, more than Rodney would have expected. Some argued for a while, but it was soon decided to proceed with Gregory's plan.

Silas stepped forward into the light holding up his belt. What little light there was reflected weakly off the red, white and silver belt buckle. "You must all remove your belts, my brothers, and hide them away. The Imperials may not know their meaning, but we cannot risk it."

There was much grumbling, but no one protested as much as Rodney thought they might. At least no one refused. The belts represented their status as Daemon Knights. It would have been wiser to discard them entirely, bury them or throw them in the lake perhaps, but many of the knights would not have accepted that. Silas had achieved as much as could be expected. Once a few other minor details had been discussed, Silas called an end to the meeting. Each knight, as he left the circle, took a turn at slapping Gregory on the back. The poor young man was going to be stiff in the morning, if not black and blue.

Instead of crawling into their bedrolls, the whole camp began the business of becoming a band of freelance Carpathian knights and their followers. With sharp knives, retainers set about removing their lord's arms from their tunics. Knights and squires alike began the task of scraping the markings from shields, helms and tack. Rodney was in the process of scraping the paint off his shield with a dagger when Aldus approached, leading the mare.

"A map, as promised," Aldus said, holding out a folded square of yellowed parchment. "Sir Silas has a copy as well."

Rodney set the shield aside and took the offered parchment. After scanning the document in the weak lantern light, he stuffed it in his tunic and gripped the old man's forearm. The wizard gripped his in return. Rodney was surprised at the strength in the wizard's scrawny arm.

"How do you plan on getting past the Imperials?" Rodney asked.

"You need not worry. I have a few tricks up my sleeve."

"Stay safe, then," Rodney said, giving his arm a squeeze.

"We shall meet again by the time you reach Drakenmount," the wizard replied before he turned and climbed into the saddle.

If we reach Drakenmount, Rodney thought as rider and horse faded into the darkness. He took up his shield and returned to absently scraping the surface with his knife. Until he was gone, Rodney had not realized how reassuring the old man's presence had been. This quest was all about magic, something Rodney and the others knew absolutely nothing about. If Gregory's plan failed, what would they do without the wizard's magic to aid them. They would be facing twenty-five times their number, not to mention a monstrous and deadly FireDrake. Rodney was not a religious man, but he mumbled a small prayer to Pathos, the God of luck, just the same.

Chapter 16

SILAS

Just like every other morning since leaving Celia, Silas had the company underway by first light, but before the sun had cleared the horizon, all seven scouts had returned. Rodney's man Tyko approached the head of the column at a dead run with that Kelatch at his side. *What now*, Silas wondered.

"A force of eight hundred is less than a league up the road and advancing rapidly," Tyko said once he had caught his breath. "Shark-tooth found tracks through the trees to the south. It would appear that as many as two hundred have circled around us during the night and are now somewhere to the rear."

"The wizard was right," Rodney said softly. "The FireDrake must have seen us."

Silas nodded his head in agreement. "We had best send a small party to parley with them before we find ourselves caught in a pincer."

"I suggest that Charles, Edward and Edgar ride out with me to meet with them," Rodney said.

"Why those three, Rodney?"

"According to what we have been told, the Imperials are small in stature. Those three men are the largest and most formidable knights in our company. If the Imperials are to judge our strength by the first men they meet, then they will be less likely to attack without cause. I think it best we impress them any way we can."

Raising a finger thoughtfully to his chin, Silas scratched at his itchy stubble. Rodney was a good knight, and his suggestion was sound, but he was far too inexperienced to face the unknown. Besides being a young and unproven leader, he was untested in battle. Though it was wise and common practice for a commander in such a situation to send his Second, Silas had not picked Rodney for the position and still questioned his abilities. It was not that he didn't like him, in fact he thought Rodney a fine young knight. His father would be proud of him, but Rodney seemed to lack fire in his heart. What would he do if the situation turned dire?

The Baron had made the choice of Second, and Silas had been unable to change his mind. Basil harbored an obvious fondness for Frederic's son that clouded his judgement. Silas had argued for a grizzled veteran like Herman to be named Second. Though not an outstanding field commander, Herman was seasoned and steadfast. Silas could depend on him to follow orders and keep his head in a pitched battle. Most of all, he would never turn tail and run. Frederic had been a fearless knight, a good commander and Basil's most trusted adviser. Was his son forged of the same metal? Could Silas risk trusting him?

Silas twisted back in his saddle. "Gregory. Ride back and ask Charles and Edward to come forward. Then pass the word along that we will be encountering Imperials very shortly and remind them all that we are a company of Carpathian freelances." He turned back to face Rodney. "I will take Herman, Charles and Edward to conduct the parley myself."

"As you wish," Rodney replied. If the young knight was insulted, or in any way resentful, he didn't show it. Silas was impressed. Maybe there was some of the father in the son after all.

The Imperials had advanced much faster than Silas had anticipated and were soon in sight. They stopped well out of bow range and then spread out in a curved line across the road, forming a barrier from the water's edge to the tree line in the south.

Silas signalled for the company to halt. He leaned over to Rodney and spoke softly. "We seem to be boxed in, outnumbered and lacking any knowledge of the opposition's battle tactics. The only thing in our favour at the moment is the fact they are equally ignorant of us and will be wary. I will endeavour to convince them we are what we say, but should I fail, the only advice I have to offer you is a hasty retreat. They do not appear to have mounts. It is possible a spearhead of mounted knights could break through their rear line and outdistance them."

"We would lose a good number of the men on foot in a retreat," Rodney whispered back.

"That is true, but I can think of no better solution. If I do not return then the decision will be yours. I do not envy you." Silas looked at Rodney for a moment, but his Second made no reply. "The enemy to the rear has most likely followed as close as they dare. After I leave, send a couple of scouts out to confirm their location. The closer they are, the better your chances if you need to withdraw quickly."

When Gregory returned with the other two knights, Silas turned to address them. "Herman and I are riding out to parley with them. Charles, Edward, you will accompany us." Silas flicked his reins and headed toward the opposing force with the other knights in a line abreast behind him.

They came to a halt twenty feet in front of the Imperial line. Silas had made a quick assessment on his approach. They were short men, the tallest being no more than seventeen hands, but they were well muscled and carried a large assortment of weapons. Axes, long knives and spears were evident, but what caught his attention was that nearly every man carried a bow. It was a relief they were only short composite bows, deadly enough at close range, but lacking the long range killing power of a long bow or the cross bow. He saw nothing capable of penetrating heavy mail at any distance.

One of the Imperials took a few steps forward, stopping just three feet in front of Silas. He stood defiantly staring Silas in the eye with his hands on his hips, waiting. It appeared that it was up to Silas to make the next move. He thought of dismounting, but decided against it. Rodney's words replayed in his mind. He would be more imposing from the saddle and the idea was to impress them.

The man standing before him wore a red band of cloth braided into his hair. When Silas glanced at the others, he noted all of them had similar pieces of coloured cloth in their hair. A few had blue, and some grey, but most wore black. Only this single man wore red. It had to signify the leader, and judging by the number of men, perhaps an officer. Silas bowed as best he could from the saddle. "I am Silas Vennell," he said in as friendly a tone as he could. "Leader of that company of freelances back there," he added, pointing back with his thumb.

The Imperial thumped his chest with his right fist. "Lieutenant Kaspar Brun of the Ninth Imperial Legion. You are trespassing in Nagualian territory. What is your business here?"

"We have come from Carpathia seeking employment," Silas replied smoothly. He watched the officer's eyes flick to the other three knights. "We have two score mounted knights and eight score armoured foot," Silas added with a smile.

"I have met many Carpathian traders," The lieutenant replied. "Your accent is not at all like theirs." His eyes flicked back to the other three knights.

Silas shrugged. "We are from the region formally known as Sidon."

Silas's words evoked a wave of snorts and snickers among the ranks of the Imperial soldiers. The lieutenant glanced at his men. When he turned back to face Silas, he wore a broad smile. "We have heard stories of Sidon bravery," he said. The snickering among the men turned into laughter. "It is said your ancestors surrendered their country without lifting a single blade. In Nagual, men prefer death to dishonour."

Silas felt a sudden flush of anger. He had to remind himself he was only playacting, and what the officer had said was true. "That was a long time ago," Silas said coldly. "Much has changed since then."

The lieutenant appeared to think Silas's last words over for a while before he replied. "Captain Beck will have to decide what to do with you. Your men can go back and wait with the others, but you will come with me."

From somewhere behind him, Silas heard the faint whisper of steel scraping leather. It was followed by the sound of a hundred bow strings drawn taut at once. Silas looked down at the arrow heads. *Broad heads only, no bodkins, good.* Silas then turned his head slowly back. Charles had drawn his blade a foot of its length from the scabbard. Silas raised his hand. "Go back and await my return." *Before you get us all killed.* Charles made eye contact with him and then slowly slid the blade back. The bows were not lowered until all three knights had turned their horses and started back the way they had come.

The officer turned and strode back toward his men. The line of soldiers opened up and Silas followed him through. The gap closed behind him as a score of the men fell in on either side. After only twenty feet they broke into a run and Silas had to urge Midnight into a fast trot to keep up. He noted with some amusement that the loose metal rings sewn to their tunics did jingle as they ran, just as the villagers had described. Glancing from side to side, he saw that not a brow among them showed even a single bead of sweat. It didn't take much longer to realize these men were used to travelling long distances at a full run. He wished he had some way of letting Rodney know that a retreat, even on horseback, could spell disaster.

They were passing the spot where he had tethered Midnight the previous evening when the soldier right next to him speculated, rather loudly, on how good horse meat would taste for supper. Midnight let out a snort as if insulted. Silas patted him on the neck and leaned down in the direction of the soldier. "If you are thinking of harming this animal you had best like the taste of steel." There was silence for a moment and then the men all laughed until the lieutenant barked at them to be silent.

When they reached the edge of the camp, the men dispersed and Kaspar ordered Silas to dismount. Following the officer, Silas led Midnight to a large tent near the centre. The great red bulk of the FireDrake towered above all else.

As they neared the tent, Midnight must have caught the beast's scent because he became restless and began digging a hoof in the dirt. A guard stood to either side of the tent's entrance. Silas held out the reins to the one on the left. The guard stepped back and lowered his spear, but after a look from Kaspar he reluctantly took them. Midnight snorted and tugged on the reins. The man had to drop the spear to hang on. The other guard set aside his weapon and moved to help steady the animal. Silas smiled at their discomfort and entered the tent.

Inside stood two more guards identical to those outside. As his eyes became accustomed to the dim light, Silas could see that the tent was spacious but sparsely furnished. On the left side lay a thin sleeping mat. On the right, a grey-haired man sat behind a small wooden desk. This man had white cloth twisted in his braids. Kaspar introduced him as Captain Beck.

Silas repeated what he had told Kaspar. He prayed he hadn't changed anything, at least nothing the lieutenant might notice. When Kaspar made no comment, Silas relaxed. He then added they would be willing to fight for as little as supplies and a small portion of the spoils. Hopefully he had not overdone it.

The captain listened to everything intently without saying a word. Silas was still waiting for a response when he suddenly felt the hairs on his arms rise. To his left a cloud of mist formed in the air above the sleeping mat. It slowly took the shape of a white haired old man. The apparition was ghostly pale, nearly transparent, with the creases of the tent showing clearly through it. The captain stood up striking his right fist to his chest. "Emperor," he barked.

The rest of the Imperials went down on their knees with bowed heads. Silas thought it wise to follow their example.

"Would you be so kind as to introduce me to your guest, Captain," the apparition said staring at Silas through ghostly grey eyes.

"Just a Carpathian mercenary," the Captain replied. "He and his rabble are looking for coin. I was just about to confiscate their weapons and supplies before sending them back to Carpathia."

The Emperor's gaze fell upon Silas once more. This time, those ghostly lips curled in a smile. It made Silas feel uneasy. "I think not," the Emperor said. "They may be of some use. You may take them on as auxiliaries. Half the normal pay, of course."

Surprise registered on the Captain's face, but he brought his fist to his chest and said, "As you command, great one."

"You may leave now, sell-sword," the emperor said to Silas with a wave of his transparent hand. "I wish to speak with my captain in private." Silas stood, bowed, and then following Kaspar's example, backed out of the tent.

Once they were outside, Kaspar turned to face Silas. "If it were up to me, I would order my men to slit the throat of every man in your camp. After you had watched all your men die, I would then kill you myself, but, the Emperor in his great wisdom has seen fit to spare your worthless lives. Though I do not believe you will prove worthy of his generosity, I am bound by his will. We march within the sun-mark. You and your men follow as best you can until we again make camp. Report back to me then, and do not keep me waiting." With that, Kaspar abruptly turned and walked away.

As he took the reins from the much relieved guards, Silas was of two minds. On the one hand he was elated with how well Gregory's plan was working, on the other he wanted to slip his dagger into the insufferable Lieutenant's belly and give it a twist. He took a quick look around. No one appeared to be paying much attention to him, so he angled south leading Midnight in the direction of the FireDrake.

The beast appeared to be sleeping and safe enough to approach. Silas was wary, but also exceedingly curious. Rodney had talked of his experience many times, but Silas needed to see one of these beasts with his own eyes. He led Midnight as close as his mount would allow.

The FireDrake lay on its side. Up close, Silas was awed by its size. It was easily the length of six or seven tall men. Yellowed ivory talons the length of a man's hand protruded from the front claws like curved daggers. The rear claws were much larger but seemed less deadly.

The creature's mouth was closed so Silas could not see the teeth. He was leaning in closer for a better look when it moved. Time seemed to stand still as he watched it slowly scratch a spot on its belly with one of its front claws. Silas noticed that where it scratched, a speck of pale skin showed through a gap in the scales. The FireDrake turned its head and opened a single huge green eye. For a moment Silas froze. It was as if the creature was staring into his very soul and in his heart he knew with certainty it possessed an intelligence equal to his own. The FireDrake snorted, closed its eye, and went back to sleep. That was enough for Midnight. He backed away, dragging Silas with him.

For the first time in his life, Silas had experienced real fear. How could any man fight such a monstrous beast? When his wits had returned, he led Midnight to the edge of camp and mounted up as quickly as possible. The vision of the FireDrake stayed with him even after crossing the rise and the Imperial camp disappeared behind him.

Chapter 17

RODNEY

Watching the men who had accompanied Silas return without him filled Rodney with dread. The last thing he wanted was the responsibility of command, especially when the order to retreat would not only be shameful, but would in all likelihood get a lot of them killed.

Once Herman explained what had happened, Rodney reluctantly sent the twins and Shark-tooth off to locate the Imperials at their rear. He then had his fellow knights dismount and prepare themselves for battle. Rodney ordered the wagons emptied and advised everyone to be ready to move hard and fast within a moments notice, in the event Silas failed. He was pleased, if not somewhat surprised, when not a single man, noble or common, complained or even questioned his orders.

For the second time, Rodney was inspecting that all had been made ready when the scouting party returned. The Dog soldiers who had managed to sneak behind them had been located less than a half league away. They had formed a line across a section of the road. At that point, the open ground between the water's edge and the high ridge that extended deep into the forest was less than five hundred feet wide. Tyko didn't think much for their chances of getting through. He suggested leading the horses south through the forest. The only problem was the half score of Imperials who had been left to spy from hidden positions among trees.

"They are keeping a close watch on us, but for which group I cannot say," Tyko said.

"Blast it, I should have thought of that," Rodney said, shaking his head. "If they saw the wagons being unloaded it will be easy enough to guess what we plan."

"We were most careful," Tyko said. "I don't believe we were seen, so they may not suspect that we are aware of them." With a crooked finger, he motioned

Shark-tooth to come closer. "Shark-tooth seems to think he can clear them out."

The Kelatch smiled and held up a long, straight piece of wood. Upon closer inspection, Rodney could see it was made up of eight shorter pieces bound together with resin and hemp. The centres had been drilled out to form a tube. Shark-tooth produced a slim sliver of wood that was sharpened at one end and had a feathery material attached to the other. He stuffed the tiny dart into one end of the tube and then raised it to his mouth. His cheeks puffed out and Rodney heard an almost imperceptible click as the dart hit the wagon about thirty feet away.

Shark-tooth walked over to the wagon to retrieve his dart. When he returned, he was wearing that disarming childlike grin. Rodney looked at Tyko with questioning eyes, not understanding the significance of the demonstration. Tyko smiled. "The dart is coated with a poison made from death flowers. It causes paralysis almost immediately. Quite deadly."

Rodney looked at Shark-tooth with new eyes. He was beginning to understand why the Balorian knights of old had refused to pursue the Kelatch into the forests. A dart that thin could easily slip between the links of even tightly woven chain mail.

"A good idea, if only we have the time," Rodney replied. "For now, just keep watch on their scouts and keep me advised of their movements." Tyko nodded. Rodney turned back the way he had come. He would have to order the wagons loaded back up again. The men would think him daft. In consolation, perhaps it would confuse the watchers as much as his own countrymen.

Two sun-marks had passed since Silas had ridden off with a small band of Imperials, and still Rodney awaited for his return or an attack. The sky was a clear pale blue and promised a day every bit as hot as the last. Conditions over the past few days had been almost unbearable, and it was not yet summer in this Gods forsaken land. Rodney could only wonder how hot it would get by the time they reached DrakenMount.

About midmorning the line of men up ahead reformed on the road six abreast and started to quick march back in the direction of their camp. The dark outline of a rider took shape in the settling dust.

"Silas," Rodney shouted, "thank the gods." Leaping into the saddle, Rodney rode out to meet him. After circling around, he fell in beside his commander. "Did all go well?" he asked, a little out of breath.

"What?" Silas replied looking distracted. "Oh, yes, even better than we expected." He was silent for a few moments before he continued. "Why was I not informed that this Emperor Gamel was such a powerful wizard?"

"I thought everyone knew. Did the Imperials tell you?"

Silas barked a short humourless laugh. "They didn't have to. He bloody well appeared like a spectre out of thin air. What was it that the wizard called it, his fetch."

"What did he look like?"

"A lot like our friend Aldus; older and somewhat frail perhaps, but otherwise they could be brothers. He thought we might be useful. So we are safe for the moment, I suppose. Our orders are to follow until they make camp." He paused for a moment, scratching the stubble on his chin. "There is an officer. Kaspar Brun is his name. Watch out for him. He's trouble sure as sunrise."

The worry etched on the older man's face was impossible to ignore. It was not something Rodney had ever witnessed there before. Something fundamental about Silas had changed since riding out that morning. What ever happened seemed to have aged him ten years. "Is there anything else I should know?" Rodney asked softly as they neared the rest of the men.

Reining in his horse, Silas moved to the side of the road. Rodney stopped and backed Thunder up to join him. Silas motioned for the column to move forward with a wave of his hand. As the other knights passed by, Silas spoke in low enough tones that only Rodney could hear.

"The FireDrake," he said. "I had the opportunity to get a closer look it, and it at me. You and your friends are brave men to have fought such a creature."

"We had little choice, and did rather badly, as you know."

Silas hawked and spat. "Nevertheless, I would not relish facing one," he said. Silas then looked from side to side and leaned closer to Rodney.

"I looked it right in the eye," he said softly.

Rodney nodded.

"You know what I saw?"

Rodney shook his head.

"My own death," Silas said solemnly.

Rodney didn't know how to respond to that, so he said nothing. After a short silence, Silas leaned back and touched a spur to Midnight's side. Rodney followed him to the head of the column.

By two sun-marks past midday the air was full of choking dust from the marching legion ahead of them. The scouts trailed behind to keep watch on the Dog Soldiers who were still following not far behind, just out of sight. Rodney and Silas concluded they were either unaware their presence was known, or they just didn't care. Either way, the Imperials had underestimated them, and that was good. It would work in their favour when the time came to act.

Four sun-marks past midday the Balorians entered the town of Onora. The bulk of the Imperial troops had already passed through, but a group of about fifty or so were clustered together in front of an inn at the middle of town. A shadow moved across the ground in front of Rodney and he looked up to see the FireDrake glide by overhead. He watched it shrink into the distance until it dropped down where the Imperials had established a camp on the road west of town. Rodney glanced sideways in time to catch Silas staring wide eyed after the FireDrake. The colour had drained from his face. It was as if he was in a trance. Silas finally shook it off and Rodney looked away before he was caught staring.

Sounds of an argument grew louder as they approached the contingent of soldiers still in town. Two men faced one another on the porch of the inn. One wore the braids of a Dog Soldier, though they were heavily streaked with grey. As the Imperial spoke, he poked his finger into the chest of a well dressed and overly plump villager wearing a Mayor's silver chain of office around his neck.

"That is Captain Beck," Silas whispered as he leaned in close to Rodney. "The one next to him with the red cloth is Kaspar, the one I warned you about."

With a tilt of his head Silas motioned for Rodney to pull out of the column. With a wave of his hand, he signalled Herman to join them. Rodney waited as Silas instructed Herman to lead the men well past the Imperial camp, and in particular, far away from the FireDrake before striking a camp of their own. He was also to pass the word, quietly, that the knights would meet once it was dark. As Herman rejoined the column, Silas and Rodney guided their mounts near enough to the inn as to overhear what was being said. Rodney had been able to hear clearly enough from where they were, but he couldn't tell Silas that.

"We have nothing left," the Mayor said, flailing his arms about to emphasize his words. "It has been a long winter and our larders are empty."

"If you do not produce the provisions I have requested, then I will be forced to order my men to take what we need," the captain replied.

"I am very sorry, Captain," the Mayor said, holding his hands out in a gesture of helplessness.

"Not nearly as sorry as you will be! Lieutenant, order your men to search all of these buildings. Start with the Mayor's fine inn here. Take whatever you can find that is of use. If anyone gets in the way, you know what to do."

The Mayor appeared to be in a state of shock. "Yes, Captain," Kaspar replied, thumping a fist to his chest. When the captain turned to leave, his lieutenant wore a satisfied smirk.

"We need to get away from these accursed Imperials as soon as possible," Silas whispered.

It occurred to Rodney that it was more likely the FireDrake Silas was anxious to get away from, but he kept that to himself. Silas motioned for Rodney to follow and they angled back toward the column, but before they got there it had stopped.

"What the blazes is it now!" Silas barked, picking up the pace. Rodney coaxed Thunder into a fast trot to keep up.

As they approached the head of the line, which had by then reached the west end of town, Rodney noticed many empty saddles. A large circle of men, made up of both knights and Dog Soldiers, had formed in a small clearing next to the last building on the street. The men were yelling and clanging their weapons together. Jason stood in the middle of the circle with a drawn and bloodied sword. A glistening red streak ran down the length of his leg from a wound high up on his left thigh. He would have one more to add to the many scars that crisscrossed his arms and legs. Across from him stood a Dog Soldier swinging a long wicked axe. The axeman was tall, for an Imperial, almost as tall as Jason, yet much broader across the chest and arms. Four still bodies lay in the bloodstained dirt at their feet. A sobbing woman lay prostrate over one of them.

Rodney leapt from his mount and shouldered his way through the press of men. The moment he stepped into the circle, however, a big gloved hand clamped on his shoulder and pulled him roughly back. Rodney turned to stare into the chiseled face of Charles Dunn. "It is a proper duel," the big man said. "You cannot interfere."

"What happened?" Rodney asked.

"It started with a hound," Charles said. Rodney looked again and saw that one of the bodies was the headless corpse of a black and brown dog.

Charles pointed to the men on the ground. "Those two Imperials killed the hound. That's when the woman and her husband came out of the building. One of the soldiers killed the man. The other was dragging the woman away when Jason jumped in and challenged them. They attacked and he ran them both through. Nice piece of work it was too. Got that gash in the leg for his trouble. That's when this big one with the axe stepped up and challenged him. Jason accepted, of course."

If Jason had accepted a challenge, then Charles was right, Rodney could do nothing but watch. It soon became evident that the man with the axe was experienced. Like Jason he had numerous scars on his forearms. The weapon he handled with such finesse looked lethal. It was about two thirds as long as a pike, made completely of metal, with a curved double-edged axe head on one end, and an iron ball on the other. He held it in the middle with both hands, swinging it from left to right in front of him as a shield. It proved very effective in blocking Jason's sword thrusts, and it didn't take Jason long to become wary of both ends. He avoided the cutting end twice only to be struck glancing blows with the iron ball.

A thin trail of blood trickled down from under his helm where the iron ball had last struck. Dark blood also leaked from between the fingers of his left hand where it clung tightly to that nasty gash in his thigh. His opponent appeared to be in no hurry. He could see Jason was in the process of bleeding to death. Jason lunged awkwardly with his sword. It was a desperate and clumsy move; very much unlike Jason, even if he was light headed from loss of blood. The axeman easily side stepped and struck Jason in the same spot at the side of his head with the iron ball. Jason dropped to the ground. His dented helm rolled into the spectators.

When the axeman raised his weapon above his head, wild cheers erupted among his comrades. He waited for even more adulation before he finally approached the fallen knight. The Imperial placed his left foot on Jason's sword and then raised the axe slowly with both hands over his head for the killing blow. Rodney swore under his breath. No doubt the axeman was intent on taking off Jason's head, but then the confident smile vanished when Jason rolled over and slammed a spur into the back of the Imperial's knee. Even as he was falling the axeman still managed to swing the axe at Jason's head, but Jason rolled again and the axe thudded harmlessly into the dirt. Jason sprang up, ignoring his wounded leg. His dagger rose and fell in one swift motion and the Dog Soldier went still.

For a moment there was silence and then Imperials and knights alike drew their weapons. Rodney heard Silas's shout from behind him. "Enough! Lower your swords and withdraw!" The knights responded by lowering their weapons, but the Dog Soldiers did not.

An Imperial officer pushed his way forward through their ranks. It was the same officer Silas had pointed out. "Stop!" he barked. "That is enough!" He looked down at the dead man and frowned. "Ramell will not be pleased." He looked at Jason, who was now kneeling in the dirt holding a bloody and dirt smeared leg. Then Kaspar's frown shifted into a grin. "You have killed one of his brothers, but it is of no great loss; he has many more."

Leaving Silas to deal with the officer, Rodney rushed to Jason's side. He was joined by Lionel in examining Jason's wounds. The cuts on his head were minor. Like most head wounds, there was a lot of blood with little real damage. The thigh wound was deep though, and would need surgery. Added to that, it was full of dirt and would soon be infected. He wrapped the leg tightly with a piece of the dead villager's tunic.

"That should hold until Garrick can have a look at it," Rodney said.

With Lionel's help, Rodney managed to hoist Jason back onto his horse. "My sister would be very angry with me if I let you get yourself killed," Rodney said.

"It will take more than this scratch," Jason replied with a maddening smile. Rodney jerked the cloth tight and Jason winced, but still managed to hold his smile.

"Please do try to stay out of any more duels until we reach camp," Lionel said as he mounted his own horse. Jason still wore that satisfied grin and Rodney just shook his head. *Dear sister, you have given me an impossible task.*

In addition to taking up a long stretch of road, the Imperial encampment sprawled across a farmer's field with total disregard for the sprouting crops being destroyed. Since the road was impassable, the company travelled along the edge of the forest skirting the Imperial camp as best they could. It was tough going for the wagons. When the Vennell wagon lagged behind, Rodney rode back to see what the problem was. As it turned out, the rear axle had split going over a large rock. He returned to the head of the column and sent Yvon and young John back to assist Silas's men in fabricating a replacement axle from one of the young conifers nearby.

Once they were well past the countless rows of Imperial tents, Silas called a halt in an area with an abundance of lush green spring grasses. The location was close enough for the Imperials to keep watch on them, yet not so close that sound would carry from one camp to the other. As a precaution against someone sneaking up close to spy on them, Silas had given orders to use the wagons and tents to form a perimeter with a large open area in the centre.

Rodney was tending to Thunder's needs as Silas's wayward wagon rolled into camp. Yvon hopped down from the seat and trotted over to Rodney with John on his heels. Rodney smiled. It would appear that each of the twins had acquired a shadow.

"A small company of Dog Soldiers is right behind us," Yvon said, "and they're moving fast."

The light was failing but when Rodney glanced back in the direction of the Imperial camp he could see the dark shapes of men. They were two thirds of the way and covering the remaining distance rapidly. He marvelled at how efficiently they moved. *It is a good thing we didn't try to outrun them.*

"I must warn Silas," Rodney said. "Tyko and Shark-tooth are scouting to the west. Send your brother to me when he returns."

Finding Silas proved difficult with all the men milling about in the growing darkness. Rodney finally caught sight of him just as the Imperials entered the camp. He counted at least a score of them and noticed a red cloth in the leader's braids. According to what Silas had told him, this marked the man as an officer, but it wasn't Kaspar; Rodney had met him after Jason's duel. Rodney cursed as he recalled Kaspar's words. It could very well be the brother of the axeman Jason had just killed.

Rodney picked up his pace, arriving at Silas's side only moments ahead of the Imperials. One quick look around was all it took to find Jason. He was sitting nearby in plain view, propped against a fallen log near the fire and looking miserable. It served him right for getting involved in such stupidity. Lionel and Garrick were with him. Being the closest thing to a physician the company had, Garrick was stitching up the slice in his leg while Lionel was admonishing him for his recklessness.

The Imperials came to a halt before the fire, but when one of them pointed in Jason's direction, the officer turned and marched straight toward him without losing stride. Silas stood between Jason and the advancing Imperial officer. Flanked by Charles and Edward to one side, Rodney and Herman on the other, they formed a wall. The officer stopped short, barely avoiding a collision.

"I want that man!" the Imperial howled. Drawing a short single-edged sword, he took another step forward. Ignoring the drawn weapon, Silas placed his hand palm out on the man's chest. The young officer's eyes burned with pure hatred. "Out of my way," he snarled, trying to shove his way through. Silas outweighed him by at least half as much again and wouldn't budge.

"I understand your anger," Silas said soothingly. "But as you can see, that man is wounded and in no condition to fight another duel."

"He murdered my brother. I claim blood rights."

"You must be Ramell," Silas said in a calm but firm voice.

The officer stepped back, wariness overcoming anger. "How is it you know my name?"

Silas smiled. "One of your fellow officers spoke of you. Kaspar, I believe was his name." The young officer's eyes narrowed and his face clouded over again. "It was Kaspar who told me how your man took unfair advantage and murdered Garm."

"I appreciate your loss Lieutenant," Silas said, "but, I can assure you that it was a fair fight, and as I have said, this man is in no condition to defend himself. I suggest you wait until he has healed to take your vengeance."

"No! I will have it now," the Lieutenant shouted, taking a single step to the side. Before he could take a second, Charles Dunn moved to block his way. The officer had to crane his neck back just to look at the knight's face. When he did, he backed away holding out his sword. Charles stood stone faced, an immovable mountain next to the smaller man.

The smile on Silas's face faded. "Very well. If you cannot wait, you may fight Sir Charles in Jason's place. It is our way."

Charles gave Ramell a broad smile. "I would be most happy to accommodate you, little man," he said cheerfully in his deep gravelly voice.

The Lieutenant took another step back as Charles drew his massive two-handed broadsword. The well oiled blade gleamed wickedly in the dancing firelight. By comparison, Ramell's short sword looked more like a table knife. Charles was a full two heads taller, and with his mail close to three times the lieutenant's weight. The hapless Imperial glanced behind him. His men had formed a defensive semicircle to cover his back, but no one else had yet drawn a weapon.

"Perhaps I will wait a few days until your man has healed," Ramell said with obvious strain in his voice.

"A wise choice," Silas said. Charles shrugged, sheathed his sword, and stepped back. As he did, Rodney noticed the rest of the Dog Soldiers visibly relax. He took a deep breath, feeling his own tension subside, but he also felt a throb in his temple signalling the start of another one of his headaches.

The lieutenant composed himself. "I demand to know why you have chosen to camp here. You were instructed to stay behind the legion."

Silas's hard grey bristled face cracked with a smile. "It is simple. We needed good fodder for our horses. The grass on the other side of your camp has been rendered useless by your passing. So, we are here where it is still fresh."

The lieutenant's eyes shifted from face to face. "Very well. I shall inform Captain Beck. There is one other matter though."

"And that is?"

"You must have noticed we travel with a FireDrake," the officer said as he strutted forward, puffing out his chest. "It is another example of the irresistible power of Nagual, but the beast needs to be fed and we were unable to obtain suitable livestock in Onora. They have only pigs, and it refuses to eat them. Captain Beck believes it will eat horse meat. You have more animals than you could possibly need, so we will take one to feed the beast. You will be compensated, of course."

Rodney watched the colour drain from Silas's face as Ramell spoke. The cause could have been the suggestion of eating horse flesh, a repulsive thought for any knight, or the mention of the FireDrake. Rodney suspected it was the latter.

The lieutenant smiled, raised his right hand, and pointed a finger at Jason. "Since that one is unfit to fight, he can ride in one of your wagons. I will take his animal."

"No one is taking my bloody horse," Jason bellowed. He tried to stand but Lionel placed a firm hand on his shoulder and forced him back down.

The other knights looked to Silas for direction, but their leader said nothing. Then Herman stepped forward. "We will not give up any man's mount for meat," he growled.

The lieutenant sneered. "I shall be more than happy to give Captain Beck that reply, if you wish, but I can guarantee you that he will not be pleased."

As much as he hated to think of any horse being slaughtered, Rodney knew he had to buy some time. Resigned to the fact there was little choice, he stepped forward. "You can have one of my draft horses. We can manage with the one if we lighten the load."

The lieutenant looked disappointed. "I suppose that will have to do, for now. Bring forth the animal."

"I will send someone around within the sun-mark," Rodney replied. *We may as well get something out of this.*

"Very well. Within the sun-mark then." Without another word, the lieutenant spun around and walked away. Even before reaching the edge of camp the whole lot of them had broken into a trot. In no time at all they had disappeared in the darkness.

Once they were gone, Silas snapped out of his trance. "Rodney, see to that horse, and then join the rest of us as soon as you can. We will await your return."

Rodney nodded and left to find Yvon. He hadn't gone far when Tyko and Shark-tooth fell into step beside him. The archer was breathing heavily and had a fine sheen of sweat on his face, but the Kelatch at his side showed no evidence of exertion at all. The more Rodney learned about Shark-tooth, the more the man became a mystery. *Maybe he is a demon after all.* "What have you to report?" Rodney asked.

"We searched for a full league and found only two sentry posts, both well hidden in the trees," Tyko replied. "The first is but a short distance away. The second a quarter league farther west. There are six men in each camp and they appear prepared to spend the night. With six, they will surely leave two on watch."

"I expected as much," Rodney said. "I must provide a horse for that blasted FireDrake's supper. You and Yvon take the grey to the edge of their camp. One of you slip into the woods on the way back. See if you can find any more sentries close enough to present a problem. Report to me as soon as you return. I will be meeting with the other knights."

Wishing he had the time to brew a cup of tea, Rodney went to his wagon and filled a mug with cool water. He tipped the mug up and drained it, wiping the excess water from his mouth before refilling it. His thirst sated, he made his way back to the centre of camp. The others were gathered around the main fire by the time he arrived.

Holding up the map Aldus had provided, Silas stood next to the fire speaking softly but clearly enough that all could hear. "This map was rendered by the wizard's own hand. It plainly shows a pass within a day from where we are now. The Kingdom of Icarus lies on the other side. Our best chance to be free of these bastards is to get through that pass as soon as we can. If we leave within the next few sun-marks, we can be out of Nagual before the sun sets again."

Rodney took a good long look at the faces of his fellow knights. Some looked doubtful, but many more nodded their heads in agreement as Silas continued. "To succeed in this, we must leave soon. With any luck, we will have reached the pass before the Imperials even suspect we are gone."

"What about the FireDrake?"

All heads turned to Martin as he stepped into the flickering light of the fire. Silas's right eye twitched, but he did not respond. After a moment of silence, Martin continued. "Is it not true the beast flies by night? Surely we will be seen before we have gone a single league."

A wave of grumbling travelled around the circle of men. Silas seemed to be losing control of the meeting. No doubt he was distracted with his peculiar fixation on the FireDrake. Rodney stepped forward. "If I may take the liberty of answering Martin's question, Sir Silas."

Silas gave Rodney the slightest of nods.

"First of all, my woodsmen are even now delivering the FireDrake's supper. I would wager that before long the creature will have a full belly and be more inclined to sleep than to fly. Wizard Aldus has mentioned their habits are such."

Jason spoke up. "Yes, the wizard told us that after a large meal they prefer to curl up and sleep for many sun-marks."

Martin ignored Jason as if he didn't exist. "I will take your word for that, Sir Rodney, but what will happen when the beast awakes on the morrow?"

Rodney held his copy of the map. "A note on the wizard's map declares this Escarpe Pass to be narrow with tall cliffs. He warns that it may be untraversable by wagon." Rodney turned to face the other men. "You've all seen the FireDrake. It is far larger than any wagon." One of the men snorted, a few others smiled, but most just nodded in agreement. "So once in the pass we should be safe enough."

Martin inclined his head and stepped back, but Rodney wasn't finished. "The real problem is their sentries. Our scouts report at least two camps of them. One just up the road and another a quarter league further west. Twelve men at least to give the alarm."

Jason's brother Garrett stood up from the flat rock he had been sitting on. "So, they have posted sentries beyond our camp. The wagons make enough noise to wake the dead." He scowled at Jason. "And my foolish brother is in no condition to walk," he added.

"I can ride well enough," Jason snapped. "Besides, wrap the horse's hooves with rags and they will..."

"If I may be so bold as to offer a suggestion," Martin said interrupting Jason. "With the aid of a few good men I think I could eliminate these sentries discreetly."

"Who would you suggest for such a mission?" Rodney asked.

"Sir Talbot and Sir Nicholas I believe are both well suited for this sort of thing."

"Now there's a pair in the dark," Edward mumbled. More than one man snickered in response. Talbot scowled at the big knight. Rodney could barely make out the shape of Nicholas Naismith in his black tunic, mail and beard. But he appeared to be smiling.

"How say you?" Silas asked.

Both men nodded their approval. Rodney looked at Talbot and Nicholas for a moment. They were both expert with knives, true enough, but this was no time to put all his trust in men he didn't know well. Then he remembered Shark-tooth's little demonstration from the day before.

"I suggest you take two of my men with you," Rodney said. "Tyko and Shark-tooth know exactly where these sentries are hidden, and I believe you will find them quite useful in other ways."

Martin's eyes flicked toward Shark-tooth and lingered there for a long moment. "Very well," Martin said making no attempt to hide his distaste.

"Do your work quickly," Silas said. "We will wait only until you return. The wagons we must leave behind, so each man will carry enough food and drink to see him through two days of hard travel. Rodney, we need a couple of men to stay behind and keep the fires up for a while. They best be good runners as they will need to catch us up. Now unless one of you has something to add, this meeting is over. I suggest everyone prepare themselves."

It was with much reservation that Rodney watched Martin and the others slip quietly out of camp. Once gone, he informed Tyko and John that they were to remain behind and keep up the facade of a full camp by adding wood to the fires and moving about.

"This you will do for three sun-marks," Rodney said. "After that, do your best to catch up. I will tie your belongings to my saddle. Without the burden of packs you can make better time."

Those who had gone to clear the way returned sooner than Rodney expected. Martin approached leading his and looking well pleased with himself. "Your Kelatch proved most useful," he said. "Killed four with those clever little darts. I for one plan on being careful not to make an enemy of that little fellow."

"I believe that would be wise," Rodney said as they joined the line leaving camp. With only starlight to guide them they would have to stay close together to keep from getting lost. As camp fires faded away behind them, Rodney yawned and rubbed his aching temple. It was going to be a long night. He would trade his sword for a cup of hot chicory tea.

Chapter 18

GAMEL

From the shade of a date palm on the palace's rooftop garden, Emperor Gamel contemplated the city he had ruled for over a hundred years. In the heart of the Olaug desert, Crystal City was a like fine gem floating upon an ocean of sand, but even though it was the largest and wealthiest city in the known world, it was a fragile thing. The sole reason for its being was the life-giving underground springs fed by the ocean many hundreds of leagues away.

The remains of an ancient inland sea, the basin of the desert was well below the level of the distant ocean. Pressure from the great ocean forced the sweet water to gush forth from five different cracks in the thick rock below the sand. All five springs were within the city walls and provided the only drinkable water for seventy leagues.

Crystal City's location had always been its first and best line of defence. A gruelling seven day march from the nearest potable water, any enemy who tried to lay siege to the Empire's capital would soon die of hunger and thirst in the blistering heat of the desert sun. There was not even a single tree or boulder for shade within sight of the city gates.

The city boasted of many fine fruit and vegetable gardens, but Gamel was the only citizen allowed the luxury of growing things simply for their beauty. His one great passion, besides an insatiable lust for power, was growing roses. The flowers in his garden were not of any ordinary variety, but an extremely rare strain of black blood-roses. As he resumed tending to his prized flowers, he caught the squeak of the door to the garden opening. It would be Lusias, his personal servant. No one else would dare disturb him in the sanctity of his garden. Not if they valued life.

Ignoring the sound of his servant's slippered feet, Gamel snipped off a rose that was nearly spent and lifted it to his nose. "Ah," he sighed. Even in a wilted condition, the aroma was intoxicating. He recalled how black blood-roses had

134

always been his long dead mother's favourite flower. An image of her face formed in his mind. Before he realized what he was doing, the rose was crushed in a tight fist. He winced as a thorn pricked his palm. Ignoring the pain, he squeezed even harder. A trickle of blood ran down his wrist. The barbs of a black blood-rose were as sharp as razors. *Bloodthirsty plant.*

The servant's soft footsteps came to a stop just a few feet behind the Emperor. Lusias had been his personal servant for nearly two years. That was much longer than any other servant had lasted, at least as far back as Gamel could remember. The young man was adept at grovelling, which was no doubt the reason for his success. It both disgusted and pleased Gamel at the same time. With a sigh he turned toward Lusias. His servant's face was very pale. Gamel could almost taste his fear. *Must be bad news. It's always bad news when he looks like that.*

"Ah, Lusias, what news of our little spy."

Lusias bowed. Keeping his head down, he raised only his eyes. They lingered on the thin trail of red on Gamel's arm before he spoke. "The man was very difficult, your greatness, but he confessed to all in the end."

"Yes, yes, of course," Gamel replied sharply. His patience was running thin and his hand was beginning to throb. "They all do, and is he a spy for King Solon as we thought?"

"Yes... your greatness," Lusias replied.

"What is wrong Lusias? You are snivelling more than usual. Out with it man." Gamel was beginning to feel annoyed. Lusias was treading on soft sand.

Some colour had returned to the servant's face, but his tone had even less confidence if that was possible. "I'm afraid the spy is dead, your greatness," Lusias said, lowering his eyes. "The torturer was a little overly zealous and..."

Lusias looked into Gamel's eyes and paused with his mouth half open. Gamel watched a bead of sweat run slowly down his servant's cheek and then he smiled. "Get quill, ink and paper, Lusias. I wish to send a message to our own agent in Icarus."

The drop of sweat fell from his cheek to his collar as Lusias replied, "Yes, your greatness, right away."

Lusias bowed as he backed away. He stumbled over a small painted rock in his haste to leave and nearly fell. Gamel reached down and snipped off another dying flower. He raised it to his nose and sniffed. The fragrance mixed with the earthy smell of his blood. "And summon my physician," he yelled to the fleeing servant.

Gamel touched the rose gently to his nose. The door closed. He didn't really care if the spy lived or died, but he hated incompetence. He would need a new chief torturer. His first task would be to eliminate his predecessor. Perhaps that would instill the proper motivation to perform his duties with diligence.

Chapter 19

JOHN

John and Yvon had to move quicky if they were going to catch up with their countrymen before they reached the Escarpe pass. With the aid of a clear night sky, travelling the road had been easy enough. John was not sure how much time had slipped away since leaving the camp, but he was exhausted. His best guess was roughly two sun-marks before dawn.

They had alternated between running and walking for most of the night. Yvon suddenly signalled for him to stop only moments before a dark shape loomed up from the side of the road. John leapt back and stumbled over the end of his longbow. He caught the flash of polished steel as Yvon drew his long knife.

The shape slowly resolved itself into a man. He held out both hands palm out. "I am a friend," a familiar voice said.

It was Liam, one of Silas's scouts. John relaxed and took a moment to inspect his bow. It looked undamaged, but he would have to inspect it further in the light of day. It was then John noticed Liam was standing on a path that forked off from the main road and into the trees.

"The way to Icarus," Liam said. "Your brother went on ahead to scout. I stayed behind at Sir Rodney's request to ensure you did not pass it by. In the darkness we nearly missed it ourselves."

Yvon's blade slid silently back into its sheath. "We are most grateful."

"Here, you must be hungry," Liam said holding something out.

John took what turned out to be a thick strip of dried auroch and greedily tore off a piece of the stringy meat with his teeth. Liam smiled and held out a goatskin. Tipping it back, John was rewarded with a mouthful of cool foamy ale. It was impossible to suppress a smile as he wiped the foam from his lips. After Yvon took a turn, he passed it back to John for another.

"Come," Liam said. "We must have a full league to make up by now."

Much refreshed, John followed as the two men set a brisk pace along a soft earthen trail that twisted through thick pines. It was much easier on John's feet than the hard packed road, but the trees soon became so dense that the meagre starlight no longer penetrated the canopy of branches. Liam stopped to fashion a torch from a thick branch and a grease soaked rag from his pack. He lit it with flint and knife, and they were soon on their way again. John chewed on the dried meat as they walked. Without the stars it was difficult to gauge the passage of time.

The trees became shorter and shorter the higher they climbed, until finally there were only stunted pines and small bushes. The torch had long since burned away, but with an open sky they could see well enough again by starlight. A little further on, and even the small bushes had disappeared to leave nothing but hard ground and bare rock face. Soft earth and pine needles gave way to a rocky surface littered with sharp stone fallen from the cliffs above. The soles of John's goatskin shoes had worn thin on their journey; after a few painful missteps he was forced to pay closer attention to where he placed his feet.

"They'll not make good time on this," Liam said. "Be needing to stop often to clear stones from the horse's hooves."

"That's true enough," Yvon replied. "We should be catching up soon."

The stars had already begun to disappear in a brightening sky when John heard the first sounds of men up ahead. By the time they reached the rear of the column, the trail had narrowed to as little as eight feet between the rock walls in places. The column was moving slower than he had been travelling and John was grateful for the easier pace, but his feet ached just the same. It felt as if lead weights were attached to his legs. Just when he thought he couldn't take another step, the men in front stopped. Overjoyed, John took the opportunity to sit on a flat rock and rub his sore feet. Word soon filtered down that they would have half a sun-mark to eat and rest.

Liam handed John another piece of dried auroch meat. "Eat it lad. It will give you strength."

John thought he was too tired to eat, but he bit off a piece and chewed it anyway. The auroch was as hard as the rocks beneath his feet, and much too salty for his taste, but before he knew it the meat was gone and he found himself wishing for more.

With a wry grin, Liam produced a wrinkled apple from his pouch and rubbed it on his tunic. He sliced it into three equal parts and offered John and Yvon each a portion. It was leathery, but tasted so wonderful that John sucked on it awhile to savour the flavour. When the line started to move, John took one last mouthful of flat beer from Liam's nearly empty goatskin and wearily followed.

By midday the steady incline of the trail levelled off abruptly and actually began to angle downward. When the column stopped again, John flopped down onto the ground, not even bothering to look for a comfortable rock. Liam and Yvon plunked themselves down next to him. They were just as tired; he could see it in their eyes.

"Be much easier now lad," Yvon said.

John looked down at his feet and sighed. "I could sleep for three days."

Neither Liam nor Yvon responded. When John glanced up, both men had their heads tilted straight back. John tried to follow their gaze but saw nothing in the blue sky between the cliff faces. Then a large dull red shape passed overhead. It was the FireDrake. An uncomfortable lump formed in John's throat. The creature was long gone before he was able to find enough moisture in his mouth to swallow it down.

By the time John had recovered from the shock, everyone was back on their feet and the column was on the move. He finally found his tongue and turned to Yvon. "Do you think it saw us?"

A humourless smile formed on the archer's lips. "A line of two hundred men and fifty horses. I would say the Imperials know exactly where we are. The real question lad, is are they willing to enter Icarus to give chase."

"Icarus," John said confused.

Yvon pointed straight ahead. "Icarus."

John suddenly realized the cliffs that had been pressing in on either side had abruptly fallen away. Spread out below was a lush green valley. "It's beautiful," he said softly.

"I pray we've not fallen from the pot and into the cookfire," Yvon said.

John looked at Yvon, not understanding.

"We are a foreign military force," the archer said. "If we are caught, at best the Icarians may decide to send us back the way we came. A poor option to say the least. At worst they will demand our surrender or try to kill us outright as invaders."

John turned back to look out over the valley. Was there an unseen army lurking in those trees just waiting to attack? He felt Yvon's comforting hand on his shoulder. Well, he had wanted adventure. Unfortunately, it was not turning out to be what he had expected.

Chapter 20

EDMOND

In the great hall of Zindale castle, Duke Edmond Meredith sat with his wife, Wynne, partaking in a late dinner. They had been discussing his cousin, the King of Icarus.

"Edmond, it is very foolish of you to keep things from me," the Duchess said, taking another sip of her wine.

"I am sorry my dear," Edmond said, setting down his knife and taking her hand in his, "but I did not want to worry you with unfounded rumours and idle castle gossip."

"I worry more when my husband tries to keep secrets from me," Wynne said softly.

"Secrets, what secrets would that be my dear?" Edmond replied. He tried not to look her in the eye but was unable to prevent himself from doing so.

His wife withdrew her hand from his. It was that I-have-you-now smile of hers that said she was not fooled in the slightest. "So what then was in the letter the King's messenger delivered so early this very morning?"

Edmond laughed. "You never cease to amaze me, my dear. I do not believe a single event will ever take place in this castle that you are not privy to the instant it occurs."

"You're stalling, Edmond."

Edmond sighed. "The King's message detailed his concerns regarding trade routes to the sea. His letter states they are being made impassable by a host of dragons, no less. Possibly his men have been drinking too much strong wine."

Edmond wanted only to allay his wife's fears, but even to his own ears his remarks sounded flippant. "The King only wishes to ensure that the Escarpe pass remains open to travel. I dispatched my own messenger to Baron Morgan early this morning requesting for him to personally confirm that it is so."

"What else? You are leaving something out, I can tell."

"The King's intelligence suggests the Empire may be making preparations to invade Icarus. He is sending three thousand regulars from Concurie, just in case his fears prove to be true. I must augment this force with two thousand men so as to match the strength of a full Imperial legion."

"And," the Duchess said, as she skewered a piece of roast chicken with a silver prong.

"I received a report a few days ago that confirms an Imperial legion is indeed nearing the Nagual side of the pass, but there could be many reasons for that. In itself, this news does not portend an invasion."

The Duchess dipped her chicken in some spiced butter sauce. "Raising and outfitting that many men will be very expensive. Will he compensate us, do you think?"

Edmond snorted. "Not very likely. But we have no choice. If we do not defend Icarus, we stand to either lose our lands to the Empire, or have my cousin find another relative to entrust with the Duchy."

A momentary flash of fear registered in his wife's eyes. "You need not worry my dear," Edmond said trying to comfort her. "I will not leave you unprotected, or leave our holdings undefended to be ransacked by the first band of opportunists that chances by. A score of my best lancers and all of the castle guard, except for Captain Doyle, will remain behind to protect you. My master-at-arms is out in the countryside conscripting every able-bodied man he can find. I have sent requests to the southern Barons, in the King's name, for a thousand armed men."

"Can you depend on them?" Wynne asked with a look of concern. "They have been quite rebellious as of late."

"Oh, they will not like it to be sure, and I dare say not a one will come in person, but they will send conscripts at the very least. No matter how disgruntled the Barons may be, they cannot afford to offend their King."

The Duchess pursed her lips. "There is still something else. Something you have been avoiding to tell me. After all these years Edmond, do you still not realize I can sense these things?"

Edmond lowered his eyes and sighed. "You are right. I cannot keep anything from you. The King has requested I personally lead the army." When he looked up, the fear in her eyes was back again. This time it lingered.

"You are too old for this sort of thing," Wynne replied testily.

Edmond watched his wife's fear turn to determination. Then he noticed his captain, Fergus Doyle, standing at the doorway to the hall. *Thank the Gods for small favours*. "Captain Doyle," he called. "Excuse me my dear, but I must speak with the good Captain."

Edmond stood, kissed his wife's hand, and ignoring the stormy look on her face, marched over to meet with Fergus. Without looking back, he placed his arm around the captain's shoulders and guided him out of the hall. He was only putting off an unpleasant and inevitable discussion with Wynne until she had him alone once more. She was a reasonable woman; perhaps it would be easier once she had a little more time to accept things as they were.

"We have word from Baron Morgan, your Grace," Fergus said. "He sent a messenger straight from the pass. It is even worse than we feared. An advance force of Imperial Dog Soldiers has entered the pass; too many for the Baron to engage with his small party. There is sure to be a full legion not far behind. It would appear the King was right. They intend to secure the pass and prepare the way for a full scale invasion. They could be in Icarus as early as dawn tomorrow." The captain frowned. "And that is not all, your Grace."

"What else, Captain?"

"Two hundred armed men came through just ahead of the Imperials. Carpathians by the look of them. They were seen entering the forest along the river. Some of Baron Morgan's men are tracking them. It could be nothing, but..."

"My gods Fergus," Edmond said shocked. "If the Carpathians have made an alliance with the Imperials, we are full of beer and waist deep in a pool of candiru fish. If Carpathia should invade from one of the eastern passes."

"My thoughts exactly, your Grace."

"Was there any more to the message, Captain?"

"Just that Baron Morgan will gather as many able-bodied men as he can, but at best he can muster five hundred, with most of those being farmers. Hearty men to be sure, but not up to facing seasoned fighters. He urgently requests your aid in the defence of his castle."

"Yes of course. Give his messenger a fresh mount and this message. In two days I will have two thousand men ready to come to your aid, but you will have to hold until then. Expect us with the rising sun the day after next."

"An Imperial legion has five thousand trained fighters, your Grace," the captain said. "We will be outnumbered two to one."

Edmond smiled. "In four days, three thousand of the King's regulars will arrive. We do not have to defeat the Imperials, just hold them for the next four days."

Fergus nodded in agreement. "There is one more thing, your Grace."

"What is that, Captain?"

"One of the Baron's men said he saw a dragon, but it was not confirmed by any of the other men."

"A dragon," Edmond said.

"Apparently a very large one, your Grace."

Chapter 21

AGNES

At the northern tip of Zindale Valley, just one league south of Moonlight Falls, Agnes Finn shared a three-room stone cottage with her widowed mother Isabel and her elder brother Shaun. Having just finished their evening meal, Isabel sat at the far end of the table engrossed in hooking the final details to the edge of a shawl. Shaun glowered down at an arrow resting between his thick fingers, while from across the table Agnes watched with deep concern. Though Shaun had his mother's eyes, he was the spitting image of their father, right down to the thick moustache he kept twisted at each end with candle wax.

Twenty four winters had passed since Isabel wed Connell Finn, and in all that time Agnes's father had done blessed little farming. If it hadn't been for her mother's hard work they would have all starved. Memories of her father were anything but pleasant. He was a drinker, gambler, brawler, and Agnes suspected, even a womanizer. As such, Connell was generally disliked by his peers, but it was Shaun who suffered for it. Even as a young child, he was smart enough to pick up on their feelings. Perhaps that was why he hated being a farmer so much.

Shaun's prize possession was the carving knife their father had given him on his twelfth birthday. Though only ten at the time, Agnes remembered the day well. She had never seen her brother so happy. He was extremely clever with that knife and could carve just about anything. Agnes reached up to touch the hardwood hair clasp he had given her last harvest feast day, the evening before their father was killed.

Connell had been hit by a stray arrow in a suspicious hunting accident. The shaft struck his heart killing him in moments. Watching his father die had changed Shaun profoundly. Agnes couldn't begin to imagine the extent of the

144

grief her brother suffered. Her father had never paid much attention to her, and given his behaviour, it was something for which she was truly grateful. Truth be told, even as a little girl she had feared and despised him.

In the days that followed, no one stepped forward to identify the shaft. Shaun kept it, even after all the fruitless inquiries. Agnes hated the thing, but could never bring herself to get rid of it when Shaun was away. She just couldn't do something like that behind his back, even if was for his own good.

Before Connell's death, Shaun had always been quick to anger, especially with derogatory remarks directed at their father; even so, his good-natured kindness and genuine deep barrelled laugh had always more than compensated for it. Agnes hadn't heard him laugh like that since the night he gave her the hair clasp.

Agnes reached out and gently touched Shaun's hand. "You need to put Da's passing behind you, Shaun," she said softly. "You've grieved long enough."

"Leave me be, Aggie. You don't understand."

Agnes glared at the arrow in his hands with loathing. "You should have thrown that accursed thing away months ago. Why do you keep it only to agonize over it again and again?" She wiped a tear from her cheek. "I truly do not understand you."

Shaun threw the arrow across the room. "There, are you satisfied now?" Agnes watched him jump up and stomp over to the door. "I am going in to town," he muttered.

The door slammed with such force that dust rained down from the dried thatch above. Isabel seemed oblivious to what had just transpired. Ever since her husband's death, she had withdrawn into her own inner world. Agnes would have expected her mother to rejoice at being rid of the man who had made her life so hard, but in her own way she still grieved as much as Shaun.

After wiping the pooling moisture from her eyes, Agnes sniffed, walked to the door, and then snatched a lantern from the wooden peg on the wall. "I will be back in a little while, mother. I'm going to see Robin."

"All right dear," her mother replied without looking up from her hooking.

While walking down the well-worn path to the Smith farm, Agnes pondered how two such completely different men, like Shaun and Robin, could have remained such fast friends. Unlike her brother, her betrothed was not a large man, in fact, he was a finger or two shorter than her. Though no one could ever tell from his tidy cottage, Robin Smith lived alone. Five winters back his parents and young sister died of red fever. As the sole survivor, Robin inherited the family farm at the age of seventeen. Since then he'd proven himself to be a successful and hard-working farmer. Even so, because of his delicate features and silver hair, most people in the valley regarded him with distrust.

Before she knew it, Agnes was standing before the door to the Smith cottage. She knocked and, when the door opened, fell into Robin's arms sobbing. Thin calloused hands rose up to comfort her. Agnes admonished herself for being such a whimpering mollycoddle. What kind of a farmer's wife fell to pieces every time there was a problem? When she finally detached her head from the side of his neck, Robin guided her gently to his table.

"What's the matter, Aggie?" he asked with his soothing voice, the same one that had comforted her for as long as she could remember.

"Shaun, what else," Agnes replied. "He's gone to town again. It's almost every night now. He'll come back late and stinking of ale. Would you talk with him. He listens to you."

Robin squeezed her hand. "I'll go to town and have a talk with him, but I can't promise he'll listen."

I must look a fright, Agnes thought as she turned her head to wipe the tears from her cheeks. When she took a breath, her eyes focussed on the bow leaning against the wall. Known for the best wine in all of Icarus, the valley was also the wintering ground for many deer and elk. Venison was a staple in the winter and valley men learned to use a bow as soon as they were able to draw one. Robin was as good a hunter as any, though he didn't seem to enjoy the kill like other men. What he did seem to enjoy was working the soil, tending the vines and spending quiet evenings with her.

While Agnes was busy thinking, Robin had pulled on his cloak. "First, I must see you home," he said. Agnes nodded her consent.

They walked back to her cottage holding hands. Agnes wished it could have lasted forever and when they reached her door she was reluctant to let go. "Tell Shaun it's only because I worry so that I sent you to reason with him."

"I will, Aggie," Robin replied.

Agnes knew he wouldn't forget, not like other men might. Most illiterates had an excellent memory, since without written word things just have to be remembered, but Robin's bordered on miraculous. He never forgot anything, and could recite conversations from years past, word for word.

When Agnes was a young girl, Baron Morgan had selected her to be trained as an assistant for his preceptor. Her father had no objections once he learned she would be well paid for it. The extra coins helped finance his gambling and drinking. With thirteen children, and the preceptor getting on in years, Agnes still visited the castle every other day to teach the younger ones their letters. Recently she had taken it upon herself to teach Robin basic reading skills as well. She had not expected him to learn common script quite so quickly. Taking to it like a duck to water, he accomplished in two moons what had taken her three years of hard work to master.

Agnes held out the lantern for Robin to take, but he smiled and shook his head. "It's a clear night. I can see well enough to follow the road to town."

Before going inside, Agnes thanked Robin with a soft kiss on the cheek. Instead of closing the door she paused to look back. By the dim light of the lantern she watched him pull his cloak tight around his thin frame. She waved to him. He waved back and then disappeared into the darkness. Agnes sighed and shut the door.

Chapter 22

RODNEY

The rocky trail ended abruptly by the edge of a large deep pool formed by volumes of cold mountain water cascading down the cliff face. A narrow but well used dirt trail continued on around the pool and then followed the stream on the other side. The scouts had gone on ahead while the rest of the company seized the opportunity to wash the dust from their faces and water the horses. The roar of the falls, combined with the tranquillity of the dark swirling pool, was almost enough to make Rodney forget they were in all likelihood still being pursued by an entire Imperial legion, not to mention a FireDrake.

According to the scouting party's report, the stream emptied into a large river half a league down the trail. A proper road followed alongside the river for yet another half league until the river veered into a thick forest which offered a secluded place to get some badly needed rest. After some grumbling they pressed on leaving the peaceful pool behind. The sun had disappeared behind the mountains by the time they located a suitable campsite far enough into the woods that cook fires would not be visible from the road. The trees, mostly oak, maple and willow, had not yet fully leafed, but were still thick enough to hide them from unfriendly eyes.

Silas took Rodney aside, unfolded his map, and pointed to their position. "According to the map, the way to Drakenmount is but a one day march from where we are now. It shows a village here, two leagues south. Mossburg. After you have something to eat, I want you to select another knight and ride to this Mossburg. We need intelligence. Gather as much information as you can, but take care; neither attract attention to yourselves nor stay overly long."

Rodney was displeased with the prospect of losing two or three more sun-marks of sleep, but he understood the need for intelligence and everyone else would be just as tired as he was. "Very well," he said. "I will leave within half a sun-mark."

Silas folded his map and stuffed in his tunic. "Good. I shall await your report."

Since Jason was in no condition to ride, Rodney asked Lionel to accompany him. He made it clear that it was a request, not an order. Lionel griped at first, but then agreed. After removing their swords, both men stripped down to tunics and trousers. To be less conspicuous, they tied long well-worn hooded capes around their necks to hide their features and cover the cut of their clothing. Once satisfied with their disguises, they saddled a couple of draft horses and set out for the village.

It was late by the time Rodney and Lionel reached their destination. The few villagers still out and about stared like starving hawks as they plodded down Mossburg's main street. As strangers, Rodney expected to be noticed, but they were drawing far more attention than was warranted. When he saw a small long haired pony hitched to a wagon, he suddenly realized why. Balorian horses were descendants of the larger breeds brought to the island by Carl Daemon and his followers. Unlike their island home, such horses might not be common in Icarus. Their mounts marked them as foreigners, not just strangers.

"We must get these horses out of sight," Rodney said as he massaged his right temple.

"We passed a stable on our way in," Lionel replied. Rodney motioned for his friend to dismount. Not wishing to look anyone in the eye, they kept their heads down while leading the horses back to the stable. Upon reaching their goal they found it closed for the night. Rodney pounded on the stable doors with his fist until one creaked open a foot and a young dirty faced boy with bits of straw in his hair peered out.

"We're closed," the boy said. "Come back tomorrow."

"I know the hour is late, but we are in need of feed and water for our horses," Rodney said.

The boy seemed to notice the horses for the first time and whistled. "Those are the biggest animals I've ever seen." He looked at Lionel and then back at Rodney. "Only know one man as tall as either of you. Not any kin to the Finns are you?"

"We are just travellers," Rodney said, "from Carpathia."

The boy nodded. "It'll be two pennies each for a stall, one more for hay, three for oats."

"Hay will be fine," Rodney said tossing him a silver coin. The boy caught it with a quick hand. "You can keep the rest for your trouble."

"Thank you, Sir," the boy said with a wide grin.

"Are you sure that was wise," Lionel whispered after the boy had led his mount into the stable. "He suspects something. He called you Sir."

"Silvers are the smallest I have, besides, the boy will be too busy worrying about how to keep the stable master from taking his extra pennies to be wondering about who gave them to him."

As they walked back to the tavern Rodney felt ill at ease. He glanced at Lionel. His friend always seemed so calm. How did he manage that? Rodney rubbed his temple again. All this sneaking around was giving him a headache. He would give anything for a hot cup of chicory tea.

The few people they passed paid little attention to men on foot and Rodney was somewhat relaxed by the time they reached the tavern. A faded sign, with of a mug of frothy ale painted on it, hung out into the street. "This looks like as good a place as any," Rodney said.

Muffled voices escaped from cracks in the grey wooden door as Rodney lifted the iron latch. He paused a moment, taking a deep breath before pulling the door open. They entered and proceeded through the large open beamed room to a dark corner. Rodney counted eleven men sitting at two of the tables. A few patrons took notice as they passed, but none overly so. As soon as they were seated, an unkempt serving woman stepped up to their table.

"What'll it be?" she asked.

"Mulled cider," Lionel replied.

"Do you by chance have any chicory tea?" Rodney asked hopefully.

The serving woman snorted. "Not from around here, are yo?. We have red wine and ale." She glanced over her shoulder and then leaned in closer. "The wine is watered, so I'd recommend the ale."

"Ales it is then," Rodney said.

"Two pennies each," she replied, eyeing them sideways. "In advance if you please."

Rodney flipped a silver coin onto the table. The serving woman snatched it up with a practised hand as she turned and walked away. She returned within moments to slam down two mugs of ale and six pennies. The ale slopped onto the coins. Rodney took one of the pennies, flicked off the moisture, and held it out to her.

"For you."

The woman smiled, exposing a mouth full of blackened teeth. "Can I get you gentlemen anything else?"

"No thank you," Rodney said. The serving woman turned and walked away with an extra swing in her ample hips. Lionel smiled knowingly at him and Rodney rolled his eyes.

The two knights sat back quietly, sipped their ale, and waited. A sun-mark passed and most of what they had overheard was about weather, last year's crop or a willing harlot named Rose. Rodney was sipping from his second glass of ale and thinking of leaving when the tavern door opened. A tall man with a chest even broader than Rodney's filled the doorway. He had to tuck his left shoulder in just to pass through.

Silence hung in the air like a cold grey cloud as the man walked across the room. A few curious eyes turned his way. One man nodded a silent greeting, but most returned to their cups or continued their conversation in lower tones. With a blank stare, the man walked to an empty table two over from Rodney and Lionel. After easing himself onto a stool, he sat with his wide back against the wall.

With his left hand the big man produced a slender piece of wood from a side pocket of his grey homespun trousers. One moment his right hand was empty, the next a glint of lantern light sparkled on the keen edge of a well-oiled knife. He ordered an ale and set to carving the wood. Rodney watched him for a while before going back to listening.

A short while later the tavern door opened once more and a young lad came in. The newcomer took off his straw hat to reveal a head of silver hair. It was strange to see hair one would expect to find on an old man framing the face of a young boy, but judging by the shadow of stubble visible on his chin as he passed by their table, he was neither. Rodney put his age closer to his own.

The newcomer stopped in front of the big man's table. "Can I share your table?" he asked, as he slid onto the stool across from his grim looking friend without waiting for a reply.

The big man looked up from his work and smiled. "So, Robin, has my sister sent you to be my keeper?"

Robin kept his eyes down and clasped his hands together on the table. "Aggie worries about you, it's true, that's why she sent me, but..."

"Ha, she worries I spend too much time in the tavern you mean," the big man said. "Just like my old Da!" The smaller man raised his head to look the other in the eye. They stared at one another for a long tense moment before the big one sighed. "I can't stand just sitting at home on that blasted farm. I'd much rather be here enjoying a mug or two."

"Farming is a good life, Shaun," Robin replied.

"You and your stupid farming. I hate it! Working your life away. Scratching in the dirt like a chicken. It's the same as throwing it away by my reckoning. Where's your spirit? Where's your sense of adventure? What kind of a man are you? Do you want to be a blasted farmer all your life?"

Robin's cheeks reddened. It looked odd against the silver hair. "Yes I do. Adventure won't keep me from starving to death."

The big one looked away for a while, seemingly intent on whatever he was carving. He turned the bit of wood slowly this way and that before speaking again, "Ground's dry now. I expect Aggie will be nagging me to do the blasted plowing soon."

"I don't understand why you hate farming so much," Robin said. "It's a blessing to be able to plow and plant," he added, just before the tavern door swung open and slammed hard against the wall. Rodney instinctively reached for the sword that was no longer strapped to his side. He settled for slipping his hand in his tunic where his dagger was hidden. He gripped the handle while trying to look calm.

A short stocky man dressed in well-worn fighting leathers strutted though the dust that rained down from the rafters. On his heels followed two similarly dressed young men who awkwardly passed long pikes through the narrow doorway. The leader surveyed the room and smiled, displaying a missing front tooth. He moved to the centre of the room and stood with his left hand resting on the pommel of his sword.

"I'm glad to see so many able-bodied valley men here tonight." The man's voice was as raspy as an old rusty door hinge. "Yes, very glad indeed. For those of you who don't know me, I'm Sergeant Lennart, and it's my duty to inform you that you are all hereby conscripted as levies in the service of our Lord the Baron Morgan."

The hush that had settled in the room changed to murmurs, mutters and oaths. Unperturbed the burly sergeant continued. "You will defend the Baron's holding, and your homes therein, from an Imperial army which at this very moment marches through Escarpe pass." Rodney shared a glance with Lionel. They had to get back and tell the others.

"Dog Soldiers," a man shouted as he leapt from a table next to the sergeant.

"With a few hundred Carpathians to boot," the sergeant replied. Rodney pulled down on the hood of his cape as Lionel muttered a low curse.

From another table an older man spoke up, "We'll need to see our families safe first." A murmur of agreement echoed through the tavern. "Then we'll get our bows and show them what valley men are made of." There was a half-hearted cheer taken up by some of the men.

"There's no time for that," the Sergeant bellowed. "The Baron will provide all the weapons you'll need."

The silver haired man started toward the door. The Sergeant moved quickly to block the way, his right hand gripping the hilt of his sword.

"I must see to Aggie," the younger man said.

"I've sent my men around to all the farms," the sergeant replied. "Every man, woman and child in the Baron's fief will be taken to the castle. Your woman will be safe; like as not she is already there waiting for you, pretty as you please."

As he spoke the Sergeant's eyes narrowed. Rodney hadn't noticed him move, but Shaun was standing next to his friend holding the curved carving knife in his hand. "Go Robin," he hissed. "I can deal with this."

Rodney looked around the room. The big one's grim look was mirrored on the faces of the other men. Sweat glistened on the pike-men's faces as they too looked nervously about. It appeared to Rodney there would soon be dead men on the tavern floor.

"Wait, Shaun," Robin said, resting the flat of his hand against the big man's chest. "Fighting the Baron's men makes no sense. They're valley men like us. If we're under attack we have to stick together."

Most of the anger seemed to drain from the big man's face as he slowly lowered the knife. The Sergeant's grip on his sword relaxed enough to allow some of the colour to return to his knuckles. "All right then, lads" the sergeant said with remarkable calm. "Form a line outside behind the others. We must make haste to the castle."

The two pike-men backed out through the door. Rodney and Lionel leaned back and watched the rest file out. Rodney was just about to believe they would go unnoticed when the sergeant turned and took a step toward them. "What are you two waiting for, a bloody invitation from his lordship? Up we go lads. Move your arses!" Rodney glanced at Lionel, who shrugged. They stood up and followed the others out the door.

The street was well lit despite the few stars visible, and only a faint haze from the half moon that managed to penetrate the clouds. Of the fifty men who stood in the street, ten wore fighting leathers; the rest had only the homespun clothing of villagers and farmers. Except for the sergeant and his two pike-men, each man dressed in leather held a large pitch torch making it much too bright to just move off into the shadows.

Rodney leaned over to whisper in Lionel's ear, "We will go along with them until we are out of town. Then we slip away and come back for the horses."

Lionel nodded as they attached themselves to the rear of the column the sergeant was forming. Rodney had hoped they would remain the last in line, but the two pike-men took up positions behind them. He leaned over and whispered in Lionel's ear again, "They are very young. When we make our move, try not to injure them too badly."

One of the pike-men pushed Rodney with the shaft of his pike. "No talking," he said in a voice that broke into falsetto half way through. Rodney's anger sparked. Lionel nudged him with his shoulder and Rodney let it go as they started marching down the street.

Once past the stables, Rodney deliberately slowed his pace. They were being led down the same road they had travelled earlier, but heading away from the Balorian camp. Their route soon veered into the trees. At the first sharp twist in the road there was a good ten feet between them and the next two men in line. Rodney stopped and bent down to adjust his boot. When the last man up ahead disappeared around the bend, Rodney sprung up and punched the nearest pike-man in the jaw. He fell like a wet sack. Before the other one could get over his surprise, Lionel struck him in the back of the head with the hilt of his dagger. The second pike-man crumpled to join the first on the ground.

The two knights turned and ran back to the stable. Rodney pulled on the doors, but they were bolted from the inside. He pounded on one of them with his fist. The stable door opened a foot and the young boy poked his head out. He was holding up a lantern. "Who is it," he said.

"We have changed our minds," Rodney said, trying to sound calm. "We will be taking our horses, now. If you are quick to bring out our mounts and saddles, there is another silver in it for you."

The boy's eyes went wide and then the door slammed shut. Lionel swore. After a lot of noise inside, the door swung wide open and the boy led out Lionel's mount. Rodney had his own saddled not a moment too soon. Even as he slid his foot into the stirrup, he caught sight of flickering torch light from the direction of the road. He flipped a silver coin to the boy and kicked his mount into a canter, which was as much as he was going to get from the big animal. It was so dark he could not see the road, so he let his mount have its head. As the pinpoints of light disappeared behind them, Rodney silently thanked Pathos that none of their pursuers were mounted.

Chapter 23

VERNON

Hunched on the throne with his chin resting on the knuckles of his left hand, King Solon twisted the waxed end of his moustache with the right. The King's flinty blue eyes were levelled on the tall grey haired man standing before him. Arms crossed, Vernon Sacarus stood to the King's right. As Captain of the Royal Guard, it was his place of honour. Filled with contempt, Vernon looked down the length of his ample nose at Baldric, the King's senior adviser. The man was flanked by three members of the royal guard on each side.

Promoted after the untimely death of his predecessor, Senior Adviser Gibbons, Baldric had held the post for less than a year. Gibbons had been ruthlessly efficient in carrying out his duties. Vernon had not only respected the old man for it, but had over the years developed a fondness for him to the point of elevating him to the status of the father he never knew. Vernon preferred to believe the feeling was mutual. It was well known the King had loved the old man too, much like a surrogate father, but what few people knew was that Gibbons had been much more than just a loyal adviser. He had in fact been instrumental in keeping the kingdom secure. He was a great man, not a back biting boot licker like Baldric.

It was well known that Vernon was the only one left in the royal court who King Solon trusted without reservation. Vernon had worked hard to earn that trust. His position as Captain of the Royal Guard was won through years of loyal service to King and country, all under the direction and guidance of Gibbons. Vernon had proved himself time and time again to be adept at making the King's problems disappear. If that wasn't enough, he had sworn a blood oath to protect the King with his life. It was an oath he would never break.

Though a remorseless sadistic killer, even by his own admission, Vernon was uncompromising in loyalty to his nation's sovereign lord, and great loyalty came with great rewards. Untouchable, with the full weight of the King behind

155

him, Vernon was free to indulge in pursuits that would have otherwise cost his head. Secure in the lofty position of King's favourite, Vernon stood patiently waiting for the King to speak.

The court was often kept waiting as Solon pondered affairs of state. Vernon didn't mind. It gave him time to reflect on his own greatness. He took great pride in his reputation as the deadliest swordsman in Icarus. Though not overly large or strong, he was incredibly fast. His blade work with a saber was unparalleled and he had never met a man who could match his speed, but his reputation was not based on that alone. His fame was largely due to no challenger having ever survived a duel with him. If not killed outright by a lethal thrust or slash, his opponents succumbed to what had seemed to be only minor wounds. Whispers of poison blades and other suspicions could never be proved, and no one dared voice such a thing in his presence.

In reality, only Vernon and Gibbons knew the truth. His dagger was coated with a poison applied as a liquid that dried clear and remained potent for more than a moon. One small prick on the finger was all that was needed to bring death within a few sun-marks. The first sign was profuse sweating, followed by dizziness, paralysis of the limbs and then a gasping death. There were faster acting poisons, but Vernon enjoyed to watch and found the effects of this one most satisfactory. Though it had never proved necessary, he carried a small brass vial of antidote hidden under his belt just in case he should ever nick himself.

The silence was broken when Solon finally spoke. "So Baldric, have there been any new messages from our little friend in Nagual?"

Baldric shook his head. "No, sire, there has been no word since the last communication."

"It has been fifteen days since then. We must conclude that our agent has been compromised and has either gone to ground or been captured."

Baldric shifted the weight on his feet and licked his lips. "Perhaps a few more days sire?"

The King's eyes narrowed. Vernon was very astute at reading faces, especially the King's. Obviously Baldric had replied a little too quickly for Solon's liking. The King's gaze stayed rivetted on Baldric until the older man finally lowered his eyes to stare at the tips of the shoes protruding from under his long dark robe. Though he made sure to conceal his pleasure, Vernon enjoyed watching Baldric squirm.

"No, we think not," Solon said. "By now, our cousin has received our message. He will add the strength of his own men to the three thousand we are sending and then secure the Escarpe pass. With our own routes to the north sea hopelessly blockaded, our merchants unable to pay their taxes and screaming for action, we cannot allow the only other route north to become closed to us as well."

"But sire," Baldric said.

Solon raised his hand for silence. "We have spoken."

Baldric opened his mouth as if to protest. Solon raised his eyebrows. The adviser seemed to think better of protesting and smiled. "I acquiesce to your superior judgement, sire."

Vernon could see the lie in Baldric's eyes. He detected fear as well, but there was something else, something he couldn't put his finger on, yet.

"You may leave us," Solon said with a sweep of his hand. Baldric bowed and backed out of the chamber. Once he was gone, the King leaned over to Vernon and crooked his finger. Vernon bent closer. "We think our adviser needs watching, Captain," Solon whispered.

Vernon smiled. "I could not agree more, your Majesty. I will see to it personally."

The King leaned back and resumed twisting the end of his moustache. Vernon bowed and left the chamber through a small door concealed by a tapestry hanging behind the throne. It felt like old times. Baldric was up to something, and whatever it was, Vernon Sacarus would find out. Then Baldric would be his. Vernon smiled. This was going to be such fun.

Chapter 24

ROBIN

A long with Shaun and the rest of the conscripts, Robin waited in the cold while Sergeant Lennart took half his men to search for a couple of deserters. Before he left, the Sergeant vowed to cut the eggs off any man who tried to follow their example. No one chose to find out if he meant it.

The sergeant returned empty handed a short while later. Eager to know what had happened, Robin and Shaun eavesdropped on the regulars as they discussed the incident. The last man in line had apparently stopped to fix his boot. That's when the others leapt out from the trees and struck the two Logan brothers from behind. One of them put up a valiant fight, but outnumbered, he was beaten into unconsciousness, which was how the sergeant had found them both lying on the road not far from town. The accomplices must have brought horses, because the pounding of hooves could be heard in the distance.

It was a sun-mark past midnight when they finally reached Montcre castle. To Robin's great relief both Agnes and her mother were waiting for them just inside the gates. The moment they passed through, Agnes came running over and flung herself at Shaun, hugging him close. When she let him go she immediately repeated the procedure with Robin. He held her tight while Shaun hugged his mother.

"I'm so glad you're both safe," Agnes said softly in his ear. "I was worried sick." When Robin finally released her, she swung a long bundle from her back to the ground. Robin recognized it as the wool blanket from his bed. "They tried to make us wait in the great hall, with the rest of the women and children, but I wanted to give you this first."

Agnes unrolled the blanket to reveal both Robin and Shaun's bows. Robin picked his up. After inspecting it, he gave Agnes a quick kiss on the cheek. "How did you ever manage to get it?" he asked, knowing the baron's men would not have allowed her the time.

158

"I threatened them," Agnes replied with a mischievous grin. Robin was confused. She must have noticed, because she leaned in close and explained. "They've seen me many times with the Baron's children. His son may still be a boy, but he has the Baron's ear and is his only male heir. It was enough to convince them to make a small side trip to your cottage."

There was little time to reply, as the reunion with Shaun's family ended abruptly when Sergeant Lennart ordered all the conscripts to the castle armoury. The musty windowless room that served as an armoury was stacked to the rafters with an array of swords, pikes, long handled axes and other things Robin didn't recognize. Most of the metal was covered in a heavy layer of rust. They appeared to have been there a very long time.

Once Robin had a good look at what was there, he thanked the Gods for Agnes's foresight. Most of the bows in the armoury were poorly crafted castoffs, some so old and dry that they were as likely as not to snap on the first draw. Being content with their own, Robin and Shaun made to leave with only a quiver of arrows apiece, but Sergeant Lennart was insistent they each take a 'hand-to-hand' weapon.

Seeing their hesitation to select one, he picked up a heavy broadsword and crooked his finger for them to follow him. Once outside the armoury, the sergeant rested the tip of the sword on a hitching post. He waited until Robin, Shaun and some of the other conscripts had formed a half circle around him.

"If one of those dirty bastards gets onto the ramparts," the sergeant said, "a bow will be less than bloody useless." To make his point, he raised the weapon swiftly and then slammed it down onto a hitching post. The post was a good three fingers thick, but there was a loud crack as it split down the middle.

The Sergeant looked at the faces of the conscripts and then handed the sword hilt first to Shaun. "You're a big enough lad to handle this skull cracker," he said.

Robin backed away as Shaun hefted the sword and swung it from side to side. He raised it over his head and then brought it down on the post. The wood snapped in two as the heavy blade passed right through it and penetrated the hard packed ground by at least three fingers.

"See that, it was made for you lad," the Sergeant said with a satisfied gap-tooth smile.

If the grin on his face was any indication, Shaun was quite pleased with Sergeant Lennart's remarks. When the sergeant turned away, Shaun leaned over to Robin. "You know, I've always wondered what it would be like to be a professional arms-man." The grin on his face faded. "Was thinking of joining up just before Da..."

Robin slapped his friend on the back. "Come on Shaun. The good sergeant will have our eggs on a spit if we keep him waiting."

When the conscripts reached their places on the wall, Robin was carrying a short sword. It was the lightest one he could find. Shaun had the broadsword along with an old battered shield he had picked out. Robin felt out of place. Shaun on the other hand, looked every bit like a formidable warrior. The sergeant placed Robin and Shaun together at the centre of the west wall. It was castellated with narrow arrow slots in each merlon. He then told them to get some sleep. Wrapping himself in his cloak, Robin stretched out on the rampart and then spent the rest of the night trying unsuccessfully to do just that.

⚽ ⚽ ⚽

The first Dog Soldiers appeared at the edge of the forest shortly after dawn. By the time the sun had cleared the eastern mountains, there were more men than Robin could count. The enemy stayed out of bow range, however, so the defenders could do nothing but sit through a long morning of watching and waiting for an attack that never came.

Just because they didn't launch an assault on the castle didn't mean the Dog Soldiers were idle. Their activities were concentrated in the forest, where they felled trees by the score. From his vantage point Robin watched as large gaping holes appeared in the foliage. Through one of the gaps he could see the top of some sort of framework being lashed together, but he couldn't see enough to make out what it was. When curiosity finally got the better of him, he turned to Shaun who was also watching through the crenel on his left. "What do you suppose they're building?"

Shaun pursed his lips and shrugged his shoulders, but it was a voice to Robin's right that answered his question. "They'll be making siege weapons and scaling ladders most likely."

Robin turned to see who had spoken. It was one of the Baron's regulars. An old greybeard with blackened teeth. He turned his head and spat. A large stream of black spittle sailed through the crenel. The arms-man wiped the excess spittle from his mouth with the back of his hand and knitted his brows. "They'll use catapults first off. Burning hay bales to keep us busy and tire us out a little. Then boulders or iron balls to breach the walls."

Robin looked over at Shaun, who just shrugged again. When he looked back, the arms-man pulled a plug of tobacco from his tunic. He tore off a chunk with his teeth. The wad of tobacco made the side of his cheek poke out. "But you can rest easy lad. They'll not be attacking any time soon," he mumbled as he chewed.

Some brownish spittle had run down the arms-man's chin as he spoke. He smiled, raised his hand once more to wipe his mouth, then his eyes bulged out as an arrow punched through his neck. Robin heard another shaft hit the stone next to his head just as Shaun yanked him back behind the merlon. The attack they had been waiting for all morning had finally arrived.

His eyes fixated on the dead man lying next to him, Robin was paralyzed with fear. A growing pool of dark blood formed around the man's head while his eyes stared blankly up into the sky. The look of shock registered on the man's face reminded Robin of the way his mother's face had looked when she died. It was one of total disbelief. Robin came out of his stupor only when he realized Shaun was shouting at him. He could barely make out the words over all the screaming and crashing of wood and steel. "Shoot, blast it. Shoot."

Slipping the bow off his back Robin notched an arrow. Too afraid to poke his head out through the crenel, he tried to look through the narrow arrow slit but his vision blurred. He knelt back down and rubbed his eyes. When he opened them, he was facing down along the rampart. Arms-men with long hooked poles were running back and forth frantically pushing ladders away from the wall. One of the pole-men fell backwards, pierced by three arrows. Another was pulled through a crenel and over the wall by his pole. Twice, a Dog Soldier managed to swing a foot over a crenel onto the rampart, but both men were cut down by the defenders.

The tops of two rough cut pine poles slammed into the opening between Robin and the dead arms-man. Robin watched the ends of the poles vibrate until a Dog Soldier's braids appeared. The next thing Robin knew, he was standing above the invader with his sword raised high. He screamed in panic as he slammed the weapon down onto the man's head. Once, twice, three times he struck. The Dog Soldier toppled back, taking the ladder with him.

Sergeant Lennart suddenly appeared at Robin's side. "Good work, lad!" he yelled, slapping him on the back. "Knew you had it in you."

An arrow bounced off the side of the merlon and stone chips stung Robin's cheek. The Sergeant ducked down and pushed the dead arms-man off the rampart. Holding his cheek, Robin watched the body join at least ten other twisted forms laying in the courtyard at the base of the wall. When Robin looked back, the Sergeant was gone. Another arms-man with a crossbow had taken his place. Once again Shaun pulled him back behind the merlon. "Stay back, blast it! Aggie would roast me alive if I let you get yourself killed!"

Still with a full quiver, Robin had yet to loose a single arrow. He peered through the slot. With so many men on the ground below, there was no need to look for a target. He sent shaft after shaft through the slot until he reached for another arrow to find but two left. Robin snuck a quick sideways glance at Shaun. He was crouched behind his own merlon with an empty quiver and the bow slung over his back. Looking the part of a seasoned warrior, Shaun held both sword and shield at the ready. Robin knew better. His friend possessed no more skill than he did himself. Perhaps Shaun's size and strength would make the difference.

"Sappers!" someone yelled. Without thinking, Robin poked his head around the merlon to get a better look. A group of men were huddled under a great wood and leather tortoise that moved with surprising speed toward the corner tower. Only their armour clad feet were visible. Robin let loose one of his arrows. The shaft glanced off the hardened leather and skidded along in the dirt.

Only a single crossbow bolt had managed to punch through the tough hide before the tortoise reached the safety of the tower wall. At that angle, to use his bow Robin would need to lean out through the crenel. An arrow flashed by reminding him of the danger in that. The castle walls were forty feet tall and six feet thick, with a steep ravine running the full length of the east wall. The castle's only weakness lay in the two square corner towers to the west. If the Dog Soldiers succeeded in digging enough earth away from the base of one of the towers, it could collapse and breach the wall.

To Robin's relief, the sappers were given little time for digging. The Baron's men had prepared for such an attack. He watched with fascination as steaming liquid spilled through the openings between the corbels, down the high wall, and over the sapper's shield. Two men beneath it went down clutching their legs. The tortoise tilted slightly as the smell of rancid oil and fat wafted up on the breeze.

After giving the oil time to soak in, the men on the tower tossed over pitch torches. The tortoise ignited, burned intensely for a while, and then collapsed as the men sheltered beneath it fled, many ablaze themselves. Robin sent his last arrow at one, but the Dog Soldier was struck by at least three shafts and he couldn't be sure if one had been his. An arrow whistled by his ear and he dove back behind the merlon.

The failed attempt with sappers seemed to take all the fight out of the Imperials and they retreated back out of bow range. Clutching the old blunt sword, his arrows spent, Robin waited the rest of the day fearfully peering through the arrow slot. He wished he knew more about fighting with an edged weapon, not that the short sword in his hand had much of an edge. At least it worked well as a club.

Just as the top of the sun dipped below the mountains, Robin snuck one last look through the castle's crenel. A cool spring breeze carried the stench of oil, pitch and burnt leather from the bottom of the north west tower. The scorch marks were barely visible as they began to blend in with the mottled brown stone of the castle walls in the growing darkness.

Two young boys came along with a bucket of hot soup, copper cups, stale bread and news from the other walls. Robin and Shaun were surprised to hear the attack had been concentrated mainly at the south gate house. They had been sure the west wall had seen the worst of the fighting, but one of the boys told them fifty men on the south wall had been either slain or wounded severely enough that they could no longer fight. It amounted to half of their total losses. The Baron set enemy casualties at four hundred, so they had managed to kill four Imperials for every valley man lost. It was all well and good, but they were outnumbered ten to one.

After filling their cups, one of the boys leaned in close. "A man on the north wall saw a giant red bird circling the castle just before the attack," he said. "A bad omen to be sure." He turned to the other boy, who nodded in confirmation. The boy leaned in again. "When the Baron heard of it, he ordered them to stop talking such foolishness. Can't say as they stopped talking though, least out of the Baron's hearing."

"You didn't hear it from us though," the second boy added as he picked up the soup bucket and they moved on to the next man.

Robin looked at Shaun, who just shrugged as he dipped the bread into his soup. Robin followed his friend's example. He wasn't really hungry but he would force it down anyway. After all, who knew when they would get another meal. One of the boys returned a short while later, this time with a bucket of cool frothy ale. Robin sipped his slowly, as he watched camp fires haphazardly flicker into existence amid the distant sounds of voices and clanking pots.

Spots of dancing light circled the castle and spread out across the valley floor. Robin stopped counting the fires when his eyes reached the tree line near the river that ran the length of the valley. Easy enough to see through the sparsely leafed trees, by the light of a large bonfire, stood a giant wooden structure.

"Mangonel," the crossbow-man next to him said. "It looks ready too. Only needs to be dragged out of the trees. Mark my words, come first light it'll be hurling missiles at the walls. Then the real fighting will begin."

Robin swallowed the last of his ale and slid back down behind the merlon. Closing tired eyes, he wrapped his arms around his legs and rested his forehead on his knees. *Then the real fighting will begin.* The words echoed in his head, over and over, keeping sleep at bay until well past midnight.

Chapter 25

SILAS

Silas sat by his small fire staring into the flames. His son lay on the other side wrapped in a wool blanket and sleeping soundly. Silas shivered before releasing a long heartfelt sigh. Growing old was proving to be an unpleasant experience. He looked down at his sleeping son, envying his youth. Then momentarily forgetting his discomforts, he smiled. Gregory was as good a son as any man could ask for. Silas took solace in the knowledge that he had sired a better man than himself. As a father, he was truly blessed.

"How can it be so blasted hot during the day and so miserably cold at night," Silas muttered to himself as he rolled a cup of mulled cider slowly back and forth between his fingers. The cup was only half full, but it was the very last of the Balorian cider, and he wished to savour it because there would be no more for a long time to come. The gentle warmth from the copper cup penetrated to his finger joints and soothed the aching stiffness. The cold and damp of the forest had seeped into his hands. He doubted he could hold a sword for very long.

With a grunt, Silas stretched out his legs. Both knees made those now familiar cracking sounds. He had long suffered the dull, annoying pain that accompanied the same sounds in his hands. His physician back in Balor had called it Articulation Sickness. It came with advancing years for many. As of late this same malady had attacked his knees and hips. Only strong cider and the warmth of a fire was of any comfort.

In hindsight he'd been a fool to come. Travelling through the rocky pass had been near torture. Several times during the long day he had been forced to dismount and walk Midnight through the loose stones and debris. If that was not bad enough, he had lost count of how many times he bent down to remove stones from the horse's hooves. He could have asked his squire Oliver to do it, but what kind of knight failed to attend to his own mount? By the time they had reached softer ground it had become unbearable just to sit in the saddle.

As tired as he felt, Silas could not allow himself the pleasure of sleep. His Second was long overdue and he was worried. Two of Rodney's men were keeping watch for him on the road. Silas berated himself once again for sending Rodney to the town. He should have sent one of the scouts, or even one of the other knights. It would be most unpleasant explaining to Basil how Frederic's only son had been lost performing such an un-knightly deed. Would he have sent a Second of his own choosing? Was it bruised pride over having Rodney forced upon him that prompted his decision? In truth, he had expected Rodney to refuse outright, or at the very least protest, but he had accepted the order without complaint. Such dutiful compliance only added to Silas's deep feelings of guilt. Rodney was more than proving his worth as Second.

Aware of someone approaching, Silas looked up to see Herman lumbering toward him. "They've returned," the big man said in his gravelly voice.

"It is about bloody time," Silas grumbled. He stood, ignoring the pain it produced in his knees. *Perhaps this is my penance*, he thought grimly. Silas took one last sip from his cup. The cider was cold and sour. He cast the dregs into the flames and the fire hissed back angrily. It matched his own mood as he followed Herman, trying to keep up to the big knight's long stride.

They caught up with Rodney just as he was leaving the makeshift paddock that had been constructed of ropes tied between trees. His Second looked exhausted. Silas felt another twinge of guilt. Like everyone else, Rodney had not slept the previous night and now he would have little sleep this night as well. Both Rodney and Lionel carried their saddles as if they were made of lead. Both also sported dark patches under their eyes.

When his Second noticed them approaching, he stopped. "We have much to report," Rodney said in a voice that sounded even more tired than he looked.

"Very good, but see to your tack first," Silas said, waving his hand in the direction they had been heading. "You both look near done in and I think a little refreshment would be in order. Your report can wait a short while longer."

The two younger knights snaked their way around the other campfires and sleeping men. Silas and Herman followed until they found Jason, who was propped against a tree stump near a small fire. The injured knight was fast asleep. Having left the tents with the wagons in Nagual, they were all sleeping under the stars.

When they stepped into the light of the fire, one of Rodney's men greeted him by lifting a steaming pot from the flames. The man was one of the twins; Silas didn't know which, as he could never tell them apart. The man filled a copper cup from the pot as the two knights dropped their saddles on a fallen log next to Jason's. An unpleasant aroma drifted by Silas's nose when Rodney took the proffered cup. When his Second took a sip and then let out a satisfied, "Ah," Silas recognized the smell. It was chicory tea; a vile drink he had never been able to stomach.

The four knights sat down around the fire. Silas stretched out his fingers over the flames to warm them, as Rodney explained all that had transpired since he and Lionel had left camp. When he was done, Silas rubbed his chin absently as he thought it through. "It sounds to me that these Icarians will be hard pressed to defend themselves," he finally said.

Rodney refilled his cup before he responded. "We saw perhaps fifty men, and most of those were serfs. They may have a garrison at this Baron Morgan's castle, but I doubt it will be adequate. Even if it is, they will have little chance against both an Imperial Legion and a FireDrake."

Silas forced the vision of the FireDrake's eyes from his mind. It haunted him still, like some spectre from a childhood nightmare. He reached into his tunic and withdrew the map. Unfolding the parchment, Silas tilted it toward the fire. "Ah, this must be it," he said touching a small square with his finger. "Montcre castle. It is northeast of the trail we must take to reach Drakenmount."

"We could offer them aid," Rodney said.

"There is nothing we can do," Silas replied. "There are too few of us to make a difference. We would only succeed in getting ourselves killed. Who would carry out our mission then? No, it is imperative we find the trail marked on this map and carry out our duty. We leave at first light, so you best get some rest. There are precious few sun-marks left so I will not keep you any longer."

Silas returned to his own fire with a troubled mind. As much as he would have liked to help the Icarians, they had to reach Drakenmount. He wrapped himself in his blanket but was unable to sleep. Despite his best efforts, he could not stop the vision of the FireDrake's eyes from reforming in his mind.

The company was on the move with the rising sun. Avoiding the main road, they travelled for most of the day along a narrow trail that followed the river. For a while, the sounds of battle could be heard to the east. Fortunately, the Imperials were too preoccupied to watch for a few hundred men sneaking around behind them, but running away with their tails between their legs did not sit well with Silas. Twice in as many days made it even worse. From the scowls on their faces, it bothered the rest of the men too.

By the time the sun had touched the top of western mountains, they were well away from the fighting and Silas felt at peace for the first time in days. The sky was clear, the air warm and the trail soft. His joints had not felt this good for a long time. He smiled, feeling like a new man. Then Rodney cried out. "Look!" Silas focussed on the trail up ahead. The entire scouting party, with the exception of the Kelatch, was bound, gagged and lashed to the trees.

"Halt in the name of the Duke!" a voice cried out. Scores of bowmen dressed in forest green uniforms stepped out of the trees on both sides of the trail. Every one of them had an arrow notched and ready. A man in oiled leathers stepped out from the trees. He had the air of a leader. "Draw weapons only if you wish to die," he said.

Silas raised his hand. "Hold!"

The man in leathers took a few steps closer. "By what right do Carpathian knights enter Icarus!"

Silas considered lying, but something in the man's voice caused him to think better of it. "We are Balorian, not Carpathian. I am Sir Silas Vennell, Daemon Knight, and leader of this company. We wish only passage through your land. I can assure you we shall cause you no trouble. Very near this place is a trail that leads into the mountains. We intend to leave Icarus by that route as soon as possible. Just allow us passage and you will never see us again."

A thin grey haired man in a deep blue tunic, with a polished silver breastplate, stepped out from behind a tall pine. "I will take over from here Captain," he said. The first man inclined his head and stepped back.

The older man walked toward them with an unmistakable air of authority and nobility. He didn't stop until he stood on the path within five feet of Silas and Rodney. "I am Duke Edmond Meredith," he said, "cousin to the King, lord of the land in which you trespass and I will decide how much trouble you are." He raised a long narrow finger and pointed it at Silas like a weapon. "You Sir, will come with me." The Duke's eyes darted to the other knights. "The rest of you will wait here."

Silas dismounted and handed the reins to Gregory. "May my Second accompany us, your Grace?" Silas asked, indicating Rodney with his outstretched hand.

The Duke's eyes flicked momentarily to Rodney. "Very well. Captain Doyle, bring them both to my tent." With that the Duke spun on his heels and walked back toward the trees.

Once Rodney had dismounted, the Duke's captain relieved them of swords, daggers and even their belt knives. He then looked Silas and Rodney up and down before speaking. "Have you any other weapons on your persons?" he asked Silas shook his head and the Captain grinned. "Well if you don't mind I shall see for myself."

Silas and Rodney lifted their arms. While poking around inside their tunics, the Captain discovered the maps. To Silas's great relief, once he had opened and examined them, he handed them back. After he ran his fingers around the tops of their boots, the Captain stepped back and smiled. "No offence, but one can never be too careful with foreigners."

Flanked by four Icarian archers, they followed the Captain down a narrow winding path through the trees until they reached an open meadow. In the centre stood a large white tent. As they approached, one of the guards opened the flap. Inside, Edmond sat on the far side of a long table. There were three empty stools arrayed on the opposite side. He motioned for them to sit. As soon as they had taken their seats, an arms-man handed them each a fine silver goblet of dark red wine. Silas took a sip. It was sweet, thick and warmed his insides on the way down.

After sipping his wine, Edmond cleared his throat. "Well gentlemen, we seem to have a bit of a problem here. My Duchy has been invaded by five thousand Dog Soldiers, and I have but two thousand men with which to defend it." He paused and looked Silas in the eye. "Then there is you. Two hundred armed men, including trained knights if what you say is true, who just happen to arrive at the same time. You will need to give me a very good reason why I should not kill you and your countrymen out of hand."

Silas looked at Rodney and then back at the Duke. He took a deep breath. "Perhaps I should start at the beginning."

"Ah," the Duke replied. "That would be an excellent place."

Silas pulled out his map and handed it to the Duke. He then proceeded to tell him everything. While Edmond looked at the map, Silas told him of Rodney's encounter with Aldus and the FireDrake Grigor; of the amulet and the sorceress; of how Aldus had drawn the maps and then left; and lastly, he spoke of the FireDrake and all that had transpired with the Dog Soldiers. He left out only his own brief encounter with the FireDrake in the Imperial camp.

There was a long silence when Silas had finished. Captain Doyle was the first to break it. "And you really expect us to believe this?"

The Duke raised his hand. "I consider myself a good judge of character." He turned his head to face his Captain. "Though I will admit it all sounds strange, I believe they are who and what they say." When the Duke turned back to Silas a wide grin had spread across his face. "Besides, his tale is too preposterous to be a lie."

Silas inclined his head. "We are in your debt, your Grace."

"Ah, well put," the Duke replied. "That brings up another matter. In three days, four on the outside, three thousand of the King's regulars will arrive. With their aid we will have no trouble dealing with these Nagual scum. Unfortunately, we do not have the luxury of waiting three or four more days."

Edmond's grin vanished as his eyes narrowed. "Baron Morgan is defending Montcre with, at best, five hundred men. I have asked him to hold for one day, and my reports say he has done that admirably. The cost has no doubt been high. He cannot be expected to hold for another, and I cannot afford to let Montcre fall. It would give Nagual a foothold in Icarus. I am desperately short of fighting men. You have two hundred armed men. My price for your lives, and safe passage through Icarus, is four days of military service."

Edmond took a sip of his wine. "With the element of surprise on our side I am confident we can, if not defeat them, at least keep them from sacking Montcre. But this FireDrake is a fly in my honey."

Silas rubbed his chin in thought. "We had decided against helping your people only because two hundred would not have made a difference against a legion, but now perhaps with your forces it may. I agree to your terms; four days of service in exchange for both our freedom and passage through Icarus."

The Duke raised his glass. "To the morrow then," he said, with a friendly smile. Silas raised his glass as well. By the sour look on the captain's face, Silas could tell he did not share his lord's enthusiasm.

"If I may speak," Rodney said.

"Of course," said the Duke.

"Though I have only limited experience concerning FireDrakes, I have given it much thought. It is true their scales are effective armour and dragon-fire is most deadly, but I have a plan that just might work to defeat one. I will need the aid of six knights, an additional twenty men, thirty coils of good hemp rope and some long stout poles."

The Duke nodded. "Twenty seven men to slay a dragon. I would call that a bargain any day. Captain Doyle, see that this good knight has whatever he needs. Now gentlemen, we need to plan our battlefield strategy."

Chapter 26

BALDRIC

With the hilt of a razor sharp dagger gripped firmly in his white knuckled hand, Baldric pressed an ear against the King's chamber door. A small piece of parchment was balled up in his left hand. The bit of parchment was a message from the Emperor. It had come by bird earlier in the day and ordered the immediate death of King Solon.

Why the Emperor needed birds was still somewhat of a mystery to Baldric. Having witnessed it several times, he knew very well of the Emperor's ability to travel in spirit. What he didn't understand was why the Emperor could not travel to the King's palace in Concurie. "It is one of the few places I cannot go," the Emperor had said. He would explain no further, and one did not press the Emperor, that is if one wished to stay alive.

The chamber guards lay slumped on the floor to either side of the door. The sleeping potion Baldric had poured into their evening ale would ensure they remained unconscious until morning. He tucked the crumpled parchment into a side pocket of the black robe that blended so well with the long shadows cast by the oil lamp down the hall. He stepped over one of the guards, lifted the latch, and then carefully tested the door. It opened smoothly without making a sound. *This is too easy. Solon is a fool who deserves to die.*

Baldric slipped silently inside the room and gently closed the door. The latch clicked back into place like a drum beat in the dead silence of the chamber. The sound was echoed by his pounding heart as he stood frozen in place listening for the King to stir. He half expected the man to leap up and scream for his guards, but there was only silence. His hand was shaking. If only he could have used poison. Baldric had never actually killed someone with his own hand. It seemed so, so barbaric, but Solon refused to eat or drink anything that his tasters had not tried first. They were highly trained and capable of detecting even the subtlest of poisons.

The outline of a grand four poster bed took shape as Baldric's eyes adjusted to the darkness. What little light there was in the chamber came from the windows above, which allowed in only a few slivers of starlight. His slippered feet moved silently across the carpets until he stood at the side of the bed. The Queen slept in her own chamber so there was only one lump under the covers. The King lay near the edge within easy reach.

Baldric was nervous and the blade quivered in his hand. Only a sun-mark before, he had crept into Baron Egan's sleeping chamber and taken his dagger. The baron would not wake until morning, thanks to the sleeping potion Baldric had slipped into his wine during supper. Baron Egan had been chastised by the King for some infraction or other the day before. That and a bloody rag found outside his door would be enough to hang him for the King's murder. No one would ever suspect Solon's loyal and trusted adviser.

Baldric raised the slender blade over the sleeping form. *Calm yourself Baldric. There is nothing to fear, Solon is a sound sleeper. If the blade finds his heart on the first stroke, he shall never awaken.* The dagger fell once, twice, three times. On the third stroke he released the handle of the blade. Solon never moved, never even made a sound. "That was easy enough," Baldric whispered to himself.

"Not as easy as you think, traitor," the King's voice boomed in the darkness. Baldric spun around just in time to be blinded by a bright light. When his eyes could once again focus, he saw the King, very much alive, standing ten feet away and flanked by a pair of guards on either side. Two of the guards held back the tapestries that had hidden a recess in the stone wall with one hand, while holding up lanterns with the other. The remaining two were pointing loaded crossbows at Baldric's chest.

"We have been watching you, Baldric," the King said with a crooked smile, "We have been watching your birds as well. The last message you sent was intercepted by one of our fine archers. But never fear, together we shall send the Emperor another."

Baldric felt something sharp prick the skin at the base of his spine. "Move, if you wish to live a little longer," the voice of Captain Sacarus whispered in his ear. Baldric complied and took a few steps away from the King's bed. "Sit," the Captain hissed when they had reached a small desk in the corner.

After Baldric was seated, one of the lanterns was placed on the desk. Before him was a quill, ink and some small pieces of parchment. He recognized them as his own, taken from his chamber. "Take up the pen and write down our words," the King said. Baldric took the quill, dipped it in the ink, and then carefully shook of the excess.

"Solon is dead," the King said. "No one suspects. His army has been recalled." As Baldric wrote he could feel the point of the captain's sword pressing a little harder with every word. "Sign it," the King barked.

Once signed the message was taken by one of the guards and handed to the King. Solon leaned in toward the light to read it. "We commend your penmanship, Baldric," the King said tucking the note into his robe. "You seem to have a multitude of skills of which we were hitherto unaware."

"What now?" Baldric asked the King.

"What now," the King replied. "Now you die."

Baldric heard the sound of tearing cloth. It was followed by a dull wet thud, accompanied by a terrible searing pain in his back. He looked down in shock as the tip of the Captain's sword protruded from his abdomen. His hand twitched, involuntarily knocking the ink bottle from the table. *That will stain the carpet* he thought as the world tilted and then went black.

Chapter 27

ROBIN

When the first rays of morning light fell upon the mangonel, Robin could see it clearly through the arrow slot. The Dog Soldiers must have dragged it out of the trees sometime during the night. He watched in fascination as the long arm swung up and released a small grey object. The object grew into a round boulder that passed over his head to crash with great force at the base of the inner wall.

A second missile sailed over the south wall. It barely cleared the heads of the defenders on the rampart to land in the courtyard embedding itself into the ground. Robin spun around at the sound of a third as it pounded through a merlon on the north wall near the tower. When the dust had cleared, most of the merlon was gone. Only a jagged finger of stone remained.

Back at the mangonel facing the west wall, Dog Soldiers swarmed over the device like bees on a hive. The arm was pulled down and then shortly after released. This time a boulder slammed into the corner of a merlon just ten feet away. The sound it made was akin to a thunder clap. Robin instinctively closed his eyes and covered his ears. When he opened his eyes again, a good portion of the merlon was gone along with the man who had been standing behind it. At this rate, there would soon be nothing left to protect the defenders along the wall. He could hear the cheers of Dog Soldiers in the distance.

There were two more thuds in quick succession. Both Robin and Shaun ducked down flat on the rampart behind their merlons. Over and over, missiles either slammed into the wall, or whistled overhead. After each strike on the west wall, Robin could hear the sound of stone crumbling down and crashing to the dirt below. For what seemed like an eternity, he lay with his hands clasped over his head wondering if the bombardment would ever end.

All too often a thud was followed by a scream. Robin shuddered each time, wondering if he knew the owner of the voice. Was it Banan, old Alex Brady, one of the Logan brothers? Was the next scream going to be his? At least Agnes was safe in the keep with the rest of the women and children. Robin wished only to awaken from the nightmare and find himself back in his cottage sitting by a warm fire next to Agnes.

A boot kicked Robin's foot bringing him to his senses. He looked up into the grizzled face of one of the Baron's regulars. He could smell the stench of the man's breath. "Get up," the arms-man barked. "The Duke is here. Every man to gates!"

Shaun glared back at the burly arms-man. Their eyes locked for the briefest of moments before the other man turned and continued down the rampart. Robin glanced back the way he had come. Most of the merlons between him and the north west tower had sustained damage. The rampart next to the tower was completely exposed for a span twice the length of a man, but the wood beams supporting the rampart had held.

Down at the west gate, scores of lancers were forming a line two abreast. The Baron himself was mounting a horse at the head of the column. His silver armour and the great white plume on his helm made him easy to recognize. Men were leaving the walls and pouring into the courtyard. They gathered to either side of the lancers. *Gods, they were going to open the gates.* He looked out at the advancing Dog Soldiers. They had stopped just out of bow range and half of them had turned back toward their camps.

Shaun put his hand on Robin's shoulder. "Come on Robin," he said.

Robin looked back toward the arms-man who had stopped to stare up into the sky. Most of the other men were doing the same. Robin cupped a hand over his eyes to try and see what they were looking at. What he saw froze his blood. A giant winged creature was coming straight at them. A cry went up from the wall. "Dragon!"

The dragon sailed over the castle so fast it was little more than a blur. The wind from its passing nearly knocked Robin off his feet. A small number of defenders regained their wits in time to let loose a few arrows and crossbow bolts, but any that struck the beast bounced off as if the creature were made of stone. Once the dragon had passed over the castle, it flew up, banked and then came back again.

When the creature had first flown by, Robin was so terrified he couldn't move, but after that first pass, something within him changed. It was as if a previously bolted door in his mind had opened. Detached from the battle, and all those around him, he watched the beast approach. Time seemed to slow down until the dragon hung motionless in the air above him. At that moment a small pink spot on its great belly caught his eye. The patch of pink grew until it seemed he could almost reach out and touch it.

Robin didn't remember having raised his bow, but it was up with an arrow nocked and drawn back. He released the shaft and the dragon suddenly shot past. A cloud of arrows flew at the beast, but not a one penetrated its thick scaly hide, except for his. He couldn't explain how he knew it was his, but he did. In the wink of an eye he had seen the shaft sink into the creature's belly clear up to the grey goose feathers. The dragon dipped as the arrow struck. The screech it made was deafening.

The dragon roared, and then turned back. Its massive dull red wings seemed to fill the morning sky. Huge green eyes locked onto Robin, and then he heard a voice. It sounded oddly feminine. *Nasty little halfling*, it shrieked inside his head, but Robin didn't have time to think about it. The dragon approached spewing forth a river of fire. The air in Robin's lungs grew so hot he thought they might burst.

"May the Gods save us," Shaun screamed, as grabbed Robin's arm and leapt off the rampart pulling Robin along with him.

Chapter 28

RODNEY

Under the cover of darkness, Rodney and his men had moved soundlessly into position. Two sun-marks earlier, Silas had sent Talbot, Nicholas and Liam to find and eliminate any sentries the Imperials had seen fit to post west of their camps. Rodney had sent Tyko, Yvon and Shark-tooth further to the north. Edmond's men would perform a similar action to the south. The Imperial Captain must have been very confident, because all six men had returned without encountering a single sentry. Silas had laughed when Nicholas informed him that the Imperials had even been so kind as to clear a staging area for them in the forest behind their camp.

Once the scouts had returned, Silas and Rodney led their men along the river to a position directly west of the castle. Silas and most of the men would remain there until the Imperials had begun their attack. They numbered near four hundred, as Edmond had placed two hundred of his archers under Silas's command. The east wall of Montcre faced a wide ravine running north and south. That left only three walls to defend. To the north lay the widest stretch of open ground between the castle and the forest. It seemed the most logical place to execute Rodney's plan.

Separating from the others, Rodney led his party further north to take up a position well back in the trees. From there they could ride forth with little danger of encountering Imperial forces. It would also give them plenty of open ground in which to work. If they were going to entice the FireDrake to fly low enough for Rodney's plan to work, they would need every bit of it.

Rodney leaned back resting one hand on the horn of his saddle. The other held a freshly carved spruce war lance. The long and slender steel tip had been ground to a sharp needle point. Lionel was to his right, with five more mounted Daemon knights waiting behind them in the predawn darkness. There was still insufficient light to see their faces, but Rodney didn't need to; he had jousted with every one of them and knew their abilities well. All five men were seasoned knights, good with a lance and expert horsemen. Lionel's brother William was a former champion, as was Silas's brother Florence. Jason's brother Garrett was the finest horseman in the order, and the only other man that could ride Thunder. Daniel Buxton and Dominic Jenour were both contenders every year for Master-of-the-lance.

Twenty more Balorians crouched close on either side, yet they were not well armed for battle. Some had bows across their backs but little or no armour. Their only other visible weapons were the daggers hanging from their belts. Rodney's party was not here to fight Dog Soldiers; they had come prepared to battle a FireDrake. Morton and six other squires carried spare war lances over their shoulders, the wood so fresh that the sap still oozed from one or two. Six men held two long stout pine poles, equally as freshly cut. The rest shouldered coils of rope and a bundle so heavy that it took four men to carry it between them.

Hidden in the trees, they waited for the dawn and a glimpse of the FireDrake. To Rodney's surprise, when the sun rose, the FireDrake was nowhere to be seen.

Lionel leaned over and spoke in a hushed tone. "Perhaps the beast has returned to Drakenmount."

Rodney allowed himself a smile. "Let us hope it is so. I must admit that I would be much relieved." He turned back to the other knights. "Unless the FireDrake appears, when the attack begins we will ride south to join up with Sir Silas."

There was much lighthearted whispering among the men following Rodney's words. They were brave men and had all volunteered to face the FireDrake, but he expected a missed opportunity would sit well enough with everyone.

After a moment of thought Rodney turned to his squire. "Mort, I am leaving you in charge of the rest of the men. You know what to do." He paused. "If things go badly, return to the Duke's camp as best you can."

The Imperials didn't attack with the dawn as Edmond had predicted. Instead they hammered at the castle walls relentlessly with three massive siege weapons. Though Rodney had never seen one before, his father had described such machines in detail. Rodney and his men watched helplessly as the mangonel did its work. There were far too many Dog Soldiers around the machine nearest them. They would have to wait and hope that most of the men manning the mangonel would leave to join their countrymen when the time came to attack the castle.

Boulder after boulder pounded the castle wall. Rodney knew the Duke would not sound his charge until the Imperials had spread out their forces. The key to their stratagem was in first eliminating small pockets of men, like those manning the siege weapons or left behind in their camps, while their main force was advancing on the castle. With any luck they could kill their commander before the Imperial soldiers knew what was happening.

Edmond was counting on the Dog Soldiers being caught in a deadly three-way crossfire between the south woods, their main camp and the castle. The Imperials had too great an advantage in numbers, so the Duke wanted to be able to do as much damage as possible and still have the option of retreating. If the enemy concentrated their forces in either direction, they were to withdraw. If they split their forces, then they would fight.

From his vantage point Rodney could not see the south side of Montcre, but both the north and west walls were near ruin. Large gapping holes could be seen along the battlements. It wasn't hard to figure out that holding for even one more day was not an option.

After a full sun-mark of bombardment, the Imperials finally attacked. To the north of the castle, near Rodney's position, they had left twenty men behind to operate the mangonel. The machine continued to launch its deadly boulders. When the Imperials reached the walls, the defenders would not be able to stop them, but there wasn't much Rodney and his men could do except possibly disable the mangonel.

Rodney nudged Thunder forward. He and the other knights had just cleared the trees when horns sounded from the west, then everything seemed to happen at once. As if summoned by the horn, the FireDrake appeared in the sky above their heads. Rodney watched in awe as it passed low overhead and then sailed on toward the castle. It was his first close look at it. This one looked every bit as formidable as Grigor, if not more so.

The Imperials had formed two lines. A larger group was to the southwest while a smaller group, of less than two thousand, formed up to the northwest. The western line had advanced to a point midway between the castle and the forest. There it had stopped. The Dog Soldiers appeared just as reluctant to get in the FireDrake's path as anyone else. Distracted, they failed to notice the volley of arrows that showered down on the unprotected backs of the men left behind in their main camp. There were less than a hundred. Taken unawares, they were quickly cut down.

Rodney turned Thunder and barked orders to his men. "Use your bows," he yelled. "Kill the men on the Mangonel."

Those with bows dropped their burdens and nocked arrows. After three quick volleys the Dog Soldiers were all down. The other men ran forward to finish off any who still lived.

"Over there," Rodney yelled pointing into the clearing. "As we planned and as quickly as you can!"

Men shouldered their bows and ran into the field with the lances, poles and ropes. Rodney didn't wait to watch. "Knights to me," he bellowed as he charged toward the castle. He couldn't afford the time to look back and see who followed.

The archers under Silas's command had advanced from the trees into the abandoned camps. They let loose two volleys into the backs of the Imperial line before the Dog Soldiers were even aware things had gone terribly wrong.

As Rodney neared the mass of Imperials, a flash of an officer's red braid drew his eye. It looked like Ramell. He was rallying his men into a formation of spear men four deep. Nearly eight hundred strong, they charged back toward their camp at a dead run. Behind the spear men, a row of archers sent a volley of arrows over their heads. Silas's men scrambled for cover as hundreds of arrows rained down. Luckily, most fell short.

Rodney swore. Another officer was leading an additional thousand from the southern lines to join up with Ramell in the assault on Silas's position. He was too far away for Rodney to be certain, but he had a feeling the second officer was Kaspar. With their combined forces they would easily overrun Silas and his men. They would be butchered to a man.

At that moment Edmond led a charge of fifteen hundred screaming men who had sprung up from the tall grass to the south. In numbers they were now evenly matched with the Imperial forces on the south side of the castle. The second thousand who had been charging toward the camp faltered. Kaspar was turning his men south toward the new threat, leaving Ramell and his men to fend for themselves.

The first of Ramell's men entered the camp. At the same time the Duke's Captain burst from the trees to the southwest leading a charge of eighty lancers. Ramell diverted two hundred of his men to his left flank to intercept them. It was then that Silas called his charge. Archers sent one last volley aloft before drawing their blades, as two scores of mounted Daemon Knights and squires thundered through the camp to hammer into the advancing Imperials. The Dog Soldiers were unskilled in fighting mounted men. Had they used long pikes they could have stopped the charge, but their short stabbing spears were ineffective.

When the two mounted groups hit the Imperial formation it disintegrated.

Rodney charged recklessly into the enemy's right flank. The tip of his lance snapped off when it struck a soldier, lifting him from the ground. Another half score of spear men went down under Thunder's roughshod hooves. Rodney cast his useless lance aside and drew his sword. That's when he caught sight of Jason in the thick of the fighting, hacking left and right from the saddle. What was the fool doing? He could barely walk! Ramell was not far away and fighting to reach him. *Sylvia, you have given me an impossible task. No one can save Jason from himself.*

Jason's horse reared and he went down in a sea of Dog Soldiers. Though Rodney wanted to ride to his friend's aid, between them lay hundreds of men locked in arm to arm combat. A horn sounded from the castle. Rodney turned his head in time to see the gates flung open and two score of lancers ride out. They formed a ragged line and then charged abreast toward the rear of the Imperial archers.

Once the lancers had cleared the gates, hundreds of men armed with bows and crossbows poured out of the castle. When they were in range, they dropped to their knees forming a line. Rodney thought he recognized the burly sergeant from the tavern standing in the forefront with raised sword. When the sword fell, a volley of arrows and bolts arched into the air to land on the heads of the Imperial archers. The Dog Soldiers turned and sent back a volley of their own. Ten of the lancers from the castle went down, but lacking the power of long bows, the shafts launched at the Icarian archers fell short. The Icarians sent another volley.

With Ramell's men overrun, the remaining Balorian and Icarian bowmen from Silas's group moved forward and began to pepper them with arrows. The Captain and about sixty lancers were bearing down on them from the southwest. Silas was not far behind with his knights, coming from the east. Even though the Dog Soldiers had superior numbers, when hit on three sides by mounted men their resolve broke. Imperials began to flee the field in ones and twos, and then en masse.

To the south, the battle was not going as well for Edmond. Rodney could see he was being forced back by the larger Imperial forces. Captain Doyle must have seen it too. He gathered his lancers and those from the castle and charged south. With their blood still hot for battle, about twenty Daemon Knights followed them. Rodney looked back to where he had last seen Jason, but could not pick him out of the mass of men. His head snapped up at the sound of a roar above him.

The FireDrake was attacking the castle. As a result the battlements were completely ablaze. Hoping there was still time to put his plan into action, Rodney pushed a Dog Soldier back with his boot and broke away from the battle. Sheathing his sword, he galloped up to the line of Icarian archers. Thunder reared up when he pulled back on the reins in front of the sergeant.

"I fight for Icarus," Rodney screamed. "Loose your arrows upon the FireDrake. We need to draw him away from the castle and to the north." Without waiting for a reply, he spun Thunder around and rode back to gather the other knights.

When the FireDrake made its next pass, it was met with a cloud of arrows. The shafts just bounced off the hard scales, but they did get its attention. It banked and flew straight at the archers preceded by a long spear of fire spewing forth from its mouth. The centre of the line disappeared in smoke and flame. The rest of the men broke and ran in every direction to escape.

Rodney and the six other knights had formed a line directly in the FireDrake's path. Once he was sure the beast had seen them, he turned and raced north. Thunder was terrified and ran as if possessed. Rodney felt the heat of the fire singe the hair on his forearms. When he looked back, only Lionel and Florence remained. Smoke billowed from Florence's mail and helm.

At first Rodney feared there had not been enough time for his men to set the trap. Then he spotted the two red flags up ahead. Between them stood seven lances, all point first in the dirt. Even though the FireDrake was almost upon them, Rodney reined in and plucked one of the lances from the ground.

The other two knights passed him as he turned to face the oncoming FireDrake. "Now!" Rodney screamed. Ropes that had been invisible in the dirt drew tight. From where the red flags had been, two forty foot long pine poles rose into the air. Between them was stretched a net fashioned from hemp ropes as thick as a man's thumb. The FireDrake hit the net with such force it ripped the poles from the ground and dragged along a half score of men still clinging to the guide ropes. Rodney just managed to get out of the way as the FireDrake's massive body crashed into the dirt, still caught in the net. One of the beast's great wings lifted twice and then lay still.

After calming Thunder down, Rodney approached the unmoving FireDrake cautiously. He kept his lance levelled at the beast's chest. One great green eye opened and then the FireDrake was on its feet. Its speed was incredible, even with one wing still entangled in the net. It was difficult to keep the lance level when Thunder reared, but he managed to do so and still keep his horse under control. Rodney charged as the FireDrake lunged with its maw wide open. The jaws snapped shut just as his lance struck its chest. Rodney was yanked from the saddle and slammed to the ground. The world tilted, blurred and then went quiet.

When he opened his eyes, the first thing Rodney saw was a row of teeth, massive teeth. The image blurred and when he could see clearly again, the FireDrake's mouth was covered in blood and its great pink forked tongue hung to one side. The eyes were closed and three lances protruded from its chest. His was helm impaled on one of the incisors. Remembering what Aldus had told him about a FireDrake's poisonous saliva Rodney quickly felt his face and scalp for wounds, but he could find none.

When Rodney turned his head, which took much effort, he saw the body of Thunder laying not far away. The poor animal's head was torn clean away. The blood on the FireDrake must have been his. A hand appeared before his face. It was Lionel. "Can you stand?" his friend asked.

Rodney gripped the offered hand and pulled himself shakily to his feet. "I feel fit enough. Is the battle over. How did we fair?"

"Yes, it is done. We routed them, but with heavy losses. Silas has been gravely injured, I'm afraid."

"What happened?" Rodney asked holding his head. It was pounding like a drum.

"The FireDrake swept him from his mount. His neck is broken."

"Take me to him," Rodney said.

Lionel led Rodney across the field to a circle of knights that had formed near the castle gates. Silas lay unmoving on the ground. He was on his back with his eyes closed as if asleep. His son knelt by his side. On the other side lay the body of Sir Maynard. The other knight's chain mail was ripped open and the broken remains of an Imperial spear protruded from his chest. His dead eyes stared out at nothing. Rodney knelt down between the two fallen knights. "Silas," he said softly.

The older man's eyelids fluttered and then opened. "Rodney," he said weakly. "Rodney, is that you?"

Rodney lifted his leader's limp hand. "It is," he said.

"I told you that beast would be my end," Silas gasped. "You are Leader now."

Rodney looked at Gregory and put a hand on the young man's shoulder. When he looked back, Silas was dead. Rodney let go of Silas's hand. "If the battle is done then we best gather the men and see to our dead."

Chapter 29

GAMEL

Wearing only a thin white silk robe, snow-white velvet slippers and a dark scowl, the Emperor stood staring into the black water of the scrying pool in his private chambers. His mood had turned foul as he watched the battle in Icarus unfold. He had chastised himself more than once for not detecting the gathering army in the forest in time to warn Captain Beck. Now Raoul was gone, along with most of his legion. Gamel regretted losing the men; not that he cared for them, or even mourned their loss, but the legion belonged to him and he didn't like giving up what was his. He wanted Icarus in ruins to prevent them from interfering with his plans. He would have gladly traded the lives of every last one of them, twice over, if it would have achieved his goal.

Gamel had recognized the false sell-sword in Captain Beck's tent two days back for what he was. Having taken a great interest in the war between Carpathia and Balor, Gamel identified the man as once being one of Balor's more formidable fighters. The man was much older, but Gamel never forgot a face. Perhaps it had been unwise, but their numbers had seemed so insignificant that he allowed curiosity to overcome better judgement. He had let them live just to see what they would do, for his own entertainment. It was an indulgence which he regretted, but one he would soon rectify.

Their new leader was interesting. Even Gamel had to admit he was impressed with how easily the young knight had defeated the FireDrake. It had been a particularly large one too. Over the years Gamel had tested his magic against them in various ways, always covertly of course, but had found magic to be totally ineffective. They were immune to everything magical. The only exception was Aedon, of course.

Until witnessing the battle, Gamel had believed the FireDrakes to be invincible. He had never before considered the possibility of sending mere men against them. In light of recent events however, he wondered if he had placed more value on them than they were truly worth. But, then again, dragon-fire was devastating. Had the beast continued the assault on the castle, instead of foolishly chasing after the knights, the castle and its defenders would have been totally destroyed. With an army of FireDrakes at his command, his legions would be invincible. These Daemon Knights had done well against a single FireDrake, but with hundreds at his disposal no one could stand against him. He would just have to train them to keep well away from the ground.

Magdalen was going to be furious, of course. The loss of the FireDrake was going to make it even more difficult to manipulate her. She had developed a fondness for the creatures. Some sort of feminine weakness he supposed. He would have to think of something to divert her anger. Perhaps revenge against her pet's killer would serve his purpose. Men she had no fondness for at all.

Leaning over the edge of his scrying pool to more closely examine the creature's remains, Gamel noticed something laying in the dirt by its great head. It was a small thing. The remains of a gauntlet lost by one of the knights during the struggle. Most of the metal trappings had been torn away and only the fingers retained the metal links. *This could prove useful.*

Movement to the right caught his eye. An emaciated mongrel sniffed at the headless corpse of a horse. The filthy creature's scarred tawny hide hung in loose folds over protruding ribs. The animal was old, arthritic and starved near to death. Somehow it managed to find the strength to tear a piece of flesh from the corpse.

Though his legion was decimated, roughly four hundred had managed to escape the slaughter. "Now let me see where you are," Gamel said to himself. A series of ripples disrupted the smooth surface of the pool. With each ripple came a new image. Various groups of soldiers scattered between the castle and Escarpe pass appeared and disappeared. "There," Gamel said finally.

The pool revealed a soldier with a tattered red cloth hanging from one of his braids. He was leading a small band of fifty-odd men north toward the pass. They halted when they caught up to a score of Imperials standing around a young lieutenant who had collapsed from his wounds. He was very pale from loss of blood. Gamel watched with interest as the first officer approached. He stopped ten feet away from the dying man.

"Captain Beck made a mistake promoting you, Ramell," the officer Gamel had been following said. A cruel smile crept onto the lieutenant's face. "You were never officer material," he said, holding out his hand to the soldier standing next to him. The soldier handed him his bow. The officer selected an arrow from the man's quiver, and in one swift motion sent the shaft straight into the prone man's heart. He died instantly.

The officer looked up at the dead Lieutenant's former men. "You follow me now," he said. No one offered any arguments.

Gamel moved his hand over the pool and the image moved to one side. On the other side was the image of the slain FireDrake. He focussed his mind on the spot and his fetch was there in an instant. The gauntlet lay just below his transparent slippered feet. He looked over at the dog, and projected his thoughts into its primitive mind. *Come here little fellow. You have nothing to fear from me. I am your friend.*

In its weakened state, the animal offered no resistance. Tail between its legs, it hobbled over and lay at his feet with a soft pathetic whine. Gamel created visions of soft tender meat in the dog's mind, until saliva dripped from its mouth. Next he placed the image of the officer's location into the animal's mind. *Pick up the glove. Yes, that's it. Now go! As fast as you can!*

As the dog lumbered off with the glove in its mouth, Gamel returned to his body to follow the dog's progress in the scrying pool. He maintained the link with the creature's mind giving it guidance when it took a wrong turn or images of food when it slowed. When the animal faltered he lent it strength. Gamel saw through its eyes; felt the pounding of the animal's heart, the excruciating pain in its joints and lungs. Just as it appeared the wretched creature could go no farther, the Lieutenant came into view. He and his men had stopped to rest by a pond next to a waterfall. The dog limped up to them and dropped the gauntlet at the Lieutenant's feet.

Gamel released the dog's mind, focussed on the image in the pool, and then closed his eyes. When his eyes opened, he was there. Fear registered on the faces of the men when they saw his ghostly image hovering over the water. Gamel smiled, savouring the taste of their fear. The officer had the presence of mind to bring his fist to his chest in salute. "Emperor!"

"What is your name, Lieutenant?"

"Kaspar Brun."

"Well Kaspar, how strong is your desire to redeem yourself?"

The lieutenant dropped to his knees and clasped his hands before him. "Your greatness, I live only to serve you." Spittle ran down his chin as he spoke. "I will kill them all for you, great one, but I need more men."

"Revenge will be yours, Kaspar. You need only follow my instructions."

"Anything you ask, great one." Kaspar's eyes were aglow with a fanatical light. "I am yours to command."

Gamel looked into the officer's eyes and saw madness there. *Very good.* "First you will select your best runner and send him to deliver this gauntlet to a friend of mine. She lives in the swamps to the west of the Hagstroms. There are still others from your legion on their way here. You will wait and gather as many as you can before proceeding through the pass. When you reach Nagual, you will head north and find the Second legion. We will speak again then."

The lieutenant slapped a fist to his chest. "As you command!"

Satisfied, Gamel returned to his body. Hungry and thirsty, he pulled on a braided cord hanging nearby. Lusias appeared even before the cord stopped moving. "Yes, Great one," his servant said with a bow.

"I am famished, Lusias," Gamel growled. "Bring me food and wine."

Lusias bowed again and ran from the chamber. Gamel looked back into the pool. Another image formed. In the plains, the Second legion was moving toward Icarus.

Chapter 30

RODNEY

When the Duke learned that the Balorians lacked a qualified healer, he sent them an Icarian Physician. The healer's first duty was to inspect Rodney from head to toe. He looked closely at his wounds, checked for broken bones, then poked and prodded all of Rodney's soft spots. Finally satisfied, the physician announced, that other than a few bruised ribs and a rather large lump on his head, Rodney was just fine. Once Morton had been similarly inspected, Rodney instructed him to make a list of the slain. As Leader, he would be expected to conduct the last rites for their dead.

At midday, those who were fit gathered at the place where the bodies of their countrymen had been laid out. Forty-three Balorians had perished in the fighting. Another forty men were injured badly enough to require surgery. The Duke's physician was seeing to the more serious injuries while Garrick tended to broken bones and the lesser wounds.

Included in the dead were seven knights. To Rodney's great relief, Jason had miraculously survived and was not among them. He was covered in cuts and scrapes however, and would have a new batch of scars on his arms and legs. The gash on Jason's leg had opened up again, so Garrick had sewn it closed and applied a salve to prevent infection. He assured Rodney that, aside from the old wound, the damage was minimal and Jason would be able to ride in a couple of days.

For many of the wounded being cared for by the physician, it would take a fortnight, if not a moon, for a full recovery. When he had everyone gathered together Rodney advised those still fit that they would leave for Drakenmount in three days, once their obligation to Icarus had ended. The injured would remain behind and return to Balor as soon as they were well enough to travel.

The knights had taken what items they wanted from the belongings of their fallen brethren. When Carl Daemon died, each one of his followers took something from his personal effects. Since then, it was a custom to honour and remember a fellow Daemon Knight. Silas's sword now hung from his son's belt. Gregory had his father's helm tucked under his arm as well. Herman's mount had broken a leg, so he had claimed Silas's horse. It was a fine animal, another destrier from the Lambert herd. In hindsight, Rodney wished he had thought of it himself. With Thunder gone he needed a new mount. Instead he had pulled the gauntlet from Silas's left hand to replace the one he had lost.

The people of Balor still practised the ancient Sidonese funeral rites. Rodney knelt by each body and placed a copper coin under their tongues. The coin was for the ferryman who would carry them across the Mirror river in the afterlife. The dead were then placed on a funeral pyre and covered in oil. Rodney stood before the pyre with his arms outstretched and his face to the sky. As Leader, it was up to him to speak with the Gods on behalf of the dead.

"Hear me Turlough, God of war," Rodney intoned. "Hear me Ulrich, God of death. I ask you to accept the souls of forty-three brave Balorians." He unrolled a list that Morton had compiled. "Sir Silas Vennell, Sir Maynard Emson, Sir Dominic Jenour, Sir William Tait..."

Pausing at William's name, Rodney glanced at Lionel. His friend bowed his head upon hearing his brother's name. "Sir Garrett Lambert..." Rodney stopped, suddenly feeling heat in his eyes. He could see Jason with a arm around Morton's shoulder. His best friend had lost an older brother and the squire his father.

After he had read all forty-three names, Rodney stepped back and nodded to Herman who, along with his brother Edward, had been standing by the mound of bodies holding burning brand. At Rodney's signal, they cast them onto the pyre. The oil caught quickly. The mound of dead burst into flames as if fanned by the breath of the Gods. Slowly, one by one, the men withdrew as the crackling fire consumed the bodies.

When Rodney noticed the twins standing nearby, he waved them over. Every one of his retainers had survived the battle, for which he was thankful. Shark-tooth had reappeared, as if by magic, once the Duke's men had released the other scouts. Rodney's grandfather had been right. Trying to catch a Kelatch was like trying to catch smoke.

"I will need another mount," Rodney said to Tyko. "See if you and Shark-tooth can find the draft horse from our wagon."

"I believe it is with the others," Tyko replied.

"Good. Bring it to me if you please. Yvon, you and John will assist me in retrieving my tack from Thunder."

Yvon and John followed Rodney as he crossed the field. It was not hard to locate the body, laying as it did next to the gigantic red lump of the FireDrake. They were halfway there when Rodney spotted Garrick. Coll was sitting on a rock next to him. The tall guardsman was stitching up a cut in the older man's left shoulder. As Rodney approached them, Coll tried to stand. Rodney couldn't help but notice the wince of pain.

"Stay still, blast it," Garrick barked as Coll sagged back down.

"How is he?" Rodney asked.

Garrick turned to Rodney. "The wound is clean and should heal well, but he has a broken collar bone. I can do nothing for that. Perhaps the physician can do more, but I doubt it. I would wager that it will be another moon before Coll can travel with any degree of comfort."

"Bah," Coll muttered. "It's nothing. I'll be as strong as an auroch in a few days."

Rodney smiled. "Father always said you were indestructible Coll, but I think we best let the physician decide." Coll turned his head and grunted.

Rodney's smile faded. "Garrick, how many more have you to tend?"

"Coll is the last. The old goat wouldn't let me take care of him until I had seen to everyone else first."

"When you have seen to his needs, please join us over by the FireDrake. I need to recover my gear from Thunder."

"I am nearly done here. I will not be but a few more moments, Sir Rodney."

Thunder's headless body was covered in crows. Rodney shooed them away in disgust, and then shuddered at what he saw. Other creatures had obviously been at the corpse as well. His once proud stallion had been reduced to nothing but carrion. A short time later, with the aid of Garrick's pike, the four of them raised the heavy body enough to remove his saddle, tack and armour.

Tyko and Shark-tooth had found the draft horse. Rodney looked the big gelding over. He had a few minor cuts and scrapes, but seemed sound. The gelding was well muscled and just as large as Thunder had been, but it was far from being a trained warhorse. The armour might fit, but Rodney would never be able to depend on it in battle as he had with Thunder. Sadness suddenly overwhelmed him. The destrier had been a gift from Sir Frederic on the day of Rodney's knighting. Thunder had been much more than just a magnificent horse; he had been a living breathing link with his father. When Rodney returned to Vincent Castle, he would now be truly alone. Thunder had sired many offspring. There were two strong mares and a three year old stallion in his stables, but it would never be the same.

As Rodney was adjusting the cinch strap, Captain Doyle hailed him. "Sir Rodney, may I have a word with you?" Rodney nodded as the captain approached. "Baron Morgan formally requests that you, and all your brave men, join us for a victory feast right after sundown. He extends to you, and your Second, the honour of seats at the head table next to himself, and my Lord Duke."

Rodney didn't feel up to attending a feast, but he could not refuse such an offer without giving offence. Such a refusal would also be unfair to his men. They had earned a good meal and a little diversion. It was just the thing to help forget the loss of so many good friends and comrades, at least for the length of an evening. It would be good for morale.

"We would be honoured to join you in your repast," Rodney replied. Captain Doyle bowed and then strode away without another word. The Captain's words had reminded him of something. Rodney had one more task yet to complete. He needed the counsel of their most senior knight. He had to find Herman.

Rodney found the big man tending to Midnight. "He is a fine animal," Rodney said as he approached.

Herman looked up. "Ah, Rodney. Yes, he is that indeed. From the same line as your own Thunder. My condolences to you on losing such a fine mount." His face clouded over. "Please forgive me. I should not have taken him. You are Leader now, and by rights he is yours." He patted the horse on the neck affectionately before offering Rodney the reins.

"I already have a replacement," Rodney replied, waving the reins away. "Silas would have wanted you to have him in any regard."

Herman tilted his head in respect. "You are most gracious, Rodney. Very much like your father."

Rodney smiled, well pleased with the compliment. "I will need to select a Second, and you are the most experienced man we have."

"I wondered when you might get around to asking," Herman replied, shaking his head. "I will tell you the same thing I told Silas. I have no head for tactics, and no desire to lead. Besides, I am old enough to be your father, and it would be unseemly to serve as your Second. I think the Baron had the right of it. You need a younger man. One with a good head on his shoulders."

"Well, it just so happens I do have someone in mind, but I would like to hear your thoughts on the matter."

"I would be most pleased to offer you my humble opinion. Who do you

191

have in mind?

⚜   ⚜   ⚜

It was much later, just after dusk, when Rodney led the Balorians through the castle's charred gate. Lionel let out a low whistle as they entered the courtyard. Many outbuildings, including the stables, had burned to the ground, no doubt the result of the FireDrake's attack. Ropes had been strung between posts to tether the horses. As he dismounted, Rodney noticed that even the ground was scorched. It was as if the very earth had been turned to ash.

Much work had been done to clear away the dead and debris, but it would take considerably more before the castle would be returned to its former condition. Captain Doyle met Rodney at the entrance to the keep in order to escort him and his men to the great hall. The inner keep, though blackened on the outer walls, seemed intact. Within the walls of the keep was a large square courtyard, in which countless tables and benches had been hastily constructed from rough cut boards. Much of the wood was charred and probably came from the west wall's ramparts, which had collapsed.

Rodney thought over his decision for the tenth time. He had never intended to ask Herman to be Second, and had been concerned that the elder knight would expect it. The big man had surprised him in that regard, and then had agreed whole heartedly with his choice of another. So far Rodney had been tight lipped about the matter. Only he, Herman and his new Second were aware of his decision.

Both Lionel and Jason were trusted friends, but Jason was much too rash and Lionel was no more a tactician than Herman. Rodney could not allow his personal feelings to get in the way of making such an important choice. He had selected the best man he could think of to lead their company in the event that he too should be killed. Rodney had put his own personal likes and dislikes aside for the good of all. He had chosen Martin as his Second, and Jason was going to be furious.

Captain Doyle introduced Rodney to his host, Baron Morgan. Though the Baron stood almost a head shorter, he had arms like a blacksmith, a chest like a war horse, and no doubt out weighed Rodney considerably. A bushy black beard, sprinkled with hints of grey, covered most of his face. It was so thick it hid most of his mouth along with the tip of his nose. The burly Baron welcomed Rodney with a bear hug that squeezed every bit of air from his lungs.

Baron Morgan introduced Rodney to his wife, the Baroness Annette, and then to the Duchess Wynne, who had just arrived from Zindale castle by coach.

The family resemblance between the two women was striking. They both had thick straw coloured hair, blue eyes, and round rosy cheeks. They appeared to be in their early forties and were probably sisters, cousins at the very least. Rodney bowed and kissed each of their outstretched hands.

His welcome from the Duke came with open arms and a wide grin. "Icarus is forever in your debt," Edmond said, before expressing his condolences for Silas in a more somber tone. "I was saddened to hear about Sir Silas. He was a brave and noble knight. I regret that I didn't have the chance to get to know him better."

"Yes, it is a great loss," Rodney replied with feeling. After a moment of silence he turned his head back, searching for Martin. His newly appointed Second was standing next to Herman, just behind Lionel and Jason. Rodney motioned for him to come forward. Martin smiled and squeezed between the other two knights.

"May I introduce Sir Martin Neville, my Second." As he spoke, Rodney watched Jason's face from the corner of his eye. First it registered shock, and then ran through three shades of purple. Rodney turned away to avoid making eye contact.

Once they had completed the formal introductions, Baron Morgan led the way to the head table. The Duke and Duchess were seated with Rodney and Martin on the Baron's right, while Annette, Captain Doyle and two other officers sat to his left. Below the head table, the remaining Balorian knights sat to the right and left mixed in with other Icarian nobles and officers. The rest of the hall was filled with the lowborn who spilled out of the open doors and into the courtyard. Among the commoners there was little segregation. The Balorians shared tables with Icarian arms-men and local farmers.

As Rodney looked around the room, he noticed Gregory seated near the doors. The knight sat next to a young Icarian maiden. Rodney recognized the two men sitting across the table from Gregory as the silver haired man and his rather large friend from the tavern. Gregory had better be careful. The big blond man was dangerous, and he didn't like the way the two Icarians were scowling at the young knight. Gregory appeared too engrossed in what the young lady was saying to take notice.

Silas's son was soon forgotten when Rodney's eyes locked onto Jason's. His friend returned an uncharacteristic blank stare, but his eyes hinted at anger that boiled beneath the facade. Rodney had been unable to bring himself to discuss his choice beforehand with Jason, though it was unlikely to have made a difference even had he done so. He would have to smooth the waters between them over the course of the next few days.

Throughout the customary speeches and toasts that preceded the feast, Rodney remained relatively quiet. Baron Morgan had opened his wine cellars and was providing plenty for all. Even though the festivities had been underway for only a short while, some of the Balorians were already displaying the inebriating effects of Icarian wine.

After draining his first glass quickly, so as to not offend his host, Rodney sipped the second slowly. He found the wine to be remarkably strong, and the first glass had left him feeling light headed. Balorians were not accustomed to such strong drink. He hoped his countrymen had the sense to not overindulge. There was a great deal of preparation to be done over the next two days before they could continue their journey. Martin seemed to be restraining himself, but Jason and the rest appeared to be emptying their glasses with wild abandon. No doubt they would regret it in the morning. Fortunately, the food arrived before any of the knights fell off their stools.

The meal consisted primarily of young juicy roast pig, honeyed duck, dried fruit and cheeses. Rodney picked at his trencher for a while and then struck up a conversation with Edmond. He had to shout to be heard over all the noise. "Between the dead and wounded, we have lost near half our company. How might I entice your Grace to join us in our quest? Perhaps you could send Captain Doyle with a few hundred archers. It seems to me we have a common foe in this sorceress at Drakenmount."

"I agree. We both seem to have a stake in it, but my hands are tied, Rodney. I await the King's men by his command. Once they arrive, I will lead them through the Escarpe pass to guard against further incursions by the Empire's forces. The King fears they are massing in the plains for a full scale invasion, and I have to agree with him. FiredDrakes hold the northwest passes. With the trade routes to the sea closed to us, the King cannot allow the Escarpe pass to fall into the Emperor's hands."

Realizing it was fruitless to try and change Edmond's mind, Rodney changed the subject. "We could certainly use more ropes and steel tipped lances. They seem to be the only weapons effective against FireDrakes."

"I would be most pleased to provide you with all the weapons and supplies you need for your journey," the Duke replied. "It is the least I can do, but lances are only useful on the ground. Have you considered ballistas?"

"FireDrakes move too quickly and are uncommonly intelligent. I believe they would recognize such a weapon for what it was and not approach near enough for it to be effective, beside which, transporting such a device through the mountains would be awkward at best."

"You are probably right," the Duke said with a sigh. "I must say that I am surprised at the intelligence you say these beasts possess. I would never have guessed they could actually communicate with a human. They seemed far less dangerous, when in my ignorance, I believed them to be just dumb beasts."

"That is why our mission is so important," Rodney said, raising his voice as the jugglers, tumblers and jesters paraded before the head table while a group of musicians played a merry piece with their lutes and lyres. Knights and officers alike banged their fists on the tables and stomped their feet, more or less in time with the music.

The Baron coughed. "Pardon me, your Grace, but I understand this was not the first occasion Sir Rodney has faced one of these monsters."

"Ah, yes, that," Rodney said. "Well, I must admit we lost our first encounter. We were lucky the FireDrake Grigor was not intent on killing us at the time."

"Well you've more than made up for it this day, I would say," the Baron replied, with a broad smile that showed a row of perfect teeth. "My men have come up with a name for you."

"They have?" Rodney said, feeling a bit embarrassed. "What is it they call me?"

The Baron's smile widened. "Drake Slayer."

"I did not kill the beast on my own," Rodney protested. "There were twenty men on the ropes and three lances in the FireDrake's belly when the deed was done, not to mention the four good knights who perished."

"Ah, that may be so, but your lance was the first," the Baron said, picking up his glass and lifting it into the air. "Drake Slayer," he bellowed.

"Drake Slayer," the others at the table echoed while lifting their glasses.

"Drake Slayer!" roared the people in the hall. "Drake Slayer."

Rodney's attention was suddenly drawn to the strange look on Edmond's face. His lips were moving, but the noise in the hall was so loud, even Rodney couldn't hear his words. Then the music and the shouting suddenly died. The hall went deathly quiet. Rodney followed Edmond's wide-eyed stare to the centre of the room. A ghostly image hovered in the air above the heads of the people seated in the middle of the hall.

The translucent milk white image of the most beautiful woman Rodney had ever seen held his eyes captive. She was dressed in a full length long sleeved gown that was cut lower at the neck than current fashion allowed, even in Icarus. She was slender, with voluminous hair that curled down both her back and across her partially exposed breasts. Between the two falls of hair hung an amulet with a large greenish stone. It was the only part of the image that had any colour. The green stone was filled with red specks that seemed to flow and change as she moved. Piercing eyes flashed as she spoke in a voice that was both harsh, and yet at the same time musical. Rodney was so enthralled that he missed the meaning of her words. Only after she stated her name did he begin to pay attention to what Magdalen was saying.

"Drake Slayer!" she spat. "I demand you show me this Drake Slayer. Show me who committed this foul murder. Show me who killed Gytha!"

Rodney pushed back his chair and stood slowly as if in a dream. The ghostly woman turned her gaze on him. For a few seconds their eyes met. The woman's face lost some of its hardness, her eyes narrowed, and for a tiny moment she looked confused, then her face sharpened as anger returned. Her mouth opened, but before she could speak Sir Florence leapt up. "I helped slay your beast," he yelled.

The rest of the Daemon Knights stood as one, and followed his lead in claiming culpability for killing the FireDrake. Then Edmond was on his feet. "Your foul creature was destroyed at my command, Witch," he shouted to be heard over the other men. "I lead these men and accept full responsibility. Your demon attacked this castle and was destroyed for it."

"I had expressly forbid it. She would not have attacked unless provoked. You lie!"

"Nevertheless, the beast did attack this castle and died for it. Let that be a lesson to you, and the Emperor. Icarus is not a kingdom to be trifled with!" A loud cheer went up in the hall with Edmond's last words.

Magdalen's lips narrowed before they curled into a cruel and humourless smile. "I would not be so quick to talk of lessons if I were you."

The sorceress glared about the room as if burning each person's face into her memory. Rodney was still entranced. Even in anger, the shape of her face was pleasing to the eye. Her skin looked as smooth as silk, with the exception of a small mole on her left cheek. That slight imperfection only seemed to enhance her beauty. Her hair resembled a living thing, as the curls danced across her chest when she turned her head.

"I shall not forget you, Sir Knight," Magdalen said. Her words had an icy edge.

"Nor I you," Rodney replied, without even thinking.

The sorceress stared at Rodney for a time and then lifted her arm and pointed directly at him. "You'll all pay. But you..." she said with undisguised venom in her voice. "I am no one's fool. The murder of Gytha is on your head, so you will be the first to suffer."

Magdalen's eyes shifted to the Duchess sitting next to him. "You and those you hold most dear." With those last words the image of the sorceress faded away, but her voice echoed on long after she was gone.

Even after the sound had died, the hall remained quiet until one of the musicians strummed his lyre. The music and laughter eventually resumed, but with less enthusiasm. Rodney paid little attention to goings on after that, and before he knew it the evening had ended.

Rodney soon found himself entering the former legion Captain's tent, which he had claimed for his own. The sleeping mat was a bit short, and his feet stuck out past the end, but it was preferable to the hard ground where most of the others would spend the night. He stretched out on the mat, not even bothering to remove his boots, and closed his eyes, but sleep was a long time coming.

He tried to move forward, but his feet were rooted to the ground. The ghostly white vision of the sorceress floated just out of his reach. She smiled, beckoning with her hand for him to come to her. Rodney tried to reach out once more just as the world shook. A familiar voice called out to him from a great distance. The image of the woman faded away. "Wait! Don't go," he yelled and then opened his eyes.

Morton leaned over him with concern etched deeply upon his face. "I am sorry to awaken you, Sir Rodney, but Captain Doyle has been waiting to see you for some time now."

Rodney sat up and blinked. The sudden movement initiated a dull throbbing in his head. He looked down at his feet to see that he was still wearing his boots. The events of the previous night came flooding back. They were camped in the remains of the abandoned Imperial camp and he had taken over the Imperial Captain's tent.

Baron Morgan had offered the hospitality of a room in the castle, but Rodney had politely declined with the excuse of wanting to be with his men. The excuse was true enough, but the real reason was his need to talk with Jason privately about Martin. Unfortunately, by the time the feast was over his friend was in such a drunken state that talking would have been a waste of time. It was just as well. Rodney's thoughts were too preoccupied with Magdalen to deal with Jason anyway.

"How long has he been waiting?" Rodney asked, rocking himself onto his feet. His legs were stiff and his mouth felt like it was full of dry leaves. The motion made his head ache all the more. *Just what I need, another blasted headache.*

"He's been waiting almost a sun-mark. I thought you would want to know."

"You did the right thing, Mort," Rodney replied as he ran his fingers through his tangled hair drawing it back behind his ears. "Bid him enter." Rodney hooded his eyes to block the bright light which flooded in when his squire pulled back the tent flap.

"He will see you now, Captain," Rodney heard Morton say, before the light blinded him again as the Icarian entered.

"A good morn to you, Sir Rodney," the captain said with a friendly smile. "I trust you slept well."

Rodney returned the smile, in spite of his pounding head. "I slept as well as could be expected. Good morn to you Captain Doyle. I see it is well past sunrise and understand you have been made to wait overly long. I do beg your pardon. You must think me a sloth, but your Icarian wine has quite a bite to it. We do not have anything like it in Balor."

"Ah, that explains why most of your country men are still abed then."

Rodney raised his eyebrows. There could still be Imperials about and it was not a good time to be caught unawares. "I hope the sentries are not included in your observations."

Captain Doyle laughed. "You needn't worry Sir Knight. I was stopped well outside your perimeter by an archer and that strange little wild-man of yours. I have also seen at least six more sentries since then."

Rodney relaxed and allowed a small smile of pride to curl on his lips. "Good! Now I expect that your visit has another purpose beside wishing me a good morn."

"It does indeed. His Grace would like you to breakfast with him. He will be expecting you at two sun-marks before midday."

The thought of food turned Rodney's stomach, but he kept that to himself. "You may tell His Grace I shall be delighted to join him for the morning meal."

"Until then," Captain Doyle replied with a slight bow and then spun around and left the tent. Morton immediately stepped back inside. "Ah Mort, pray tell me where is the sun."

"Less than three marks before midday."

"Gods! I am to breakfast with the Duke at two. I must make myself presentable. Saddle my horse while I bathe in the river."

"Your mount will be ready when you return, Sir Rodney."

Morton obviously did not share Rodney's sense of loss over Thunder. Rodney gave the squire a smile and a slap on the back. "Good lad," he said. Morton beamed back a broad smile of his own, before he ducked out of the tent.

A short while later, Rodney was shaking the water from his hair. It was badly in need of cutting. After tying it back with a strip of leather placed across his forehead, he pulled on his damp tunic. Though heavily stained, at least the garment no longer smelled of sweat and wine after a thorough rinsing in the river. He would have preferred a clean tunic, but all his spare clothing had been left behind with the wagons in Nagual. Perhaps later, when he had more time, he could purchase new clothing in Mossburg.

True to his word Morton had the gelding saddled and waiting when Rodney returned to his tent. Gregory stood next to him with the reins of his own mount in hand. "Mort tells me you have business at the castle this morning," the young knight said.

"Yes, I am to breakfast with the Duke."

"I would like to accompany you, if I may, just to the castle grounds."

Rodney smiled. "Might this have something to do with that comely young maid I saw you conversing with last night?"

Gregory blushed. "Aye, it would."

"Well, beware that big farmer she was with. I've seen him before and he seems handy with a knife. I'd watch my back if I were you."

Gregory smiled. "Oh, that is just her brother, but I thank you for the warning and will be careful none the less."

"Very well, let us be off then. Mort, advise Sir Martin of where I have gone. He is in command during my absence. Oh, and keep an eye on your uncle. If he starts any trouble seek out Lionel or Herman for assistance."

When Rodney and Gregory arrived at the castle gates, they found them open and two young lads waiting to tend to their horses. The knights dismounted and handed their reins to the boys. Rodney was late and in a hurry. Hopefully, Edmond would not be insulted by his tardiness.

Gregory stopped when they entered the inner courtyard. Off to the left was a table shielded from the sun by a large awning. At the table sat the Baroness Annette and Duchess Wynne. They appeared to be having breakfast together. In the daylight, Rodney could see that even though they were getting on in years, and somewhat plump, they were still both striking women. The young woman tending two young children nearby, however, outshone them both. She was the very same maiden Gregory was seeking.

"I think that here we part," Rodney said, putting a hand on the young knight's shoulder. Gregory didn't seem to be listening, so Rodney just left him standing there and walked toward the keep.

Captain Doyle was waiting impatiently near the door to the hall. He wasted no time in ushering Rodney inside, and announcing his arrival. Baron Morgan and the Duke were sitting at the head table, drinking from fine silver cups and nibbling on cheese from a matching silver platter. As soon as Rodney was seated, more food was brought in, and a cup boy filled his cup with heated wine. He sipped it slowly while eating but soon found his cup empty. Remarkably his headache was gone by the end of the meal.

When the meal was over, they discussed the appearance of the sorceress on the previous evening. Then the Baron inquired about the route Rodney's company would take to Drakenmount, and the supplies they would need for the journey. Rodney was just about to make another request for aid, in the form of additional archers, when an Icarian arms-man burst into the hall. He was out of breath from running hard. "A dragon," he gasped. "Another dragon approaches the castle, my Lords!"

As if on cue, a woman screamed. The scream had come from the courtyard. Rodney scrambled with the others to get out of the hall. They arrived just in time to see a massive FireDrake set down in the centre of the courtyard near the table and canopy. The Baroness swooned, falling heavily to the ground. The young maiden was frantically trying to push the screaming children under the table. Gregory drew his broadsword and stepped between the FireDrake and the women, but the beast swatted him aside as if he were an insect. When it flapped its great wings, dust flew into Rodney's eyes blinding him. When his vision cleared the FireDrake had taken flight. The Duchess hung from one of its hind claws while Gregory's young maiden hung from the other.

By the time Rodney reached the spot where Gregory lay, it was too late to do anything. The FireDrake was almost over the inner wall. Two bowmen on the wall raised their weapons. "Don't shoot you fools!" Edmond screamed. "You might hit Wynne!" The bowmen lowered their weapons as the FireDrake cleared the wall and was gone.

Rodney bent over to help Gregory to his feet. The young knight appeared to have suffered nothing more serious than having the wind knocked out of him. A servant approached Edmond and handed him a small package. "The beast dropped this, your Grace," he said.

The object was wrapped in a waxed cloth and neatly tied with a red ribbon. The Duke pulled on the ribbon and removed the wrapping. Inside was a small rolled parchment. He opened it with a single practised motion. "It is from the sorceress," he said.

After reading it, the Duke gave the message to the Baron, who read it and then in turn handed it to Rodney. Rodney unrolled the note. *I gave you fair warning Drake Slayer. Your woman will not be harmed, but you will go to your deathbed without ever setting eyes on her again.* It was signed *Magdalen.*

Chapter 31

ALDUS

The night Aldus left the Balorian camp he cast a concealment spell around himself and the mare. The spell was a simple one learned early on as Pewlin's apprentice. He had selected that particular concealment spell, not because it was the best one for the job, but because it required only a small trickle of magical energy to maintain. More importantly it did not require using Gweneal. A portion of the amulet's magic was still bound to the spell shielding Grigor from the sorceress. Aldus was worried that using more might attract unwanted attention. Halflings could sense magic when it was nearby or of great strength. Over the years Aldus had taken great care to maintain absolute obscurity as a practitioner of the magical arts. He had especially kept Gweneal a secret until his recent visit to Balor.

Spells would work against Magdalen because she was not directly linked to Aedon, but they would not be effective against a FireDrake; no other magic save Aedon's would ever be. Even so, it was more than enough to fool the eyes and ears of ordinary men. It worked on the minds of those around him. When he passed by, the sound of hooves became cricket chirps. The grass and shrubs disturbed by horse and rider would appear to be caused by a whirling dust devil or sudden gust of wind. In any case, whatever was seen and heard would be forgotten within moments.

With the exception of drokas, used by desert traders to haul their goods, Imperials held a longstanding contemptuous attitude toward using animals for any purpose other than food. It was an inclination for which Aldus was most grateful. Keener senses were not so easily fooled by simple illusion. It would take much stronger magic to fool the ears of a horse, the nose of a dog or the eyes of an owl.

Aldus paused by a large grassy mound just outside the Imperial camp to ensure the FireDrake was still in residence and not aloft where she might notice

202

him. With a wave of his hand he cast another minor spell to enhance his vision. For a brief time his eyes shape-shifted into those of an eagle. Objects that had been far away and blurred became enlarged and in crisp focus.

The FireDrake's great bulk was clearly visible in the dancing light of the many campfires. An area had been set aside for her in the centre of the camp. She appeared to be asleep. *What luck.* Any dragon could sleep for days if left alone and even should she wake, with all that light around her she would be blind to the darkness. Even a FireDrake's eyes had limitations. Aldus smiled, and was about to ride on, when a Dog Soldier stepped out from behind the mound.

Crouched over, with his feet slightly apart and an arrow nocked in his bow, the man watched and listened for what seemed to Aldus an incredibly long time. A bead of sweat ran down the wizard's forehead and into the corner of his eye. The stinging salt made him blink. The soldier took another step closer. Just a few more and he would walk right into the mare. Aldus held his breath, praying the horse would remain calm, and then tensed when he heard a voice directly behind him. "I told you, Fugol, it was just the wind."

Gods, there is another one right behind me.

"I smell an animal, Esau," the first one muttered. "It smells like one of those creatures the Carpathians ride upon."

"That is quite a nose you have there, Fugol. You can tell how near an animal is now by its stink on the wind."

An angry look flashed across Fugol's face. He took a half step forward but then stopped. He grunted, and then melted back behind the mound as quickly as he had appeared. Without a backward glance, Aldus flicked the reins gently and moved forward.

Aldus encountered no other sentries, but it was some time before he was able to relax. With such a near escape, he decided to keep the concealment spell in place even after he was well away from the Imperial camp. So it was, when passing through Onora a few hours later it was still intact. In front of the last building, at the west end of town, a large black and brown dog leaped out of the darkness and barked. The mare reared and Aldus nearly slipped out of the saddle. The spell of concealment fell away as he fought for control of the frightened horse. When horse and rider appeared out of nowhere the dog jumped back, barking all the louder. Aldus cursed at the dog and then recast the spell with a little more strength this time. Even so, it did not quiet the dog.

A light appeared, followed by a gruff voice. "Hey boy, what are you yapping at." A short stocky man in his night dress stood in an open doorway.

The man had obviously been roused from his bed. His hair was askew and he rubbed an eye with his knuckled left fist. An oil lantern hung from his right hand, casting a glow out into the gloom. "There's nothing there, you useless hound. Get back here. I suppose if I don't let you inside you'll keep me awake all night."

The dog looked at where horse and rider had been, let out a soft whine, and then bounded back to its master. The man slapped the hound on the rear with the flat of his hand as it passed through the doorway. The light of the lantern winked out with the closing of the door.

The concealment spell stayed intact until Aldus reached the trail to the Escarpe pass just before dawn. Once the mare was watered, he fed her a handful of oats and then left her to graze on the tall grasses by the lake. He watched the sky brighten, while washing down a meal of bread and cheese with the last of his Balorian cider. He was bone tired and the cider was making him drowsy, but a safer location would need to be found before he could risk sleep.

After refilling the empty cider skin with lake water, Aldus mounted and started up the trail leading to the pass. A sun-mark later he found a secluded spot where the trees formed such a thick canopy that not a single patch of blue sky showed through. Confident they would be invisible from the air, Aldus dismounted and unsaddled the mare. The horse snorted as if to say it was about time she had some rest. The wizard smiled and rubbed her withers. She shivered and shook her head. When he stopped, she whinnied and butted him gently with her head.

"You will have to make do with that, old girl," Aldus said as he whirled a finger in the air. The mare's eyes went wide as a band of air solidified around her forelegs, but she soon calmed down when Aldus dumped two handfuls of oats in front of her nose. With the mare securely hobbled he lay down to sleep. A saddle made a hard pillow but he was so tired he fell fast asleep almost instantly.

Intending to rest for only a few hours, Aldus was surprised to awake in near total darkness. Fishing a candle lantern out of his pack, he lit it with a small spark of the force electric which he had gathered from the air and condensed onto the tip of his finger. Heading out after saddling the mare by candle light, he travelled all night and well into the next day, resting again in a small stand of willows near a pond on the Icarus side of the pass. He started out again at first light the following morning.

By the end of the fourth day Aldus was safely into the evergreen forests of the Hagstrom mountains, where no country lay claim. The mountain wilderness stretched all the way to Drakenmount and beyond for hundreds of leagues to end at the ice cliffs of the northern sea. An hour before sunset he entered a large clearing. It looked like a comfortable place to camp so he unsaddled the mare and let her run loose. Being seen was no longer a worry, as it was unlikely the FireDrake travelling with the Imperials would fly this far to the northwest.

After collecting enough dry wood, Aldus built a fire on the windward side of two large rocks at the north edge of the clearing. It was then that he noticed Gweneal growing warmer. It could only mean that Grigor was approaching. The FireDrake had returned to Drakenmount to molt, as FireDrakes must do twice each year to replace their scales, and for a half moon could not fly. Grounded, and without their protective armour, they were at their most vulnerable. It had been a moon since Aldus and Grigor had parted company. The wizard searched the star filled sky but could not see his friend. *Maybe I have enough time to make some tea.*

The fire was blazing nicely and Aldus was reaching for the tea kettle when Grigor's voice boomed inside his head. *Aldus, it is good to see you again!*

Sparks and ash flew from the fire as the FireDrake landed nearby. Aldus hastily brushed bits of burning cinders from his robe before it could catch fire. Grigor took a few steps forward and then laid his massive head on the ground before the fire, oblivious to the various burning coals lying beneath him.

Aldus caught a fleeting glimpse of the mare galloping off down the trail. Now that Grigor was here, he would have had to let it loose anyway, so it was just as well. *You seem fit enough my friend,* Aldus said. *What news?*

Very little has changed since last I left Drakenmount. Most of the females are content with the sorceress. A number of them have flown to the south at her request, to prevent the humans from entering the Hagstroms. It's as if she no longer needs the amulet to force them to do her bidding. Oh, a few of the females are openly against her but they will not commit to action. As for the males, they will do nothing as long as they are left alone.

Aldus scratched the thick hair on his chin. *It is as I feared, we will have no aid from the other FireDrakes, but what of the elves?*

Grigor snorted and a cloud of dirt mixed with hot ash flew up from the fire. Aldus brushed dirt and ash from his beard as Grigor replied. *I may be elf-kin, but I will never understand my little cousins. They are content to wait. To stand by and let events unfold without interference. They will take no action either for or against us.*

Aldus scratched at a piece of burnt twig tangled in the hair under his left ear. *Well, not against us is something I suppose. You've done what you can and now I must see what can be learned in Penardun. If you will be so kind as to watch over my body, I will travel to Penardun to see what I can learn.*

Grigor opened his mouth and pulled back his lips, exposing double rows of teeth the size of daggers. It was what passed for a smile with a FireDrake. *Never fear my friend, no harm will befall you while Grigor is here.*

Projecting one's fetch was more a matter of concentration than magic, though it required both. Aldus relaxed and stared into his tea cup. Soon the image of a black, ice encrusted fortress appeared in the yellowish brown liquid. The thaw had only just arrived in the higher reaches near Drakenmount and with the setting sun what had melted during the day was quickly freezing once more. The scene of foreboding dark walls changed to one of a small dim chamber. Satisfied, Aldus shut his eyes. When they reopened he was there, or at least his ghostly fetch was.

As Aldus floated a foot above the floor, a beam of star light from a narrow opening in the outer wall provided just enough light to see. In this form he was somewhat limited in what he could do. To increase his night vision or create more light would require drawing more power from Gweneal, and doing so would alert Magdalen to his presence. He could not afford that, so he let himself drift up through the ceiling and into the room above. It was much the same as the one below, so he drifted through the wall to his right and found himself at the end of a long corridor. Two thick candles in sconces at the far end provided just enough light to see.

Somewhere in the ancient keep countless books of magic were hidden. As a young man, in the company of Pewlin, Aldus had travelled in the flesh to Penardun twice; both times in a fruitless search for the fabled library. Since Gweneal came into his possession he had travelled there in spirit a few times. His last visit was before Magdalen seized the amulet and took possession of the keep. If not for Gweneal, his fetch could not travel within leagues of Penardun, due to the presence of Aedon.

The corridor was on the upper floor of the west wing where the finest rooms were to be found. The many doors lining both sides of the corridor appeared to be made of ordinary oak, but were anything but ordinary. Thousands of years old they were preserved by a magic Aldus did not know. All the doors were closed, and probably locked, not that it mattered to a fetch, but one could not be sure that passing through an ensorcelled door would lead to the other side. His fetch floated slowly along the hall, pausing to poke its head through each closed door.

Near the end of the hall his search finally bore fruit. On the other side of the door stood his quarry. The sorceress was standing before a scrying pool as motionless as a statue. Her eyes were closed as if asleep. She was obviously in a trance and projecting her own fetch into another place just as he was doing.

Aldus drifted closer to examine the amulet Magdalen held clutched in her hand. She was vulnerable, but what could he do? He would risk using Gweneal if he knew of some way to snatch the amulet and spirit it away. The problem was that he did not know of a way. Giving up on the idea he floated about the room to see what he could learn, but found nothing of interest. He drifted back to the sorceress and paused to take one last look; then her eyes opened and she screamed.

Chapter 32

MAGDALEN

As the Icarian hall faded away Magdalen found herself in a state of confusion. Everything she understood about what was right told her she should feel only hatred and contempt toward Gytha's killer, but righteous anger had been thwarted by something in the way he had looked at her. She couldn't explain it. What was happening was all very strange. She didn't understand her feelings. It was most disturbing. For some inexplicable reason she did not want to think about it, and at the same time she could not just put it out of her mind.

Fortune had stepped in and offered a simple solution to her dilemma, and Magdalen had been quick to embrace it. Above all else, she was a woman of her word. She always said exactly what she meant, did exactly what she promised, and expected no less from others, even in the face of overwhelming evidence that she belonged to an extremely small group of people who valued truth above all else. While she made the transition to her body, a plan of retribution was taking form.

Sensing the warmth of her body, Magdalen opened her eyes and then recoiled in shock at the ghostly face of a fetch that loomed before her. Even as the scream left her lips, the anger she had previously been denied supplanted her initial shock. The fetch began to fade as it backed away. Magdalen would have to act quickly before it disappeared entirely. By the time she recalled an appropriate spell, the fetch's outline had already lost its milky colour and was turning grey. Aedon grew warm in her hand as she cast a crimson net of fire over the fading image. She pulled the net tight with a thought and then let go of her rage and calmed herself.

As a satisfied smile formed on her lips, Magdalen felt her body relax. She had acted in time and the interloper was now held securely in her net. It had regained its luminous quality, but with an additional red hue that was a reflection of the fiery bands that held it prisoner. At first glance she had mistaken it for the Emperor's projection, but closer inspection revealed that it was not. The man was aged, but not so ancient as that treacherous old fossil Gamel.

It seemed like her apprenticeship with the Emperor had begun a lifetime ago, but it was only seven years before that Gamel's fetch had visited Magdalen for the first time. She had been incredibly naive back then, but he had seemed so kind, so benevolent, and knew everything about her: her joys, her suffering, even her dreams. He had known just what would entice her too, offering power, security, riches, and a special place at his side in the palace at Crystal City, complete with all the comforts of a princess. Even though it seemed like a bard's fairy tale she believed his every word and accepted his offer willingly. Not until years later did she understand the price she was expected to pay.

At the time it had seemed an easy enough decision to make. Magdalen had never known a father. The man who had sired her abandoned his wife and daughter. She had been too young to even remember his face. After a lengthy illness, her mother passed away a few years later. Magdalen was left in the care of her mother's elder brother, the town cobbler. He was a reclusive man with no wife or children of his own. The years of misuse she suffered under her uncle's roof still sparked anger and even fear deep down inside. The physical scars she bore from the experience were as nothing, compared to those locked away where none could see.

Her past seemed so unreal to her now. She snorted. At one time, she had even numbered Gamel among her friends. The Gods alone knew how precious few of those she had known in all her twenty-five years. Thinking of it only reminded her that earlier in the day she had lost another, so she forced unpleasant thoughts of the past from her mind and returned her attention to the business at hand.

"I do not believe we have met," Magdalen said sweetly, as she walked slowly around the glowing image. "My name is Magdalen, but then I think you already know that." The fetch showed no response to her name, confirming her assumption.

"You are no doubt wondering how I have managed this." She laughed and shook her head. "Penardun has a very extensive library, you see, and its books contain the most powerful of spells, like this net of spirit-fire I used to trap you."

The old man's eyes flashed at the mention of the library. Magdalen smiled with satisfaction. "You seem surprised. I think you know things that are of interest to me, old man. Let me demonstrate another spell. One that will grant me access to your memories. Very shortly I will be privy to all you know. It would be only fair after all. I am at a disadvantage, you see, as you seem to know much of me, yet I know nothing of you." Magdalen could feel the fetch struggling against its bonds. "Don't worry," she said soothingly, "I will be as gentle as I can."

Coming to a stop facing the fetch, Magdalen drew another trickle of power from the amulet as she forced the magic to reach across the void into his mind. At first the probes were subtle, like tentacles of smoke. She probed here and there, trying to locate his secrets. Unfortunately, her efforts met with an iron wall of will. "You must realize that if I keep you here long enough your body will grow weak and die. Do not resist and I will release you unharmed."

Loosening the net enough to allow the fetch to speak, Magdalen waited for a reply, but none was forthcoming. "I am going to get what I want," she said, "one way or another, so why put yourself through unnecessary pain?" Still nothing from the fetch. "Very well," she said, reluctantly lifting the amulet off her chest. "We will do this the hard way."

This time Magdalen drew more power. She could feel the heat of the magic in the joints of her fingers. The fetch convulsed despite the net. Then, like opening a dam, his memories flooded forth in a deluge of information. At first it came so fast she was forced to slow the flow enough to make some sense of it. Images and thoughts paraded before her in between veils of mist. People and places she did not recognize flowed by until finally a face she knew appeared; the Drake Slayer. With the image came a thought, and in the thought was a name; Rodney Vincent.

Her mind had become one with the old man's memories. The Drake Slayer was riding toward her flanked by two other knights. All three had drawn swords and appeared to be attacking, but before she could tell what was happening the image changed into one of a jousting tournament. Though she couldn't see his face, she knew that the jouster with the red griffin was Rodney Vincent.

From out of the mist to Magdalen's right a woman's face appeared. The shape of her eyes and mouth reminded Magdalen of the Drake Slayer. An unmistakable family resemblance. A sister perhaps. A thought came to her, yes, one of two sisters. The face faded to be replaced by a hazy view of the sea. She was standing on the deck of a ship. Looking down she saw long thin fingers gripping the ship's rail. She felt the rise and fall of the deck beneath her feet just as the image grew dark.

So involved in what she was doing, Magdalen had failed to keep track of time. Though she wanted to learn more, the fetch had reached its limit for being away from the owner's body. Whoever he was, the old man was losing contact with his physical body. Soon he would lose the ability to return entirely. His mind was drifting into darkness. Magdalen knew she had to leave. The fetch's owner would die if she held it any longer.

With a sigh, Magdalen withdrew her probes from his mind and then released him from the net. The fetch slumped, and for a moment it appeared she had waited too long, then it slowly began to fade until it finally disappeared. Only when Aedon had cooled to its normal temperature, that of an elfin body, did Magdalen realize her mistake.

How could I have been so blind? Even at rest Aedon was not approachable by the kind of magic used to project a fetch, unless she allowed it. That was how Gamel had calculated its approximate location at Drakenmount in the first place. The only possible way a wizard could have sent his fetch so close to Aedon was if he possessed magic just as powerful. That could only mean another elfin amulet. As if she didn't already have enough to worry about.

Chapter 33

RODNEY

One of the more gravely wounded squires was found dead in the morning. After being informed of it upon his return from the castle, Rodney took the time to personally interview every one of his men. It would be pointless to start out on such a perilous and difficult journey with anyone who was less than fit. By the time Rodney had finished tallying up those he deemed sound enough to journey on to Drakenmount it was late in the day.

Of the original party, forty-four were dead. Another thirty-nine were wounded severely enough to require time to heal before they could travel, let alone fight. That left thirty-three knights, counting himself, twenty-eight squires and fifty-six arms-men. A total of one hundred and seventeen men to face the sorceress. Rodney didn't even want to think about the possibility of facing FireDrakes.

As the reality of his situation set in, Rodney laughed out loud. One FireDrake had very nearly destroyed a castle and scores of Icarian archers, along with six Daemon Knights. By Rodney's calculations it would take every Daemon Knight in Balor to face a horde of FireDrakes, and even then success was most doubtful. As for approaching the sorceress's lair unnoticed, a band of sneak-thieves would be more suitable to the task. Surely there were simpler ways of committing suicide.

Thinking of Magdalen brought back the haunting vision of the night before. It was impossible for Rodney to accept that so lovely a woman could be the evil black-hearted sorceress Aldus had described. Rodney shook his head. At least he had finally spoken with Jason, not that it had done any good. As stubborn as always, Jason had not taken Martin's appointment well. He even went so far as to imply Rodney could no longer count him among his friends.

The voice of Gregory interrupted Rodney's thoughts. "Sir Rodney, I beg your pardon, but these men have requested an audience with you."

Rodney looked over the young knight's shoulder at the two Icarian commoners who stood a few steps behind him. He recognized them as the men who had sat across from Gregory at the feast, and again as the same two from the tavern. The big one stood defiantly with arms folded across his chest and a dark scowl on his face. The other kept his eyes down while nervously twisting the rim of the soiled straw hat in his hands. Both men wore bows strung over their backs. Suspended by a rope from the big one's hip hung a broadsword. It appeared to be a solid enough weapon, though it was badly rusted and looked as dull as a plow blade.

In spite of having a lot on his mind, Rodney was curious. "What do they want?"

Gregory motioned to the men to come closer. When they stepped forward, he placed his hand on the big one's shoulder. "This is Shaun Finn," Gregory said. "His sister Agnes was taken with the Duchess this morning."

"Ahhh, the maiden," Rodney replied.

Gregory's eyes glazed over as he cleared his throat. "The same." He then placed his other hand on the smaller man's shoulder. "This is Robin Smith. Her betrothed."

Rodney raised an eyebrow at that. He tried to read Gregory's face but then Shaun spoke out of turn. "Gregory here says you are marching to the witch's lair. We will go with you to see Aggie safely returned."

The Icarian's lack of respect grated on Rodney's nerves. "This is no spring outing," Rodney said a little harsher than he had intended. "We can't be wet nursing a couple of farmers."

"I can fight as well as any man here," Shaun replied quickly, "and Robin and I both hit what we aim at. You'll not lack for meat with us around, and from what I've seen you've few enough bowmen."

Rodney shared a look with Gregory. "Baron Morgan's Sergeant has vouched for their steadfastness and skill," Gregory replied to the unasked question. "They both held their positions on the west wall until the collapse of the rampart."

Rodney was impressed. It took uncommon bravery to stand your ground in the face of dragon-fire. He levelled his gaze at the two Icarians. Robin lowered his eyes again, but Shaun glared back in defiance.

Rodney finally turned back to Gregory. "Very well. They may join our ranks, but they will be your responsibility, Gregory." The young knight nodded and turned to leave. "Oh, and by the way," Rodney added, "please find that man a scabbard and a whetstone for his sword. It is a disgrace."

As Rodney watched the three men walk away, he noticed Coll striding across the camp and moved to intercept him. His arm was trussed up in a sling. Rodney had put off the unpleasant task of delivering what he knew would be unwelcome tidings. Coll would be returning to Balor with the rest of the wounded. As he drew near he waved Coll over. "Would you be so kind as to join me for a walk in the woods?" Rodney asked. He wanted to be away from the others so they could have a private conversation.

"Be happy to," Coll replied.

Once away from the camp, Rodney put it to his retainer plainly. "Coll, you cannot accompany me to Drakenmount. I need you to lead the wounded back to Balor."

Coll's smile vanished and he looked crestfallen. "But I...," was all Coll managed before Rodney cut him off with a raised hand.

Rodney placed a hand gently on his uninjured shoulder. "I am told your injury will take some time to heal, and I can think of no one else I trust to get the others back to Balor safely."

"There are three squires with the wounded. Surely one of them can take command, so I will certainly not be needed for that."

Even though Rodney had already made up his mind, he checked his list for Coll's benefit. There were three wounded squires, Raynold Vennell, Pierce Jenour and Noel Austin. "They are too young and inexperienced. The oldest has only just turned seventeen. You know as well as I, it will be a difficult journey. I need someone with sound judgement in command."

The elder man sighed. "I suppose you're right at that."

Now that Coll had accepted his lot, Rodney spelled out what he wanted done as they walked. Coll and the others were to wait in Icarus for a fortnight, or longer, to allow the wounded time to heal. Rodney stressed they were to wait even longer if the Imperial troops were still a threat.

"Only when it is safe are you to lead our countrymen home," Rodney said. "The Duke has promised wagons suitable for travelling the pass, along with horses and supplies." Rodney unfastened a small pouch of gold coins from his belt and handed it to Coll. "This is to purchase passage from Celia to Balor." Coll took the offered pouch with little enthusiasm.

When they emerged from the trees, Rodney heard the angry voice of Captain Doyle. He was shouting at Morton in front of Rodney's tent. The captain was forcefully tapping his index finger on the young squire's chest. Rodney swore and picked up his pace. One of the captain's men spotted Rodney approaching and tapped his superior on the shoulder. The grim faced officer spun around and marched toward Rodney, followed by six of his men. They stopped almost nose to nose.

"The Duke requests that you attend him at once in the great hall," the captain said. "Plans must be made for the journey to Drakenmount."

Six armed guardsmen made it obvious that Edmond had issued a command, not a request, and turning it down was not an option. Rodney was barely able to hold his temper in check. The urge to strike the captain was overwhelming. Morton was his Squire, and striking him, even with just a pointed finger, was a great insult. If they had been in Balor he would have instantly demanded that Captain Doyle either apologize to his squire, or provide Rodney satisfaction through a duel. Rodney stared back in silence, letting the anger flow away just as his father had taught him.

When Rodney finally responded, it was in a cool calm voice. "I will find my Second and be there shortly." Without waiting for a reply he turned and walked away. Rodney could sense the captain and his men following behind at a discreet distance.

By the time he found Martin, Rodney had given up on his calming exercises and had gravitated into a foul mood. His Second was conversing with a group of his friends. "I am to meet with the Duke, and you will accompany me," Rodney said.

"You must excuse me, gentlemen," Martin said to the knights with a flourish of his hand, "but duty calls." The smiles that appeared in response to Martin's flippancy melted under Rodney's cold stare.

On the way to the castle Rodney reconsidered his choice for Second. Martin was just too full of himself for Rodney's taste. Along with misgivings, the thought occurred to him that with good reason he could still change his decision.

The knights killed in battle had left six young squires without mentors. Rodney had given the task of finding knights willing to take them on to Martin. Perhaps his Second would provide a convenient excuse to replace him. Rodney made a show of smiling and tried to sound friendly. "Have you seen to that matter of placing the squires we spoke about this morning?"

"But of course," Martin replied with that infuriating, greasy smile of his. "Sir Benjamin will take Sir William's squire Anton. Sir Charles has taken Sir Maynard's squire Perce. Sir Joel Neville..."

Rodney kept up his false smile as his Second continued on to the last squire. So far Martin was carrying out his duties commendably, and he had the feeling Martin knew what Rodney was about with the question. That Martin was both intelligent and perceptive was not in doubt.

When they arrived at the hall, they found both the Duke and Baron Morgan bent over a large map which had been spread out on the high table. "Ah, Sir Rodney," the Duke said. "Good of you to join us." Edmond's sarcasm was not lost on Rodney. He no doubt held him responsible for his wife's abduction.

After a respectful bow, Rodney indicated Martin with his hand. "You have met my Second."

Martin bowed to the Duke and flashed a quick, toothy smile. "Some wine?" the Duke asked.

Both knights nodded and were given cups of Montcre Castle's fine red wine. Rodney took a sip. It tasted wonderful. He had never cared for cider but was quickly developing a taste for Icarian wine.

"This vile witch must be stopped at all costs," the Duke announced, "and as you can understand I must secure Wynne's release. To that end I have decided to accompany you. I will bring two hundred of my best archers, just as you requested."

"Of course," Rodney replied with a slight bow.

The Duke replied without looking at Rodney. "I will of course assume command."

Rodney was not surprised, and in fact had been expecting something like it, but he was also not about to turn their quest for the amulet into a rescue mission for Edmond's wife. "I am sorry, your Grace, but I cannot agree to that."

Edmond placed his hands on his hips and looked Rodney in the eye. He had to tilt his head back to do it. "You do not have any choice in the matter. You are not in Balor, but Icarus. You are on my land and in no position to bargain, Sir Knight."

"I cannot turn over command of my men, or my mission, to anyone other than another Daemon Knight. If you refuse us passage through Icarus then we must find another route. I understand your need to rescue the Duchess, and deeply regret her abduction, but I cannot do as you ask."

The Duke's face clouded over. "Will you at least show the western route to the accursed witch's lair?" he said.

"No," Rodney replied.

The Duke's eyes narrowed. "You must realize I could just take it."

It was Rodney's turn to look Edmond in the eye. "I thought we had an agreement," he said. "Is the word of an Icarian Duke so worthless?" he added with an edge of contempt. Edmond's face turned bright red. From the corner of his eye Rodney saw the Baron scowl as his hand moved toward his sword.

The tension was broken when Martin stepped in. "Ah, if you will forgive my boldness," he said with an easy smile, "perhaps we do have something to bargain with after all. Surely we can come to some agreement on a partnership. Cooperation for information as it were."

The Duke rubbed his chin with his forefinger before he replied. "We could share command perhaps."

Rodney shook his head. "You know as well as I that in any military campaign there can be only one leader, otherwise there is only chaos."

"Blast it," the Duke said. "Very well, you have me over a barrel. Until we reach the witch's lair, you will be in command."

"Agreed," Rodney said as he pulled the map Aldus had given him out of his tunic. Once Rodney had shown Edmond the key points on his map, the Duke called in a scribe who set to work making a copy.

"I have received another message from the King," Edmond said. "He has dispatched an additional five thousand men. I am instructed to await their arrival, and then lead our combined force through the pass. Since I cannot wait, Baron Morgan will stay behind in my stead. He will lead the King's forces when they arrive."

Edmond turned to the Baron. "Galen, you will march through Nagual toward Drakenmount as a diversion, while Sir Rodney and I travel through the western mountains unnoticed. Once you have crossed the plains, lead your forces through the pass shown on this map. You will approach Drakenmount from the southeast, while we come from the northwest."

The Duke stroked his chin with the forefinger of his right hand. "Do not attack, but wait for word outside the witch's fortress. If a messenger is not forthcoming, look for a signal fire to the west. Only then are you to attack. While she is distracted, we will enter her lair and rescue Wynne."

Edmond turned to Rodney. "Once we reach Drakenmount, our partnership is dissolved."

"Agreed," Rodney said. "You have your mission, and we have ours."

The Duke held out his hand. "So be it," he said. Rodney clasped his forearm and the deal was done.

Chapter 34

GAMEL

Rays from a setting sun cast wondrous multicoloured beams of light through the stained glass windows of the Imperial palace. Every bit of glass in the palace was of the finest quality to be found in all the known world. Each one of the thousands of individual pieces had been made by the city's artisans. An endless supply of fine sand and lamp gas from beneath the desert floor had over the years enabled the city to establish itself as a major centre for glass production. The abundance of fine quality glass to be found throughout the city was how it had acquired its name. Artisans from all over the continent travelled to Crystal City, just to study under the guild's glass masters.

The Emperor was paying little mind to what light filtered through the high windows of his chamber as he soaked in a lavish marble bath. Another form of beauty had attracted his attention. Two young maidens clad in gossamer thin silks held up an ornate full-length oval mirror at the foot of his bath. The Emperor's gaze wandered away from the image in the mirror of four men leaning over a large map, to the young girl on the left. She lowered her eyes and trembled under his stare.

Gamel's thin lips curled into a pleasant smile. Though he had long ago lost the desire for women's flesh, he still took pleasure in gazing upon their beauty. Only his prized black blood-roses were as beautiful as this young maiden. His thoughts drifted back to the long ago days of his youth, when he had possessed both the vigour and a more than an average interest in the fairer sex.

After a time of wistful reflection on younger days, Gamel's eyes returned to the mirror. He focussed his thoughts. The already fading image morphed into the interior of a legionary command tent in the southwestern Olaug plains. Brodulf Grim, Captain of the Second Imperial Legion, leaned forward with the knuckles of his fists resting on a modest travel desk. He was addressing two of his lieutenants. They looked vaguely familiar. *What are their names, ah yes now*

218

I remember, Milo and Lanzo Beald, the two sons of my former General.

The Second Imperial Legion was camped one day north of the Escarpe pass. After what must have been a gruelling forced march, the legion had been waiting there for the past two days. Gamel watched with interest as the captain informed his men of the defeat of the Ninth Legion in Icarus.

"We travel ten days without rest to get here and now we are to turn back," Milo said. "Why do we not march on Icarus and avenge the honour of Nagual?"

The captain's eyebrows rose to midway on his forehead. "Have you become so bold as to question the orders of the Emperor?"

The young officer lowered his eyes. "No sir."

"Our orders are clear. We wait for Lieutenant Brun and his men and then march north. We are to join the Seventh and Third legions north of the Vanir pass to await the arrival of General Hael."

"Why would we be going north, Captain?" Lanzo asked. "There is nothing in the northern Olaug Plains but tribesmen and endless grass."

Milo's eyes went wide. "Lizard spit!" he said. "The Vanir pass leads to Drakenmount. Surely we are not going there?"

Captain Brodulf shrugged. "I stopped asking questions like that a long time ago, Lieutenant. I suggest you do the same. Believe me it will be much better for your health in the long run. Now return to your duties."

The two brothers slapped fists to their chests and marched out of the tent. The image of Brodulf frowned down at the map on his table just as a loud knock on his chamber door disturbed Gamel's concentration. He nodded to his servant Lusias, who moved to open the door. The image in the mirror faded back to Gamel's own reflection as General Gunther Hael entered the chamber. The General stopped next to the two maidens. He smiled at each of the women briefly while his eyes followed their curves from their necks to their feet. Then he turned to face Gamel.

"Ah, I see we share the same taste in women," Gamel said in his fatherly voice, "but there is nothing better than a hot scented bath to soothe tired old bones. Why don't you join me, Gunther?"

The General bowed his head slightly. "A most kind and generous offer, your greatness, but I really must return to my duties. Perhaps another time."

"Ah well, suit yourself, General. To business it is then. But first, Lusias pour the General some wine. We are civilized men after all. It is a good Icarian vintage, you will enjoy it I'm sure."

Gamel's manservant hurried to the general and offered him a cup which he then proceeded to fill right to the rim. "I want you to leave in the morning for the Vanir pass," Gamel said, as Gunther raised the cup to his lips.

The General's eyebrows went up in surprise, and his wine sloshed over the side of the cup. Gamel's manservant was there instantly to wipe it from the spotless marble floor. Gamel set his own cup aside. "You will take the Fourth, Fifth and Eighth legions."

"I do not understand, your greatness," the General replied. "Just this morning our intelligence indicated that another five thousand Icarian troops have left Concurie. Surely we will move to reinforce the Second Legion."

"I have already contacted Captain Brodulf. The Second Legion will march north to the Vanir pass. The Icarian army will also be moving north and then on through the Vanir pass. Once they have entered the pass, the remaining men from the Ninth Legion will follow them, but before they do, I want you to give the lieutenant in charge this." Gamel nodded at Lusias, who produced a small object wrapped in black velvet and presented it to Gunther.

"What is it?" the general asked, holding it up to examine.

"For your own safety," Gamel said, "I strongly suggest that you do not open it." He was rewarded by the slightest hint of fear that flashed across Gunther's face. "The lieutenant's name is Kaspar Brun, and I have a special job for him and his men, but that is not your concern. Once the way is clear, you will lead your forces south."

The general smiled. "I think I understand, your greatness. We will have twenty thousand men and a rich unprotected valley to plunder."

"That is correct. It is easy to see why you are my general." Gamel's sarcasm appeared lost on Gunther. "Once you have secured the valley I will have more instructions. You may go now."

The general bowed, handed his still full cup to Lusias, and then backed out of the chamber. Gamel stood up, looked down at his frail body, and then sighed. "Lusias, my robe," he barked. His manservant draped a gold trimmed white robe over Gamel's bent skeletal frame. Gamel stepped out of the bath and Lusias handed him a cup of wine. Gamel took one sip and handed it back. "That will be all. You may all leave me now," he said with a wave of his hand.

After the door clicked shut, Gamel turned back to the pool. The milky water began to darken, first to a muddy grey and finally to the colour of the blackest ink. He looked down into the dark pool as an image of two men on horseback appeared. They were the same two Balorian knights he had been watching earlier. That image disappeared and another image of twisted trees formed in the pool. A bent form, almost as misshapen as the trees, turned to face him.

Knowing what to expect failed to prevent Gamel from blinking. The face staring back would make a hardened Dog Soldier cringe. The witch Agilina was a grotesque creature. The careless misuse of powerful magic over the centuries had distorted her features so much she barely resembled anything human.

"Greetings Agilina," Gamel said.

"What do you want now?" the witch croaked.

"I have a little job for your pets."

"Why not use the bitch's FireDrakes," she whined. "Why bother with poor old Agilina Barbota."

"One of my legionnaires is on his way to you. He should arrive in a few days. I would appreciate it if he was allowed to reach you in one piece. He will have in his possession a glove. It recently belonged to the leader of some troublesome Balorians. Use it for your pets to get the scent. I have added a little something to increase its potency."

"What am I to do with your man afterwards?" Agilina asked.

Gamel smiled. For all her years Agilina was like a little child. If only Magdalen could be so easily manipulated. "You may consider him a gift, to do with as you will." Agilina's face cracked into a crooked smile. It was a disturbing sight. Even after many years, it still had the power to send a chill down his spine.

"I have been having doubts about Magdalen as of late," Gamel said, as an afterthought.

The witch laughed. "I told you she'd be trouble from the start. But would the great Gamel listen to poor old Agilina? Nooo."

"I think it is time for you and I to formulate new plans."

The hag's smile broadened.

"We will speak of it again," Gamel added as he withdrew his fetch. When he had returned to his body, he stood for a long time reflecting on how he had trained Magdalen, guided her in recovering Aedon, and then how the ungrateful little whelp had betrayed him. No one had ever done that before, and lived to tell of it. Well, it was his own fault. He had let her beauty cloud his judgement and she had proven to be far more devious than he would ever have given her credit for.

You are not smart enough to outwit Gamel Cola, my dear. I will have Aedon, and then the other three. Soon I can cast off this old, shrivelled shell. With all four I will be immortal, a living God, and you sweet Magdalen will worship at my feet. In chains if necessary.

Chapter 35

AGILINA

Agilina stood hunched over a limp form laying in the soft, moist earth just outside the door to her home. The smell of rot and decay permeated everything around her, not that she noticed or cared. What light spilled from the open doorway glinted off the metal rings attached to the Dog Soldier's tunic. His braids were covered with mud and his clothing torn and stained. The left side of his face was swollen and caked with dried blood, but he was still alive.

It was a struggle to remove the soldier's armoured tunic. Once it was free, Agilina set it aside with his pack before cutting off the rest of his clothing with a small, sharp knife. Ancient gnarled fingers probed the unconscious man's body in search of broken bones. Pleased at finding nothing of consequence, she smiled.

"You did well, my Sweet," Agilina said to the darkness. "Now take him inside."

A shadow moved at Agilina's side, all but invisible, until a shaggy black arm wrapped itself around the man and lifted him into the air. The light from the doorway was blocked momentarily as a tall bear-like form carried the unconscious man through the opening. Darkness made little difference to Agilina. With eyes like a moor cat she hunted through the clothing unhindered.

Not finding what she was looking for, Agilina slid her hand into the pack. "Ah ha," she muttered at the feel of cold steel against her skin. "There you are." Withdrawing a large metal-clad glove, she cast the pack out into the darkness.

222

The thud of it striking something solid was answered by a low snarl, followed by the sound of ripping cloth. Agilina sucked in a deep breath of thick swamp air. "Come to me" she intoned. "Come to me, my darlings."

Dark shapes appeared between the twisted trees and shadows at the edge of the small clearing surrounding her home. One leapt out over the tangled roots of a misshapen black spruce. Saliva dripped from long canines, which protruded from an elongated snout. Though it walked upright like a human, the creature had such a prominent hunched back its front claws nearly touched the ground. Even shaped as it was, it stood taller than any normal man.

The creature came to a stop an arm's length away. Blood red eyes glowed as it snarled and snapped. Spittle splashed onto Agilina's tattered dress and shoes. A stringy piece of rotted meat hung from the fur near its mouth. As fierce as it looked, when the eyes of beast and hag met, it was the beast that backed away and whimpered. Agilina's face split in a satisfied smile, exposing rotted teeth and a fat black tongue.

When Agilina raised her arm, the creature stepped forward to timidly sniff the leather and steel glove she held in a calloused dirt-stained hand. Similar beasts, of varying shapes and sizes, ventured out of the darkness to sniff at it in turn. One, even more bestial than the rest, in that it walked on all four limbs, raised its wolf-like head and howled long and hard. As if they had been waiting for it, the others joined in with snarls and howls of their own until the clearing was filled with their horrific clamour.

"There!" Agilina screamed, pointing a crooked finger to the east. "To the Hagstrom mountains. Seek the owner of this scent and rip out his heart." The howling increased in intensity. "Kill those with him and feed, but bring me back a few alive," she added rapping the nearest snout with her fist. "Alive mind you. Now go!"

Her creatures bounded off into the swamp in a frenzy of howls. It was impossible to tell if their enthusiasm was due to anticipation of the feast to come, or fear of disappointing their master. By the time Agilina reached the doorway the sounds had faded into the distance. She knew they would run all day and all night, stopping only long enough to feed upon whatever prey they happened to encounter along the way. Though none of them could truly speak, most had enough human in them to understand her words. The rest would follow the more intelligent ones blindly.

She entered her hut and closed the door. An eight foot long wooden slab dominated the centre of the one room hut. Three large rusted metal cages stood to one side against a mud wall. A rough wooden table piled with jars and other things rested against the adjoining wall. The first of the cages was empty. Its door hung open. The second cage contained a thin and half-starved grey wolf that growled weakly as Agilina approached. The third held a blue-black moor cat, a fine specimen who's cold predator eyes followed Agilina's every move. It was no doubt hungry as well, but unlike the wolf, its only other reaction was a lazy flick of its tail.

The stench of urine, faeces and rot would have driven any sane person from the hut in disgust, but Agilina was accustomed to the odour and barely noticed. She walked to the middle cage and bent down, her face within two fingers of the bars. The wolf snarled, baring his teeth, and then lunged, snapping at the rusted metal to leave the bars glistening with saliva.

In response, Agilina cackled. Turning to the table, she poured a yellow powder from a dusty jar onto a chunk of brownish meat that had been almost indistinguishable from the table's surface. Using her knuckles as a pestle she kneaded the powder into the meat. Once satisfied with her handywork, she dropped the tainted meat through the top bars of the wolf's cage. In the three days since it had been caught in her trap the animal had eaten nothing. It almost choked in an attempt to swallow the corrupted meat whole.

Agilina waited patiently for the powder to do its work. After a short time the animal's eyes glazed over and it sunk to the floor of the cage. With the hapless animal laying immobile in its own filth, Agilina swung the cage open and dragged it over to the big wooden slab.

Except for a stained loin cloth, Gamel's soldier lay on the table naked. Agilina bound the unconscious man's wrists and ankles with thick leather straps, which were in turn fastened to the sides of the slab. She pulled a strap across his chest and yanked it tight. A moan escaped from the man's lips. Agilina ripped off his loin cloth and stuffed it in his mouth before pulling another strap over his lips and chin.

With seemingly little effort for one so old, Agilina hauled the wolf onto the slab. As she lay it across the man's legs, his eyes opened. Agilina grinned. "Much stronger than I look, eh." One look at the hag's face and the Dog Soldier's eyes rolled to white as he fainted. Agilina cackled with glee as she leaned over the two limp forms.

Reaching under the collar of her ragged dress, Agilina withdrew a polished piece of amber that hung from her neck by a thick cord. She wouldn't lose this one, not like she had the other. It had taken decades to charge the amber with enough magic to continue her work after losing the elfin amulet in the swamp. Clutching the stone firmly in her palm, she voiced the words as she had countless times over the centuries.

A golden glow formed around the slab. The man's body began to blur until he was no longer recognizable. His flesh then seemed to melt and flow into the body of the wolf. As it did, the wolf's body swelled. Legs grew longer and thicker, as did its chest, neck and head. When the last of what had been a man disappeared, there was but one lump of flesh and fur that slowly solidified into another of Agilina's creations.

The wolf-man opened its eyes and snarled. When its crimson eyes locked on Agilina it lunged, only to stop abruptly two fingers from her neck. Agilina could hear the crackle of her dark magic as it took hold of the beast's mind.

"You are mine," she said. "And now we both know it, eh." The beast backed away and lowered its head in submission. Agilina tucked the amber stone back under her dress and smiled. She so enjoyed her work.

Chapter 36

ROBIN

For ten gruelling days Robin had marched through the rugged Hagstrom
mountains along with a force of three hundred and twenty men. Every
muscle in his legs and back ached. Despite a strong reluctance to work the farm,
Shaun had always been a tower of strength. He could carry a dressed elk farther
than any other valley man, without even breaking a sweat, yet even he looked
worn as he trudged along wordlessly at Robin's side.

Conditions had gone from bad to worse ever since leaving Icarus.
Inclement weather aside, the real trouble had started six days back, when the
trail they travelled turned west. After much deliberation and arguing amongst
the nobles, they had abandoned the trail in favour of a forest route along the
Hagstrom's eastern slopes. The treacherous, rocky terrain had since proved to
be most unsuitable for travel.

Growing up among the foothills of Zindale Valley had not prepared Robin
for the closeness of the sheer cliffs and towering jagged peaks that were the
Hagstroms. Had it not been for the flat top of Drakenmount, periodically visible
above the other peaks, he was sure they would have become lost in the endless
twists and turns. A score of scouts set out each morning just to blaze a trail that
the main party could follow.

The entire company had long since descended into a foul humour, with the
nobles demonstrating the foulest. Robin, along with the rest of the commoners,
avoided them as much as possible. The cause of their displeasure was a
combination of unforgiving terrain, thick clumps of nearly impassable forest and
a damp bone chilling cold. The route proved hardest on the nobles. The trees
were small and grew so close together that for most part they were forced to
walk. It was something the nobility had neither the boots nor legs for.

All in all, the mountains were proving too rough for the Balorian horses.
Seven had come up lame over the past six days and had been subsequently put

down. The knights seemed to mourn each one lost as if it had been a dear family member. Talk of making use of the meat resulted in bared steel and threats of violence. A ridiculous way for grown men to act over stock, but then nobles were strange that way. Another horse was found dead early that very morning. To Robin's way of thinking, the knights were better off for not having to suffer through the ordeal of coaxing such an ungainly animal up the steep slopes, or through forest too dense for their wide bodies. The smaller Icarian horses, like the two Duke Edmond and Captain Doyle rode, were much better suited for the task, as were the short sturdy Icarian ponies they used for pack animals. At least they could be handled by one man.

Another growing problem was an ever widening rift between the Icarian and Balorian nobles. When they departed Icarus, the Duke was riding at the head of the column alongside the Balorian leader. After a loud and heated argument between them a few days back, however, the company had split in two. Adamantly refusing to ride with the knights, the Duke was keeping company with his archers. Robin was not privy to what their differences were. One man argued it was something to do with the Duchess, another that is was over leadership. Robin wasn't about to lose any sleep over it. Who could understand nobles anyway. They seemed to get upset at the most absurd things.

Since leaving Icarus, Robin and Shaun had been travelling in the company of Gregory's men. When the Duke segregated his archers, Gregory came to speak with Robin and Shaun. He offered them the choice or joining their own countrymen or travelling with his men. Robin and Shaun both agreed their best chance to rescue Agnes lay with the knights, so they elected to stay. Since then, any contact with the Duke's men had resulted in nothing but silence and dark looks.

To make matters worse, the temperature had been dropping steadily since leaving the main road. The dry, warm spring air of the valley and foothills was all but a memory. Breath left their mouths in billowing clouds of smoke. When they stopped for the night, frost covered men's beards and eyebrows like lard icing on a cake. As the days grew colder, more and more toes and ears had succumbed to frostbite. With that thought, Robin slipped his stiff hands under the scarf he had wrapped around his head and felt his ears. His hands felt as cold as ice. He took that as a good sign.

The scouts had chosen a campsite protected from the icy winds by a large slab of rock. Somewhere in the distant past it must have slid down from the mountain. The area was heavily treed, but slides of gravel and dirt had cut swaths through the trees leaving large open areas suitable for building warm fires. Gregory walked over from the fire he shared with other nobles to relay the welcome news that they were just three days south of Drakenmount, and to offer them some wine. It was easy to see why Gregory's men were so loyal.

The first thing Robin did after starting a fire was to remove his boots and hang them over the flames to dry. When they stopped steaming he slipped them back on. It was the first time in two days he felt warm. Lazing before the fire next to Shaun, sipping mulled wine with the eight other Vennell men, Robin could almost forget how exhausted he was. Gregory had warned them it would be their last for some time, so they were doing their best to enjoy it. From now on they could look forward to nothing but water.

Thinking back, Robin was grateful Sir Gregory had agreed to speak for them. At the same time, he was plagued with jealousy over his obvious interest in Agnes. The young knight had proved to be a likeable sort, and to Robin's chagrin he found it impossible to dislike him. Regardless, he was resolved to not let petty jealousy endanger Aggie. After all, they were just three men desperate to save a women they all cared for. The fact that one was a noble, and the other two serfs, made little difference.

Fires from the Icarian camp were visible through the thin line of trees which separated the two camps. Even though there were two hundred of his countrymen nearby, if it were not for Shaun, Robin would have felt very much alone. He glanced at the faces of the foreigners who shared his fire. No matter how friendly these men were, he and Shaun were outsiders. He watched his boyhood friend poke at the base of the fire with a long branch that he had peeled the bark from with his knife.

"Never imagined it would be like this," Shaun said as he pulled the stick out of the fire and blew on the smoking end.

"What do you mean?" Robin asked.

"I've always dreamed of leaving the farm on some grand adventure. You know, seeking my fortune, fighting for my country, being a hero, that sort of thing. Thought travelling would be all fun and exciting." Shaun shivered and pulled his blanket tighter around his broad shoulders. "Can't say this is all that much fun." He turned his head and spat. "Even bloody farming was better than this. At least I was warm."

Robin could hardly believe his ears. Even tired and depressed he couldn't help but smile. He was about to remark on Shaun's sudden change of attitude when he heard the sharp snap of cracking wood. It seemed to have come from somewhere in the stand of pine behind them.

"What was that," Robin whispered.

Shaun cocked his head to listen. "Just the frost," he said, resuming his poking at the fire.

Not feeling very reassured, Robin kept an eye on the trees while continuing to sip his cooling wine. It was too dark to see anything, but he watched anyway. Something was wrong. Robin couldn't say how he knew it, he just did. A wolf howled in the distance just as he set the cup on a flat rock by the edge of the fire to warm. "Wolves howling," he said. "It'll be a cold night when the wolves howl."

Shaun laughed. "Don't need wolves to tell me that," he said and then bolted straight up. "What was that?"

Robin shielded his eyes from the fire and scanned the woods again. A movement between two trees caught his eye. "In the woods!" someone screamed, just as a large black shadow burst out of the trees.

Because it stood on its hind legs, Robin at first thought it to be a bear. That was, until he caught sight of the distorted face. No natural creature could possibly look like that. Before anyone could act, the nightmarish beast tore into the man sitting next to him. Primal self preservation drove Robin to leap over the fire to safety.

With the flames between him and the beast, Robin watched in horror as another man was ripped apart even as he drew a dirk to defend himself. Shaun was at Robin's side with his sword raised. Firelight reflected off the sharp edge of the blade. Fumbling, his hands shaking with fear, Robin finally managed to string his bow and let loose an arrow. It struck the monster full in the chest, but the beast continued to rend and tear at the doomed man.

Shaft after shaft plunged into the beast, until Robin reached for another arrow and found the quiver empty. His spare arrows were rolled in cloth tied to his pack, which in his panic he had left on the other side of the fire. It was immaterial anyway. The incredible number of broken shafts protruding from the beast seemed to have little or no effect.

Screams of men and horses mixed with howls of beasts. Its coat glistening with something dark and wet, a great black war horse leapt through the fire scattering the burning wood. With glowing embers laying all about, Robin was momentarily blinded by so many points of light in the darkness. He rubbed his eyes in frustration. When his vision cleared, he could see the Balorians forming a semicircle around two larger fires in front of the big rock. Each man held a weapon in one hand and a burning log or branch in the other. The great slab of stone reflected the light all around them. In the glow, Robin counted no less than a score of the shadowy creatures darting in and out with incredible speed for such misshapen hulks. They were like nothing he had ever seen before. Some had heads like wolves, while others resembled bears or panthers. One looked almost human. It was by far the most terrifying.

A low growl drew Robin's attention back to what was left of his own fire. Having torn everyone else apart, the beast Robin had peppered with arrows turned its beady red eyes toward him and Shaun. Then it charged. Robin reached down and snatched up a smoldering log that lay by his feet and threw it in the face of the oncoming beast. It howled in pain, but kept coming with its fur singed and smoke billowing behind. In what he knew would be a useless attempt to fend off the beast, Robin raised his bow just as Shaun leapt in and plunged his broadsword into the creature's belly right up to the hilt.

The beast howled in pain as it raked Shaun savagely with its claws. Shaun went down with the beast on top of him. Robin turned in a frantic search for another burning log, but saw nothing but dying embers. A foul smell filled his nostrils and pain akin to fire ran down his back. He tried to run, but his legs gave out and he fell face first to the ground. There was more pain as sharp rocks dug into his cheek. Shouts, growls and screams pounded in his head. He tried to rise, but didn't have the strength. Then everything went silent. He felt himself floating upon a dark cloud. The last thing he remembered was being vaguely aware of that awful odour growing stronger.

Chapter 37

RODNEY

Within the arc of firelight that danced across the sheer rock face behind them, a score of grim faced men stood shoulder to shoulder in a rough semicircle before two blazing fires. They were all that remained of the Balorian company still able to stand and defend themselves. Though distant firelight still flickered weakly beyond the line of trees separating the Balorian and Icarian camps, it was impossible to tell if any of their allies remained alive.

Rodney held a long, slender sword in his right hand and a thick, makeshift torch in the other. The blade had belonged to Jason's cousin Earnest, who had been killed in the first wave. Rodney had pulled the sword from the dead knight's scabbard after one of the beasts fled with his own embedded between its ribs.

Glowing red eyes dotted the darkness beyond the firelight's reach. It seemed as if they had been fighting these nightmarish creatures for half the night, yet Rodney knew that no more than a half sun-mark had passed. A sword in each hand, Jason stood to his right. Dark unnatural blood stained the tips and edges of both weapons. Rodney recognized the long slightly curved blade in Jason's left hand as Sir Gavin's, so he too must have fallen.

At least the beasts were keeping their distance for the moment. Rodney knew it wasn't their blades, but fear of fire holding them back. Unfortunately, the fires were dying, and there was nothing left within reach to use for fuel. They had already thrown in everything that would burn, including their saddles. Since it was extremely doubtful any of the horses had survived, they would have been of little use anyway.

It was easy to figure out the beasts intended to make their final assault once the fires were reduced to glowing embers and the men were blind in the darkness. What puzzled Rodney was why he seemed to be their preferred target. For every beast that charged another man, two launched themselves directly at him. The men struck down while at his side seemed to have just been unfortunate enough to place themselves between him and a charging beast. Lionel had been such a victim. Badly mauled while fighting at Rodney's side, he lay with the rest of the wounded against the great slab of rock.

Time after time, something from Rodney's worst nightmare leapt out of the darkness to grapple with him. Twice he had gone down under their weight, only to be saved by Jason's deadly blades. Rodney could feel their sticky blood and gore congealing on his face and arms.

Between attacks, Rodney caught glimpses of other men defending themselves desperately with whatever weapons were to hand. Taken completely unawares, they had armed themselves with swords, bows, knives, axes, burning brands and even stones taken from around the fires. Shark-tooth was the only able bodied man not engaged in battle. After exhausting his darts, he had sat down cross-legged in front of the fire directly behind Rodney and began chanting Kelatch gibberish. Rodney could only assume he was praying to whatever gods his people held dear.

A loud scream from the Icarian camps drew Rodney's eyes back to the flickering lights on the other side of the trees. The Icarian campfires were dimming and he didn't think much of their chances. Arrows seemed useless and the Icarians had little else in the way of weaponry.

A nearby growl forced Rodney to refocus his attention on his own problems. So far the beasts had come at him one at a time. Most withdrew when wounded or threatened with fire, but the more human-like creatures would not stop until they had been hacked to bits. Pieces of the dead lay everywhere, but from what he could tell only a half score of beasts had been slain.

The last two had been dispatched by Jason while they had Rodney pinned to the ground. Like most of the knights, Rodney had continued to wear his mail even in the bitter cold. It had cost him a little frostbite on the back of his neck, but if not for that foresight he would most certainly be dead. As it was, with every move his shoulder ached where the last beast had nearly succeeded in biting through the steel links.

Like a death shroud, the darkness drew closer as the last flames of the fires flickered out. The glowing red eyes that roamed back and forth seemed grow in size and number. Rodney braced himself for the final assault, but just as the beasts moved in for the kill the clearing became awash with intense white light. It was instantly followed by a deafening crack of thunder.

At first Rodney thought a bolt of lightning had come to ground. Unlike a lightning flash, however, it did not fade away. It took a few moments for his eyes to adjust, but even through squinted lids he could see the number of beasts was far greater than he had feared. Though many were hunched over mangled bodies of men or horses, their maws bloody from feeding on the flesh, the rest were arrayed in front of him on the verge of attacking.

Startled by the sudden light, the beasts shielded their eyes with long hairy arms. Rodney watched, stunned, as half them burst into flame. The mystery was solved when a FireDrake roared past no more than fifteen feet above the ground. The force of its passing was such that Rodney was nearly thrown to the ground. By the time he regained his composure, the few beasts that had escaped the dragon-fire were fleeing into the forest.

With a deafening roar, the FireDrake swooped by once more leaving a wall of flame in its wake. Its dragon-fire was directed into the trees along the edge of the clearing and incinerated everything before it. After a moment of relative silence, the white light faded, but even so, the whole area remained illuminated by burning trees. Plumes of black greasy smoke curled up from smoldering mounds that dotted the clearing. Thick smoke drifted up from everywhere only to disappear where it blended into the upper darkness. Speechless, Rodney stared at the scorched lumps that were once men and beasts.

The FireDrake returned to land just twenty feet from where Rodney stood; the wind rolling off its wings fanning the flames of all that was still burning. An arrow bounced of the FireDrake's chest. Then a large rock. Only then did Rodney notice the white haired man straddling the creature's neck.

"Hold!" Rodney screamed.

Yet another arrow bounced off its head.

"Hold, I say!" Rodney screamed again.

The missiles stopped.

Grigor's head lowered to the ground and Aldus slid down from a modified Balorian saddle attached to the base of the FireDrake's long neck. The wizard looked at Rodney and smiled. "I was beginning to get worried."

"I thought I recognized Grigor," Rodney said, returning the smile as the two men gripped forearms in the universal warrior's greeting, "but I was not sure until I saw you. I would have hated to see you spitted by an arrow in payment for saving our lives. What were those monstrosities? More of Magdalen's doing?"

The smile on the wizard's face faded. "No, though they are abominations created by magic, they are not hers. There are other players in this game. Very dangerous ones."

Aldus looked down at the gore that had been transferred from Rodney's arm to his own. His eyebrows rose as he looked at Rodney's bloodstained clothes. "You are injured?"

"Only a bruised shoulder," Rodney replied. "The blood is not mine."

When the wizard's eyes went to Rodney's shoulder he frowned. Following his gaze, Rodney saw Shark-tooth standing a few feet behind him. He was wearing his customary smile that always gave the impression he was keeping secrets. Something wordless passed between Shark-tooth and Aldus, then the Kelatch walked away.

Rodney turned back to find Aldus facing the FireDrake. The wizard nodded to Grigor and then looked toward Rodney. "Excuse me Sir Rodney, but Grigor wishes to speak with you. Would you allow me to make that possible?"

After Rodney gave his consent, the wizard reached over and touched him lightly on the forehead. At first it felt like his ears were filling with water, but then he heard a voice inside his head. *You present me with a bit of a puzzle, Sir Knight. There is something very different about you. Something I do not yet fully understand. Just the same, it pleases me to see you well.*

"And I you," Rodney replied, as he marvelled at the deep musical timbre of Grigor's voice.

A claw-full of those vile creatures that attacked you are still nearby. I can smell their foul stench, Grigor added with an audible snort, *but you may rest easy for I will track them down to ensure they trouble you no more.*

I will remain with our friends here, the voice of Aldus replied in Rodney's mind. *We will meet again at Drakenmount in three days.*

Grigor's huge emerald eyes locked onto Rodney. In that brief moment he understood what Silas must have felt that day in the Imperial camp.

Please try to stay alive, Sir Knight, the FireDrake said. *Beside the fact that Aldus believes your presence crucial to freeing my kind from bondage, I wish to solve this puzzle of who and what you truly are.*

Unsure how to respond, Rodney just said, "Good hunting, friend Grigor."

Grigor lifted into the air with two beats of his massive wings and then disappeared into the darkness with only a few more. *Fare you well,* were his parting words.

Aldus touched Rodney's forehead and the fullness in his ears drained away. "Come," the wizard said, "we have much to talk about, but first I must see to healing your countrymen. There must be many in need of my services."

"True," Rodney replied. "Unfortunately, far more are in need of funeral rites."

❂   ❂   ❂

After administering to the wounded, Aldus had rejoined Rodney by his fire. From somewhere within his robe the wizard produced a pot and to Rodney's delight a pouch of chicory tea. While they waited for the water to boil, Aldus explained how he had come to arrive just in the nick of time. "I had little choice. She had me caught in a web very much akin to dragon-fire."

Rodney nodded even though he did not fully understand the import of what the wizard was saying. Aldus poured some of the chicory root into his hand as he talked.

"I could feel her thoughts probing into the remotest recesses of my mind. It took every bit of strength I had just to bury the knowledge of you and Grigor. Still, she nearly broke through my defences. Then, just as I was failing, she let me go."

"Why would she do that?" Rodney asked. "Perhaps you have misjudged her intentions."

Aldus laughed. "Do not fool yourself, my friend. The amount of power Magdalen wields boggles the mind. Even were she a decent sort, that much power would corrupt anyone. No, as long as Magdalen holds the amulet we are all in danger."

Something about the wizard's words bothered Rodney. What about the amulet in his possession? Why should one be any less corruptible than the other? Rodney had to fight down the urge to defend Magdalen just on principle. Aldus having just saved their lives tipped the scale, but even so it was a battle he had only barely won. In the meantime, the wizard had dropped the chicory root into the pot of steaming water and stirred it with a thin stick before setting the pot on a rock to steep.

"Now where was I?" Aldus said, clasping his hands together. "Ah yes, after she let me go, I found myself adrift in the void without the strength to return to my body. A white light appeared, promising peace and blissful sleep. I was about to enter its warm embrace when a voice called out to me. The voice grew louder and more insistent until finally I recognized it. It was Grigor. He brought me back from the abyss."

The aroma of chicory drifted by Rodney's nostrils and he smiled in anticipation as Aldus filled two copper cups. The wizard offered him one, which he accepted eagerly. Raising it to his lips, Rodney breathed in the steam before taking a sip. "Ah," he said lifting the cup to Aldus, "a very fine brew."

Aldus nodded absently. "To make a long tale short," he said, "I awoke in great pain. It was as if my very soul had been ripped from my body and crushed. Until then I had not realized the true extent of Aedon's power."

"Well, you look as fit as last we met," Rodney said, as he rolled the warm cup in his hands and then stretched his shoulder. "A knight could use such a healing gift as yours."

"If only it were that simple. A wizard cannot heal himself directly, you see, so all I could do was put myself into a healing trance and let nature take its course. Grigor stood guard over me. Only yesterday did I awake. But, enough of my adventure. By that purpling around your neck, and the look on your face, I can see there is yet one more healing to perform."

Rodney smiled. "I would be most grateful."

Chapter 38

ROBIN

Robin's world was spinning. It didn't stop until a sudden jolt sent a nauseating wave of pain down his left arm. Another jolt sent a similar wave down his back and left leg. Opening his eyes revealed only blackness and resulted in setting the world to spinning again. Reaching out with his right hand, Robin grabbed at a tangled mass of coarse hair. *Must be on the back of one of the horses.* Another wave of pain forced an involuntary pull on that handful of hair. The owner beneath let out a growl. His hand froze as a horrifying realization hit him like a punch. He was on the back of one of those terrifying beasts that had attacked the camp. The thought was too much for him. When another jolt sent new waves of pain down his arm, he willingly let his mind drift back to the welcome bliss of unconsciousness.

The reprieve was short lived. Robin awoke once more, this time engulfed in pain. His leg felt as if it were caught in a vise. He screamed. The outcry was answered by a snarl and new pain exploded in his head as his body was slapped abruptly against the rough bark of a tree. He blacked out for a time. For how long he couldn't tell. When his senses returned he was lying flat on the ground. After discovering that the slightest movement caused intense pain throughout his entire body, he kept very still. His left eye remained in total darkness, but he could see shadowy images with the other.

Reaching up very slowly with his right hand, Robin felt the swollen lump that was the left side of his face. His hair was caked in something crusty. Dried blood. His blood. The fingers of his left hand were completely unresponsive. When he tried to lift his left arm, the pain in his wrist was so intense he nearly passed out again. His left leg was on fire. He could still move it, even wiggle his toes, so at least it wasn't broken.

A small gap in the thick cloud cover exposed a three-quarter moon. Enough light filtered through to allow Robin to see his immediate surroundings. As his vision sharpened he detected another body lying next to him. The face was swollen and unrecognizable, but the handlebar moustache was unmistakable. "Shaun," he croaked softly. "Shaun, wake up."

His friend remained motionless. Ignoring the pain, Robin slid closer. Being careful not to jostle his left hand, he bent over so his ear was next to the unconscious man's mouth. He was rewarded by the faint brush of air. *You're still breathing. Thank the Gods.* Robin shook Shaun over and over, but there was no response. The growls grew louder and he pushed himself back against the tree in fear.

Twenty feet away, three wolf-like beasts hunched over what remained of a corpse. Their snouts were wet and glistened in the moonlight. They snapped and snarled at each other as they fed. Robin wanted to scream but swallowed down his terror instead. A little closer, but facing away from him, a fourth beast sniffed the air. Its silhouette appeared more human than the others. Robin shuddered, an act which sent another wave of pain down his back. They had to get away before the beasts began to look toward them for their next meal.

Darkness returned as the moon once again disappeared behind cloud. Robin reached over and made several attempts to rouse Shaun. Just as before, there was no response. He finally gave up and slipped quietly behind the tree. Robin hesitated, unsure of what to do. He couldn't just leave Shaun to the mercy of these beasts, but what else could he do. He was barely able to move himself.

The sound of creatures fighting over their meal helped Robin make up his mind. If he could just find the others, they could come back for Shaun. Being very careful not to make a sound, he rolled over onto his stomach and crawled slowly forward. Every move was agony, but he gritted his teeth and kept moving. The loud snap of breaking bone spurred him on in spite of the pain.

When he could no longer hear the creatures, Robin finally forced himself to stand. Searing pain shot up his arm. Carefully cradling his left hand inside his tunic, he took a step and cautiously shifted the weight to his left foot. His leg held but still felt like it was on fire. Touching it gently, he could feel the ridges of claw marks that ran the length of his leg, across his buttock and around to his back. The wounds were not deep, but were covered in crusted blood, inflamed and incredibly painful.

Ignoring the pain, as best he could, Robin limped slowly forward, awkwardly trying to step lightly as if stalking a deer. After what seemed like an eternity he arrived at a frozen stream. The ice was thin enough to break with the heel of his boot. He dropped onto his belly and took a long drink from the cold, clear water. It chilled him inside, but soothed his dry throat and renewed his strength. Taking a handful of cold mud from the stream bed, he smeared it on the back of his left leg. It felt wonderfully cool. He then rubbed some on his head as well. It eased the pain. He only wished he could reach his back. His head snapped up painfully in response to a howl in the distance. *They are coming for me. I've got to hide.*

On the other side of the stream stood a large redwood with low wide branches. He picked himself up and hobbled across. The ice shattered beneath his weight and freezing water filled his boots, but with all the pain he barely noticed. On the other side he began a slow one-handed climb up the tree. Needles and branches rubbed against his wounds, but fear drove him on. He had climbed only about three times his height when he heard a twig snap. It sounded very close and he went still. There was another snap. This time it came from directly below him.

A snorting, sniffing sound drifted up from the base of the tree. On the verge of panic Robin held his breath. There was a howl in the distance. It was answered by a second, followed by the sound of something crashing through the trees. The noise faded into the distance and Robin finally took a breath. Resting his head against the rough bark, he closed his eyes and tried to relax.

In the throes of a nightmare, with horrible monsters chasing him, Robin tried to run but his legs were sticking to the ground like glue. He turned, rolled over, and then fell. A sharp pain in his ankle made him yelp as his one good eye opened to blink at the bright morning light. He lay on the soft, damp forest floor. *Lucky for me the moss is so thick and soft.* He tried to stand, but the moment he put weight on his right foot he collapsed in pain. He reached down to his ankle to find it already beginning to swell. *Must have landed badly when I fell out of the tree.*

Dragging himself to the edge of the stream, Robin filled his belly with water and then plastered more mud on his leg and backside. Using a forked stick as a crutch, he started to hobble down the mountain following the stream. By midday he had stumbled into the same clearing where they had made camp the night before. *Gods, was it only last night.*

At first Robin feared the worst. His companions were gone and only the charred bodies of the dead remained. Then he realized that they had somehow managed to set a section of the forest on fire. *Must have been how they drove them off.* He crossed the clearing; on the way he noticed many boot prints leading north toward Drakenmount. He bent down by one of the dead fires to feel the ashes. They were stone cold, which meant his companions were long gone.

In his present condition, Robin had no hope of catching up. He flopped down on a rock in total despair and covered his face as a strong wind stirred up the ashes. When he opened his eye, a shadow had fallen across him. A sinking feeling settled in his gut like an iron weight. Had the creatures found him? He reluctantly turned his head, shielding his one good eye from the sun. What he saw was even worse than he had imagined. Towering over him stood a massive FireDrake.

Somewhere in his mind, Robin heard a voice. *A little halfling.* Falling backwards, too exhausted to even scream, he prayed the end would be quick. Huge claws closed around his body. The pressure on his wounds was so unbearable he hardly noticed the sensation of being lifted into the air as his mind drifted into oblivion.

Robin awoke to find himself sprawled out on a cot in a small stone-walled chamber with a high curved ceiling. Even with only one eye there was more than enough light to see by. A survey of the room failed to reveal the source of the light, until he realized the light emanated from the stone walls themselves. Both walls and ceiling gave off a glow which made the room as bright as a cloudy day.

Lifting his right hand to his face, he marvelled at how remarkably clean it appeared. Even the dirt under his nails had been scrubbed away. He found a bandage on his head that extended across his forehead and covered the whole left side of his face. He became aware of the absence of pain as he drew his fingers through what hair poked out from under his bandages. It had been cleaned and oiled. His hand came away smelling of lilac. Propping himself up on one elbow, he looked down at the rest of his body. His left leg was wrapped in bandages and both his left forearm and right ankle were in splints.

A shuffling sound drew Robin's attention away from himself. His eyes widened in shock as the most delicate and beautiful girl he had ever seen walked through an opening in the wall that he had not noticed. The girl set a wooden tray down beside his cot. The wonderful aroma of cooked food wafted by his nose. The sound of his growling stomach seemed to amuse the girl. Her smile had the effect of making her look even more beautiful, if that was possible.

"I must inspect your bandages," the girl said in a singsong voice. Robin could not stop himself from staring as she carried out her duties. Once satisfied, she smiled again. "Eat, you need to regain your strength." Before Robin could think of a reply, she had left the chamber through the same nearly invisible doorway.

Robin stared at the spot where the girl had vanished until hunger got the better of him. He picked up the wooden spoon and began eating what looked like some kind of stew. It was warm and slightly spicy. He couldn't remember ever tasting anything better and the bowl was soon empty. After the stew was gone, he set to work on the half loaf of bread by tearing off strips and dipping them into a bowl of honey.

With a full stomach, Robin lay back and quickly fell into a light sleep. When something brushed against his cheek, he opened his eye to find himself face to face with that wondrously strange girl again. Her bright eyes lowered to his. Her smile was dazzling.

"Where am I?" Robin asked.

"Drakenmount," she replied in that singsong voice. Robin pushed himself up in alarm.

The girl frowned. "You are safe," she said, placing a hand on his shoulder and gently pushing him back down. Long red hair fell forward exposing a long slender pointed ear. Sensuous lips curved into a broad smile when she noticed him staring.

"What... Who are you?" Robin asked, unable to avert his eyes from her ear.

"I am Ethlfled," she said, tucking her hair back behind both ears. "A Red Elf."

Robin was speechless. He just stared open mouthed until she laughed. Her laughter was like sweet music.

"Pardon me for staring," he finally managed, "but until now I thought elves only existed in children's fables."

"I can assure you I am quite real," she replied.

"Forgive me, but I have never met anyone like you before," Robin said sheepishly. "My name is Robin."

"Greetings, Robin."

"Can you tell me how I came to be here?"

"Grigor brought you in three days ago."

"Three days," Robin said under his breath. "Well I would like to thank this Grigor. He saved my life. I remember being attacked by monsters, and then by a dragon. It was horrible."

Ethlfled covered her mouth with her hand and giggled. "Now eat your food and get some rest," she said. "Tomorrow I will show you Drakenmount and perhaps you will meet Grigor."

Chapter 39

GAMEL

The Emperor stood in his chamber, hands clasped together, waiting. The door was barred, the windows shuttered and a spell in place to prevent the slightest sound from escaping the room. An ensorcelled mirror hung from a brass hook embedded in the marble pillar next to the scrying pool, its sole purpose to display the reflection of anyone using magic to scry within a league of the mirror. There was another magic practitioner, one of considerable power, who had taken an interest in Gamel's affairs. The raw force of magic unleashed near Drakenmount during the night had awakened him from a sound slumber. Yes, it had been powerful magic indeed to accomplish that.

Gamel raised his eyes to the mirror. Two familiar faces were reflected on its silvery surface. He looked down at the same two faces reflected in the scrying pool. *They should be here soon.* He did not mind waiting. He had waited centuries for his schemes to bear fruit. What were a few moments compared to that?

Almost simultaneously two ghostly images flickered into existence. They floated in the air a foot above the black, placid liquid of the pool. The two shimmering fetches could not have been of greater contrast to Gamel's senses. One, immaculate and captivatingly beautiful; the other disgustingly filthy and repugnant. As a connoisseur of beauty, he found it ironic that of the two it was the beauty he mistrusted.

"Magdalen, my dear," Gamel said in as smooth and fatherly a voice as he could muster. "As promised, Agilina's pets have destroyed that pitiful company of knights, and, at no small cost I might add. Surely a little gratitude is in order. Many of her creations have been sacrificed for your safety."

"And what thanks do I get, eh," Agilina screeched.

"Destroyed indeed," Magdalene said, ignoring Agilina's comment. "My FireDrakes report that a number of them still live. The survivors have already reached Drakenmount, nearly at my very door."

A cold, hard lump of anger rose up into Gamel's throat, but he refused to allow it to show, even in the slightest. *Your FireDrakes! They should be mine you treacherous, spoiled, ungrateful child.*

"Surely a handful of weary and wounded men will pose no threat to a sorceress of your great power," Gamel replied, trying to look both concerned and injured at the same time. "You command FireDrakes; the greatest force in the known world. Have them dispose of these pathetic knights."

"I will see to them, you can count on that, but what of the army that marched out of Icarus ten days ago? It nears Vanir Pass even as we speak."

"Never fear my dear," Gamel replied pleasantly with a wave of his hand. "As I am sure you already know, my legions are in position to intercept them."

"Yes, I am aware of your men. They should be more than enough to crush the Icarian army. That is unless they bungle it, like they did in Icarus. What I want to know is what you are waiting for. Why let them get so close? I know you too well, Gamel. You are up to something."

Clever girl. "Timing my dear, just timing. My general has orders to take them the moment they enter the pass. They will be trapped and easy prey for my Dog Soldiers."

"Very well. Then there is nothing else to discuss." With that Magdalen's fetch faded away.

"Nasty bitch," Agilina spat, once the image had completely dissolved. "If only I could get her on my table, she would make a fine specimen. I'd have a little fun first of course. Perhaps split her pretty nose and cut off her ears." Agilina's eyes widened with apparent glee. "Her hair would make a nice shawl," she added, following with a fit of manic laughter.

Gamel looked in the mirror. Only Agilina's disgusting face remained. He let the facade of a friendly disposition he was projecting fall away. The lines of his face hardened to a countenance that felt more comfortable. It was not necessary to hide his true nature from Agilina.

For a moment he allowed himself the indulgence of imagining Magdalen's lithe body stretched out on Agilina's slab. He could not suppress a smile of satisfaction. Of course he would not let Agilina mar such beauty. Dealing with Magdalen would be a pleasure he reserved solely for himself, but Agilina had the right of it.

Though he was possibly the most patient man alive, even his patience had limits. It was time that something was done about his lovely former student, but first, the amulet had to be taken away from her, even if it meant that someone else would get their hands on it. What was stolen once could be stolen again. It would only be another delay, but this time he would not trust the task to another halfling. It was too dangerous.

Gamel looked up at the misshapen fetch hovering above him. "You may soon have your wish, my dear Agilina," he said absently. "We have much to discuss, you and I." The witch looked at him warily. She kept one eye squinted shut, but listened intently.

Chapter 40

VERNON

Though only late spring, the Olaug Plain was already hotter than Concurie at the height of summer. Vernon wiped the dust and sweat from his brow. He longed for the cool baths of the King's palace, with its lovely pleasure girls waiting to take care of a man's every need, and if one of the girls had gained a few bruises when he was done, it was of little matter. One or another was always slipping on the wet tiles. It was an occupational hazard after all. Visions of the palace shattered as the irritation of dust caked on the inside of his nose made him sneeze violently.

"May the Goddess bless you," said a voice at Vernon's side.

Vernon glanced over at the man riding next to him. Though they were of the same height, Galen Morgan was at least twice Vernon's size. Astride a magnificent snow white stallion, with his well oiled leathers, polished silver armour and that hideous white plume on his helm, even Vernon had to admit the backwoods Baron was an impressive sight.

Since leaving Icarus, each day had grown hotter than the last. It galled Vernon that in the last nine days under the merciless sun he had not seen the baron lose a single drop of sweat, while he himself shed buckets. He failed to understand how a man of such bulk had no need to perspire, so it was with great satisfaction that he watched a tiny bead of sweat leave a trail in the dust as it ran down the side of the Baron's face. *So, he is human after all.*

Gratified that he was not the only one suffering the effects of the heat, Vernon twisted around in the saddle to better see the line of men and wagons which stretched as far back as the eye could see. The tail of the column was obscured by a cloud of dust in the distance. As he thought of all the surprises they had in store for the witch and her troublesome dragons, Vernon allowed himself the pleasure of a smile. They were too far back to see at that moment, but just knowing they were there lifted his spirits. Twenty springalds of his own design. The giant crossbows had been intended for use in clearing the northeastern passes, but they would serve just as well here. He would eliminate the vermin at their source.

Following the springalds came twenty wagons heavily laden with fire hardened darts. They were as long as a spear and twice as thick. As luck would have it, Vernon had been presented with an opportunity to test them at Montcre. Galen had provided targets constructed of thick wooden planks covered in scales taken from a slain dragon. A disappointing exercise at first. The wooden darts proved to be inadequate for penetrating the rock hard scales. They were not found wanting however, once the Baron's blacksmiths had refitted the shafts with needle-sharp steel tips.

The Baron's craftsmen had worked in shifts, day and night, until every dart was fitted with a shiny new tip. Even Galen took a turn at a forge. Vernon had found it amusing how Galen, stripped to the waist and covered in soot, suited so well the role of a common blacksmith. Most unusual for a noble, even one like Galen who was so far removed from high society. Perhaps his dear mother had not been chaste. The previous Baron would not be the first noble to be made cuckold by a commoner. In this case, perhaps by his blacksmith.

"The witch will not catch us with our britches down this time," the Baron said when he caught Vernon looking back.

Vernon was impressed with Galen's resourcefulness if not his refinement. That in itself said a lot for the captain's opinion of him, since he had never met a noble he did not in the end hold in complete and utter contempt. The King of course was the one exception. "To be sure," Vernon replied, offering his countryman a smile but nothing more to encourage idle conversation.

By the Duke's decree, Galen was to lead the Icarian forces. Unperturbed, Vernon let it be known right from the start he would follow Galen's orders only so long as it suited him. When Galen protested, as Vernon knew he would, he presented the Baron with a letter. It bore the King's seal, and stated plainly that Vernon spoke with the King's authority in all matters pertaining to national security. Hence, Galen led by his leave, and when the battle started, it would be Vernon who took command. Galen couldn't argue with the King's seal and had grudgingly agreed. Vernon kept it to himself, but if Galen had not accepted his terms he would have run him through before they set one foot outside of Icarus.

The scouts had returned earlier to report the column would reach the entrance to the pass long before nightfall. Galen had been eager to forge ahead, but Vernon insisted they camp on the Olaug side of the pass. He did not want to risk leading the King's troops to a potential slaughter within confined quarters. They would proceed only when he was satisfied the route was properly scouted. All kinds of traps could be laid. Galen had reluctantly agreed to wait. Vernon knew it meant they might be forced to march through part of the next night, if they were to arrive on the morning the King's cousin was expecting them, but tired men were better than dead ones.

"Look, another dragon," Galen barked.

Shielding his eyes with his hand, Vernon gazed up into the cloudless sky. It took him a while to locate the dull red spot that could only be a dragon. "It's the third we've seen today," he replied.

"We'll not be surprising the witch, that's for certain," Galen said. "I hope this pass is too narrow for dragons."

"You should be hoping it is wide enough that boulders cannot be dropped on our heads," Vernon replied. The disdain in his voice was an obvious insult. Galen didn't seem to possess much of a military mind. Perhaps he should stay to smithing. He sensed the Baron's struggle to bite back his words as the big man grunted a reply.

It pleased Vernon that this backwoods noble understood his place in the scheme of things. He would hate to have to kill him just before the battle. After all, it would be bad for morale. As they rode on in silence, Vernon once again let his thoughts return to the pleasure girls of the palace baths.

Chapter 41

RODNEY

It was a demoralized and ragged remnant of the original company that arrived within sight of Penardun near dusk on the thirteenth day out of Icarus. The wizard had tended to their wounds three days back, but those who had suffered the most grievous injuries were slow to recover their strength. Three more days of travel without proper rest had made a bad situation worse. Many of the men were not strong enough to keep up on their own, requiring those who were to exhaust themselves assisting others.

On the morning after the beasts attacked they made an early start, once a few words had been said for the dead. The weather had improved and by midday it was warm, but before nightfall it had begun to rain. Though the sky to the east remained clear, the damp coastal sea air crossing over the mountain shed its moisture in an endlessly chilling drizzle. Halfway through the next day, Rodney took Aldus aside to ask him for help.

"There must be something you can do to give us strength. If not that, then perhaps you can at least do something about this endless rain."

Aldus frowned and scratched his beard. "Such things can be done of course, but it requires a great deal of magic."

"I have seen you heal men who would have otherwise died without your intervention. Surely what I ask is no greater than defeating death."

"Healing requires only small amounts of magic, administered here and there in the subject's body. What you are asking for requires very much more. As it is, the magic unleashed to deal with those were-beasts has already alerted Magdalen to our presence and put us all at great risk. She will be watching closely. Anything I do now will only serve to pinpoint our exact location. We might as well walk up to the gates of Penardun and say here we are."

It was pointless to argue about something of which he was totally ignorant, so Rodney spoke no more of it. They marched for another day and a half until what had been drizzle turned into sheets of bone numbing sleet. The thought of another cold wet night was disheartening to say the least. If there was ever a time when Rodney had felt more worn and miserable, he could not recall it. Just lifting his feet required sizable effort. As luck would have it, when it was time to call a halt, Tyko stepped out of the trees with most welcome news. The bowman had found them a dry, sheltered place in which to camp. It lay in a small glade nearby. A large, natural overhang of rock with ample high ground beneath it to get them all out of the rain. Upon hearing of their good fortune, the men picked up the pace with renewed vigour.

Upon seeing the place, Aldus cautioned that they would still be visible from the air so it would not be prudent to light fires. Convinced that without the warmth of a fire none of them would be of any use in the morning, Rodney instructed some of the men to gather branches and small bushes to seal the open end of the outcrop. Once they had a secluded area, small fires were lit inside. The result of their construction proved to be somewhat close and smoky, but bearable none the less, and certainly superior to spending the night freezing in wet bedrolls.

Moving aside a small bush, which functioned as a door, Rodney crawled back outside. Aldus followed and then joined him in surveying their handywork. The only visible light they could detect escaped from the little doorway.

"With the bush back in place it should be adequate," Rodney said. He moved it back in place to demonstrate, then glanced at Aldus with raised eyebrows in a silent question.

There was a long pause before wizard replied. "It will suffice." Then his head jerked up. "FireDrakes approach. Quickly, we must get back inside before we are seen."

The wizard yanked the bush away and crawled back in. Rodney followed pulling the makeshift door back into place from the inside. They waited, listening carefully. After a time, they both finally relaxed and returned to their fire. Rodney had already decided against posting a sentry, for there was not a man among them who wasn't in dire need of both warmth and rest. Aldus agreed that it was just as well with FireDrakes about.

So few had survived the attack of three days back, it seemed to Rodney that what little faith his fellow knights may have held in his ability to lead must have died along with all those men. Over the past three days they had gravitated into one of four distinct groups. Each of these had their own unofficial leader and kept their own counsel. For the most part, so far, they just talked amongst themselves. The challenge to his leadership that Rodney was expecting had not yet come. His feelings on the matter were twofold: on the one hand he was duty-bound to lead, while on the other he would gladly turn the responsibility over to someone more capable.

The were-beasts, as Aldus called them, had nearly wiped out the Icarian archers. Since arrows had proved so ineffective, they had suffered the worst casualties. Of the Icarians, only the Duke, Captain Doyle and nine archers remained. Edmond sat by their fire conversing with his countrymen. He cast the occasional sour glance Rodney's way. Though they had not spoken of it, Rodney knew Edmond blamed him for what had happened, and as leader Rodney would have to accept the responsibility.

A snort of laughter came from the direction of Martin's followers. It was the first merry sound Rodney had heard in three days. He could see his Second's grinning face in the firelight next to Talbot and Nicholas. Four others sat with their backs to Rodney. He didn't need to see their faces; they would be Martin's squire Brian, his brother-in-law Owain, Sir Herbolt and Sir Joel.

Just past Martin, leaning against the stone slab of the overhang, sat a grim faced Sir Herman. For the past three days Silas's cousin Duncan had grumbled about how Herman was the eldest, had the greater experience and should therefore be named Leader. When Herman failed to pay heed, he tried to enlist Gregory to his cause. To Rodney's relief, the attempt proved unsuccessful. The young knight would stay loyal to whom he referred to as, *my father's duly appointed successor.*

Duncan was hunched forward, across the fire from Herman, speaking in whispers. Rodney wondered what Duncan would think if he knew how easy it was for Rodney to listen in. On either side of Herman were his brothers, Edward and George. George's squire sat cross-legged next to him polishing his sponsor's sword. The other three knights at Herman's fire were Sir Lewis, his brother Gavin and Sir Claud.

Unlike the other three, it was quiet around Rodney's fire. Only the crackling of the flames disturbed the silence. As he looked from man to man, he saw naught but tired glum faces. Shark-tooth was the only exception. He still wore that silly grin. The two young squires, Karl and Miles, sat with far off stares., arms wrapped tightly around their legs, their hairless chins resting upon their knees. Each had lost his sponsor and they were no doubt worrying about their futures, if not their very survival.

John and Garrick sat next to Yvon, who was lost in grief. His brother had been torn apart before his very eyes. Angry red lines ran across Yvon's face from hair line to chin. They still remained, even after the wizard had healed the wounds received when the bowman had leapt upon the were-beast that had slain Tyko. John was trying to comfort him with little success.

Morton and Jason sat to Rodney's right, while Gregory was to his left. Since the death of his father, the young knight had attached himself to Rodney and was seldom far from his side. Rodney was beginning to feel like a surrogate father, even though there was but eight years between them. Along with his squire Lewis, Jason had lost his last surviving brother, Ernest. Since leaving Balor, he had lost every male member of his immediate family with the exception of Morton. A cruel blow of fate it was, that left Martin as his next closest living male relation.

Lionel had been badly mauled, and though the wizard had healed his wounds, he had been as weak as a kitten ever since. Over the past three days, he had needed Jason's constant support just to be able to walk. Rodney was worried about him. The far off look in his eyes bespoke of injuries that could not be seen. Calling out the names of his wife and son, he lay in a fitful sleep near the fire among the few surviving Balorian commoners. Their lords were all dead, yet they still seemed to have faith in Rodney's leadership. Perhaps they just didn't have any other choice. Rodney sighed and then went back to watching the flames. The ghostly vision of Magdalen came to mind. He closed his eyes to allow himself the pleasure of enjoying it.

Chapter 42

MAGDALEN

Magdalen watched with great interest as the images in her scrying pool swirled and changed. A smile slowly formed on her lips as the men cut and dragged branches to block the entrance to the little den they had fashioned in the side of the mountain. They were close by, only a few sun-marks on human legs.

Agilina's horrid creatures had done their work well, if not completely. Magdalen counted only forty men, and most of those appeared too weak to be a threat. *Fools. Haven't enough of your country men died? Did your mothers teach you no sense at all?*

When she recognized the pompous Icarian Duke by his thin face and wispy yellow beard, Magdalen grinned. Even more gaunt than she remembered, he didn't look so fine now in tattered clothing and covered in filth. Come to rescue his wife, no doubt. Magdalen was still cross with herself for leaping to conclusions and abducting her by mistake.

Seeing the Drake Slayer curtailed Magdalen's amusement. It was his hands that were stained with Gytha's blood. Questioning the Duchess had confirmed as much. The other woman was only an innocent servant and could offer little more. If the Icarians had remained at home, Magdalen would have already released them, but her hands were tied. She couldn't let them go now, not while it could be construed that such release was secured by the force of arms. There would be no end to it. She might as well hand Aedon over to Gamel and become his slave. The thought made her shudder.

Should the Icarian Duke be killed, which seemed most likely if he didn't turn back, she would release his wife and her servant. Magdalen felt no animosity toward the women, just these arrogant men. It was them she wanted to see punished, but most of all, she wanted the Drake Slayer to suffer as Gytha had suffered at his hands.

Magdalen followed the Drake Slayer's movements. He was standing all alone just outside the shelter they had constructed. As she watched, an odd thing happened. He turned his head and spoke as if there was someone standing next to him. Magdalen frowned. It was most curious. The knight looked up and then a bush moved of its own volition. Was the knight a wizard? No, she didn't think so, but how could she explain the bush? The realization struck her like a blow. The Drake Slayer was in the company of a wizard, or another sorceress. Someone powerful enough to shield themself from her scrying spell.

The fetch she had encountered not so long ago came to mind. Could it be the same old man? Did he truly possess one of the amulets? If so, she shouldn't be able to scry within a league of him. It was a natural defence the elves had built into each amulet to protect them from halflings. Unless, unless he knew a spell to counter the defence. No, not counter it, alter it in some way to render himself invisible to scrying without giving away the presence of the amulet. Clever. That would certainly explain things. No matter, he was dangerous regardless. The image changed to the interior of the shelter. She watched the Drake Slayer as he removed his mail and then his cloak. When she caught herself admiring his shape, she growled in frustration. What was the matter with her? This man had murdered Gytha. She could never let herself forget that.

With a wave of her hand the image in the pool became a FireDrake in flight. Though late at night, the magic of the pool made the image as clear as if it were only dusk. It expanded to reveal four females she recognized as part of a group she had sent south to guard the passes near the sea. They were most likely returning to shed their scales. Well, she had one more little task for them to perform before they could return to their warm caves in Drakenmount. Grasping Aedon with her right hand she called out to them. The FireDrakes in the pool immediately altered their course toward Penardun.

Magdalen released the amulet, strode out of her chamber and down the hall. Half way to the end of the hall she stopped to run her hand over a section of the stone wall. It looked and felt like stone, but that was only an illusion. This was the secret door to the library. To her knowledge it was the only way in, or out. The concealment spell was still in place, but with a little added touch of her own. Magdalen had always found if wise to be prepared, and thanks to the Librarian's advice she no longer needed Aedon to force her way in.

Upon reaching the end of the hall, Magdalen paused to withdraw a blackened torch from its holder. Gathering the force electric on her finger tip, she set the pitch-soaked wood ablaze. Glowing torch in hand, she made her way up the winding steps that led to the large, flat rooftop of the west tower. When she opened the door, the four females were already perched on the tower's edge waiting for her.

Females were preferable to males, who resisted her every command and forced her to use the amulet to compel them. It was so much easier with females. They were much smarter anyway. *Just like with humans*, she mused.

Magdalen projected her thoughts equally to all four. *Hannah, Gaynor, Naomi, Salome, thank you all for answering my call.* The Drakes responded with greetings that seemed genuinely friendly and warm. Yes, she very much preferred the females.

Did you notice the men hiding like rodents under the rocks in that little glen to the west? You would have flown over them on your way here.

Yes, we saw two of them, Gaynor replied. She was the largest of the four, and by FireDrake custom therefore the leader.

Two you say. Well, there is one among them I seek. Let me show him to you. Magdalen recalled the image of the Drake Slayer from the feast in Icarus and then projected it directly into their minds. *Have you seen this man?*

Yes, I have seen that one, Naomi, the smallest of the four replied.

I recognize him as well, Hannah added.

Good, I want him brought back here to me, alive, Magdalen said. *He is the human who killed your sister Gytha.*

Poor Gytha, Naomi said. *She never did get along well with humans.*

Magdalen shook her head. *I ordered her not to get involved in any fighting. They must have done something to anger her.*

Gytha always did have a temper, Hannah said. *I warned her more than once it would be the death of her.*

Magdalen's face hardened. *I will make the killer suffer before he dies.*

That will not bring Gytha back, Naomi said.

And what of the others? Gaynor asked.

Destroy them if you must, or just chase them away, Magdalen replied with a wave of her hand. *It makes no difference to me, but be wary when you communicate with each other. I suspect there is a halfling with them and he may be able to hear you.*

All four females lifted off in unison and disappeared in the inky blackness. The force of their passing blew back Magdalen's long curly hair and extinguished her torch. Once the wind had died, she pointed at the torch. A hot spark jumped from her finger and the flame came back to life. She frowned as she stared off into the darkness. *I told them they would pay. It's not my fault they have chosen to ignore my warning.*

Chapter 43

SHAUN

Disoriented and confused, Shaun awoke with his mind in such a fog he could barely remember his name. There was a vague memory of being attacked by monsters, plunging his sword into one, and then nothing. When his eyes opened, he was on his back staring up at the rough-hewn rafters of a low thatched roof. The edges of his vision were oddly blurred. He blinked a few times but it didn't seem to help.

A hard flat surface was pressing against his back. He attempted to sit up, but couldn't move. Since he couldn't turn his head, he rolled his eyes from side to side. On his right was a dilapidated table, piled high with glass vials and various other things he could not recognize. To his left stood three large, rusted cages. Their doors were hanging open and all three were empty. The sight of them angered him, but he didn't know why.

Wherever he was, the place reeked. The scent of so many different animals, rot, urine and faeces, all assaulting his nostrils at the same time. It seemed strange that he could pick out each individual odour and identify it. There was something else too, something akin to old, soft cheese that had gone sour. He wrinkled his nose at the smell and his tongue brushed against a large pointed tooth. When a quick search with his tongue found a mouthful of similar teeth, he panicked. With all his strength, he strained against his unseen bonds. His efforts were rewarded by the creak of old leather, but he still couldn't move.

"Ah, so you are awake, my Pretty" a raspy voice said. The sour, cheesy smell grew stronger as a grotesque face hovered before his eyes. The image was blurred at the edges, but he could clearly see the face of an old and filthy hag. Her hair was a knotted tangled mess, with twigs and debris poking out at odd angles. The hag's smile displayed a row of teeth that were little more than rotted stubs. Her breath was the source of the cheesy odour. It filled his nostrils as she spoke. He snorted, trying to clear the foul stench from his nose.

"Yes," the hag said, "I've been saving the big cat for someone special. Could see right off you were the one. Turned out quite well too."

Shaun felt a rough hand caress the hair on his chest and he shuddered. The hag burst into malicious laughter that ended in a coughing fit. When it subsided, she cleared her throat and spat. The hag's face appeared before him again, and Shaun felt pressure suddenly release from his forehead. When he raised his head, he was shocked by what he saw. His naked body was covered from head to toe in a thick blue-black fur. When he shivered, the fur rippled exposing yellowish tips.

In a state of shock, he watched as the old woman unfastened a series of leather straps, first from his waist, and then his legs and arms. He raised his right hand, but it was not really a hand anymore. There were still fingers, but they were short, as furry as the rest of him, and much too thick to be of any use. When he flexed them, long curved ivory claws the size of small daggers slid out. The tips were wickedly sharp and looked far more deadly than any knife he had ever seen. That thought triggered a memory. Where was his carving knife?

Surprisingly, the panic Shaun felt previously was replaced by a feeling of well being. In fact, he was feeling better than he had ever felt before. He watched the claws slide in and out a few more times, and then rolled smoothly off the table to land in a crouch before the wretched old woman. Raising a deformed hand, he allowed his claws to extend to their full length. As Shaun stared at the hag's wrinkled leathery face, intense hatred welled up inside of him yet he held it in check. First he needed information, but when he tried to ask for his knife all that came out was a snarl.

"I see it is time for your first lesson, my Pretty," the old hag said. She clutched at something hanging from her neck. Shaun fell to the ground as if crushed by a mountain. Screaming in agony, he squirmed amid the filth of the dirt floor. After what seemed an eternity, the pain stopped. Shaun leapt to his feet panting, but stayed well back from the hag.

"Ah, but you are a smart one," the old woman said. "I can see it in your eyes. Left a pinch more human in you than the others, I did. Needed one that could think for himself, you see."

The old woman turned her back on Shaun and shuffled over to an open doorway. "Come," she barked from outside. When Shaun didn't move, she lifted the amber stone from where it hung from her neck and dangled it menacingly. "Need another lesson, my Pretty," she said in a shrill raspy voice.

Shaun bounded out the door on all four limbs like an animal. Once outside, he stopped almost immediately. Before him towered a great, black bear-like beast. It stood a full eight feet tall with arms and legs as thick as tree trunks.

"Oh, that's old Sweet, my Pretty" the hag said. "He's the pack leader, but then I'll just leave the two of you to sort that out." With that the hag fell into a fit of cackling.

The moment Shaun looked into Sweet's eyes, the black beast's lips peeled back exposing long yellowed canines. When it growled, Shaun extended his claws and snarled back without giving it a thought. In response, Sweet charged. Shaun leapt to one side and as the beast passed raked it with his claws. Sweet bellowed in obvious pain, but then turned and snapped at Shaun's neck. It took amazingly little effort for Shaun to avoid his teeth. Sweet charged at him again. This time, as the other rushed by, Shaun jumped onto his back. He buried all four sets of claws into Sweet's back and sides. Then he sank his fangs into Sweet's thick neck. A hot liquid filled his mouth. They fell to the ground as Sweet rolled in an attempt to dislodge his tormentor, but Shaun would not let go and kept his jaws locked onto the back of the beast's neck.

Sweet stood once more and waved his huge, hairy arms behind his head in a vain attempt to dislodge Shaun from his back. Shaun bit down all the harder. Sweet shuddered, and then dropped like a felled tree. The two of them lay unmoving for a time before Shaun released his hold. When Shaun stood, Sweet crawled slowly off into the trees. Scores of red eyes dotted the darkness around him. They backed away from his glare, none wishing to challenge. Shaun had never felt such power. He tilted his head back and roared. He barely noticed the old woman by the door to the hut.

"I knew you were the one," she said clapping her hands, "I knew it." Shaun glared out into the trees to the sound of the hag's shrill laughter.

Chapter 44

RODNEY

Bone tired, most of Rodney's companions had long since found a place to curl up for the night in the comfort of their dry shelter. All but four had given in to fatigue and were fast asleep. Herman leaned against the rock wall polishing his sword. Captain Doyle stared into his fire through half-closed eyes and appeared to be in danger of falling over at any moment. Across from Rodney, Aldus stirred the coals of their fire with a stick, sending small burning embers drifting up into the air.

Visions of Magdalen still dominated Rodney's waking thoughts, if not his dreams. When his mind had returned to where he was, the face of Aldus brought back the memories of the attack three nights past. Had the wizard and Grigor arrived any later, or not at all, they would all have perished. They owed him their lives, but at the same time, they would not have been in harm's way, if not for the wizard in the first place.

Rodney struggled with his thoughts until Aldus broke the silence. "What is troubling you, Sir Rodney?"

"I would like to thank you once again for saving our lives," Rodney said, leaving out the more disturbing thoughts of Magdalen.

"There is no need for thanks," the wizard replied, waving his hand absently in the air, "and I really cannot take all of the credit."

"I understand, we owe Grigor a debt as well."

"That is not what I meant," Aldus said, raising his eyes to meet Rodney's. "There is something I have been reluctant to mention, simply because it is still a mystery even to me."

Rodney felt his eye twitch. It was accompanied by a dull throb in his right temple. "Oh, and what is it you have waited so long to tell?"

The wizard replied without looking at him. "I will need to start at the beginning. Do you remember the day we first met?"

David Korinetz

"I shall never forget it," Rodney replied with the hint of a smile on his lips. "It is not every day I am granted the opportunity to battle a FireDrake."

"Then you may recall I spoke of a dream which brought me to Balor."

Rodney nodded. "I do recall some mention of such."

"This very moment is part of that dream," the wizard said, sweeping his arm to encompass the whole chamber. "I saw these forty men." He lifted a finger and pointed to Jason's helm where it lay on the ground beside the knight. "The black crossed swords on our sleeping friend's helm, and a rather large man sitting across from me. His face was hidden, but then that is the way these things work most of the time. There are always secrets mortal men are not meant to know."

A smile curled on the wizard's thin lips as he pointed to Rodney's belt. "The one thing I could see clearly was the red dragon on his belt buckle. The symbol of a Daemon Knight."

Rodney looked down. Out of habit, he had strapped the belt back on after removing his mail.

"I now know without a doubt that you are that man," Aldus said. "I am also convinced it is you and Sir Jason here who will accomplish this task."

An uneasiness settled into Rodney's gut. The wizard was expecting more from him than what might be possible. As if reading his mind, Aldus spoke again. "Every man can only do the best he is able. That is all anyone can ask of him. Even himself."

"That sounds like something my father would have said," Rodney replied, after a half-hearted laugh. "I cannot say I understand it all, but you have my thanks for telling me just the same."

Though the wizard had gone silent, Rodney had the feeling he wasn't finished yet. Being as tired as he was, Rodney was content to wait. The wizard would either tell him in his own good time, or not. He didn't have to wait long.

"As I told you the night of the were-beast attack, I had only just recovered from an ill-advised visit to Penardun that same day. I was still weak, and spent the day trying to make up for as many missed meals as I could." Rodney hid a smile, having witnessed the wizard's amazing appetite.

"I had just begun my third meal of the evening, when I heard a voice chanting." Aldus tapped his temple with his finger. "It was much the same as when Grigor speaks, but it was not another FireDrake because he could not hear it. I knew not the meaning of the words, for it was in a tongue I am unfamiliar with, but the message was clear; you and your countrymen were in danger. So, I saddled Grigor and we flew until we sighted your fires. The rest you know."

While Aldus scratched at something in his beard, his eyes wandered down to the sleeping Kelatch. Shark-tooth wore that same childish grin even in slumber. After a long pause the wizard's eyes returned to Rodney. "I remember hearing something very similar while in the throes of my Wizard's Dream. The voice sounded a lot like our little, dark friend here, but I can detect not a drop of elfin blood in him. So you see, it remains a mystery. I just thought you should be privy to all I know." That said, his smile returned. "Now we both best get some sleep, for we will be needing to rise all too soon."

The throbbing in Rodney's temple had intensified. A half hearted attempt to smile was defeated by a wide yawn. If all had gone to plan, the Icarian army had already set siege to the keep. Rodney and his companions had been hard pressed to reach Drakenmount on time, but they had. It was a cruel act of fate that would put them so near and yet too weak to strike. Was there something else he could have done? Other options he had missed?

According to plan, a covert assault would begin a sun-mark before first light. Success hinged solely on gaining entrance to Penardun unannounced and undetected. The only way of achieving their goal was to rappel down from the cliffs above the keep in the predawn darkness. Proper timing would allow for enough light to find handholds yet still remain invisible against the rock face. Aldus had assured Rodney that unless Magdalen used a spell she could see no better in the dark than anyone else. Recalling the old wizard's amazing eyesight, Rodney found it far from reassuring. FireDrakes would be another matter. If even one was present, no one would go unseen.

Rodney lifted his hand to stifle another yawn just as Aldus leapt up and screamed, "FireDrakes!"

A section of their blind was suddenly ripped away before Rodney knew what was happening. The force of it blew smoke and ash everywhere. Men screamed as they leapt up from their bedrolls in panic. Rodney stood up and drew his sword just as a man-sized claw wrapped around his body. The sword fell from numb fingers as he was dragged out from under the overhang. His arms were pinned so tightly to his sides that he was barely able to breathe.

Herman charged out through the gaping hole in the blind. The big knight's sword was high above his head. There was a clang akin to steel striking stone as the blade came down on the claw holding Rodney trapped. The FireDrake roared. It jerked Rodney aside like a rag doll and then lowered its massive head. A wall of red-hot fire engulfed Herman. As the knight disappeared in the flames, Rodney felt himself lifting into the air.

The light of the burning brush below Rodney's feet exposed two more

FireDrakes just landing near the overhang. He caught a fleeting glimpse of Jason and Martin standing shoulder to shoulder, poised to defend the entrance with shields up and swords drawn. Rodney wanted to warn them back but he could hardly breathe, let alone speak. He watched helplessly as the two FireDrakes extended their long necks. Dragon-fire flowed from their mouths and under the rock, incinerating the remaining branches that still partly blocked the entrance. Screams echoed in his ears along with the pounding in his head as he was carried off into the night.

Unsure of which direction or how far they flew, Rodney's thoughts were hazy from lack of air. Finally the pressure relaxed on his ribs and he gulped in a breath. Pain exploded in his head and spots danced before his eyes. The spots had barely cleared when he was dumped onto a hard, wooden surface. The wood felt strangely smooth and warm. He tried to stand, but was too weak and dizzy. All he succeeded in doing was to aggravate the pain in his head.

"Well, well, well," said a vaguely familiar feminine voice. "I see our honoured guest has arrived. I have a special room prepared just for you, Drake Slayer."

Looking up, Rodney saw the face from his dreams, but this time it was in the flesh, and all the more beautiful for it. She smiled, but only with her mouth. When their eyes met the smile faded. She touched the amulet that hung between her breasts and a flash of bright red light blinded him. "Bring him," he heard her say. She said something else too, but the words were slurred as dizziness overcame him and he lost all awareness of his surroundings.

The side of Rodney's head felt like it was being pounded by a blacksmith's hammer. When he opened his eyes he found himself alone in a darkened chamber. Then, from seemingly out of nowhere, Magdalen's ghostly image loomed before him, much the way it had in Icarus. The image abruptly changed, turning into flesh and blood again. Then, to his horror, that wondrous red hair rose up of its own accord to become slithering snakes that coiled and hissed about her head. Full, pink lips stretched thin and wide as they darkened to a deep shade of crimson. Those red lips then parted to expose long, pointed teeth, just like those of a FireDrake. Her arms shot out to form wings as scales replaced flesh. Once the transformation into a multi-headed FireDrake was complete, each one of the heads bent low with an open maw. He passed out just as dragon-fire engulfed him.

Awareness crept slowly into Rodney's mind. He could feel beads of sweat streaming down his face. When he opened his eyes, he was once again in the iron grip of a FireDrake. It held him fast as fire spewed forth from its giant maw. He watched helplessly as first Herman, Jason and then Martin were consumed by fire. He could neither look away nor close his eyes until they were nothing but ash. Their screams echoed in his mind until he thought he could stand no more. Then the claws began to close. Tighter and tighter they squeezed, until he heard a rib crack and then another.

With a flash of red light, Rodney found himself back in the darkened chamber. He could see only by what little light radiated from the glowing red manacles clamped around both of his wrists. Magdalen appeared again, but this time nothing untoward happened. She was just watching him. Was he awake? No longer able to differentiate nightmares from reality, he couldn't be sure. Rodney squinted to see her better. She was so beautiful. His throat too dry to speak, all he could manage was to mouth the word, "Why?"

Magdalen's smile faded and then so did she. Rodney was left facing a blank stone wall. He took the opportunity to get his bearings. He was hanging from unnatural chains that ended in tightly fitted manacles made of the same ghostly material. By their red glow they appeared fresh from a forge yet were as cold as ice against his skin. He raised both arms in an attempt to relieve some of the pressure on his wrists. A trickle of fresh blood ran down his arm from where the manacles had rubbed the skin raw. It matched the colour of the chains. Rodney had only a few precious moments to think about it before the chamber went dark and the nightmare of fire and death returned.

Chapter 45

MAGDALEN

Magdalen stood before the full-length mirror in her sleeping chamber. Stone-faced, she watched the reflection of three men as they were consumed by fire. The image changed to the Drake Slayer, bound in unbreakable chains forged from Aedon's magic. As tears mixed with the sweat on his face, Magdalen frowned. This was not what she had envisioned. She had expected to savour her vengeance. Now to hand, it didn't taste nearly so sweet as she had imagined. The longer she watched, the more anger grew steadily within her until she felt a shortness of breath and a flush in her cheeks. The Drake Slayer did not beg for mercy, nor did he scream in utter terror. He was in agony, without a doubt, but not in a way that gave her any kind of satisfaction.

The despair of witnessing the deaths of his friends seemed to completely overshadow any sense of physical pain her spells were inducing in his mind. What was wrong? The magic of the amulet penetrated his mind easily enough, laying bare his innermost thoughts. She could sense what he felt as if they were her own feelings. She had not experienced such emotions since the death of her mother. It was most disturbing.

The Drake Slayer's most inner secrets were not what she had expected. His high capacity for compassion came as a complete surprise. There were many people in his life for whom he cared deeply. His thoughts of her had been shocking to say the least. By all rights he should be hateful, cringing in fear, begging for his life, not thinking of her in the way he did.

The fool is besotted. Magdalen shook her head. *Do all men think with their loins, or is he just an addlebrained imbecile?* No, she could see he was neither weak minded nor weak willed. Insane perhaps? That might explain it, but for some reason she couldn't accept that either.

A slight shuffling noise at Magdalen's side disturbed her concentration. She turned an angry face toward the elf standing attentively at her side. She had been unaware of his presence but was not surprised by it. "What is it now, Merflyn?" she barked. "I am very busy."

"Pardon my intrusion, mistress," the librarian said, in that annoying singsong voice, "but why not just kill him and be done with it? You do not seem to enjoy his suffering, which believe me I can truly understand. What I can not comprehend is why you continue with this when it seems to distress you so."

"Why!" Magdalen exclaimed. "This man killed Gytha! Do you not feel grief for your slain kin? Anger at her murder?"

"I fail to see what torturing this human will accomplish. His suffering and death will not bring Gytha back, nor will it ease my grief. No matter what you do to this poor man, Gytha will still be gone. Please enlighten me if what I say is not true?"

Magdalen had no reply. She turned back to the mirror to avoid the elf's accusing gaze. After a few moments of silence Merflyn spoke again. "If I had need to place blame upon someone's head for Gytha's death, I might point the finger of accusation toward the one responsible for sending her away from the safety of her home. Perhaps it is your own guilt you wish to slay."

"You go too far," Magdalen screamed, as her cheeks flushed with anger. Merflyn simply raised an eyebrow.

Considering that the elf was as much in thrall to the amulet as any FireDrake, his total lack of fear was frustrating to say the least. What good was having power over him, if he didn't care? She calmed herself. "I wish for him to suffer as much pain as possible. It is only in his mind, after all. I should think that would appeal to your delicate sensibilities, Merflyn."

"Another living creature is suffering great pain. Be it real or not. I can take no pleasure in that, mistress. Besides, what is reality but what we believe it to be. If no one believes in me, do I truly exist?"

It was pointless to argue with an elf, so Magdalen swallowed her retort. He was probably a thousand years old, and so skilled that none but another elf could hope to win a war of words with him. Further conversation would be fruitless and only serve to sour her mood even further. "Never mind! Just leave me. Go back to Drakenmount. I do not want you here."

As Merflyn bowed and backed gracefully from the chamber, Magdalen waved her hand and the image in the mirror was replaced by her own reflection. She gazed upon herself for a moment and then straightened the folds of her dress. Pulling back her scarlet hair, she turned slightly to better see her profile.

The smile that had crept unbidden into place melted as her face clouded over. *What am I doing? What I look like means nothing.* She let her hair fall back and raised her hand. The mirror shattered and she stormed out of the chamber in disgust.

Shaking with anger, Magdalen plucked a torch from the wall as she walked down the hall. It ignited at her touch and burned unnaturally bright, as if fuelled by her rage. She made her way down the slippery stone steps that led to the lowest level of Penardun. When she reached the bottom, the damp repugnant odour of the corridor assailed her nostrils. She put the back of her hand to her nose. What had once been the keep's main food storage area was now rank with mould and decay from neglect.

Upon reaching the third door, Magdalen slid back the bolt and then paused to straighten her dress. When she realized what she was doing, her anger intensified. Grasping Aedon tightly, she drew a small amount of power into her lungs and then exhaled sharply toward the ancient wooden door. It swung open to slam violently against the stone wall.

Warm yellow light from her torch flooded into the chamber. With buckled knees, the Drake Slayer hung by his wrists, thrashing from side to side. Sweat stained pink with blood dripped from his fingers. She waited until the thrashing stopped and his eyes had begun to open. She fought back pangs of pity that nagged at her viciously. His lips began to move, but Magdalen raised her hand and cried, "Stop!"

The Drake Slayer blinked and then squinted. Having suddenly forgotten why she had come, Magdalen stood in silence until Gaynor's voice boomed in her mind. *A large army of humans has entered the valley.*

Magdalen relaxed, almost feeling relieved. *I should have known better than to trust that weasel Gamel. Gaynor, meet me on the roof of the tower.*

"Well," Magdalen said regaining some of her composure. "It appears the rest of your friends have finally arrived, but do not fear, I will return once they have been dealt with." She waved her hand and the Drake Slayer slumped forward. "There will be no more dreams for now." She took one last look at him as he hung limply in the chains. Her hand moved in a slow downward motion. The chains grew in length until the knight lay in a heap on the damp stone floor with his hands loose at his sides.

"I wish for you to be well rested when I return," Magdalen said, before she spun around and left the chamber. When her foot touched the first step, she waved her hand again as an afterthought. The door squealed on its hinges as it slammed shut. There was a snap as the bolt slid back into place. As she climbed the slick steps, Magdalen pushed all those disturbing thoughts of the Drake Slayer from her mind. She would deal with him later.

Chapter 46

JOHN

John awoke to a fiery hell, and at the centre of it all stood Wizard Aldus with intense silver light radiating from his outstretched hand like a miniature sun. The ground beneath John's feet shook, opened up and then swallowed him whole. Buried in dirt, he struggled until lack of air forced him to stop. Just as he was on the verge of suffocating, the ground opened up again and spit him out. In turn, he coughed and spit out a mouthful of dirt.

Burning bits of debris from what was left of their blind lay scattered all around the shelter. As John gasped for air he noticed a body lying next to him. He blinked the dirt from his eyes. It was Yvon. For a moment he feared the worst, and then an arm twitched. John thanked the Gods that his friend was still alive, but didn't have much time to think about it before he was hauled roughly to his feet by Wizard Aldus.

After releasing John's arm, the wizard bent back down. "We are safe for the time being," he said, while struggling to pull a groggy Yvon to his knees, "but we must make haste. It will be dawn in a few sun-marks."

The others had begun to come around. Every last one of them was covered head to toe in dirt and ash. John glanced down at his own dirt smeared arms. Only the wizard remained untouched. An ash-covered hand grabbed the wizard's arm and spun him around. It was Lord Vincent's Second. "What happened?" the knight asked

The wizard stared at Sir Martin's hand until he released his grip and stepped back. Then Aldus smiled. "I buried us," he said. "It was the only thing I could think of to save us all from the dragon-fire. Once they were gone, I simply reversed the spell."

"I saw one of the beasts take Rodney, but what happened to Herman?"

Martin asked. "Did they snatch him too?"

The wizard's smile faded. "I regret to say that I acted too late to save him. I'm afraid he is gone."

The other knights who had gathered round Sir Martin lowered their heads. "What do we do now?" Sir Jason asked, breaking the silence.

"Why, you go to Penardun," Aldus said. "To climb down the cliffs as planned."

"What about you?" Martin asked ,obviously suspicious.

"You need not worry about me. I will get there, but by other means. Go to Penardun. Find Sir Rodney. He will know what to do."

Sir Martin looked to Sir Jason. "Until we find Rodney, I will lead." He paused, but Sir Jason offered no response. "Jason, will you act as my Second?" Undisguised surprise registered on Sir Jason's face. Then a smile crept into place and he nodded his approval.

It had taken nearly two sun-marks to reach the high cliffs overlooking Penardun. They would never have made it in time, if not for Shark-tooth's keen eyes. He could see like an owl in the dark.

Leaving Captain Doyle and the Icarian archers to set the signal fire, the rest of the party wasted no time in beginning their descent. They started down in pairs, with each person tethered to another by a short rope. The Duke was determined to come along and ended up paired with Shark-tooth.

John had climbed down only fifty feet before managing to get his right foot stuck in a narrow crack. He had no choice but to back up. As his left foot slid across the smooth rock face, his right foot pulled free from the crack in which it had been wedged. Only then did he realize his mistake. His grip on the small outcrop above was insufficient to bear his full weight. Still hundreds of feet above the keep, his hand slipped and he felt himself topple backwards. He hoped that when his body hit the rooftop it didn't make too much noise.

As the rope around his waist went tight, John heard a grunt from above just before he slammed back hard against the rock face. The rope slid up to his chest, making it difficult to breathe, until a rough hand grabbed his arm and pulled him up enough to relieve the pressure. His foot found purchase on a small ledge. At the same time his hands grabbed someone's leg.

"Easy, lad," he heard Yvon say. "You will take us both down if you continue to thrash about like that."

John was too winded to reply. He felt Yvon's rough hand again as it took his own and guided it to a crack in the rock. He grabbed hold and felt something brush against his arm as someone moved down beside him. "You will be fine now, John." It was the voice of Sir Jason. "We are through the worst of it. It's all cake and cream from here."

"Thank you, Sir," John replied, as he looked down. It was still too dark to make out much more than shadows below, but the sky was getting brighter by the moment. They would have to get off the rock face soon or risk being seen. The surface became rougher, offering plenty of handholds. He reached the roof in short order without further incident. Once everyone was safely down, Sir Martin divided the men into search parties. To John's surprise, the Duke gave no argument and followed orders like everyone else.

It wasn't long before one of the men located a likely entrance. They moved quietly to gather around a small door and drew their weapons. Sir Martin nodded to his friend Talbot who yanked it open. Everyone froze. A thin, dark form was standing on the other side. The knights recoiled as a young man stepped boldly through the doorway. His features were delicate, his skin pale and the tips of pointed ears protruded slightly through a crop of red hair. "Greetings," he said in a singsong voice. "Welcome to Penardun. My name is Merflyn and I am here to help you."

"Am I dead?" the voice of Lord Vincent croaked.

"Rodney, thank the Gods you are still alive," Jason said through the door.

"I am," Lord Vincent's voice croaked again. To John it seemed to be more a question than a confirmation.

There was a rattling of wood and metal as Sir Talbot worked on the lock, then a click and the door creaked open. Sir Martin held up his torch. Blinded by the light, Lord Vincent raised a manacled hand to shield his eyes. John was shocked at his condition. While Lord Vincent blinked to clear his vision, Sir Jason rushed forward. He took Lord Vincent's left hand and pulled it to the side, stretching out the chain attached to his wrist. Sir Jason's sword fell three times before he cursed and sheathed his blade.

John and Yvon moved in and knelt beside their Lord. Gently slipping an arm under his neck, Yvon raised Lord Vincent's head. With his free hand Yvon opened his waterskin and poured some of the liquid over Lord Vincent's dry cracked lips. He swallowed down what managed to get inside greedily. Yvon poured more over his head and face.

Lord Vincent opened his eyes. "Yvon?"

"Yes my lord," Yvon replied.

Lord Vincent turned his head. Sir Jason and Sir Martin were standing side by side. "Now I know I am truly dead," he said. "In life you two could not share the same room without trying to kill each other."

"I cannot cut your chains," Jason said. "They are harder than my sword. We will need to find blacksmith's tools or some such to set you free."

"You will not break those chains with any tools made by human hands," a singsong voice said. John looked up. Merflyn stood in the doorway behind Sir Talbot. He held a small, glowing object in his outstretched hand.

"Use this," the elf said. "It was made before Aedon and will unlock the chains that bind your friend."

Jason stepped forward and snatched the key from his hand.

"Who is he?" Lord Vincent asked.

"An elf," Martin whispered.

Merflyn smiled as Yvon lifted Lord Vincent's hand and Jason held the key up to the lock. "The key is too big," Jason said.

"Just touch it to the lock," the elf replied.

John gasped as the key melted into the opening of the lock. When it seemed solid again, Jason turned it. There was a click. The manacle sprung open and fell away. Both chain and manacle flickered and then vanished. The second soon followed. Merflyn held out his hand and Jason reluctantly handed back the key.

"You must hurry," the elf said. "Magdalen is on the roof at the top of this tower. Many will die if she is not stopped."

The key disappeared into the folds of the elf's clothing and then he stepped back into the passageway. "Wait," Sir Martin said as he leapt past Sir Talbot in pursuit. A moment later the knight returned. "He is gone," he said with a shrug of his shoulders.

"Are you fit?" Sir Jason asked Lord Vincent. "Can you walk?"

"Yes, I think so. Just help me up."

John and Yvon each grabbed an arm and pulled the knight to his feet. "I thought you all dead," he said, as they guided him through the doorway.

Jason laughed. "It was Aldus. The old wizard saved us all. He tricked the FireDrakes into thinking we were roasted by pulling the very ground over our heads. We very nearly suffocated, but as you can see we survived."

"I can't tell you how glad I am to hear you all survived." The smile faded from Jason's face at Lord Vincent's words.

"Herman was caught in the dragon-fire," Martin said softly. "The wizard could not save him."

When the reached the stairway Sir Martin took the lead. As they made their way up the slippery steps, he and Sir Jason quickly brought Lord Vincent up to date on what had happened since his capture.

"After leaving the Icarian archers to cover our backs and light the signal fire," Sir Jason said, "we climbed down the cliffs. That's when we met our friend Merflyn."

"The elf led us to the Duchess," Sir Martin added. "The women were locked in one of the chambers on the top floor."

"They were terribly frightened," Sir Jason said, "but otherwise unharmed. The Duke and most of the others are there with them now. The elf then brought us down here to free you."

"I am afraid you failed to inform us of your plans for dealing with the sorceress," Sir Martin said.

"Gods," Lord Vincent mumbled. "I had not thought. I was so intent on getting here I made no plans at all."

By the time they reached the top of the stairs, Lord Vincent was walking on his own, although still shaky on his feet. From the other side of the thick wooden door came the unmistakable roar of a FireDrake. It was followed by a boom of thunder that shook the stone landing beneath their feet. Sir Martin tried to open the door, but it was jammed. "Stand back," Sir Jason said.

Yvon pulled John back down a few steps. He could feel the Kelatch and Sir Talbot pressing at his back.

Arms locked together, Sir Martin and Sir Jason rushed the door with Lord Vincent close on their heels. They must have thrown their backs into it, for the heavy wooden door swung open and all three men spilled out onto the roof amid smoke and flame.

Chapter 47

MAGDALEN

Magdalen burst through the door and onto the roof just as Gaynor landed on the tower wall. Ignoring the FireDrake, Magdalen stepped as close to the edge as she dared and mouthed a spell to enhance her vision. Less than a league away, thousands of men were forming battle lines. Still more were pouring in from the Vanir pass at the far end of the narrow valley. They would be outside Penardun's walls within a sun-mark. She could never allow them to get that close.

When her eyes had returned to normal, Magdalen backed away from the edge of the low stone wall that encircled the tower's rooftop. Feeling more secure with the tall stone wall of the stairwell at her back, she turned to face Gaynor. *Where are the Emperor's legions?*

Gaynor shook her head. *A small number of them, no more than a few hundred, followed these other humans into the pass. At first it appeared the rest would do the same, but then the majority turned south. They are now many leagues away and will not be coming to your aid.*

Magdalen's face reddened. *I knew that old weasel was up to something. I was a fool to trust him.* Gaynor had the grace to remain silent. *It is now up to the FireDrakes to defend Penardun.* Magdalen lifted the amulet from her chest. She focussed on projecting her message backed by the power of Aedon. It would need to be strong enough to reach every last FireDrake at Drakenmount. *Penardun is under attack! Defend me!*

Three dull red specks arose instantly from the forest that lay a few leagues to the west. Those specks swelled quickly until Magdalen recognized them as Hannah, Naomi and Salome. As the females neared the tower, many more similar specks appeared in the sky around Drakenmount. Soon FireDrakes were

272

arriving from every direction. So many had perched on the tower's roof that even the ensorcelled cedar timbers creaked under their weight. A score of agitated FireDrakes circled over Magdalen's head and still more could be seen making their way from Drakenmount.

Magdalen couldn't wait any longer. She raised her hand and pointed in the direction of the massing army. Her outstretched arm glowed as crimson magic danced like fire along the length of it. Leaving nothing to chance, she used the full extent of Aedon's power to compel the FireDrakes. Nothing in either this world or the next would be able to stop them. *Attack them. Drive them away. By the power of Aedon I command it!*

The sound of score upon score of massive wings beating the air was deafening. The force of the downdraft pushed Magdalen back, pressing her hard against the door of the stairwell. She watched as nearly two hundred FireDrakes converged over the army in the valley, in the form of a red cloud.

Once individuals were no longer discernible, the desire to both see and hear what was happening was overwhelming. Magdalen took a few steps forward and closed her eyes in concentration. She could feel the power of the amulet engulf her as her fetch sped toward the battlefield.

When her eyes opened, Magdalen was practically on top of the attacking front line, hovering thirty feet above the ground. She knew that as a fetch she could not possibly fall, but was instantly struck by a wave of dizziness all the same. Heights had always been her bane, even as a child. To shake it off she focussed on how the FireDrakes attacked the advancing lines of men with their dragon-fire.

Though they rarely hunted together, FireDrakes possessed a dragon's bird-like instinct to flock. So rather than attack singularly, they swooped down as a group. They came in high, diving down along the edge of the sprawling Icarian army. At the last possible moment, their great wings would extend and they would soar directly over the heads of the men below at breakneck speeds. The wind of their passing alone was enough to knock many men from their feet.

Every third man in the front line held a large red and silver shield. As the wall of dragon-fire approached them, the shield bearers raised them up above their heads. The men around them darted underneath to hide from the flames, not that it would do them any good. Nothing could withstand dragon-fire.

Crossbow bolts and arrows filled the sky like swarms of buzzing insects as her winged warriors soared by. Magdalen smiled. Bolts and arrows were useless against their armoured bodies. The fools may as well have been throwing feathers.

To Magdalen's consternation, even though the battlefield below was nothing but trampled mud and black ash, the majority of the enemy front line remained intact. She floated down to take a closer look at one of those odd shields. As if noticing her ghostly fetch for the first time, the men backed away in fear. Magdalen screamed in rage when she recognized what was rivetted to those shields between polished strips of steel. They had been fireproofed with FireDrake scales. The Icarians had stripped poor Gytha's body of its scales. *Butchers! Monsters!*

The cloud of FireDrakes banked and then came back for another pass from the southeast. To Magdalen's further horror, when the lead FireDrake dove in close enough to unleash its fire, two long poles sprung up from the ground in his path. The danger became immediately apparent when she caught sight of the heavy nets that hung between the poles, but it was too late to warn the FireDrake who became entangled and then slammed into the ground. Magdalen's milky white hand covered her mouth to stifle a scream. The quick-thinking FireDrake managed to burn away parts of the net and launch itself back into the air, but the strokes of its wings were laboured and one hind leg hung limp.

More poles sprung up as the rest of the FireDrakes drew near, disrupting their assault. For the most part they were able to veer to either side and avoid the nets, but not before one more FireDrake was caught. It was a large female. She hit the ground with bone crushing force and did not move. At least they were aware of the danger and with the next pass flew well above the reach of the nets, but the result was to make their dragon-fire less effective.

The FireDrakes reformed for another pass. Amid the flames, the men below were frantically pulling long, heavy shafts from wagons and loading them into what looked like giant crossbows. Magdalen had thought them to be siege weapons for assaulting Penardun. She was unfamiliar with such things, and had therefore paid them little attention until one fired. The massive bolt passed between two drakes missing a wing by mere fingers.

An ear piercing scream signalled that yet another FireDrake had fallen victim to the nets. It was a small FireDrake who, lacking the range its larger brethren had with their fire, had come in too low. When it crashed to the ground, men armed with long spears swarmed over it like bees on a hive. *This must be how Gytha died.* Magdalen turned her head, not wishing to witness the poor creature's destruction. Another FireDrake screamed as it too struck the ground. This one had been hit by one of the heavy bolts. In a frenzy, it bit at the shaft protruding from it chest as it thrashed on the ground. Men scrambled out of the way to avoid being crushed.

Near the wounded FireDrake was a wagon filled with more of the giant bolts for the deadly weapons. The morning sunlight reflected off their steel tips. Magdalen tried frantically to project her thoughts, *Burn the wagons!* She watched helplessly as the FireDrakes attacked again without paying the wagons any special attention. Either they had not heard her words, or they were in such a frenzy that they did not understand. Something had to be done, but as a fetch Magdalen lacked access to Aedon's power, so she took the only option open to her and fled back to her body.

When Magdalen returned to the tower, a large male FireDrake was just landing in the centre of the roof. Her thoughts were still on the battle and she paid him no mind. She didn't stop to wonder why this particular FireDrake was not with the rest. She wanted desperately to recall them before any more were killed, but then how could she stop the army from marching on Penardun? Would she be able to face them alone with only the power of Aedon? It was either that or see more of the FireDrakes slaughtered.

The big male took a step toward her. Magdalen turned her head. She had little patience with the males. They were always so difficult. *What is it?* Only then did she really look at him, and see the white haired old man riding upon the FireDrake's long neck. Raising her hand instinctively, Magdalen drew on Aedon's power just in time to block the blast of silver light that shot toward her. Red and silver fire crashed midway between her and the old man with incredible force. Even the ensorcelled wood of the tower's roof could not withstand it. A twenty-foot circle was left scorched black and smoldering.

The wizard leapt down from the FireDrake's neck. He hit the ground and rolled with an agility surprising for one of his apparent age. Magdalen hurled a bolt of crimson fire. The old man was knocked off his feet. He lay unmoving. Even though his face was blackened and his hair burnt, she recognized him as the owner of the fetch that had visited her a fortnight before.

As she examined his face, Magdalen's eyes were drawn to the amulet hanging from his neck. It was a twin to Aedon, right down to the glowing bloodstone in the centre. *I am sorry old man, but I can see now that letting you go was a mistake.* With no other option, Magdalen drew power from the depths of the amulet's magic and threw a lethal bolt of raw energy to finish him.

Magdalen had completely forgotten about the FireDrake, and just as the magic was leaving her fingers he leapt forward. Though immune to other forms of magic, Aedon's power would kill him as easily as it would the old man. Magdalen tried frantically to pull the magic back. She had no desire to see another FireDrake killed, but it was too late. All she succeeded in doing was to reduce its strength. The bolt struck the FireDrake full in the chest. He was driven back along the roof skidding to a stop with his tail hanging over the edge. He lay there, an unmoving heap.

Magdalen spun around at the sound of the door behind her slamming against the stone wall. Three men came tumbling out. One fell to the ground and did not get up. The other two recovered quickly and charged at her with drawn blades. She brushed them aside with a wave of her hand as easily as if they had been insects. The third man was slow to regain his feet. He was unarmed, but Magdalen wasn't taking any chances. When she raised her hand to strike, hot magic danced on her fingertips, yet when she saw his face, she hesitated. It was the Drake Slayer. How was that possible? Nothing could have freed him from those chains.

She was not sure why, but Magdalen found it impossible to destroy him. As she stood fixated on his eyes, the magic on her fingertips died. Something she didn't understand was holding her back. Then she felt a tug on her neck as Aedon was torn from her hands. Dazed, she turned to face the man standing next to her. His features were hidden by a helm with crossed swords decorating the nose guard. The amulet dangled from the unbroken chain gripped tightly in his hand. Her hand went to her neck. How was that possible? Magdalen balled her right hand into a tight fist. She still possessed her own natural power, even though it was like a candle to Aedon's sun. She could feel the magic pooling in the palm of her hand.

Magdalen, a voice boomed in her mind. She turned expecting to see one of the FireDrakes, but instead it was the wizard. He was back on his feet. Smoke still rose from his hair and beard. In his hand was the other elfin amulet. She cast the ball of magic at the wizard knowing full well it was a futile gesture. He blocked it easily with an open palm. Magdalen felt her stomach drop.

The wizard made a chopping motion with his hand and her power drained away. He raised his hand and twirled his finger. Magdalen's arms were crushed to her sides by the very air around her. Rough hands clamped onto hers and pulled them roughly behind her back. A thin piece of fresh leather cut unkindly into her soft skin as her wrists were tightly bound behind her back.

"Bring the amulet to me, Sir Jason," the old man said.

The man who held Aedon walked over to the wizard and dropped it into the palm of his hand. Without another word the old man walked back to the fallen FireDrake. The knuckles on his hand whitened as he gripped Aedon tightly. She watched its power flow gently into the FireDrake. It was strange to see another use its magic. The FireDrake's huge body quivered and then he opened his eyes. The wizard smiled. *Welcome back, my friend.* The smile faded as he turned toward the valley and held Aedon aloft. *Enough! FireDrakes return to your home!* Magdalen did not need to look. She knew they would obey.

The wizard turned back to face her. *I am not a vengeful man, but you leave me with little choice. You are far too dangerous.* He raised both amulets above his head and touched them together. Red and silver light entwined and then snaked out to strike her forehead. Her head snapped back with the blow. It felt as if a door had slammed shut in her mind. She blinked in shock. She had fully expected to die the moment the magic struck. It was what she would have done in his place. Then the horror of what he had done sank in. She was totally cut off from her magic, helpless. Only the Gods knew what these men would do to her now.

Chapter 48

RODNEY

R odney stood next to Edmond amid his entourage, on the carved granite steps leading to the doors of Penardun's inner keep. Those around them had formed a semicircle with the Duke at its centre. Rodney was to the left, along with Jason and the other surviving Balorian knights arrayed at his side. On Edmond's right stood the Duchess, Baron Morgan, Captain Sacarus and a handful of other Icarian nobles and officers.

The entire Icarian army had gathered to hear Edmond speak. The chatter of thousands of voices echoed off the ancient stone walls. Men lined the ramparts and spilled out through the great stone archway which served as the entrance to the elfin fortress. Even the expansive grounds of Penardun could not contain them all, and thousands more stood outside the tall walls. Rodney could hear the men outside calling up to those on the walls, pleading with their fellow countrymen to tell them what was happening inside.

With his hands on his hips, Rodney gazed out upon a sea of unfamiliar faces. Though still suffering the effects of his ordeal, his strength and vigour were rapidly returning. Edmond raised his hand for silence. Once the noise level had dropped enough that he could be heard, the Duke nodded. Captain Doyle led the nine surviving archers from the front ranks to stand before them.

"Kneel before me," Edmond said in a loud clear voice that all could hear. Captain Doyle knelt on the first step, the archers on the ground behind him.

The Duke drew his sword. "For outstanding courage in battle and selfless service to Icarus; in the name of King Solon I name you Sir Fergus Doyle, Knight of Icarus." He touched the former Captain lightly on the head with the flat of his blade. "Arise, Sir Knight."

Sir Fergus stood and walked up the steps to take a place among the Icarian

278

nobles. Facing his countrymen, the former captain made a fist and raised his arm. The army, to a man, responded with cheers and hoots. If Icarus was anything like Balor, it was not every day a commoner received such an honour, not to mention the stipend and land that would accompany the title. It would bestow on every common man the faint hope it was possible that he too could achieve titles and wealth.

The Duke looked down at what remained of the two hundred archers who had followed him to Drakenmount. "For your bravery and contribution to the rescue of the Duchess, I hereby award each of you twenty gold crowns." With that, the Icarian army cheered even louder. Gold had that effect on men.

Smiling at their enthusiastic response, the Duke turned to face Rodney. "For our Balorian friends and allies, without whom we would never have succeeded, I declare you all honorary citizens of Icarus with all the rights and privileges thereof."

To even more cheering, Rodney and Edmond gripped each other's forearm. Edmond then pulled himself toward Rodney throwing his arms around him in a seemingly heartfelt embrace. "My thanks, Sir Knight" he whispered in Rodney's ear. It seemed all past animosity had vanished with the safe return of his wife.

Still fuelled by all the excitement, the Icarians let out another round of cheers. Rodney was embarrassed at having done nothing either to save the Duchess or recover the amulet. He smiled weakly as Edmond backed away. Galen stepped forward to offer his hand. Rodney took it and braced himself to have every bit of air squeezed from his lungs, but Galen let out a belly laugh and just slapped him on the back.

"Wizard Aldus," the Duke said. "We all owe our lives to you, but I must admit I know not how to reward a man of your stature. If there is anything you desire that is in my power to grant, it is yours."

Rodney looked at Aldus. All signs of his battle with the sorceress were gone. His robe was as clean as ever. His hair and beard were the same, though a little shorter than before. Standing next to him was a young man with his head bandaged and one arm in a sling. The wizard placed his hand on the young man's shoulder. "I ask only for your leave to take on young Robin here as my new apprentice. He has a talent for my art."

"With my blessings," the Duke replied.

The young maiden who had been abducted along with the Duchess was standing next to the wizard's new apprentice. Gregory was at her side. Her head resting against his shoulder spoke volumes. It was then Rodney recognized the wizard's new apprentice as the maiden's betrothed. Rodney had thought him killed by were-beasts. By the look on the maiden's face as she laughed at something Gregory was saying, they were betrothed no more.

When Edmond called for the sorceress to be brought forward, Rodney forgot about anything else. Magdalen was half led and half dragged forward by two burly guards. Her hands were still bound in the same leather straps. The men called her vile names and groped her as she was led past them. Some even spat upon her.

Suddenly overcome with seething anger, Rodney felt the pressure of a hand on his wrist. He glanced to his side. Though Jason's eyes stared straight ahead, his hand was clamped on Rodney's holding it firmly in place. Glancing down, Rodney realized he held a white-knuckled grip on the hilt of his sword. A hand's width of the blade was visible above the top of the scabbard. He had no recollection of when he had started to draw the weapon. Rodney relaxed and let it slowly slide back into the sheath. Only then did Jason release his hand. It was all done so casually he suspected no one had even noticed.

Rodney's eyes drifted back to Magdalen. Somehow she had managed to maintain an air of dignity even under such severe conditions. Though her hair was dishevelled, her clothing scorched and torn, she was still a vision of beauty. When she was forcibly turned to face the Duke, Rodney winced at the angry red welts around the bindings on her wrists. She was helpless. From what Aldus had told him, she was permanently cut off from her magic; a sorceress no more. Aldus had been left with no other choice. With her magical ability intact she would always be a threat. It was the only way he could allow her to live.

Edmond raised his hand for silence. "For horrendous crimes committed against the King and the good people of Icarus; for the many crimes you have undoubtedly committed against other nations of Coronis; in the King's name, I sentence you to death. You will be burned for the witch you are."

Rodney watched in shock as the Icarians stepped back in a wave of bodies, exposing a thick wooden stake. Bundles of dark, oil-soaked wood were stacked around it.

"Do you have any last words before the sentence is carried out?" the Duke asked.

Magdalen raised her chin. "I was taken from my home by military force in an act of war. I am accused of crimes that in the context of war are no crimes at all. I claim the right to trial by combat! If you have any honour at all, you will grant my request."

"Ha!" Edmond spat. "Do you think me a fool? Or do you truly believe that there is a man here who would raise his hand to defend you?" There was an uproar of laughter among the men, which was soon echoed outside the walls.

"I need no man to fight for me; I can defend myself. Just untie my hands and give me a sword!" All the Icarians within the sound of Magdalen's voice laughed all the harder.

"I see your game," Edmond replied. "You will not be unbound. You think to escape the flames by manoeuvring one of us into running you through. I am afraid that you are going to be disappointed, for you will burn."

Rodney could stand no more. "Wait," he bellowed. Every eye within the sound of his voice turned to him as he stepped forward. "I will stand as her champion." He looked into Magdalen's eyes, but she only glared back defiantly. "If she will have me."

All of Penardun went deathly silent. "You cannot be serious, Sir Rodney," Edmond finally said in wide eyed disbelief. "Surely you jest."

"I have never been more serious in my life," Rodney replied. He walked down the steps to stand before Magdalen. "Do you accept me as your champion."

"If you expect gratitude from me, Drake Slayer," Magdalen replied coolly, "you will be disappointed."

"I expect nothing, my Lady," Rodney replied flatly, "save the honour of defending you."

"Very well," Magdalen said, "as I seem to have no other choice, I accept you as my champion."

Rodney drew his sword, turned her sideways gently, and then sliced the leather strips from her hands. She made no sound, but her eyes betrayed her pain as she moved her hands close to her chest and rubbed her wrists.

"I will stand for the King," Captain Sacarus said.

The Duke looked at the Captain and then stepped over to Rodney's side. Leaning in he spoke softly into Rodney's ear. "Vernon is my cousin's champion. He is deadly with a blade and will give you no quarter. No man has yet to survive a duel with him."

After stepping back, Edmond raised his voice. "I can see you are not quite fit, Sir Knight. Withdraw your offer now and no one will think the less of you."

"I will stand," Rodney said.

The Duke shook his head slowly and lowered his voice again. "Very well, it is your life. If you are determined to throw it away, then there is nothing more I can do." Edmond raised his voice once more for all to hear. "Clear a circle for Trial By Combat."

The Icarians formed a near perfect thirty foot circle in the centre of the grounds. Rodney watched Vernon remove his upper armour, padding and tunic. The Captain then stepped into the centre of the circle. He held a heavy saber in his right hand and a long thin dagger in his left.

After borrowing Jason's sword and shield, Rodney stepped forward, but Sir Fergus quickly grabbed his arm and pulled him aside. "I see you are unfamiliar with Icarian duelling rules. You may wear no armour above the waist and can use only sword and dagger." He pulled a thin dagger from his belt and held it out. "You can use mine if you wish."

Rodney dropped the shield and reached for the dagger. A hand shot out to grab his wrist before he could take it. The hand belonged to Nicholas. "Take mine instead," he said holding out the hilt of his dirk. Rodney took the proffered weapon in his left hand. It had a wide guard and felt heavy, but well balanced. An ideal blade to fend off another. There was also a notch cut out just above the guard. *A sword breaker.*

Nicholas leaned in close as Rodney took the blade. "Beware his dagger," he said in a whisper. "It has a poisoned edge." Rodney's eyes narrowed as he looked closer at the Icarian's dagger.

"Mind your own as well," Nicholas added with an evil grin. "We thought to even the odds. Thanks to your Kelatch, my dirk is now as deadly as his little darts." With that, the other knight released the weapon and backed away.

"My thanks," Rodney said. He looked at the blade in his hand and could just barely make out a slight staining along the edge and on the tip. It glistened as if still damp. After Morton helped him remove his mail, padding and tunic, Rodney stepped back into the circle.

Having never seen each other fight, both men were cautious. They exchanged a few light blows, each taking the other's measure. At first Rodney was confident. The Captain was at least ten or twelve years his senior, so Rodney had the advantage of both size and age, but by the way his opponent moved, he assessed his agility to be closer to Jason's.

If Rodney hoped to save Magdalen's life, he was going to have to end the match quickly. He flicked his sword to the left and then turned his wrist, swinging the sword in from the right. The blade flashed toward his opponent's head. Vernon ducked under his sword, as expected, so Rodney spun around to his right and swung his sword backhanded in a downward arch. It was Lionel's trick. Unfortunately it didn't work. Vernon sidestepped easily, and in the same fluid movement plunged his saber into Rodney's left side. The Captain then stepped back with a smile of satisfaction on his thin lips.

The dirk fell to the ground as Rodney clutched the wound in his side with his left hand. Dark, warm blood ran freely between his fingers. Rodney was having difficulty holding up his sword. Vernon swung his saber, casually knocking Rodney's blade from his hand. Rodney dropped to one knee. The spectators went quiet. All Rodney could hear was the sound of thousands of men breathing.

The Icarian rested the tip of his dagger on Rodney's right shoulder. He felt a slight burn as the blade's poisoned edge bit into his skin. A flick of his wrist was all it would take to end Rodney's life by slitting his throat, but Vernon took a step back. He seemed to prefer to let the poison do his work. Rodney's lips had already gone numb and his vision was beginning to blur. Everything seemed to be slowing down. He saw Nicholas's dirk lying at Vernon's feet. Rodney let himself fall forward with his right hand extended. His hand closed with the dirk in his fist.

By the saber's long shadow, Rodney knew Vernon was standing over him, even though the captain made no move to disarm him. He obviously thought Rodney too far gone to be a threat. Rodney was going to die, but if he took the captain with him, Magdalen might still be saved. He tightened his grip on the dirk. Pooling the last of his strength, he coiled his muscles, turned, and then drove the blade toward Vernon's unprotected inner thigh. The blade went in all the way to the hilt, with its tip protruding from the other side. Vernon gasped. The saber hit the ground as he staggered back. Rodney could see the disbelief on his face. He took another step back and then fell just as Rodney blacked out.

When Rodney opened his eyes he was greeted by Shark-tooth's grinning face. He was applying some horrible smelling goo to Rodney's right shoulder. Already the feeling was returning to his neck and his vision had cleared. Aldus knelt to his left, tending the wound in his side. The same two guards still held Magdalen between them. "Release her," he croaked, as he forced himself to stand.

The guards glanced at the Duke, who nodded his consent. "You can let her go," he said. "Just post a guard at the gates with instructions to detain her should she try to leave."

Once released, Magdalen looked at Rodney for a brief moment before turning away. The men parted before her as she walked straight-backed across the grounds and up the steps. At the archway leading into the keep she paused to look back. Their eyes met for one last time before she stepped inside and was swallowed by shadows. Jason put a hand on Rodney's shoulder as he stared stone-faced after her.

Chapter 49

SYLVIA

Chin resting on the knuckles of her right hand, Sylvia sat alone at the head table in Vincent Castle's great hall. A cup of mulled cider long turned cold sat untouched as she stared longingly at three letters resting on the table next to the cup. The seal on one was broken. It was from Jason and she had read it twice. Of the other two, one bore her brother's seal and was addressed *To my dear sisters;* the other was to Elinor from Lionel.

The letters had arrived in the most unusual way, being delivered by a FireDrake no less. The creature had landed in Vincent Castle's courtyard and dropped a waterproofed satchel. It left the castle, pausing in a field nearby only long enough to burn and devour two sheep, before flying off toward the mainland. The satchel was brought to the bailiff Albert Beane, who opened it to find a half score of letters. He kept the three that were addressed to his Lord's sisters, and sent a rider out to deliver the rest. Because Rodney's letter was addressed to both Sylvia and Elinor, he sent riders to escort them back to Vincent Castle. Sylvia had saddled her gelding, Smoke, and returned with the messenger as quickly as she could.

When Sylvia had arrived, the bailiff handed her all three letters and then left her in the great hall to wait for Elinor. Once she was alone, Silvia took her small knife and broke the seal on Jason's letter. She breathed a sigh of relief when she recognized the writing to be in his own hand. It was written in the Carpathian script that Balor shared with its mother country. Jason was a man of few words so, even though it covered little more than half the page, for him the letter was long. Three sun-marks had passed since then and still Elinor had not arrived.

Sylvia picked up the small bell from the table and rang it twice. Rodney's young page Walter appeared almost immediately. He must have been waiting just outside the door. "More cider, my lady?" the boy asked.

"Perhaps later, but first I want you to run out to the front gate and see if my sister has arrived." Walter bowed and backed out of the chamber. She could hear his footsteps as he ran down the corridor. *Good lad.*

Sylvia drummed her fingers on the table for a time, then she picked up Jason's letter and opened it.

My dearest Sylvia. There is so much to tell you and my hand so clumsy with a quill. First of all, Rodney, Lionel and I are all alive and well. We have succeeded in our quest, but it was at great cost. It is with regret that I must tell you of the deaths of Ernest, Garret and young Lewis. There are many men who will not be returning to Balor, but that is enough of death. You will be pleased to know that cousin Martin and I have resolved our differences. One day, I believe, we may even be friends.

I must speak to you of Rodney. Your brother has been touched by love in a most cruel way. He returns a whole man, but not the same man that left Balor only two short moons ago. I think it best you and I quest at Vincent Castle for awhile when we return. You need not worry for me, I am well and long only to hold you in my arms once more. Forever yours, Jason.

What did Jason mean about her brother being touched by love, and in a cruel way? Where was Elinor? Sylvia could not stand to wait any longer. She set Jason's letter down and picked up the one with Rodney's seal just as Walter returned. "Well?" she said, wincing at the shrillness of her own voice.

"There has been no sighting of Lady Elinor, my Lady."

"Thank you, Walter, you may go."

The moment Walter had left the hall, Sylvia cut Rodney's seal with her knife. Just because Elinor did not mind to wait, didn't mean she had to. Sylvia took a deep breath and then opened the letter.

My Dear Sisters. I hope this letter finds you both well. It will take us more than a moon to reach Balor, and Grigor has offered to deliver any letters we wished to pen. As you have no doubt both read your husband's letters first, I will not dwell overly much on what has happened. We are delayed in leaving Drakenmount, as we await the return of Grigor and Wizard Aldus. They led a host of FireDrakes south to prevent the Emperor's legions from invading Icarus.

Coll and many of our country men await us in Icarus. We have lost our mounts, but Duke Edmond has been kind enough to provide us with transport for the journey home. Too much has happened to tell it all in a letter, and my hand is stiff from writing. As you know, a sword is much more to my liking than a quill. May the Gods watch over you both until our return. Rodney Vincent.

Sylvia set the letter down. She was still no wiser as to what Jason had hinted at. Sylvia picked up Lionel's letter and set the edge of her knife against the seal, only to withdraw the knife a moment later and put the letter back down. She drummed her fingers on the table and then picked up the letter once more. *This is wicked,* she thought, as her knife sliced through the seal. She opened the letter and began to read.

Dearest Darling. Little William has been slain some fifteen days back in Icarus, and many more good knights are no longer with us. We have fought men, beasts and a sorceress. This Magdalen was not at all what we had expected. She was such a wondrous beauty, she even rivals your sister. Rodney was besotted with her to the extent he fought and killed the Icarian King's champion in a duel to spare her life. He nearly lost his own in the process, and the Duke warns it is no longer safe for him in Icarus having killed the King's good friend. As his reward, she did walk away without so much as a single word of gratitude and has since disappeared. Rodney has searched for her to no avail. Even Wizard Aldus cannot find her. Physically, Rodney is well but he has been sullen and intractable ever since.

I myself was grievously wounded by foul beasts some four days past, but thanks to Wizard Aldus I am right as rain once again. We still have many days of travel ahead. I expect we shall be home by late summer. I look forward to the day I can look upon Philip and your pretty face once more. I never thought to say this, but I even miss our little spats. Lionel.

Placing Lionel's letter down on top of Rodney's, Sylvia picked up Jason's letter and stuffed it in the pocket of her riding jacket. She no longer wished to be in Vincent Castle when Elinor arrived. She could not begin to imagine what her sister would say when she found her letter opened and read. Perhaps a few days in Riverside was in order.

About The Author

David Korinetz lives at the South end of Lake Okanagan in beautiful British Columbia. At one time a prairie fish plant worker, machinist, aircraft mechanic, avionics technician, estimator, computer programmer and technical writer, after half a century of mucking around David finally turned to writing Fantasy fiction. FireDrakes was his first novel, and at the time of its second printing, the third book in the Daemon Knight series is nearing completion.